JEAN GENET

Querelle of Brest

Translated by
Gregory Steatham

ff

faber and faber

First published in Great Britain in 1966
by Anthony Blond Limited, London
Published in 1973
by Faber and Faber Limited
3 Queen Square London WC1N 3AU
First Faber paperback edition 1990

This edition published in 2000

The translation is from the de luxe edition of
Querelle de Brest
illustrated by Jean Cocteau

Printed in England by Mackays of Chatham plc, Chatham, Kent

A CIP record for this book is available from the British Library

ISBN 0-571-20367-1

2 4 6 8 10 9 7 5 3 1

to Jacques G.

The idea of murder frequently evokes the idea of sea and seafarers. No precise image of sea and seafarers may at once spring to mind: it is rather that Murder surges over our thought in breakers of emotion. If we suppose seaports to be the theatre of recurrent crimes, then the explanation is simple and need not detain us; but the chronicles are numberless from which we learn that the murderer was a man of the sea – either in reality or in imagination – and if the latter, then the crime will have less affinity with the sea.

The man who wears the uniform of a sailor is in no way pledged or bound to obey the rules of prudence. His disguise most certainly precludes him from taking part in any ceremonial that attends the execution of a preconceived or ritual murder. At the outset, therefore, we can lay down the following postulates. Uniform envelops the criminal like a cloud: it enables him to span the Seven Seas with long undulating muscular strides; to personify the Great Bear, the Pole Star or the Southern Cross. It (and we are still referring to the disguise that cloaks the criminal) permits him to return from dusky continents where the sun sets and rises, where the moon connives at murder under the roof of bamboo huts that huddle beside slow-rolling rivers alive with alligators; it allows him to move and act as part of a fragmentary mirage, to hurl his weapon at the very moment when one of his feet rests upon a beach in the Antipodes and the other is poised over Mediterranean waters; it grants him in advance the power of oblivion, since sailors are said to return from 'far distant shores'; and it permits the wearer to look down on land-lubbers as so much plant-life. It soothes the criminal. It enwraps him in folds – the tight-fitting folds of his jumper and the more ample folds of his trousers. It rocks him to sleep. It lulls the victim already under its spell to dreamless sleep.

We shall have much to tell of the physical attractions of the sailor. We ourselves have fallen under his spell and witnessed scenes of seduction. In the very long sentence beginning 'Uniform envelops the criminal like a cloud', we indulged in a facile prosody, each one of the postulates being merely an argument in favour of the author's natural proclivities. It is, therefore, under the compulsion of some curious inner motivation that we set down the ensuing drama. We would add that this story is addressed to inverts. The idea of love or lust is a *natural* corollary to the idea of Sea and Murder – and even to a greater extent to that of so-called *unnatural love*. No doubt the sailor, who is transported by ('animated by' is the more exact in our opinion, as we shall discover at a later stage) the desire and urge to murder, was first apprenticed to the Merchant Service, in which he had to endure the rigours of long voyages, nourished on ships' biscuits and the lash, paid off in some Godforsaken port, signed on again to handle some questionable cargo.

In a town of fogs and granite, however, when we come in contact with the stalwarts of the Fighting Navy, it is difficult not to imagine them as capable of any crime. All these lithe and lusty lads, licked into shape for and by a training in seamanship (intentionally fraught with risks and dangers, we like to think), with the stamp of their calling in their rolling gait and in the sturdy set of their shoulders, in the quiffs, profiles, outlines, and their rollicking provocative buttocks. Yet even a crime must be justified by their participation in it, since they are bound to enhance every action with a natural grace and nobility. Whether they descend from the heavens or ascend from some realm where they have consorted with sirens and other more fabulous monsters, these sailors, when ashore, inhabit solid buildings of stone – barracks, arsenals, or palaces – in strong contrast to the fluid, nervous, almost feminine irritability of the restless ocean (don't sailors sing in their shanties of the consolation of the waves?): they live by jetties loaded with chains, bollards, buoys, and other maritime paraphernalia to which, even when at the extremist ends of the earth, they know themselves to be anchored. To match the nobility of their stature, they are provided with arsenals, forts, convict-prisons converted to modern use, all architecturally magnificent.

Brest is a hard and solid town, constructed of grey granite hewn from Breton quarries. This rock-like quality anchors the port, giving the sailor a sense of security, for it provides him with an advantageous launching-point when outward bound and a haven of rest after the perpetually boisterous billows. If ever Brest seems less austere, it is when a feeble sun gilds the waterfront, where the façades are as noble and grand as those in Venice; or again, when its narrow streets are thronged with a tumult of carefree matelots; or finally, under fog and rain.

The action of this story starts three days after a despatch-boat, *Le Vengeur*, had anchored in the Roads. Other warships lie round her: *La Panthère, Le Vainqueur, Le Sanglant*, and further out, *Le Richelieu, Le Béarn, Le Dunkerque*, and more beside. Former ships-of-the-line bore these historic names. On the walls of a little side chapel in the church of

Saint-Yves in La Rochelle hang a number of *ex-voto* oil paintings, each depicting a ship that had been lost at sea, or saved from being wrecked, with such names as *Le Saphir, Le Cyclone, La Fée*, or *La Jeune Aimée*. These ships and their names had little or no influence on Querelle when he passed by them as a child, yet we must mention their existence.

Brest will always be 'the town of La Féria' for ships' companies the wide world over. When far from the shores of France, sailors refer to this brothel among themselves, but never without a smirk, a bawdy jest, or an outrageous guffaw, as if relating stories of ducks in China or the queer habits of the Annamites. They speak of the proprietor and his wife in some such terms as the following.

'I'll take the parts off you at dice – the way they do it at Nono's.'

'That bloke'd do anything for a bit of crumpet – he'd even take a load from Nono.'

'He's the sort of sod who fucks off to La Féria to trade his pearly gates.'

The name of 'La Féria' coupled with that of 'Nono's', even if that of 'the Madam' is unknown, must have gone all round the world, as a whisper on the lips of sailors everywhere or as a term of ribald sarcasm. On board ship there is never a man jack who knows exactly what takes place in the boss's room or what precisely are the rules of the game which has given it such a reputation; but not a rating among them, not even the rawest recruit, will fail to put forward his own explanation: every matelot will have it be understood that he alone possesses the real secret. So this establishment in Brest ever appears in the most fabulous light, bathed in mystery, and sailors bound for that port will secretly dream of this house of ill-fame which they mention only with the craftiest grin.

Georges Querelle, the hero of this story, speaks of it less than most. He has not long since learnt that his brother Robert is now the Madam's lover. The letter giving this piece of information had reached him at Cadiz.

'Dear Bro.

I send you these few lines to let you know that I was after getting back my dockyard matey's job, but there was nothing doing. My face didn't fit there or anywhere else. You know how it is. I felt fed up, fucked up, and far from home. To get sailing again I went round to Milo's place, and not long after I clapped my peepers on the missus up at La Féria and soon saw that I had clicked. I was all for it and now I'm quids in – on the nest again last night. Her old man don't give a fuck who goes with his trouble and strife – they are only business partners as you might say. Suits me. I'll be seeing you when you get a spot of leave. Hoping this finds you as it leaves me in the pink.

(signed) Robert.'

It rains sometimes in Brest during September. Wet weather makes the light linen clothes – open shirts and blue jeans – stick skin-tight to the muscular bodies of the men working in the port and arsenal. It happens, of course, that the weather is fine on certain evenings when the groups of masons, carpenters, and mechanics surge out from the shipyards. They are dog-tired. They walk along with dragging steps, and even if they lighten their gait the weight of their heavy tread only squelches with greater pressure into the puddles and the splash sends the drops bubbling up into the air all around them. Slow and ponderous, they move across the bows of the lighter, more rapid, hither-and-thither roving matelots out on the razzle, who are from that time on the chief adornment of the town. Brest will scintillate til daybreak with their dazzling antics, their incandescent gusts of laughter, their songs, their fun and skylarking, with their cat-calls and insults and wolf-whistles at the girls, their kisses, and the gaiety of their three rows of tape and their pom-poms.

The workmen are returning to their huts or lodgings. All through the long day they have toiled (your servicemen, soldiers or sailors, never have the feeling that they have toiled) in the multiple confusion of co-operative enterprise, dovetailing their respective ploys, each performing his allotted task towards the completion of a job which visibly unites them in close affinity. And now they are returning homewards. They are linked by an obscure comradeship – obscure to them – for it has an underlying tinge of hatred. Few of the men are married, and the wives of those few live some distance away. Towards six o'clock in the evening the workmen pass through the iron gates of the Dockyard and Arsenal. They walk up in the direction of the railway-station where the canteens are, or down the road to Recouvrance where they have rented a furnished room in a cheap hotel. The majority are Italians, the rest Spaniards, with a sprinkling of Maltese and French.

It is among such an orgy of fatigue and relaxed limbs, such a debauch of male lassitude and slack muscles, that Sub-Lieutenant Seblon of *Le Vengeur* delights to saunter.

* * *

In former times, there was a cannon trained continuously upon the convict-prison. Today that same cannon - its barrel only - stands upright, mounted, in the middle of the very court-yard where once the convicts used to be mustered for the galleys. It is an amazing fact that, to punish a criminal in bygone days, they used to make a sailor of him.

Went past La Féria. Saw nothing. Never have any luck. Over in Recouvrance I caught a glimpse of an accordion lying across the rounded thigh of a sailor. It's a sight I frequently see on board and never tire of - a squeeze-box throbbing in and out between the hands of a sailor.

'*Se brester*', to breast oneself for a course of action. Derivation: *bretteur*, a breaster: one who squares up to his opposite number, one who 'picks a quarrel', in fact.

When I learn - as often as not from the papers - that a scandal is afoot and on the verge of breaking, or when I'm simply afraid that it may break upon the world, I make preparations to fly: I always believe that I shall be suspected of being at the bottom of it. I feel that I must be possessed of the devil from the very fact that I've *imagined* certain incidents which could well involve me in scandal.

As for the lads, the bits of rough stuff I hold in my arms, on whom I pour out all my tenderness and whose heads I cover with passionate kisses before tenderly covering them up again in my sheets when all is over, these young toughs provide no more than a passing thrill and experiment combined. After being so 'overwhelmed by my loneliness' - a state of mind that makes me so different from others - is it really possible that I may someday hold naked in my arms, and continue to hold close-pressed to my body, the young men whose mettle and daring place them so high in my esteem that I long to throw myself at their feet and grovel before them? I dare hardly believe this, and tears well up in my eyes in gratitude to God above for allowing me such happiness. My tears make me sentimental. I melt. With my cheeks still wet with tears, I roll about, I overflow with tenderness for the flat lean cheeks of these young toughs.

The severe and at times almost condemning glance - a glance that seems to pass judgement - with which the homosexual appraises every good-looking young man he may encounter, is in reality a quick but intense meditation upon his own loneliness. In that one short cursory glance is concentrated a constantly recurring and deep-seated despair that is wrapped up with the fear of seeing himself rebuffed. 'It would be so lovely . . .' he thinks to himself. Or, if he doesn't think it, then it is expressed in the pucker of his eyebrows and the condemnation of his black look.

If some part of his body happens to be naked, then He (that is Querelle, whose name the officer never commits to paper, and this not merely for the sake of prudence as far as his brother-officers and his seniors are concerned, since in their eyes the contents of his private diary would be quite sufficient to damn him) is bound to be examining it. He searches for blackheads, or looks to see if any of his nails are split, or tries to discover a latent pimple. Vexed if He can discover no blemish, He thereupon invents one. As soon as He has nothing better to do, He turns to this game for amusement. This evening He is making a careful examination of his legs, on which the coarse dark hairs are silky in spite of their vigorous growth, and by their profusion give the effect of a sort of mist from foot to groin, thereby softening the sheer blatant crudity of the sinewy, almost knotted muscles. It astonishes me that such a sure sign of virility can provide so soft and heavy a covering for his legs. He is smiling no more than is his wont. He amuses himself by applying the burning tip of his cigarette to scorch his hairs, then He bends closer over them to sniff the smell of singeing. His body in repose is the great passion of his life – not an exultant, but a moody passion. Leaning over his body, He becomes lost in admiration of it. He gazes at it as if he were using a magnifying-glass. He observes its minutest irregularities with the scrupulous attention of an entomologist studying the peculiarities of insect-life. But if He so much as moves a muscle, what a superb and dazzling revenge does his whole body take as it glories in the interplay of its perfect components!

He never lets his mind wander, but pays careful attention to what He is doing. At every moment of the day or night. What need has He of dreams? His interest is in the actual. He never answers: 'My mind is elsewhere.' And yet the childishness of his apparent preoccupations amazes me.

With my hands in my trousers pockets, I would only have to say to him, in lazy fashion, 'Just give me a gentle shake, enough to let the ash fall from my cigarette', and, like a ham-fisted pugilist, He would lunge out at me and clout me on the shoulder. I snort with rage.

I should have been able to keep my sea-legs or cling to the gunwale – we were pitching and tossing a bit – but I quickly, in my excitement, took advantage of the rolling of the ship to sway from side to side and allow myself slowly to be shifted along by each lurch, and always in his direction. I even succeeded in bumping up against his elbow.

A cruel mastiff – a phantom hound devoted to its master yet ready to leap at one's throat – seems to be his constant attendant, and at times to be moving between the calves of his legs so that the creature's flanks become inextricable from his leg muscles. It seems ready to bite, for it is always growling and baring its fangs, and so ferocious is it that one expects at every moment to see it tear out his manhood.

After these few scattered extracts taken, but not entirely at random, from a private journal which first suggested his character to us, we would like you to look upon the rating Georges Querelle as the creation of the officer's loneliness and segregation from the world, and therefore as a solitary figure comparable to the Angel of the Apocalypse, whose feet repose upon the waters of the sea.

By long and constant meditation upon Querelle, and of allowing his imagination full play in discovering the most ravishing ornaments of his physique – his muscles, bumps and hollows, teeth, and hidden genitals – the rating has become an angel for Lieutenant Seblon (as we shall find out later, he describes him as 'the Angel of Loneliness'), that is to say, as turning into a character less and less human, as something from another world, ethereal, remote, about whose person is wafted a mysterious music unrelated to any known harmony, a haunting music that remains after all earthly harmony has been assimilated and distilled. In this rarefied atmosphere the vast angel of his creation is free to roam, slowly, unwitnessed, his feet resting upon the waters of the sea, but his head – or where his head should be – in the multiple confusion of the rays of a supernatural sun.

Lieutenant Seblon, before going on shore for the first time in Brest, picked up a pencil at random from his desk, sharpened it most carefully, and then put it in his pocket. On second thoughts, he took along some gummed labels, for it had occurred to him that perhaps the slate partitions might be too black or too coarse in texture to allow what he would scribble on them to be read by others for whom it was intended. Once ashore, he parted company with his ward-room friends on some minor excuse and went into the first urinal he saw, that at the top end of the Rue de Siam. He undid his flybuttons and, after a careful survey of the other occupants, he wrote out his first message: 'Young man passing through Brest would like to meet sailor with big prick.'

He tried, with little success, to decipher the obscene inscriptions and other graffiti on walls, and became enraged to find so noble an edifice besmirched with crude political slogans. Returning to his own scrawl, he read it over to himself and in so doing became as excited as if he had come upon it for the first time. He thereupon added an illustration – exaggerating the crudity of the design – of a male organ of outsize dimensions. Then he walked out with as much unconcern as if he had been relieving himself and nothing more. In this mood he made a full tour of the town, deliberately going into every urinal.

Though they themselves might well deny the fact, the strangely close resemblance between the two brothers Querelle served as an attraction to others and not to themselves. They came together at night, as late as possible, in the one and only bed of a furnished room not so very far from where their mother had lived in poverty. They would consort again, perhaps, in their mutual love for their mother, but so deep down in the subconscious that they had no clear vision; and they faced up to each other again in their almost daily quarrels. In the morning they parted without exchanging a word. They appeared to wish to ignore one another. Already, at the age of fifteen, Querelle had smiled with the vivid smile that was to single him out for the rest of his life. Of his own free will he chose to consort with thieves and spoke their slang. We must try to bear this fact in mind in order to understand Querelle better, for his mental make-up and his thought processes, indeed his sentiments, are dependent upon and assume the pattern of a certain stylized syntax and its unconventional pronunciation. We find in his vocabulary such slang expressions as: 'Let the ribands rip!'; 'I'm squatting on me bollocks.'; 'You can't come copper.'; 'Chop-chop!'; 'He's caught the boat up.'; 'Take his picture as he climbs aloft!'; 'He's shot his roe.'; 'See here, baby, I'm on the dot.'

These expressions are never proclaimed: they are muttered under his breath, vicariously fetched from deep down inside him invisible, as it were, and kept in the dark. Since the thought behind them is never properly shaped, his words can hardly be said to throw much light upon Querelle or, if we may dare to say it, they keep him in the shadows, and prevent him coming into the full light. They seem, in some contrary way, to go in at his mouth, pile up inside him and there leave a deposit of thick mud. From this deposit a transparent bubble comes to the surface at certain times, and explodes gently on reaching his lips. In fact, what bubbles up from the depths is a slang word or expression.

The Police who control the town and port of Brest are under the authority of a District Commissioner. When our story opens Inspectors Mario Lambert and Marcellin Daugas are working together at Police HQ, united by a singular friendship. The latter is little more than an excrescence to Mario, (the police are always recognized as going about in pairs) heavy enough in all conscience, and none too gay, but sometimes, surprisingly, a source of great comfort to his colleague. However, it was a companion of a very different calibre whom Mario had chosen to be his close associate, one nearer and dearer to him and more crafty by far – more easily sacrificed, too, should the occasion arise – a young fellow known as Dédé.

As in every town in France, there is a *Monoprix* in Brest.

This emporium was a popular stamping-ground for Dédé and a group of sailors, who could always be found wandering about from counter to counter, usually lingering longer at the one where there was something they really hankered after – and occasionally bought – more often than not, strange to relate, a pair of gloves.

To complete the picture of Brest, the old-time control by the Admiralty had been replaced by the services of the *Préfecture Maritime*.

'During his two years' service in the Marines, his insubordinate conduct and his depraved behaviour earned him 76 convictions. He used to tattoo recruits. He stole from his messmates, and indulged in strange practices with animals.'

Extract from the trial of Louis Menesclou, 20 years of age, executed 7 September, 1880.

'I formed the habit of following exciting court cases,' he is reported as saying, 'and Menesclou's poisoned my mind. I am less guilty than he, for I neither raped my victims nor cut them up in pieces. And my photo is certainly superior to his, for his is not wearing a tie, whereas I obtained permission - as a favour - to keep mine on.'
Declaration before the Public Prosecutor of the murderer Felix Lamaitre, 14 years old. (15.7.61)

'And those that are beloved, being ashamed to do any vile thing before those that love them, for very love will stick one by another to the death. As appeareth by the example of him, that being stricken down to the ground, his Enemy lifting up his Sword to kill him, he prayed him he would give him his death wound before, lest his friend that loved him, seeing a wound on his back should be ashamed of him.'
Plutarch, Pelopidas, trans Sir T. North.

A pair of blue-jeans - possibly his own but more likely pinched from a sailor - concealed his lovely feet now motionless and arched after the final stamp that had made the table shake and all the glasses reverberate. He was wearing polished black shoes, cracked and crinkled at the point reached by the rippling eddies of blue linen that ran down from their source at his belt. His body was encased, close-fittingly tight, in a turtle-necked, dirty white woollen jersey. His parted lips slowly began to close. Querelle looked as if he were just about to put his cigarette to his lips, but his hand came to rest half-way up his chest, and his mouth remained half open. In this expectant attitude he gazed at Gil and Roger, united by the almost visible thread of their glances and by the freshness of their smiles. Gil seemed to be singing for the lad, and Roger, like the leading spirit in some secret debauch, to be choosing this young eighteen year old mason for the pleasure of his voice to be the hero of a village romance for this one night.

The way Querelle studied the couple had the effect of isolating them. He consciously kept his lips parted. His smile became more pronounced at the corners of his mouth, but almost imperceptibly. A faint tinge of irony began to spread over his features, then over the whole of his body, until leaning back against the wall in an attitude of utter abandon, it was suffused with the spirit of supercilious irony, or perhaps of simple amusement. Altered fractionally by the lifting of an eyebrow (matching his crooked, slanting grin), his smile took on a malicious expression as he examined the two lads. The smile vanished from Gil's lips, as though he had deflated a small balloon in each cheek, and at the same moment died on Roger's lips; but, four seconds later, in drawing in his breath again and taking up his refrain, Gil, once more atop the table, resumed his smile, and this brought back again and sustained, until the last note of the song had died away, the smile on Roger's lips. Never for an instant did the eyes of either wander from the eyes of the other. Gil was singing. Querelle pressed his elbows against the walls of the bar-room. He began to take stock of himself in this position, and was subtly aware of the opposition between his living, bodily weight, the cascading tumult of his dorsal muscles, and the shadowy but indestructible mass of the wall behind him. In the dark shadows a silent struggle ensued between these two opposing forces.

Querelle was well aware of the beauty of his back. We shall see how, a few days later, he was to dedicate it to Lieutenant Seblon in secret. Almost without seeming to make any movement, he began rubbing his shoulder-blades up and down the stony surface of the wall. He was strong. With one hand, leaving the other in the pocket of his oilskin coat, he raised his fag-end, still alight, to his mouth. The suspicion of a smile hovered on his lips. Robert and the other two sailors were intent upon the song, but Querelle kept his smile. To coin a phrase, Querelle was conspicuous by his absence. After letting a little smoke drift in the direction of his thoughts (as though he wanted to veil them or show a touch of insolence as far as they were concerned), his lips remained parted over his even teeth. He relished their dazzling whiteness, now faintly dimmed by the surrounding gloom and the shadow cast by his upper lip. Staring at Gil and Roger, now reunited by glance and smile, he was unable to make up his mind to withdraw into his shell and close his parted lips over his pearly teeth. They had the same restful effect on his wayward thoughts as the blue of the sea has on our eyes. Meanwhile, he was ruminatingly running his tongue over his palate, and very lively it was.

One of the sailors made as if to button his coat, having turned up the collar. Querelle had not yet accustomed himself to the idea, never properly formulated, of being a monster. Deep sunk in thought, he was reviewing his past behind his ironic smile, tender and at the same time frightened, according to the extent that this past became confused with what he himself now was. Thus might a youngster, miraculously transmogrified into a crocodile, yet with the light of his soul shining in his eyes, examine his crinkled body – supposing he were not fully conscious of his maw and its enormous crunchers – look at his solemn, gigantic tail, with which he strikes the waters and the beach, or frisks against that of other monsters; the tail, which is an extension of himself, endowed with the same touching, heart-rending – and indestructible – majesty that informs the train of the daughter of an Imperial House as she trails it behind her, embroidered with crests and lace and battles of yore and a thousand dastardly crimes. He experienced the full horror of being alone, spellbound by an immortal magic in the midst of the every-day world. It was accorded to him alone, as a terrifying privilege, to perceive his monstrous participation in the realms of great muddy rivers and deep jungles. He was afraid lest some light, emanating from the innermost depths of his soul, might not be illuminating him, might not, in some way from inside his scaly carapace, be giving off a reflection of his true being and rendering it visible to those who would be constrained to give him chase.

At certain spots along the ramparts of Brest, trees have been planted, and these form alleys which have been dubbed, derisively no doubt, the the 'Bois de Boulogne'. Here, during the summer months, a few bistros are open where you can take your drinks from wooden tables swollen by rain and mist, under the trees or behind hornbeam hedges. The sailors had disappeared with a girl under the shade of these trees; Querelle let his mates have first dip, then he came up to her as she lay staring at the moon. He made as if to lower his flap, when of a sudden after a momentary, a charming hesitation of his fingers, he buttoned it up again. Querelle was perfectly calm. He had only to give the slightest turn of the head to left or right to feel his cheek rub against the sharp upturned collar of his oilskins. This contact reassured him. He knew himself to be clothed, marvellously clothed.

Later, when he was taking off his shoes, the scene in the bistro came back to his mind, but he lacked the necessary equipment to register the true significance of any event. Only with difficulty could he put his thoughts into words. He only knew for certain that it had aroused a faint tinge of irony in him. He had no notion why. Knowing the severity, the austerity almost, of his features and their pallor, this irony, gave him what is commonly called a sarcastic look. For a moment or two he had remained amazed by the mutual understanding that was being established, accepted, almost to the extent of becoming tangible, in the eyes of the two lads; the one singing up on the table there with his head bent down towards the other, who was sitting and gazing up at his pal.

Querelle took off one of his socks.

Quite apart from any material benefit he might derive from his murders, he was enriched by them in other ways. They left behind in him some sort of muddy deposit, and the stench of this muck served to deepen his despair. From each one of his victims he had preserved some rather dirty object: a pair of scanties, a brassière, a bootlace, a handkerchief, all of them objects sufficient to disprove his alibis and therefore capable of convicting him. These relics were first-hand evidence of his triumph and his success. They were the shameful reality, which is the basis behind all illuminating and incomplete appearance. In the sailors' world, where men are brimming with virility, pride and good looks, they are the drab equivalent of the following: a greasy, tooth-broken old comb kept at the bottom of a pocket; imperfectly whitened full-dress gaiters that look as deceptively clean as white sails seen from a distance; a pair of becoming but badly made slacks; amateurish tattooing; a crumpled handkerchief; socks with holes in them. What for us was the strongest memory of Querelle's expression can best be described in an image that springs readily to mind: that of a prisoner's heavy hand dangling from, or a shred of coarse material attached to a delicate strand of wire with barbs spaced so advantageously that there should have been no difficulty in avoiding them.

Almost in a whisper and despite himself, Querelle said to one of his mates in passing his hammock, 'Those two kids are a case, aren't they?' 'Which two kids?' 'Eh?' Querelle raised his head. His mate didn't seem to have caught his meaning. The conversation petered out.

Querelle pulled off his other sock and turned in. Not that he wanted to sleep, or think over the scene in the bistro. Once he was stretched out, he had at last the leisure to allow his thoughts to centre round his own affairs; but he must look sharp about it, however tired. The owner of La Féria had to have two kilos of opium if Querelle could contrive to get them through to him. The customs' officials opened every sailor's case or bag, down to the smallest package. With the exception of the officers, they made a thorough search of every man jack as they came ashore. Without the trace of a smile, Querelle's thoughts leapt to the Lieutenant. The enormity of his bright idea struck him just as his thoughts were taking an individual shape that he alone would have expressed as follows: 'Should have got the picture right away, as soon as those lollipop peepers of his gave me the up and down! He was as nervy as a cat shitting on its cinder-box. He's got me where I want me, you bet!' He would surely be able to turn to his own account the clumsily concealed passion betrayed, but to him alone, by the Lieutenant. 'Trouble is he's a bit of a cunt. A queer like him could easy get me cells.' And there came, almost stealthily filtering through into his mind, the memory of a recent scene when, in his presence, Lieutenant Seblon had answered his Captain back peremptorily and almost in a tone amounting to impertinence.

Querelle was delighted to think that his brother was now in clover, living a soft life of oriental ease and luxury as the Madam's fancy-man, and at the same time enjoying the full confidence of her condoning husband. He closed his eyes. His mind slipped back into the dim and distant recesses of the past where he became at one with his brother. As he identified himself with Robert, there emerged from this confusion first, certain words, and then, thanks to an over-simplified thought-process perhaps, clearer and more vivid ideas. These rose to the surface of his mind as he began to disentangle himself from his brother, and little by little goaded him to devise strange acts and work out a whole scheme of single-handed deeds. His thoughts crystallized slowly and took shape till they became uniquely his own, and in the process it seemed to him that he was partnered by Vic, for he had mysteriously crept into the picture. And Querelle, who had lost something of his independence in these dreamlike quests and yearnings after Vic, at once assumed his own character as he gradually became himself again and ceased his blindfold gropings after the indecisive limbs which in some insubstantial way had come to assume the substance and consistency of spunk. He discovered that his hand was gently closed round his penis, but he was barely conscious of having stroked it. He certainly had no erection now. While still at sea, he had announced to his mess that once they were in port at Brest, he was going to come his load; yet that evening he had not so much as given a thought to kissing a girl.

Querelle was the living spit and image of his brother. Robert was the closer-knit, perhaps, and much the warmer-hearted - a subtle distinction by which it was possible to recognize them apart, but one which would never be taken into account by a flouted girl. For our own convenience, we have found it essential to look forward in time to a certain day in the life of Querelle - and we know the very day and exact hour - when we finally made up our mind to tell his story. The word 'story' can hardly be said to fit the bill if interpreted in the strict sense of recounting a single escapade or a whole series of his adventures that have already taken place. Step by step we should have come to realize that Querelle - already flesh of our flesh and bone of our bone - was beginning to grow, to develop his personality within our deeper conscience and derive sustenance from the best in us, above all from our despair at not being in any sense part of him, yet having so much of him in ourselves. Having discovered this much of Querelle, we were most anxious that he should become a hero to those who may hold him in contempt. While we follow his fate in so far as in us lies, follow his destiny and development, we shall come to see how he lends himself to this plan in order finally to come into his own during the final stages of our narrative, in a conclusion which seems to be the fulfilment of his own desires and of his own destiny.

The scene we are about to describe, only slightly transposed, is the actual event which first revealed Querelle to us. (We are still speaking of the ideal and heroic character, the fruit of our secret passion.) We are able to write of this particular event that it was comparable to the Visitation. Doubtless it was only some time later that we recognized it as being 'big' with consequences, yet there and then we may be said to have experienced an anticipatory thrill. Finally, in order to be palpable to you, to become the character in a novel, Querelle must be shown as existing outside ourselves. Only in this way will you be able to appreciate the apparent – and real – beauty of his body, his attitudes, his exploits, and their slow disintegration.

The further you go down towards the port, the denser the fog appears to grow. So thick is it at Recouvrance, after crossing the Penfeld bridge, that the houses – walls, chimney-stacks, roof and all – look as if they are floating in the mist. There is a sense of desolation in the narrow alleys that lead down to the quayside. The disconsolate rays of a wan sun, haloed with the buttery gleam to be observed at the half-open door of a dairy, occasionally filter through. On you go through the vaporish twilight till you are confronted once more by the semi-opaque yet ever-enticing wall of fog, a protection now fraught with dangers: a drunken sailor reeling home on a heavy pair of legs, a docker stooping over his girl, a lurking tough armed, perhaps, with a swiftsure knife; me, you, all of us, our hearts pounding.

The fog brought Gil and Roger closer and closer together. It inspired them with mutual confidence and comradeship. Though they were barely conscious of it, their isolation instilled in them a hesitant sense of bravado, as yet a little fearful, a little tremulous: indeed, a delightful feeling such as children have, walking along with their hands in their pockets, when their feet collide and touch and become entangled.

'Have a care there! Shit! Now it's safe to go on.'

'The quayside must be hereabouts. Keep your eyes skinned!'

'Why skinned? You've got the jitters and no mistake!'

'Not me! But there are times when . . .'

At moments they were aware of feminine footsteps coming towards them, at others their eyes were held by the steady glow of a cigarette in the swirling mist, or again at others they would divine the presence of a pair of lovers locked in a close embrace.

'What's that? – "Times when" what?'

'Come off it, Gil, anyone'd think you were mad with me. It's not my fault, surely, if my sister wasn't able to show up.' And, after two more steps in silence, he added in a lower tone, 'You can't have been giving Paulette much of a thought when you were dancing with that dark girl last night.'

'What the fuck's that got to do with you? Certainly I danced with her, so what?'

'Oh! You didn't just dance with her, you went off with her after!'

'And what about after? I'm not yet spliced to your sister, chum. Who are you to preach to me? All I told you was to see she came along.'

Gil was speaking in fairly loud tones, but none too distinctly, so as to be understood only by Roger. Then he lowered his voice again, and a note of anxiety crept into it.

'Then what about what I told you?'

'Nothing doing, I tell you, Gil, and that's the truth.'

They turned to the left, in the direction of the Naval Stores. A second time they bumped up against one another. Automatically Gil put his hand on the lad's shoulder and let it rest there. Roger slackened his pace, hoping that his pal would stop. How was he to bring him to the point? A desperate feeling of love and devotion was draining the strength from his body, but at that moment someone passed by. Would there never be a moment's peace when he could have Gilbert entirely to himself? Gil removed his hand to thrust it in his trousers' pocket again, and Roger thought that he had been abandoned. All the same, in the act of removing it, Gil could not help pressing harder on the lad's shoulder as he let go his hold: it was as if some sort of regret at taking it away added to its weight.

All of a sudden, Gil got a hard on.

He was aware of the drag of his slip against his imprisoned penis. The idea behind the word 'shit' (not yet one of wonderment) slowly began to take effect upon him, pervading the whole of his body as his cock began to stiffen, bending like a bow inside the fabric, till at last, despite the fine-woven mesh, it stood erect, firm and solid. Gil did his utmost to call to mind a more precise picture of Paulette's face, when of a sudden his focus shifted as he tried to concentrate, despite her intervening skirt, upon what lay between the thighs of Roger's sister. Feeling the urgent need for physical support, easily, immediately accessible, he said to himself with a certain cynical mental reserve, 'Here's her brother, close beside me in the fog!'

It was then that he was struck by the thought of how delicious it would be to penetrate the warmth of that dark, furry-edged, invitingly half-open slit, from which emerge waves of strangely hot and heavy odours, even when it belongs to a corpse already cold.

'I'm gone on your sister, y'know.'

Roger smiled broadly and turned an open face to Gil.

'Oh! . . .'

The sound Gil made was both gentle and raucous, seeming to rise from the pit of his stomach, and yet to be only an anguished sigh fetched from the base of his standing phallus. He certainly felt there was a direct and immediate connecting link between the base of his cock, the back of his throat, and the muffled raucous groan.

We should like these reflections and observations, which cannot fully round out and delineate the characters in this book, to encourage you to become, not so much onlookers, as the very characters themselves. These creations would then, little by little, detach themselves from your own specific actions.

Gil's penis was becoming more and more rampageous. His hand had tight hold of it in his trousers' pocket, pancaking it there against his stomach. His prick had assumed the importance of a tree, of an oak, with moss round its bole and self-lamenting mandrakes pushing up between its roots. (Sometimes on waking up with a cock-stand, Gil would jokingly refer to it as 'my dingle-dangle'.)

They went on for a few more steps, but at a slower pace.

'So you like her, eh!'

It needed so very little for Roger's smile to illuminate the fog all round him and for the stars to sparkle in full brilliance above him. It made him deliriously happy to sense so close beside him the sound of Gil's saliva pressing against his lips with amorous desire.

'You get a kick out of that, don't you?'

Turning to face him, teeth clenched and hands still pocketed, Gil forced the lad to step backwards until he found himself up against a buttress of the rampart; this he did by pushing him back with his stomach and the upper part of his body. Roger kept on smiling, barely retreating, hardly withdrawing his head before the outstretched face of the young mason, who was crushing him with the full weight of his vigorous body.

'This puts a grin on your face, don't it?'

Gil took one of his hands – not the one grasping his cock – out of his pocket. He clapped it on Roger's shoulder, and so close to his neck that the thumb brushed against the cool skin of the boy's cheek. With his shoulders supported by the wall, Roger let himself slip a little, as if weakening. He never lost his smile.

'Now you're getting a kick out of this, aren't you?'

Gil was pressing forward with a vengeance, almost with the impetus of a victorious lover. There was something of the seducer's cruelty and laxity about his mouth, set off by a tooth-brush moustache, and his features suddenly took on so determined a look that Roger's smile, by the merest drooping of the corners of his mouth, was tinged with sadness. With his back to the wall, he was ever so slightly slipping forward – always with the faint sadness of his smile lending a look of resignation to his face – to be inevitably overwhelmed under the monstrous wave that was Gil, who would go under with him, one hand still in his pocket, clutching at the last flotsam.

'Oh!'

Gil gave vent to another faraway, raucous groan similar to the previous one.

'Oh, I wanted to fuck your sister, you bet! I swear if I'd got hold of her now the way I'm holding you, I'd put it up her and no mistake.'

Roger made no reply. His smile faded. His eyes remained fixed on Gil's face, where the eyebrows alone looked unforbidding, under the powder of cement and chalk.

'Gil!'

And his thoughts were: 'This is really Gil – Gil Turko – a Pole. He's not long out from the Arsenal, back from his work on the jetty along with the other masons. And now he's real worked up!' Close to Gil's ear, the words intermingled with his breath as it pierced the fog, he murmured:

'Gil!'

'Oh! Oh! God, how I wanted her! Think how I should have fucked her, good and proper. You – you're so like her – same little mug.'

He moved his hand nearer to Roger's neck. Finding himself so completely the master in the very midst of the thick blanket of fog, Gil Turko felt a further desire to be harsh, crisp, imperious. To tear aside the fog, to rid himself of it by a brisk and brutal gesture, by a ferocious look, would perhaps be sufficient to reaffirm his virility, for otherwise he would automatically be in a sloppy state of humiliation when he returned to his quarters later that night.

'You've got the same eyes. It's a shame you're not her. Hullo! What's this? Are you coming now?'

As if to prevent Roger from 'coming', he flattened his stomach closer still to the lad's, pushing him against the wall, while his free hand kept hold of the charming head, supporting it above the sovereign billows, certain of his power, above the element that was Gil. They remained motionless, the one shoring up the other.

'What are you going to tell her?'

'Try to get her to come along tomorrow.'

Despite his lack of experience, Roger realized the true worth, and almost the real meaning of his mixed feelings when he heard the sound of his own voice; it was utterly dead.

'And what about what I told you?'

'I'll do my best about that too. Are we going back, Gil?'

As they beat a hasty retreat, the sound of the sea suddenly broke on their ears. Throughout the whole of this scene they had been near the edge of the water. For an instant they were, each of them, terrified at the thought of having been so close to danger. Gil forked out a cigarette from his pocket and stopped to light it. Roger caught a glimpse of the beauty of his face framed by his large hands, thick and covered with powder, their palms illuminated by the delicate and trembling flame.

THE LIEUTENANT'S MUSINGS.

As he might a spray of lilac, Menesclou the murderer, they say, drew down within his reach the slip of a girl whose throat he was about to slit. It is by his hair and his eyes – the full power of his smile – that HE (Querelle) draws me on. Does this signify that I am going to my death? That his love-lock and his teeth are envenomed? Does this signify that love is a perilous cavern? Finally, does this mean that HE is leading me on, and '*for that*'? When, on the point of my going down on 'the Querelle Rocks' should I have the strength to be able to sound the siren's wail of warning.

(Inasmuch as the other characters may be by their nature incapable of the lyricism with which we invest them, the more efficient to reconstruct them within you, the reader, Lieutenant Seblon must be regarded as being solely responsible for the part he plays.)

I should adore it – and how ardently I desire it! – if, under his royal livery, HE were simply a young tough! Oh, to throw myself at his feet! to cover his instep with kisses!

With a view to rediscovering HIM, and, counting on absence and the emotion of return to give me the courage to address HIM intimately – by a familiar name – I pretended to go away on a long furlough. But I was unable to stick it out. I came back. I saw HIM again, and I gave HIM an order to carry out, almost vindictively. I really wouldn't mind what liberties he took: he could spit in my face, be the first to establish christian name terms by using mine. Should I say to HIM, 'You called me by my christian name?' The blow HE would strike me with his fist, straight between the eyes, would enable me to catch this oboe murmur: 'My familiarity is royal and accords me every right.'

By giving the ship's barber express orders to clip him a crew-cut, Lieutenant Seblon hoped to achieve a virile appearance – not so much to save his face as to be treated as 'one of the lads' (so he believed) among his ship's company. He was not then aware that it made them shun him. He was a well-built man, broad-shouldered, but he was deeply conscious of the presence of something feminine in him, something contained, it sometimes seemed to him, inside a tomtit's tiny egg about the size of a pale blue or pink sugared almond, and, at others, spilling over to course all through his veins and fill his body with milk. Being only too well aware of this, he had come to believe in his own weakness and that his body possessed the fragility of a huge, unripe nut whose kernel was composed of that pale whitish stuff children call milk. This core of femineity – and the Lieutenant acknowledged it with infinite sorrow – was at any time capable of spreading to every feature, overflowing into his eyes or to the tips of his fingers, and drawing attention to his every gesture by enfeebling it. He took particular pains not to be caught tatting, or in the act of making a typically feminine gesture, counting imaginary stitches or scratching his head with an imaginary knitting-needle. He gave himself away, it so happens, to everyone when he gave his men the order to pick up Arms, for he stressed the word 'Arms' so lovingly that his whole personality appeared to be kneeling before the prostrate form of a handsome lover. He never smiled. His fellow-officers found him severe and slightly puritanical; but behind his hard exterior they believed they could recognize an astonishing distinction from the way in which, despite himself, he pronounced certain words with an air of preciosity.

'Oh, the happiness of clasping in *my* arms a body so beautiful, even though it is big and strong, taller and stronger than mine.'

REVERIE: Would it be like this? HE goes ashore every evening. When HE returns, his blue-cloth trouser-legs – wide, and covering his shoes despite the regulations – spotted, with spunk perhaps, and spattered by the dust of the roads that he has swept up with the frayed bottoms. As for these trousers, they're the dirtiest pair I've ever seen on a matelot. If I were to demand an explanation from HIM, HE would smile as he chucked his cap behind HIM:

'That! Oh, that's all the chaps who go down on me. While they're giving me a chew they spurt all over my flap; it's their spunk, that's all.'

HE would appear to be very proud of it. HE wears these smears with shameless and glorious audacity; they are HIS decorations.

Though it may be the least 'elegant' brothel in Brest, where no sailors of the Battle Fleet ever go – at least not the sort likely to add any glamour or lustre to it – La Féria is certainly the most notorious. It is a Cave of Harmony, decorated with purple and gold, whither repair to seek their solace sailors from overseas, lads of the Merchant and Coastal Navies, and men from the docks. Whereas matelots go there to have a 'lay' or a 'short time', stevedores and others say: 'We drag ourselves along there to get rid of our dirty water.' When night falls, La Féria further fires the imagination, for it has all the excitement of a dazzling crime.

There is always a lurking suspicion that two or three street-arabs are on the watch, standing at their vantage-point in the mist-shrouded urinal on the opposite side of the street. Sometimes the front door of the brothel is left ajar, and from its blue aperture issue the strains of a mechanical piano, percolating in spirals of music into the semi-darkness, to uncurl and curl again round the wrists and throats of the workmen who happen to be passing by. But in the glare of daylight a more detailed appraisal can be made of this ramshackle, dirty, grey-fronted and shuttered, shame-ravaged, jerry-built erection. Viewed by the gleam of its single red lamp, behind its lowered Venetian blinds, who can help but imagine it oozing with lavish luxury, bursting with breasts, with milky thighs pressed into tight-fitted clinging black satin, crop-full of gorgeous bosoms, of crystals, mirrors, scents, and champagne, of which the sailor dreams as soon as he approaches the red-light purlieus.

This particular door was astonishing. It was a single thick panel, plated with iron, embossed with long sharp spikes of shining metal – of steel perhaps – their points directed towards the street. It was at once so disdainful and so mystifying that it acted as the perfect foil to an anxious soul thirsting for love. For the docker and the stevedore, this door was a symbol of the cruelties that attend the rites of love. If guardian it truly was, then perforce it must be the protective covering of a treasure such as only the invulnerable dragons or intangible genii could hope to pass through unscathed, without bleeding to death upon its spikes – unless, of course, it should respond to an 'open sesame', or a gesture from you – serviceman or stevedore, or whatever you may choose to be this night; and, by the same token, a fortunate and blameless prince transformed by magic into the rightful heir-apparent to these forbidden domains. To be so heavily protected, the treasure needs must be of great danger to the outside world; or, being by its very nature so fragile, must require the self-same protection as is accorded to virgins. The stevedore might grin and joke about the sharp pricks pointed directly at him, yet this would never for an instant prevent his becoming – by the charm of a word, physiognomy, or gesture – the forceful master of an imaginary virginity. And on the very threshold, if he were not already, to put it plainly, in a state of erection, he would become aware of the presence in his trousers of his prick, still soft perhaps, yet reminding him – the ravisher at the door – of his prowess by a slight throbbing at its extreme tip that spread slowly to its base and on down into the muscles of his buttocks. And, within his still flabby weapon, the stevedore would be aware of the presence of a midget but rigid sex, something like the 'idea' of a 'hard'. All the same, this would be a solemn moment, as he stood gazing at the door, and then heard the sound of its rusty hinges closing behind a client.

This door had other virtues for Madame Lysiane. When it was bolted and barred, she, the Mother Judge, would be transformed into an oriental pearl hidden inside the nacreous casket of an oyster, able to open, and close, its valve at will. Madame Lysiane possessed the soft contours of a pearl, a muffled gleam emanating not so much from her milky colouring as from an inner deposit of tranquil happiness heightened by the light of an inner peace. Her form was rounded, rich, and polished. The myriad ministrations of petty duties, innumerable little attentions and countless frettings, the wear and tear of a patient economy, all had been necessary to build up the fullness of her ample figure. It was inevitable that Madame Lysiane should be the epitome of sumptuous splendour. The door itself was guarantee of that. Its pointed spikes were ferocious guardians, even against the winds of heaven. The Mother Judge passed her life at a leisurely pace, within the confines of a feudal castle, and its character was frequently reflected in her mind. She was happy. Only the most subtle eddies of life outside found their way into her, to clothe and cosset her exquisite plumpness. She was magnificently grand, superbly disdainful. Far removed from sun and stars, frolics and dreams – but thriving on her own sun, her own stars, her own frolics and her own dreams – slippered, wearing mules with high Louis XV heels, she revolved slowly among her girls without so much as touching them; she climbed the stair, passed along the corridors hung with gilded leather, crossed the room and the salons, the astonishing salons we shall attempt to describe, glittering with lights and mirrors, upholstered, decorated with artificial flowers in glass vases and with daring pictures on the walls. Moulded by the passing of time, she was beautiful. Robert had now been her lover for more than six months.

'You'll pay for them in cash?'

'I've told you so once.'

Querelle stood frozen by Mario's looks. His looks and his general attitude expressed more than mere indifference: they were glacial. In order to appear to ignore Mario, Querelle deliberately stared at the proprietor of the establishment, straight in the eye. His own immobility was beginning to bore him too. He regained a little assurance when he made as if to take a step; this slight loosening of the muscles reacted on his body just as he was thinking: 'I'm nothing but a matelot – got nothing but my pay – I'd best find a way out of the shit. After all, there's nothing wrong in it – I'll try and rustle him for a bit on the quiet. He's got nothing on me – and even if t'other's a dick, I don't care a bugger.' But Querelle felt himself unable to make the slightest impression on the proprietor's imperturbable calm, since he showed scarcely any interest in the stuff that was offered him, and none at all in the person offering it. The lack of movement and the almost total silence among these three characters was beginning to weigh on each one of them. His thoughts came in approximately these words: 'I've not let on that I'm Bob's brother. All the same he'd never dare shop me.' At the same time he appreciated the boss's quite out of the ordinary strength and the handsome looks of the dick. Up till now, he had never encountered any real rival in the male world, and if he could hardly be said to be taken aback by what he was confronted with in these two men – unaware of his own mixed feelings as we have already described them – at least he was suffering for the first time from the indifference of men towards him. He spoke again.

'There's no stink on around here, by any chance?'

It had been his intention to show a certain disregard for the stalwart who never took his eyes off him; but he did not dare to make too pointed a reference to him. He did not even dare so much as indicate Mario to the boss with his eyes.

'You can trust me. You'll get your rake-off, I can promise you. All you've got to do is bring along five kilos of dope and the money's yours. Got it? So cheer up, lad.'

And with a very slow, almost imperceptible movement of the head the boss nodded towards the counter against which Mario was leaning.

'That's Mario over there – don't worry about him, he's part of the House.'

Without so much as a twitch of his face muscles, Mario held out his hand. It was hard and solid, armed rather than graced with three gold rings. Querelle was the shorter by a matter of an inch or so. He was aware of it as soon as he set eyes on the sumptuous rings, the breath-taking sign of tremendous virile strength. He had no doubt whatever that the realm over which this character lorded it must be a terrestrial one. His thoughts leapt with a twinge of melancholy to the treasure he possessed hidden for'ard in the soaking wet Despatch-boat out in the Roads, for there lay all that was essential for him to be the equal of this blatant male. These thoughts calmed him a little. But was it possible that a policeman really could be as rich and as handsome as he? And that, thanks to the forceful strength of this 'outside-the-law', (for so he imagined the boss of the brothel to be) beauty beyond his natural looks was added? He thought, 'A flat-foot, he's no more than a flat-foot.' But such a thought, which slowly unwrapped its full meaning to Querelle, did not calm him, and natural jealousy and antipathy yielded to admiration.

'Salut!'

Mario's voice was broad and thick, like his hands – except that it carried no sparkle. It struck Querelle slap in the face. It was a brutal, callous voice, one capable of stirring up and scattering the scum of the earth. Speaking of it a few days later, Querelle said to the detective:

'It's like a smack in the face with a raw steak.'

Querelle gave him the broadest of smiles and held out his hand, but not a word passed his lips. Then to the boss he said:

'My brother's not turned up yet, has he?'

'Not as far as I know. Haven't the foggiest where he is.'

Fearing that he might make a slip, or rile the boss, Querelle took the matter no further. The main reception room of the brothel was silent and empty. It almost seemed as if it were taking careful and solemn stock of the present confabulation. At three o'clock in the afternoon the ladies of the establishment would be having their meal in the refectory. There was no sign of anyone about. On the first floor, in her room, Madame Lysiane was doing her hair, by the light of a single bulb. The mirrors were vacant, blank, astonishingly near to being unreal, having nobody and nothing to reflect. The boss took a sip and emptied his glass. He was quite exceptionally stalwart. If he had never been exactly handsome, in his youth he had no doubt been a fine upstanding male specimen, despite the presence of blackheads in his skin, a few hardly noticeable dark wrinkles on his neck, and here and there a pockmark or two. His dapper moustache, trimmed in the American style, dated back to the days of 1918. Thanks to the doughboys after the Armistice, to the black market of the period and the traffic in women, he had been able to amass sufficient money to purchase La Féria. Lengthy service overseas and subsequent bouts of freshwater fishing had deeply tanned his skin and bronzed his face. His features were hard-set, the bridge of his nose firm, his small eyes dark and lively, his pate bald.

'How soon do you reckon to bring it along?' he asked Querelle.

'I'll have to make my arrangements and get the bag out; but that's not worrying me. I've thought of a dodge.'

With a flicker of suspicion, glass in hand, the boss threw a glance at Querelle. 'Oh, you have, have you? But – and get this into your noddle – I don't want to find myself shipped, s'welp me God.'

Mario was not in the picture, and made no movement whatever. He was standing against the counter, with his back reflected in the mirror behind him. Without saying a word, he removed his elbow from the counter – a pose that had lent him a most interesting aspect – and went to lean against the pier-glass not far from Nono, where he had the appearance of leaning up against himself. Finding himself facing the two men, Querelle felt a sudden pang, a sort of heart-rending sensation such as killers know. Mario's good looks and quiet reserve disconcerted him: they were on too grand a scale. Nono, the boss of the brothel, was far too massive. So was Mario. The lines of their two bodies met to form one continuous pattern, and this terrifying confluence blurred the individual shape of their heads and their muscular physique. It seemed impossible for the boss not to be a snitch; but it was out of the question for Mario to be anything but a cop. In his inmost being Querelle felt himself to be trembling, vacillating, almost on the point of losing his identity by vomiting and thus getting rid of all that was his real self. Feeling faint in the presence of the overpowering display of flesh and muscle that he dimly perceived towering above him – as he might when throwing his head back to appraise the height of a giant pine – an ever-shifting conglomeration that merged into one shape only to separate again and become two, crowned by Mario's good looks but dominated by Nono's bald pate and his fractiousness, Querelle remained tongue-tied, his lips parted, his palate dry.

'No, no, I'll steer clear of the shit my own way,' he said.

Mario was wearing a neat double-breasted brown suit and a red tie. Like Querelle and Nono, he was drinking white wine, but he showed no interest in the conversation. He was a proper unit of the Police Force. Querelle recognized authority in his strong legs and chest, and absolute power inherent in his sober movements; everything about him bespoke an undisputed moral authority, a perfect social organization, a revolver and the right to use it. Mario was the Master. Once more Querelle held out his hand, and then, pulling up the collar of his oilskin coat, he made off towards the back door. It was preferable, in fact, that he should make his exit by the small door into the yard at the back of the house.

'So long!'

As we have said, Mario's voice was broad and even in tone. On hearing it, Querelle felt reassured in some strange way. No sooner had he left the house behind him than he was forcibly compelled to satisfy himself by proof positive of his own stature and aura as a member of the Fighting Navy, to touch and feel on and about him the tangible attributes of the uniform he was wearing. First he considered the stiff upturned collar of his oilskin coat, which protected his neck like impenetrable armour-plating. He imagined it as a massive ruff, for inside it he could feel how delicate his neck was despite its being so strong and proud and firm, and he took delight in the delectable hollow where it was joined to his body – the perfect point of vulnerability. He began to flex his knee joints till he could feel the touch of his trouser-legs against them, and very soon he was striding out like a sailor whose one desire is to personify the typical matelot. He adopted a proper rolling gait, inclining now to the right, now to the left, without too obvious a movement of the shoulders. He thought of hitching up his oilskins and thrusting his hands through the slit pockets so that he could feel his naked belly, but he changed his mind and, instead, he put a finger up to his cap and tilted it to the back of his head, almost to the very nape of his neck, in such a way that it rubbed against the edge of his upturned collar. These tangible proofs that he was still a sailor through and through reassured him considerably and had a comforting effect. He felt sad and rather wicked. He was not wearing his customary smile. The fog moistened his nostrils, and freshened up his chin and eyelids. He was now forging straight ahead, boring a hole in the yielding texture of the mists with his weighty body. The greater the distance he put between himself and La Féria, the stronger he knew himself to be, fortified as he was by the full power of the Police force and under their friendly protection, since he endowed his conception of 'Police' with the muscular strength of Nono and Mario's good looks. For this was his first encounter with a police officer. At last he had seen a flat-foot face to face; he had gone up to him and shaken his hand. He had just registered a pact by which neither would split on the other. He had not come across his brother in the brothel, but in his stead these consummate monsters, these two trumps. While he gained in strength from the might and power of the Police the further he drew away from La Féria, never for one instant did he cease – very much the reverse – to feel himself a sailor. Querelle, in some obscure way, knew that he was very near to attaining perfection; clad in awe-inspiring uniform, cloaked in the folds of its fabulous prestige, he conceived of himself as being not so much the killer, as the seducer. He proceeded down the Rue de Siam with giant strides. The fog was chilling. Increasingly did the forms of Mario and Nono merge together and instil in him a feeling of submission – and of pride – for deep down the sailor in him felt strongly opposed to the policeman: all the more, therefore, did he seek to fortify himself with the full might of the Fighting Navy. As if pursuing his real self – ever about to overtake it, yet ever in pursuit – he put his best foot forward and strode along at a spanking pace, now certain of his identity. His body was fitted with guns, iron-clad, armed with torpedoes, easy to manoeuvre though heavy enough in all conscience, bristling and bellicose. He was now LA QUERELLE, a huge destroyer, a greyhound of the ocean, a vast, intelligent, thrusting mass of metal.

'Keep clear, you bastard!'

His voice clove the fog like a siren in the Baltic Sea.

'But you can't keep . . .'

And suddenly the young man – polite, buffeted, thrown aside by the wake of Querelle's impassable shoulder, considered that he was being insulted, and said:

'At least you can keep a civil tongue in your head! Or use your eyes!'

Did this mean: 'Keep your eyes open'? For Querelle, it signified. 'What course are you steering, where's your navigation light?' He turned right about.

'My lights?'

His voice was harsh and decisive, ready to show fight. He was well aware that he carried guns. He didn't bother about anything else. He hoped to appeal to Mario and Norbert – and no longer to that fabulous personage that their combined virtues called so vividly to mind – though in reality he placed himself under the protection of this personage. However, he did not yet openly admit it to himself, and for the first time in his life he invoked the Navy.

'See here, chum, you're not looking for a spot of trouble with me, by any chance? 'Cos any matelot'll tell you that you can't get away with that, never. D'you hear what I say?'

'But I'm not looking for anything. I was just passing . . .'

Querelle stared at him; he was under the protection of his uniform. He had hardly clenched his fists before he was acutely aware of every muscle and nerve in his body rushing to their battle-stations. He was strong and ready to spring. His biceps and arms were vibrating. His whole body was flexed for a fight in which he would measure up to his adversary – not this young man intimidated by his swagger – but to the power that had subjugated him in the room at the brothel. It never entered Querelle's head that he wanted to fight *for* Mario, and *for* Norbert, just as one fights for the beautiful princess against the dragon. This fight was to be a trial of strength.

'Don't you know you shouldn't try and capsize a Navy bloke?'

Never before had Querelle summoned such a witness to his aid. Sailors proud of being sailors, imbued with *esprit de corps*, had only made him smile. In his eyes they seemed as ridiculous as the braggarts who brazenly shout the odds and end up at Calvi. Never had Querelle said: 'Look at me, I'm a lad from the *Vengeur*', or even: 'Me, a French matelot . . .' but now, having gone so far, he did not feel in the least ashamed of his words, but rather derived considerable comfort from them.

'Clear off!'

As he shouted these two words, he gave a more scornful twist to his whole expression by pulling down his mouth at the corner nearest the civilian, and with his face contorted in a fixed jeer, he waited, hands in pockets, until the young man had turned on his heel. Then, glorying in his strength, and a trifle more severe than before, he continued on down the Rue de Siam.

When he arrived on board, Querelle saw ready opportunity for just retribution. He was seized by a sudden and violent fit of rage, when he noticed that one of the sailors on the larboard deck was wearing his cap in the very way – or so it struck him – that he alone should wear it. He made up his mind that the cap must have been stolen as he looked at the very break in it where the lock of hair flared up like a flame licking the riband, indeed the crest of hair which is now as legendary as the white fur bonnet of Vacher, the slayer of shepherds. Querelle went up to him, fixing his cruel eyes directly on those of the rating, and rapped out sharply:

'Square your cap off!'

The rating did not understand. A little taken aback, vaguely frightened, he stared at Querelle without budging. With a sweep of the hand, Querelle sent the beret flying on to the deck, and, before the wearer could bend down to pick it up, rapidly, revengefully, Querelle hammered his face with his fists.

Querelle enjoyed extravagance. It would be easy to believe that he had a real feeling for the common shibboleths, that first he experienced something of the glory of being a Frenchman, then that of being a sailor, in so far as a male is proud of national and naval prestige. We must look back at certain events in his childhood: not because these events dominate the whole psychology of our hero, but to make plausible an attitude that does not jump to the mind as merely a simple question of choice. Let us first consider how his character was influenced in his early days. Querelle grew up in a vagabond world, a world of carefully studied attitudes in those approaching the age of fifteen. Typical were the tricks of ostentatiously displaying the roll of his shoulders, of keeping his hands thrust deep in his pockets, of swinging the turn-ups of too-tight trousers from side to side as he walked through the streets. Later on, he shortened his steps, keeping his legs well flexed so that the insides of his thighs rubbed against each other, and holding his arms well away from his body to make it look as if this was due to over-developed biceps and dorsal muscles. It was not till shortly after his first murder that he adopted a characteristic peculiar to himself: a slow, ambling gait, keeping both his arms stiffly stretched to their full extent, ending in two clenched fists held together in front of his flies, but without actually touching them. His legs always kept well apart.

The quest for a characteristic attitude to define Querelle once and for all and prevent him from being confused with any other member of the crew, brings into sharp relief a form of terrifying dandyism. As a boy, he used to enter into amusing competitions with himself and apply himself to pissing in an ever higher and longer arc. One night, on leaving a brothel in Cadiz, with Vic in much the same state of mild intoxication as himself, we find him pissing in front of the prison windows; each had unbuttoned the other's flap and was holding the other's cock in a tight grip. Querelle's face was eloquent – we can best explain that by saying he had discovered a soul-mate in this mutually shared and conclusive harmony – it was lyrical. Querelle smiled on reaching him, a smile that hollowed his cheeks a little: a sad smile. It could be called ambiguous, intended for the giver rather than the receiver. Sometimes, in thinking of its effect, the sadness Lieutenant Seblon would have found in this smile could be compared to that of watching the most virile among a group of choir-boys, standing firmer on his feet, with sturdier thighs and neck, and chanting canticles to the Blessed Virgin in a male voice. He was the cause of astonishment to his companions, a cause of uneasiness because of his strength, very largely, and his peculiar stance, though his bearing was commonplace. They watched him approaching, on his face the slightly strained look of a sleeper who listens to the sob of a mosquito prevented by the gauze from getting through the mosquito-net and incensed by the impenetrable and invisible resistance. When we read: '. . . his whole appearance was subject to ever-changing expressions; from being ferocious, it would become gentle and often ironic; his attributes were those of a sailor and, standing up, his legs are always wide apart. This killer has travelled far and wide . . .', we know that this description of Campi, beheaded 30 April 1884, fits him like a glove. Moreover, it is exact, since it is an interpretation of him. All the same, his mates could say of Querelle: 'He's a rum chap', for he presented them almost every day of their lives with a disconcerting and scarifying portrait of himself. He would make his appearance among them with the glorious uncertainty of an act of God. A sailor of the Fighting Navy possesses a sort of candour which he owes to the shining example of naval heroes of the past. If he wanted to go in for smuggling, or any other form of trafficking, he would not know how to set about it. Idly resenting the boredom of his job, he performs duties that seem to us like an act of piety. Querelle was for ever on the alert. He had no real regrets for his life as a corner-boy; he had never really given it up, and, under the protection of the French flag, continued with his dangerous exploits. As a youth, he had consorted with stevedores and merchant seamen. He played their game as well as they did, and felt at home among them.

Querelle strode along, his face moist and burning, without thinking of anything in particular. He was feeling a bit uneasy, haunted by a vague, unformulated thought that his exploits would have no value whatever in the eyes of Mario and Nono, who themselves represented (and were for each other) the quintessence of value. On reaching the Recouvrance bridge, he went down the steps leading to the landing-stage. It was then that the thought occurred to him, while actually passing the Custom House, that he was letting his six kilos of opium go at far too cheap a price. But the one thing essential was 'to get himself on the right side of his mates'. He went on as far as the quayside to wait for the liberty-boat that would be coming to fetch officers and ratings returning to the *Vengeur*, at anchor out in the Roads. He looked at his watch: ten to four. The liberty-boat would be alongside in ten minutes time. He took a turn up and down to keep himself warm, but chiefly because the shame he felt compelled him to keep on the move. All of a sudden he found himself at the foot of the supporting wall of the coastal road that circles the port, and from which springs the main arch of the bridge. The fog prevented him from seeing the summit of the wall, but, judging by its slope and the angle at which it jutted from the ground as well as by the size and quality of the ashlars – details that he was quick to observe – he guessed that it was of considerable height. A feeling of nausea, similar to, if not so strong as that brought on by the presence of the two men in the brothel, once more turned his stomach a little and tightened his throat. No matter, even supposing his obvious and almost brutal physical strength really was subject to the sudden fainting fits that cause people to be termed delicate, never in his life would Querelle dare to acknowledge this as a sign of a delicate nature – by leaning up against the wall, for example: but all the same a disconcerting impression that he was about to be engulfed did make him try to take a grip on himself. He walked away from the wall and turned his back on it. The sea was in front of him, hidden by the fog.

'A queer sort of chap,' he thought, raising his eyebrows.

Standing stock-still, his legs wide apart, he became plunged in thought. His lowered gaze travelled over the insubstantial grey surfaces of the mist, as he tried to distinguish the dark, moistened stones of the jetty. Little by little, but with no proper method, he began to think about Mario's diverse peculiarities. His hands. The curve – he had stared at it long enough – from the tip of his thumb to the tip of his first finger. The thickness of his wrists. The width of his shoulders. His indifference. His fair hair. His blue eyes. Norbert's moustache and his round shiny bald pate. Mario again, one of whose finger-nails was entirely black, a very beautiful black, like lacquer. There may be no such thing as a jet-black flower, yet the end of his crushed finger did put you in mind of a black flower.

'What are you doing here?'

Querelle sprang to salute the vague form standing in front of him. Especially did he salute the severe voice that came to him through the fog with all the assurance of coming from a place full of light and warmth, official, encircled with gold.

'I'm under orders to report to the Naval Police, Lieutenant.' The officer came closer.

'But you're ashore, how's that?'

Querelle held himself correctly to attention, but he contrived to pull down his sleeve over the wrist on which he was wearing the Lieutenant's gold watch.

'You'll return by the later pinnace. I shall want you to take an order to the Paymaster for me.'

Lieutenant Seblon scribbled a few words on an envelope and held it out to the rating. He also gave him a few minor instructions in too sharp a tone of voice. Querelle noticed it. A smile flickered over his still trembling upper lip. He was both uneasy at the officer's unexpectedly early return and happy at this return, above all happy at meeting there, on the spot where he had just recovered from his panic, the Lieutenant of the ship in which he was a steward.

'Go!'

In this word alone there was a note of regret. It was unlike the Lieutenant's usual clipped speech, and bore no trace of the quiet authority that a firm mouth ought by nature to have given it. Querelle smiled to himself. He saluted and made off in the direction of the Custom House; then once again he climbed the steps to the main road. That the Lieutenant should have caught him unawares, before there was time for proper recognition, was deeply wounding, for it ripped open the opaque envelope which, he liked to believe, hid him from view. Further, it was now working its way into the cocoon of daydreams he had been spinning for the past few minutes, and out of this he drew an astonishing thread: this new venture of his was visible and taking place in the world of men and things, and was already becoming mixed up with the drama he half anticipated, much as a tubercular suspect guesses from the taste in his mouth that there is blood mingled with his saliva.

Querelle pulled himself together quickly enough. This was necessary to safeguard the integrity of his inner domain into which the highest-ranking officers had absolutely no right to be poking their noses.

Querelle rarely responded even to the most distant familiarity. Lieutenant Seblon, whether he believed it or not, never did anything to establish any terms of familiarity with his steward. Besides, this was all part of the excessive defence-mechanism adopted by the officer who, while making Querelle smile, left it open to him to take the first step towards intimacy. As bad luck would have it, this veiled intimacy only served to put him out. A few moments ago he had smiled because his Lieutenant's tone had been a little overdone. Now, however, lurking dangers made the old Querelle part his lips. If he had gone off with a gold watch from a drawer in his cabin, it was only because he had thought that the Lieutenant had really gone away on a long leave. 'He'll have forgotten all about it when he comes back after such a length of time. He'll just think he's lost it,' had been his thoughts.

As he climbed the steps, Querelle let his hand drag along the iron guard-rail. Suddenly there came back to his mind the picture of those two fellows of the brothel, Mario and Norbert. A snitch and a cop. If they did not denounce him right away, it would be even more terrible still. Very likely the police forced them to play a double game. The picture of those two trump cards grew larger and larger. They became so monstrous, threatening to swallow him up. And what about the Customs? One was within one's rights to defraud the Customs. A spasm similar to the one that had just made his stomach retch ended in a belch that never properly exploded. Slowly he returned to a calmer state, achieved almost without his being aware of it. He was saved. A little further still, and he would be sitting down up there on the top step by the edge of the road; he might even go to sleep, and rest after so splendid a discovery. From this moment on he forced himself to think in more precise terms.

> 'That's the ticket. Now I've got it straight. I must find me a lad who knows the ropes (he'd already decided on the choice of Vic), one who can let down a piece of string from the top of the wall. Once I'm off the boat I'll hang about on the jetty for a while. The fog's thick enough. Instead of passing straight along through the Customs, I'll edge over to the foot of the wall. Up on top there, on the road, there'll be a bloke to lower the end – and I'll be able to tie the packet to it. The fog'll hide me. My mate'll give it a heave and take it up. Then I've nothing hot on me, if the cops pull me in.'

A great peace settled down on him. He experienced the same strange emotion that he had as a child at the foot of one of the two towers that rise close to the port of La Rochelle. It was a feeling both of power and powerlessness. Of pride, in the first place, at the thought that so lofty a tower could be the symbol of his virility, so much so that when he stood at the base of the rampart with his legs apart in order to piss, it appeared to him as his own prick. He would sometimes skylark with his pals, when two or three of them were pissing against it, coming out of the movies after dark, and jokingly say:

'That's just about Georgette's mark!'

or:

'With one that size in my trousers, I'd take on all the old bags in La Rochelle.'

or:

'You see, this old fellow we're speaking of is the grand old man of La Rochelle.'

But when he was by himself, at night or during the day, his emotion was even stronger. While opening or buttoning up his flap, his fingers felt they were imprisoning – deliciously, with the utmost precaution – a treasure, the very soul of this giant prick; or supposing his own virility drew its strength from that of the stone phallus, then he would feel quietly humble when faced with the unruffled and incomparable power of all that is masculine. Querelle knew he had it in him to bring the opium safely and with the utmost care to the strange ogre composed of those two magnificent bodies.

'Only I'll need a proper bloke to help me, for it'll be thanks to him I'll bring it off.'

Querelle imagined in a muddle-headed way that the whole success of the venture depended upon this one sailor, and, even more confusedly, upon the peace of mind afforded by his ideas about Vic, remote as they were and as insubstantial as the dawn, but focused on Vic, whom he would enrol for the job, since it would be through him that he would eventually come through to Mario and Norbert. The Boss seemed open and frank; the other was too handsome to be just a flat-foot; the jewels in his rings were far too good for that. 'What about me, and my jewels? If only that card could see 'em'. Querelle thought about the jewels hidden away in the despatch-boat, then of his testicles, full and round and heavy, which he stroked every night, and kept safely tucked away between his hands while he slept. He thought of the stolen watch. He smiled: that was the real Querelle, coming into flower, blossoming, showing the underside of his delicate petals.

* * *

The workmen went and sat down round a bare wooden table in the middle of the barrack room dormitory, between the two lines of beds. On it were two steaming bowls of soup. Slowly Gil took his hand off the fur of the cat lying stretched on his knee, and then put it back there. Some little part of his shame was flowing out into the animal, and being absorbed by her. In this way she comforted Gil, as a dressing staunches a wound. Gil had not wished to show fight, when on coming back, Theo had begun ribbing him. So much had been clear from the tone of his voice, so suddenly humble when answering. 'There are some words you must never use.' His replies were usually tense and sharp, almost to the point of hurting, and Gil had been all the more conscious of his shame when he heard his humbled voice spreading like a shadow round Theo's feet. As a sop to his pride, he had told himself that one does not fight with a cunt, but his spontaneously gentle tone was proof that he had given in. His pals? What in fuck's name did it matter what they said? Shit the lot of them! As for Theo, well, it was common knowledge that Theo was a queer. Tough, and a bit nervy, but a queer. No sooner had Gil started to work in the shipyard than the mason had smothered him with attentions; various friendly acts which were in themselves very often masterpieces of subtlety. He plied him with glasses of syrupy white wine in the Recouvrance bistros. But behind the terrific slaps on the back from that steely hand, Gil could sense - and trembled at feeling it - a lurking, gentler hand; he wanted to chastise in order to comfort. Besides, Theo had been trying to take the piss out of him for the last few days. He was furious that he had not yet had his way with the lad. Sometimes, while at work, Gil would look across at him, and it was rare not to find Theo's eyes fixed on him. Theo was a splendid worker - held up to respect by his fellows - and, before placing it in its bed of cement, he pressed his hands lovingly over each stone, turning it over, choosing the best-looking surface and always fitting the rougher side of each ashlar facing inwards, so that the finer face was exposed and destined for the façade.

Gil took his hand off the cat once and for all, picked up the animal and gently put it down on the sawdust-covered floor near the stove. By so doing he might perhaps make his companions believe that he was by nature gentle. He even wanted his gentleness to be provoking. Finally, on his own account, he must give the appearance of wishing to divorce himself from any excessive counter-mood induced by such an affront. He went up to the table and sat down at his place. Theo did not look at him. Gil saw his thick bang of hair and bullish neck bent over his white china bowl. He was talking and laughing exuberantly with one of his mates. The sound of their mouths lapping up spoonfuls of hot thick soup predominated. Once the meal was over, Gil was the first to rise, and, taking off his sweater, he hastened to wash up. For the next few minutes, in his open-neck shirt, with sleeves rolled up above the elbows, his face reddened and moist from the steam, his bare arms deep in greasy water, he might have been a female dish-washer in a restaurant. For a moment or two he imagined that he was no longer just an ordinary workman. For several minutes he felt himself to be some strange and ambiguous being; a youth acting as serving-maid to the masons. To stop any of them coming along to tease her and smack her bottom with loud shouts of laughter, he forced himself to be brisk and busy. When he came to take his hands out of the revoltingly tepid water they no longer had the soft look, even despite deep furrows, that the white plaster and cement lent them. He felt rather ashamed of his workman's hands: white rime round the frosted quicks and nails crusted with cement. He had been storing up too much shame over the last few days to give a thought to Paulette, let alone to Roger. He was unable to think of them in a kindly way; his feelings were too shame-ridden, and a sort of sick-making steam threatened to settle over all his thoughts, tainting and dissolving them.

Meanwhile, he had come to regard Roger with hatred. In such an atmosphere, hate became ever more noxious and grew as fast as he rid himself of his shame, squeezing it out, forcing it into the remotest corner of his conscience where, however, it brooded and made its presence felt like a persistently aching abscess. Gil hated Roger for being the cause of his humiliations. He hated his pretty little phiz that gave rise to Theo's wicked innuendoes. He hated him for coming down to the shipyard the previous day. Even if he had smiled at him all through the evening while singing from the tabletop, it was simply because Roger alone knew that the last song was the one that Paulette liked to hum, and because he was addressing his sister through an accomplice:

> 'He was a careless, laughing sod,
> Who had no fear of man or God.'

Some of the masons were playing cards on the table now cleared of bowls and white china. The stove was chock-a-block. Gil wanted to go out to pee, but, in turning his head, he saw Theo coming across the room and going on to open the door, obviously on his way to the same place. Gil stayed where he was. Theo shut the door behind him. He went out into the night and fog, dressed in a khaki shirt, his blue jeans a patchwork of faded and washed-out hues, very pleasing to the eye; Gil was wearing a similar pair, by which he set great store. He began to undress. He peeled off his shirt, leaving himself in a singlet from which his muscles bulged through the wide cut-away of the armholes. With his trousers round his ankles, he could, when he bent down, see his own thighs. They were thick and solid, well developed by bicycling and football, smooth as marble and just as hard. In his thoughts Gil let his eyes travel up from his thighs to his belly, the muscles on his back, and then to his arms. He felt ashamed of his strength. Had he accepted to fight, 'on the level' of course, that is to say without recourse to punching, but simply wrestling, or 'no holds barred' using foot and fist, he would surely have defeated Theo; but the latter had the reputation of having an uncontrollable temper. In his rage he would have been capable of getting up in the middle of the night and coming on padded feet to cut his victor's throat. It was due to Theo's reputation that Gil had lain low despite the many insults. He did not want to run the risk of having his throat slit. He stepped out of his dropped slacks. Standing for a moment in front of his bed in his red slip and white singlet, he gently began to scratch his thighs. He wished that his companions could see his muscles and thus believe that he had refused to fight out of generosity, so as not to bring about the downfall of an old favourite. He got into bed. When his cheek was on the bolster, Gil began to think of Theo with an ever incensed disgust, as he imagined what he had been like in the days of his youth. Most certainly he must have been a fine specimen. In his maturity he was still pretty vigorous. 'Anyone in the building trade,' he would say sometimes, 'is bound to have a pretty hot grip.' He meant to say, 'is bound to be pretty hot stuff'. His face, with its hard, virile, and still unspoilt features, was delicately striated with an infinity of minuscule wrinkles. His small but brilliant dark eyes had a twinkle in them, but on certain occasions Gil had caught them cocked at him, and overflowing with an extraordinary gentleness, and that more often than not when the gang had knocked off work for the evening. Theo would be scouring his mitts with a little soft sand, and then he would raise his head to have a good look at the work in progress, at the rising wall, at the discarded brick-trowels, the planks, the wheel-barrows, and the buckets. Over all these objects – and over the workmen – a grey mantle of impalpable dust had settled imperceptibly, giving a uniform colour to the whole yard, composite and lifeless, now that the commotion of the day's work was over. The still of the evening was accentuated by the effect of the deserted yard lying under a sprinkling of grey. Clumsy after their day's work, tired-out and in silence, the masons would drift away from the yard with dragging footsteps, almost with an air of solemnity. None of them was more than forty. Dog-tired, haversack over left shoulder, right hand in trousers pocket, they were leaving the day behind and passing into night. Their belts uneasily held up trousers made for braces; every ten yards or so they would give these a hitch, readjust the front of them under the belt while letting the back gape wide, always showing that little triangular tongue and its two buttons intended for fastening to a pair of braces. Under a dense and brooding calm, they would return to their sleeping-quarters. None of them would be going with girls or to the bistro before Saturday, but, once abed and at peace, they would let their manhood take its rest, and under the sheets store up its reservoir of black force and white liquor; would go to sleep on their side and pass a dreamless night, one bare arm with its powder-dusted hand lying along the edge of the bed and showing the delicate pulsation of the blood in its bluish veins.

Theo would trail along beside Gil. Every evening he offered him a cigarette before setting out to catch up with the other lads, and, on occasion, his whole expression would undergo a change, as he gave him a great clout on the shoulder.

'Well, young 'un, you all right?'

Gil would make his usual non-committal movement of the head. He would just manage a smile. Gil felt his cheek grow hot against the bolster. He had lain there with his eyes wide open, and by reason of his ever increasing desire to piss; his mounting anger was aggravated by impatience. The corners and rims of his eyelids were burning. A bang on the back makes one sit up, and, in anticipation, causes an involuntary pushing forward of the body, but it may cause the giver of the blow or clout to jump, dance, or get an erection; in short, to live. Further, the recipient may be forced to pull in his stomach, or to stumble, fall, and die. We call the aspect of life beautiful, and that of death ugly. But more beautiful still is that which causes one to live to the full right up to the moment of death. Police, poets, domestics, and priests rely on abjection; they draw from this well, it circulates in their blood and nourishes them.

'Being a policeman is just a job like any other.'

In giving this answer to the slightly scornful friend of long standing who was asking him why he had joined the police, Mario knew very well that he was lying. He was by no means an out and out womanizer, despite the fact that he was well in with women of easy virtue. When he was with Dédé, the hatred he felt all round him caused his duties as an arm of the law to weigh heavily. This hatred irked him. He wanted to disentangle himself from it, but it enveloped him; what was worse, it flowed in his veins. He was afraid of being poisoned by it. Slowly at first, then with impetuosity, he became more and more involved with Dédé. Dédé would be the antidote. The Police in his veins would circulate less and less, would grow weak. He felt himself a little less responsible for it. The blood in his veins would then be less black than might be supposed to judge from the scorn of the guttersnipes and the vengeance of Tony.

Could it be possible that the prison of Bougen was filled with beautiful female spies? Mario always hoped that he would be called in for a case involving stolen documents of international importance. In Dédé's room, Rue Saint-Pierre, Mario was sitting, feet on the floor, on the divan-bed covered with a simple fringed blue cotton bedspread pulled over the unmade sheets. Dédé sprang on to the bed in such a way that he found himself on his knees in front of the motionless figure of Mario. The police officer never uttered a word. Never a muscle of his face twitched. His staring eyes were fixed on something very important straight in front of him, beyond the mirror above the chimney-piece, beyond the wall, and beyond the town. His two hands were spread out quite flat on his knees, on the hard flat surface made by the knees of a man who sits a little forward with his legs well under his body. Never before had Dédé seen him sitting in such a severely rigid position, the set of his features so hard, tense – sad even – and wicked, from the fact that his lips were so dry and tight-pressed that they might have been two extra wrinkles on his face.

'And then what's to do? What's likely to happen? I'll go down to the port, I'll have a good dekko, I'll see if he's about . . . What d'you say?'

Mario's face never relaxed. A peculiar warmth seemed to animate it, without heightening the colour; it was pale, but the lines were so close set, acutely bisected here and there and so criss-crossed that they seemed to light it up with an infinity of stars. It looked as if Mario's whole life was surging upwards, mounting up from his calves, parts, torso, heart, anus, guts, arms, elbows, and neck, right up into his face. Thence it sought desperately to escape, to go on out and evaporate into the night, after exploding in a thousand sparkling pin-wheels. His cheeks were a little hollowed, making his chin look firmer. His eyebrows were not contracted, but the eyeballs were slightly protuberant and this threw a yellowish half-moon of shadow between the lids and the bridge of his nose. Mario was rolling round his mouth an ever increasing quid of saliva, which he dared not, knew not how to swallow, but had to press against the inside of his lips. There all his commingled fear and hate were massed, at the upper aperture of his body. His blue eyes looked almost black under brows which had never appeared so ash blond. Their very brightness troubled Dédé's deep sense of peace. (For the lad was far more peaceful than his friend was agitated, profoundly agitated, as if he alone had dredged up to the surface of his face the mud deposited in both of them. This new force of purpose in Mario lent his features a desperately grave cast, with an underlying suspicion of bewilderment, like that so often observed on the face of renowned heroes. It looked as if Dédé had recognized this and could find no better means of displaying his gratitude than by accepting his purification with a delicious simplicity, by becoming endowed with the vernal grace of April woodlands.)

We were saying that the extreme brightness of Mario's eyebrows troubled the young fellow's peace of mind, for he could not be sure how so light a colour was capable of casting a shadow over so dark and stormy an expression. The desolation was too profound to be explained by a shaft of light. And this whiteness of the eyebrows troubled (we use 'trouble' here in its most exact sense of 'stirring up mud') his peace of mind, the purity of his peace of mind – not because he knew that Mario now went in fear of his life because he had arrested a stevedore, but because he was watching the policeman endure unmistakable signs of acute mental struggle – by making him realize, in some vague way, that there was every hope of seeing joy return to his friend's face, as long as it still showed signs of such enlightenment. The ray of light on Mario's face was, in point of fact, a shadow. Dédé put a bare forearm – his shirtsleeves were rolled up above the elbow – on Mario's shoulder and gazed attentively at his ear. For a moment his eye was caught by the downiness of the cropped hair, from the nape of the neck to the temples; recently cut, it gave off a delicate light, like silk. He blew gently on the ear to free it of a few longer fair hairs that fell from the forehead. None of this made Mario change his expression.

'It's a shame you've such a dead-pan look. What do you suppose those chaps will do?'

He was silent an instant or so as if reflecting, then he added:

'And what's a darned sight worse is that you never thought to have them arrested. How come?'

He leant back a little way to get a better view of Mario's profile, for his face and eyes gave no flicker of life. He was not even thinking. He was simply allowing his gaze to lose itself, to evaporate – and his whole body to be carried away in this dissolution. Robert had only just told him that five of the most determined characters among the stevedores had sworn to get his skin. Tony, whom he had arrested in a manner voted disloyal by the lads of Brest, had been released from the prison of Bougen the previous evening.

'What do you want me to do?'

Without shifting his knees, Dédé had contrived to lean back even further. He was now in the attitude of a young nun at the moment of visitation, about to fall on her knees at the foot of an oak, stunned by the revelation and by the splendour of grace abounding, and, casting herself backwards to withdraw her face from a vision that seared the eyelids, the very eyeballs, and blinded them. A smile played over his face. Gently he put his arms round the policeman's neck. With the softest of little dabs he pecked at, without ever touching them, forehead, temples, and eyes, the rounded tip of the nose, and Mario's lips, yet always without actually touching them. Mario felt that he was being subjected to a thousand pricking points of flame, darting flickeringly to and fro.

'He's covering me with mimosa,' he thought.

Only his eyelids fluttered, no other part of his body twitched, his hands on his knees never moved, his penis gave no sign of rising. All the same, the child's unaccustomed tenderness was having a considerable effect on him. It reached him in a thousand little warm shocks (painful in that he never knew where to expect them) and he allowed it slowly to swell his whole body and assuage it. Dédé might have been kissing a rock. The intervals between kisses grew longer. The youngster then drew away his ever-smiling face and whistled. Imitating the twitter of a sparrow on all sides of Mario's rigid and powerful head, from eye to mouth, from neck to nostrils, his mouth went here, there, and everywhere, shaped like a hen's beak. He whistled now like a blackbird, now like an oriole. He smiled through his eyes. He was having great fun in trying out the fullest range of birdsong. It saddened him to think that he was both himself as well as the birds, and that he was sacrificing them upon this burning but immobile head, so obviously turning to stone. He was vainly trying to work his will upon Mario's, to fascinate him with these birds. Mario felt anguished at finding himself the objective of something so terrifying: the smile of a bird. He derived certain solace as he thought.

'He's powdering me with mimosa!'

To the birdsong was added a light pollen. Mario had the vague feeling of being held captive in one of those fine-meshed veils, sprinkled all over with widely-spaced spots. Then he retired well within himself, sinking down to regain that region of flux and innocence that can perhaps be given the name of limbo. In his anguish, he escaped from his enemies. He had every right to be a policeman, a plain-clothes man. He had a right to let himself slip back into the old complicity that united him with this young urchin of sixteen. Dédé hoped against hope that a smile might make the head burst open and imprison the birds; the rock refused to smile, to burgeon into flower, to cover itself with nests. Mario was closing up on himself. He was aware of the child's airy whistlings, but he was - ever on the watch as he had to be - so far retired into his inner thought, as he tried to face up to fear and destroy it by ruthless analysis, that it would take him some little time to be aware of his muscles and bring them into play. He began to feel that he was safely ensconced behind his rigid features, his pallor, his immobility, as if behind walls and bastions. He was behind the ramparts of the Police Force, protected by outward rugosities like so much camouflage. Dédé darted a kiss to the corner of his mouth, then bounded to the foot of the bed. Perched there in front of Mario, he smiled.

'What's up with you? Are you feeling rotten, or are you up to something?'

In spite of his desire to do so, he had never been to bed with Dédé, never - so well aware was he, being himself of much the same nature, of the untrustworthiness of the young: never had he so much as made a sign capable of misinterpretation. His fellow police and those over him knew of his dealings with the kid, who, to them, was no more than a copper's nark.

Dédé had no answer for Mario's ironical behaviour, but his smile began to fade away without altogether disappearing. His face was pink.

'What's come over you? You've not gone potty, have you?'

'Oh, you're not sore with me, are you? I kiss you 'cos you're my pal. You've been scowling away there for long enough. I'm only trying to cheer you up a bit.'

'Haven't I got a perfect right to sit and think for a minute, eh?'

'You're no more use than a lump of lead when you're like that. It's not a cinch that Tony wants to do you.'

Mario made a gesture of annoyance and his mouth hardened.

'You're not thinking I've got the wind up, by any chance?'

'I never said so.'

Dédé's tone was resentful.

'I never said as much.'

He was standing up in front of Mario. His voice was hard, rather common, coarse, more like a yokel's. It was the sort of voice he might have used to a horse. Mario turned his head. He looked at Dédé for several seconds, and everything that he said during the ensuing scene seemed to be spoken in a voice far crisper than the puckered asperity of his lips and eyelids. He tried to put the full force of his will-power into his expression, that the youngster might get it fixed firmly in his head that he, Mario Lambert, Inspector of the Flying Squad, assigned to the Brest Central Police Station, did not consider himself as finished. For over a year now he had been working with Dédé, who passed on information about the secret life of the docks, the thefts, the pilfering of coffee, minerals or other goods, for the men of the waterfront paid little heed to the kid.

'Cut along.'

Motionless in front of him, looking far stockier now that his feet were planted far apart, Dédé stared at the policeman with sulky lips. Suddenly he swivelled round on one foot, keeping his legs extended like a compass, and, in reaching out to the window where his coat was hanging on the hasp, gave such a heave to the upper part of his body that he seemed endowed with a strength hitherto unsuspected. It was as if he had taken on his shoulders the full weight of some vast invisible vault of the heavens, shrouded in star-spangled obscurity. For the first time, Mario noticed that Dédé was strong, that he was now a little man. He was ashamed of having shown signs of fear in his presence, but he speedily re-entrenched himself behind the prestige of the Police, which can justify every kind of behaviour. The window looked on to a very narrow street. Facing it, immediately across the way, rose the grey walls of a coach-house. Dédé put on his coat. When he spun round back again with a similar briskness, Mario was standing before him, hands in pockets.

'Have you got it straight? No reason to go nosing in too close. I've told you, no one suspects that you work in with me, so there's no need to shift your ground.'

'Don't you worry, Mario.'

Dédé finished dressing himself. He wound a red muffler round his neck and fitted a small grey cap on the top of his head, the way village lads still wear them. He pulled out a cigarette from a number of loose ones in his coat pocket and nimbly popped it into Mario's mouth, followed by another into his own, with never a trace of a smile, in spite of what it brought to mind. And then, with a quick change of mood, he put on his gloves, gravely, almost with solemnity. They were the only visible sign of his poor riches. Dédé adored these filthy objects almost to the point of veneration and never carried them negligently in his hand, and always drew them on with the greatest care. He recognized the fact that they were the sole distinguishing feature by which he himself, from the depths of his self-imposed, and therefore moral, dereliction, touched upon the social world, the only certain world of opulence. These few gestures, this pre-determined action by its very precision, brought him once again into proper relationship with the world. He was amazed that he had let himself go just now to the extent of kissing and all that had led up to it in the way of playfulness. He felt as ashamed as if he had dropped the proverbial brick. Never before had he shown Mario – nor Mario him – the least sign of affection. Dédé was solemn by nature. In his dealings with the policeman he had always gone about collecting his evidence solemnly, and as solemnly given his report each week at some spot along the ramparts pre-arranged by telephone. For the first time in his life he had given full rein to his imagination. 'Yet I've not been drinking,' he thought to himself.

When we say he was solemn by nature, we do not mean that he ever went out of his way to wear a solemn look. It was rather that his inherent gravity made it hard for him to force himself to be light-hearted. He would never have dared, for instance, to do half the things that lads of sixteen thought nothing of: his attempts took the form of mild little jokes, such as time and time again holding out his hand and quickly snatching it back just as his pal was going to shake it, making fun of girls' tits, shouting 'Beaver!' when he passed a man with a beard, and so on. This time he really had put a bit of himself into what he had done, and, mixed with the shame, was a feeling of freedom of action. He struck a match and held out the little flame to Mario with a deeper solemnity than his knowledge of this rite warranted. Since Mario was the taller, the little fellow offered up his face at the same time, in all innocence, and partly shadowed by the screen of his hands.

'And what'll you find to do with yourself?'

'Me . . . ? Nothing. What do you want me to do? I'll be waiting for you.'

Once again Dédé looked at Mario. He gazed at him for several seconds, his mouth dry and half open. 'I'm in a funk,' he thought. He took a long pull at his cigarette and said:

'Good.'

He turned to the mirror to adjust the peak of his cap and pulled it a bit more over to the left. In the mirror he saw the whole of the room in which he had lived for the last year or more. It was small and chilly, and on the walls were pinned photos of boxers and movie stars clipped out of the papers. The only vestige of luxury was the lamp he had fixed above the divan; an electric bulb in a pale pink glass tulip. Within and all about him, Dédé felt the presence of despair. He did not despise Mario for being afraid. For some time past he had come to know that it made him feel twice the fellow he was if he acknowledged his own funk by saying out loud, 'I've got the jitters, the shivers . . .' Often enough he had to run away, fleeing before a dangerous and armed rival. He hoped that Mario would accept the challenge and fight, having decided himself, should a suitable occasion arise, to do down the docker who had just been doing a stretch. To save Mario would be to save himself. And it was natural enough for anyone to be in a blue funk as far as Tony the docker was concerned. He was a fiend and a brute, capable of every kind of double-cross. All the same, it seemed strange to Dédé that the Police should fear a bloke of that sort, and for the first time he had qualms that this invisible power, his ideal, which he served and behind which he took shelter, might be composed of merely human weaknesses. And, as this truth dawned on him through his own failings, he felt himself all the feebler, but – and how strange it was! – at the same time stronger. For the first time he was taking thought, and this made him a little afraid.

'What about Headquarters? Haven't you said anything to them?'

'Don't worry your head over that. I've told you your job, now get on with it.'

Mario dimly feared the lad might betray him. The voice in which he answered showed signs of softening, but he quickly caught up on that, even before opening his mouth, and his words were sharp and clipped. Dédé looked at his wrist watch.

'It's just on four,' he said. 'It's already pitch dark. This is something like a fog . . . can't see more than five yards.'

'Well . . . what are you waiting for?'

Mario's voice was suddenly more commanding. He was the master. Two quick steps had been quite sufficient to take him across the room and bring him, with the same ease of movement, in front of the mirror, where he combed his hair. Once more he became that powerful shadow – flesh, bone, muscle, jaunty and young, in which was contained his own proper form and sometimes that of Dédé's. (Dédé used to say to himself with a smile on his lips as he watched Mario approach their meeting-place: 'What I really like about him is that I lose myself in him.' But on other occasions his pride had rebelled against total engulfment. He would attempt a feeble gesture of revolt, but a smile or sharp word of command was enough to put him back once more in Mario's shadow.)

'All right.'

For his own satisfaction, since he alone was conscious of his act of violence, he put weight behind his words. Stock-still for a moment as proof of his absolute independence, he exhaled a little smoke in the direction of the window at which he was staring. Then, keeping one hand in his pocket, he turned abruptly towards Mario and, equally abrupt, looking him straight between the eyes, he stiffly tensed his arm and held out to him his other hand.

'So long.'

His tone was dismal in the extreme. Mario replied with a more natural calm:

'So long, young 'un, don't hang about too long.'

'You won't get the blues, will you? I've not had them all this while.'

He was at the door. He opened it. His few remaining tattered clothes hanging from the door-hook billowed out sumptuously, while the stench given off by the open latrines of the landing engulfed the room. Mario noticed this sudden, swirling magnificence of the clothes. With a certain annoyance, he heard himself saying:

'You're being too theatrical.'

He was moved, and could not hide his feelings. On certain days, he was thrown into momentary perplexity by a deep-rooted sensibility when he caught sight of, not formal and definitive beauty, but a dazzling manifestation of what can only be termed poetry: a docker would smile in such a way as he pocketed a pinch of tea in the warehouse, under his very eyes, that Mario all but went on without saying a word, feeling hesitant for a moment, as though in some way he resented being the copper and not the thief. This hesitation never lasted long. Hardly had he taken a step to move away than he was struck by the enormity of his behaviour. He was the servant of law and order, and this was in danger of being irreparably overthrown. A huge breach was already there. One could almost say that he only arrested the thief out of some aesthetic quirk. All at once his habitual demeanour would be threatened by the grace of the docker, but once Mario was aware of this threat and of its cause, one could go further and say that it was out of hatred of the man's beauty that he finally arrested the thief.

Dédé turned his head and at the same time sent a last minute farewell from the corner of his eye, which his companion took as a sign of secret understanding of his thoughts. He had scarcely closed the door when he felt his muscles go soft and his extremities weaken as if he were about to execute a graceful bow. It was similar to the feeling that he had experienced a few minutes earlier while he was playing around Mario's face and had suddenly felt weak, but he had quickly regained control of himself, though he had longed, with his neck already bending forward, to lay his head languidly on Mario's thick thigh.

'Dédé!'

He opened the door again.

'What's up? Tell me . . .'

Mario came towards him and looked him straight in the eye. He whispered gently:

'You know I can trust you, don't you, mate?'

With astonishment in his eyes and his mouth half open, Dédé looked at the policeman without answering, without seeming to understand.

'Come in and see . . .'

Mario drew him gently into the room and closed the door.

'It's understood you'll do your best to try to find out what's going on. But I trust you. Nobody must get the wire that I'm here in your digs. Got it?'

The policeman put a large, gold-beringed hand on the little nark's shoulder, and then pulled him close against his body.

'We've been working together long enough, eh, mate, and now it's up to you to look after yourself. I count on you.'

He kissed him on the forehead and let him go out. This was only the second time since they had come to know one another that he had called the young fellow 'mate'. It was a word in common use when one among his own gang addressed him, but above all it sealed the bond of friendship between the two men. Dédé went out and down the stairs. His natural toughness very soon enabled him to throw off his gloomy mood. He went on out into the street. Mario had listened to his well-known step – quick, crisp, decided – as he went down the wooden stairs of the sordid furnished hotel. A couple of strides, for the room was small and his stride naturally long, brought him to the window. He pulled aside the thick cotton curtain, yellowed by smoke and dirt. Before him were the narrow street and the opposite wall. Darkness had fallen. Tony was beginning to assume more menacing proportions. He was in every shadow, every drift of the thickening fog into which Dédé was being swallowed up.

Querelle jumped ashore from the ship's boat, other sailors after him, and among them, Vic. They were coming from *Le Vengeur*. The boat would be there to take them back on board a little before eleven. The fog was very thick, so much so that the time of day seemed to be standing still; having laid siege to the town and invested it, the fog looked like remaining in possession for more than twenty-four hours. Without a word to Querelle, Vic made off in the direction of the Customs shed, through which the sailors had to pass before climbing the steps leading up to the level of the highway; the quayside, as we have said, being immediately below. Instead of following Vic's lead, Querelle plunged into the fog towards the bastion wall that supported the highway. With a subtle smile hovering on his lips he waited a while, then he walked along the base of the wall, letting his ungloved hand brush along it. Suddenly he felt his fingers touch something flimsy. Then, taking hold of the cord, he tied the end of it round the packet of opium that he was carrying under his oilskin coat. He gave the cord three sharp little tugs and up it went, slowly bumping against the wall face on its way to Vic as he pulled it up to the top.

The Admiral in command of the Port was considerably perturbed the following morning when he was informed that a young sailor had been found on the ramparts with his throat cut.

At no time or place had Querelle been seen in Vic's company. While on the liberty boat they had not spoken to one another, or hardly, and that without standing still. Querelle had put him wise. As soon as he rejoined Vic on the highway, he took back the length of cord and the packet of opium. Directly they were walking side by side, Vic's stiff blue coat sleeve rubbed against his, and Querelle felt the presence of death throughout his whole body, the presence of a murderer. At first this came upon him slowly, rather like the mounting of amorous emotion, and almost, it would seem, through the same channel, or rather through *the negative of that channel*. In order to avoid the town and to give his general gait an even more suspicious look, Querelle decided to hug the wall of the ramparts. Piercing through the fog, his voice reached Vic's ears:

'Follow me along here.'

They continued along the highway as far as the castle (where Anne de Bretagne once lived), and there went across the Dujot Courtyard. There was not a soul to see them. They were smoking. Querelle was smiling.

'You've said nothing, have you?'

'I've told you as much. I'm no fool.'

The Courtyard was deserted. Yet no one would have been in the least surprised to see two sailors passing through the postern-gate on the ramparts and entering into the world of trees almost obliterated by fog, the world of brambles and dead foliage, ditches, mud, and paths obscured by damp undergrowth. For no matter whom, they would have been simply two young lads chasing a bit of skirt.

'We'll cross over to the other side, see? We must avoid the fortifications.'

Querelle was smiling all the time. He was smoking. As long as Vic matched his long, heavy stride, as long as he kept pace with him, he was filled with surprising confidence. Querelle's powerful yet silent presence instilled in Vic much the same feeling of authority as he had experienced during the armed drill exercises that they had practised together. Querelle continued to smile. He let the stirrings of this emotion which he knew so well develop inside him, knowing that very soon now, at a chosen spot where the trees were dense and the fog thick, it would take full possession of him, drive out all conscience, all spirit of self-criticism, and would empower his body with the perfectly timed, controlled actions of the criminal. He spoke:

'My brother'll see to it that all goes through smoothly. We're quids in with him.'

'I didn't know your brother was in Brest.'

Querelle did not answer. His eyes became fixed, as if to observe more closely within him the exact state of his own emotion. The smile left his face. His lungs swelled. His head reeled. He no longer existed.

'Yes, he's in Brest. He's at La Féria.'

'At La Féria! You're kidding. What's he on there? La Féria's a queer sort of joint.'

'Why?'

Not long did any particle of Querelle remain within his body. His body was an empty shell. Facing Vic was no one; the murderer was about to attain his perfection, thanks to the disposition in the dark night of a group of certain trees forming a sort of chamber, or chapel, down the centre of which ran the path. Inside the packet of opium there were also some jewels, stolen when with Vic.

'That's what they say, isn't it? You're more in the know than me.'

'What of it? He goes to bed with the Madam.'

A little bit of Querelle returned to the tips of the fingers and lips of the murderer: Querelle's furtive ghost once again saw the features and sovereign behaviour of Mario supported by Norbert. It was imperative for him to pass over this wall, at the foot of which he was growing pale, dissolving. Either by climbing over it, or by breaking through and accomplish this by forcing his way across with one great heave of the shoulder. 'I, too, have my jewels,' he thought.

The rings and the gold bracelets belonged to him alone. They were enough to confer on him sufficient authority to perform a sacred rite. Querelle was now no more than a tenuous breath, hanging from his own lips and free enough to detach itself from his body and cling to the nearest and spikiest branch. 'Jewels! The cop's covered in jewels. I, too, have my jewels. And I make nothing out of them.'

He was free to leave his body behind – that admirable support for his testicles. He was well aware of their weight and their symmetry. Using one hand only, unruffled, he opened the blade of the hasped knife in the pocket of his oilskins.

'But only after the boss has had a go at him himself.'

'So what? Supposing he goes nap on that?'

'Shit!' Vic appeared nonplussed. 'If somebody made you that proposition would you accept it? Would you?'

'Why not? If I had a mind to it. I've done worse than that.' A pale smile came to Querelle's lips. 'If you saw my brother, you'd fall for him. You'd let him do it.'

'That would hurt.'

'You bet your life it would!' Querelle stopped. 'Want a fag?'

The breath, about to be exhaled, flowed back into him and he became Querelle once more. Without so much as having moved his hand, with a fixed stare, paradoxically directed inwards on himself, he saw himself make the sign of the Cross. Having made this sign – a warning sign to the public that a feat of mortal hazard was about to be undertaken by the acrobat – Querelle could not draw back. He must above all remain on the alert until the act of murder had been accomplished; he must not take the sailor unawares by a movement of brutality, for it was to be supposed that Vic was not yet used to being assassinated and might cry out. The criminal has to match himself against life and death; for if there was a cry, then the blow might fall anywhere. On the last occasion, at Cadiz, the victim's blood had smeared Querelle's collar. He turned to Vic and offered him a cigarette and lighter with a restricted gesture, hampered by the parcel he was holding under his arm.

'Light your own – you light up first.'

Vic turned his back to get out of the wind.

'And he'd like you because you're a good-looking little bitch. If you sucked his prick like you draw on your pipe, he wouldn't half enjoy it.'

Vic blew out a puff of smoke, and, holding out the lighted cigarette to Querelle, he said:

'All the same, I'd be surprised if he got the chance.'

Querelle sniggered.

'Oh, yes! What about me? Don't I get first whack?'

'Come off it.'

Vic made as if to go on, but Querelle stopped, barring his way by sticking out his leg to trip him. As if he were chewing his cigarette, he said:

'Hold on. Tell me, aren't *I* as good as Mario?'

'Which Mario?'

'Which Mario? It's thanks to you that I've got past the wall, isn't it?'

'So what? What are you getting at, you silly cunt?'

'Don't you want it?'

'Come off it, stop playing the old arse fiend . . .'

Vic never finished the sentence; in a flash Querelle seized him by the throat, dropping the packet, which fell on to the path. When he relaxed his grasp, with an equally precipitate action he whipped the open knife from his pocket and severed the sailor's jugular vein. As Vic had the collar of his oilskins turned up, the blood, instead of spurting over Querelle, poured down the inside of his coat and over his jersey. The sinking man was convulsed in the throes of death, his eyes protruding, his hand executing the most delicate gesture and his body assuming an almost voluptuous attitude, sufficient at any rate to resuscitate in this foggy landscape the downy atmosphere of the room where the Armenian had been murdered, and his image was recreated in Querelle's eyes by Vic's gesture. Querelle supported him firmly against his left arm and gently laid him down upon the grass of the pathway. There he expired.

The assassin stood upright. He was the sole object in a world where danger did not exist, since he himself was objectively there. A beautiful, motionless, dark object, whose cavities were echoing in their emptiness, for Querelle could hear the rushing upsurge gurgling as it escaped from their depths to envelop and protect him. Dead, perhaps, but still warm.

Vic was not a dead man, but a youth whom this prodigious object, sonorous and empty, with a mouth half-open and half-hidden, with eyes hollow and inexorable, with hair and garments turned to stone, with knees enveloped perhaps in a thick fleece curled and rippling like an Assyrian beard, whom this object with unreal fingers, wrapped in mist, had a moment since done to death. The tenuous wisp of breath, to which Querelle was reduced, remained clinging to the spiky branch of an acacia, where it waited in suspense. The assassin sniffed twice very quickly, like a boxer, and pouted with his lips so that Querelle might enter that way by flowing into the mouth, rising to the eyes, seeping down to the finger-tips and thus re-fill this object. Querelle turned his head, gently, without disturbing the poise of his body. He could hear nothing. He bent down to tear up a handful of grass and clean the blade of his knife. He imagined that he was squashing strawberries in freshly-whipped cream and wallowing in them. He raised himself up from this recumbent position, threw the bunch of blood-stained grass on to the dead body, and, bending down a second time to retrieve the packet of opium, resumed his walk under the trees, alone.

To maintain that the criminal, at the instant of committing his crimes, believes that he will never be caught, is false. Doubtless he does not bother to define the full horror in store for him as the result of his crime: yet all the while he knows that his act must inevitably condemn him to death. The word 'analyse' is a trifle trite. It is possible, by some other process, to discover the workings of this self-condemnation. Querelle must be regarded as a joyous moral suicide. Incapable, in fact, of knowing whether or not he will be arrested, the criminal lives in a state of uncertainty, of which he can rid himself only by denying his act, that is to say, by expiation, and further, by self-condemnation (for it would certainly seem that it is the impossibility of confessing to murders that leads the criminal to panic, or to metaphysical or religious terror).

At the bottom of the ditch, at the base of the ramparts, Querelle was standing up, leaning against a tree, cut off from the world by the fog and the night. He had replaced the knife in his pocket. He was holding his cap in front of him, at about the level of his belt, both his hands spread out flat, the pom-pom against his belly. No longer was he smiling. He was now comparing before the Court of Assizes the tales he made up after every murder. As soon as he had committed the crime, Querelle had felt the hand of an imaginary policeman upon his shoulder, and he had walked slowly along all the way from the place where the corpse lay to his present position, crushed by the astonishing fate that was his. After going some hundred yards, he left the little track and plunged in among the trees, where brambles grew all round a small mound below the battlements that girdled the city. He had the frightened look, the downcast mien of a guilty man under arrest, yet deep within him lay the conviction – linking him with a policeman in arrogant affiliation – that he was a hero.

The sloping ground was slippery, and covered with thorny bushes. 'Let it slide, up my backside,' he thought, followed almost at once by other similar tags:

'As far as you're able, Mabel.'

'Up my crack, Jack.'

'Here's my prick, Dick.'

'Reach the shit – split.'

When he reached the bottom of the deep ditch of the fortifications, Querelle stood still for a moment. A light wind stirred and rustled delicately among the dry, brittle pointed tips of the grasses. The unusually crisp texture of the sound only served to accentuate the solitariness of his situation. He walked on through the fog, in the opposite direction to the scene of the crime. The wind still sighed among the sedges with a faint hissing, as soft as the sound of air in the nostrils of an athlete or the fleeting swish of a flying trapezist. Querelle, dressed in a light blue silk vest, proceeded slowly, his figure moulded by the bright blue tight-fitting jumper strapped at the waist by a leather belt, studded with steel. He was conscious of the perfectly balanced harmony of his muscles combining to make his body into an ineffably silent and statuesque whole. Two police officers walked on either side of him, invisible, triumphant, and friendly, exuding the while a cruel tenderness for their prey. Querelle walked on for several yards through the surrounding fog and the crisply whispering grasses. He was seeking a quiet spot, remote as a cell, secluded and solemn enough for a proper place of judgement.

'As long as they don't pick up my traces,' he thought.

He regretted the fact that he had not, by carefully stepping backwards on his tracks, helped the trodden down grass to stand up again. But he quickly perceived the absurdity of his fears, at the very moment of hoping that his step had been so light that every blade of grass had, in the course of nature, returned to its upright position. Then surely nobody would find the corpse till much later on, towards early morning. It would probably be found by artisans on their way to work; they are the discoverers of crimes abandoned by the wayside.

The foggy weather did not trouble him. He was fully aware of the marshy stench, for its outstretched pestilential arms enfolded him. He kept going on and on. For a brief moment, he feared the approach of a couple of lovers, strolling down among the trees, but that was something highly improbable at that season of the year. Leaves and grass were damp, and the gaps between the branches interlaced with cobwebs moistened his face with their droplets as he brushed against them. For several seconds the eyes of the murderer marvelled at the astounding stillness of the forest, where the vault of hanging creepers gilded by a mysterious sun in a dim yet sparkling air filtered through from immensely far-distant blue skies, and where the depths were illuminated by the infinitely variable lights and shades of all waking dreams.

At length Querelle found himself beside the trunk of a huge tree. He went up to it and prudently walked all round it, before leaning up against it with his back turned on the scene of the murder, where a corpse was on watch. He took off his cap and held it in front of him as before. Above his head he could only guess at the marvellous disorder of the interweaving, small, dark branches that shredded the fog and held it captive. From the innermost depths of his being was already rising to his clearer consciousness the tremendously convincing presence of the accusing finger of Fate. In the silence of an over-heated room, chockful of eyes and ears and gaping mouths, Querelle distinctly heard the droning, hollow, and more than vengeful voice of the President of the Court:

'You have cut the throat of your accomplice. The motives for this murder are all too evident . . .' (Here the voice of the President and the President himself became confused. Querelle shirked a definition of his motives by avoiding any attempt to sort them out, and by refusing to seek their origin in himself. He allowed his attention to wander away from the Court proceedings and, instead, he pressed himself more closely against the tree trunk. The full splendour and magnificence of court ceremonial appeared to his mind's eye, and in imagination he saw the Public Prosecutor rising to his feet.)

'The nation demands the head of this man! Blood calls for blood!'

Querelle was in the box. Braced against the tree, there passed before him in due array further details of the proceedings in which his head was at stake. All was going well for him. He was protected by the tree and its myriad branches intertwined above his head. He listened to the frogs croaking from distance to distance; but on the whole everything was so calm and quiet that to the agony of facing the jury was superimposed the agony of loneliness and silence. Since the crime itself was a point of departure (total silence, the silence of death desired by Querelle), around him had been drawn (or, more exactly, issuing from him, since it was the tenuous and immaterial continuity of death) this network of silence in whose web he was fast bound. With increasing intensity he took refuge in his vision. He examined it in more precise detail. He was there, and yet he was not. He was present at the projected condemnation of the guilty man in the Court of Assizes. He followed it word by word, and indeed pronounced it. Occasionally his lengthy and active reverie was cut across by such clear practical thoughts as: 'Have I really no stains on me?' or 'Supposing someone has just reached the spot . . .', but a fugitive smile flitted across his lips and drove away his fears. Too much trust, however, must not be put in the security of a smile, in its power to dissipate the gloom. A smile can induce fear, first on your teeth bared by receding lips, and give birth to a monster whose foul features will bear the exact imprint of the smile on your lips, but later the monster will continue to develop inside you, to clothe and inhabit you, till it ends up by becoming something far more dangerous than could ever be supposed from a phantom begotten of a smile in the dark.

Querelle was now hardly smiling. Tree and fog protected him against darkness and vengeance. He returned to the scene of the trial. Lord of all he surveyed, at the foot of the tree, he bade his imaginary double pass through the whole range of fear, horror, trust and flight, shudders and blenching. Recollections of what he had read came to his aid. He weighed up the reaction of the jury. His counsel rose to speak. Querelle would have liked to lose consciousness for an instant, to take refuge behind the buzzing in his ears. He must delay the closing scene. The jury would soon be returning. Querelle felt himself grow pale.

'The Court condemns you to death.'

His surroundings were obliterated. He himself and the trees diminished in stature, and he was startled to find that he was wan and weak at the knees in face of this new turn of events: just as startled as we should be if we heard that Weidmann was no giant with forehead towering above the cedars of Lebanon, but a timid young man, wan, pale as wax, of no more than ordinary height when placed between two powerfully-built police officers. At first, Querelle was no longer aware of anything but his terrible misfortune at being certifiably alive, then later, of the buzzing in his ears. In fact, his simple way of considering this misfortune is comparable to his behaviour one day when faced with death, on the occasion when the grave-diggers exhumed the body of his mother in order to bury her in a different part of the cemetery. He had arrived on the scene very early in the morning to find himself alone, confronted by the coffin which the workmen had just removed from its hole in the earth. The grass was wet, the ground slippery, and the cold intense. He could hear a bird singing. He sat down on the coffin in which his mother was decomposing. The smell of the rotting body emanated from between the badly-fitting planks without his resenting it, for it mingled naturally with the smells of the grass, the newly-dug earth, and the damp flowers. For a moment the child's thoughts turned to that awe-inspiring phenomenon, the decomposition of the mortal remains of a loved one: a misfortune that leaves one's own being and enters into the natural order of the universe.

Querelle shivered. His shoulders were getting a little cold, as were his legs and feet. He was standing at the base of the tree, cap in hand, holding the packet of opium under his arm, protected by his thick cloth uniform and the stiff collar of his oilskin coat. He put on his cap. In some indefinable way he felt that all was not yet finished. It still remained for him to accomplish the last formality; that of his own execution.

'Must I really carry out my own execution?'

It was as if a celebrated murderer, a short time after his totally unexpected arrest, were to say to the judge, 'I felt on the point of being picked up . . .'

Querelle pulled himself together, walked a few steps straight ahead and, using his hands, clambered back up the mound where the wind was singing in the grass. A few branches grazed against his cheeks and hands, and it was then that he felt profoundly sad and experienced a feeling of nostalgia for his mother's caresses, since the spiky branches were gentle, velvety, and, with the fog almost adhering to them, they recalled to him the soft light on a woman's breasts. After a short while he was back again on the path, then on the road, and he went back into the town by a different gate from the one he had gone out from with the sailor.

'I'm fed up with being on me jack.'

He was hardly smiling. He was abandoning out there on the grass, fogbound, a strange object, a little heap of starkness and quiet emanating from a still invisible and gentle dawn, an object, holy or accursed, waiting at the base of the outer walls for the right to enter the town after expiation had been duly accomplished, after the requisite period for purification and humility. The corpse would have the pale features he knew so well, from which all lines had been smoothed away. With long, easy-moving strides, displaying unmistakable signs of his customary athletic bearing, which caused any passer-by to remark, 'There goes a well set-up lad,' Querelle, his soul now quiet within him, took the road leading to La Féria.

The presentation of the story of this last adventure was given purposely in slow motion; not with the intention of instilling terror into the reader, but of giving the murder the effect that is sometimes to be derived from an animated cartoon. Moreover, the latter method would best suit the display of the extraordinary malformations in our hero's soul and body.

After committing his first murder, Querelle had experienced the feeling of being dead, that is to say, of inhabiting a profoundly remote region - more exactly, the depths of a coffin - and of wandering aimlessly about an ordinary tomb in an ordinary cemetery, and there imagining the daily lives of the living. They had seemed to him curiously insensitive and pointless, since he was no longer their pretext, no longer the central object of their generous affection. His human form - what is known as the fleshly envelope - continued meanwhile to be active on the earth's surface, among insensate humanity. Querelle therefore began to consider committing another murder. Since no act is perfect, in the sense that it is always possible for an alibi to be proof of guiltlessness, as in the case where he had committed a theft, Querelle now perceived in each crime one detail, which, in his eyes only, might well become an error capable of undoing him. Living in the midst of his errors provided the impression of nimble agility, of cruel insecurity, for he seemed to be flitting from bending twig to bending twig.

Querelle had already resumed his usual smile by the time he reached the first lights of the town. When he entered the reception room in the brothel, he was simply a stalwart sailor with clear blue eyes, out on the spree. He paused for a few seconds while the music was playing, but one of the girls lost no time in coming towards him. She was tall and fair and very thin; she was wearing a black tulle dress designed to fit tightly round the hips, and, drawn closely over the region of her cunt - and concealing it the better to excite - was a triangle of long-haired black fur, almost certainly rabbit, shabby and in places worn away to the plain skin surface. Querelle stroked the fur with a light touch of the hand while all the time looking the girl in the eye; but he did not go upstairs with her.

After delivering the parcel of opium to Nono and receiving the five thousand francs for it, Querelle knew that the moment had come for him 'to perform his own execution'.

This would be capital punishment. Even if a logical chain of events had not led Querelle to La Féria, there is no doubt that the murderer would have contrived, in mysterious and secret self-communing, some other sacrificial rites. Once more he smiled on looking at the thick nape of the proprietor's neck as he bent over the divan to examine the opium. He looked at his slightly protruding ears, the bald and shiny top of his head, the powerful arch of his body; and, when Norbert stood up again, his large-boned fleshy face with its heavy jowl and squashed nose came very close to Querelle's. Everything about this man of well over forty gave the impression of brutal vitality. Below his massive head could well be imagined the body of a wrestler, hairy, tattooed perhaps, and most certainly odorous. 'This would certainly be capital punishment.'

'You there, what are you really after? Why d'you say you want to go with the Madam? Out with it!'

Querelle discarded his grin in order to appear to smile expressly at this question and wrap up his answer in a smile which this question alone could have provoked and from which his smile alone would succeed in removing the sting. He therefore broke into a laugh as he answered, with an unembarrassed movement of his head, and in such a way that his voice could only act as a slap in the face for Nono.

''Cos I want her.'

From this moment on, every feature of Querelle's face cast a spell over Norbert. It was by no means the first time that a well-developed young lad had asked to sleep with the wife in order to go to bed with the husband. One thing worried him; which of the two would bugger the other?

'Come on then.' He pulled out the dice from his waistcoat pocket. 'Highest has it.'

Norbert crouched down and threw along the floor. He rolled a five. Then Querelle took the dice. He was very certain of his powers. Nono's well-trained eye noticed that Querelle was just about to cheat, but before he had time to interfere the number 'two' was sung out by the sailor, almost as a shout of victory. For a moment Norbert remained undecided. Was he dealing with a twister? Or . . . To start with he had thought that Querelle really wanted to go with his own brother's mistress. His fraudulent trick had proved this was not so. Yet the lad certainly didn't look like a homo. A little worried, all the same, by the deliberate concern that his prey showed in going to his perdition, he lightly shrugged a shoulder as he rose to his feet, a grin on his face. Querelle also stood up again. He looked all round him, smiling with amusement the more he relished the inner sensation of secretly proceeding to his destruction. He was going to his doom with despair in his soul, but at the same time with the inner certitude, still unexpressed, that this form of execution was vitally necessary to him. Into what would he be transformed? A bugger? He was terrified at the thought. What exactly was it like to be buggered? Of what stuff was he made? Exactly what light would it throw upon his character? It might turn him into some new kind of monster, but what would be his feelings? One is said to be 'like that', when one gives oneself up to the police. Mario's good looks were really at the back of everything. It is sometimes said that the smallest event can transform a whole life; this coming event would have just such importance. 'There won't be any gum-sucking,' he thought. And again, 'I'll stick my arse out and that's all.' This last expression had for him much the same resonance and overtone as, 'I'll stick my prick out'.

What would his new body be like? To his despair, however, was added the comforting certainty that this execution would wash him clean of the murder, which he now conceived of as an ill-digested piece of food. In the end he would have to pay for the performance, and he was prepared for the solemn occasion that every infliction of death must be. Every infliction of death must be a dirty business; where would it be possible to wash himself clean? And purge himself so thoroughly that nothing of his past self remained. And then be re-born. But to be re-born, he would have to die! After that he would go in fear of nobody. The police could doubtless seize him and see that his neck was severed; precautions must therefore be taken not to give himself away, but in front of the fantastic tribunal which he had fabricated in his own mind, Querelle would no longer have cause to answer any question, since he who had committed the murder would be dead. Would the forsaken corpse then come back through the gates of the town? Querelle could hear the long, rigid object complaining, wrapped always in its narrow shroud of fog, and whispering an exquisite melody. Vic's dead body was bewailing its fate. It demanded funerary rites and a decent burial.

Norbert turned the key in the lock of the door. It was a huge shining key and it was reflected in the mirror opposite the door.

'Drop your slacks.'

The proprietor spoke with supreme indifference. He began to undo his fly buttons. Already he had ceased to have any feelings for a lad who had pulled a fast one to make certain that he would be properly fucked. Querelle remained standing in the middle of the room with his legs wide apart. Women had never meant much to him. Sometimes, during the night, when sleeping in his hammock, his hand mechanically sought out his cock and gently caressed it till the outcome was a discreet masturbation. During the process he seldom set his thoughts on any precise image. The stiffness of the prick in his hand was enough to excite his thoughts, and, when the climax approached, his mouth assumed such a twisted shape that his face hurt him and he could never be certain that his features would not remain like that for ever, with his mouth contorted.

He watched Nono unbuttoning his flies. There was a moment's silence while his eyes became riveted on the boss's finger as he tried to force one of the buttons out of its buttonhole.

'Well, have you made up your mind?'

Querelle smiled. He began mechanically to undo the flap of his sailor's trousers.

'You'll go at it easy, won't you?' he said. 'It seems you can bloody well get damaged at this game.'

'Come off it, it's not the first time you've been slipped a length.'

Norbert's voice was dry, almost wicked. Querelle's whole body stiffened under an access of rage and thereby became extremely beautiful; head aloof, shoulders tensed and motionless, buttocks diminished, thighs tight compressed (rucked up, as it were, under the strained position of the legs, forcing the parts up and out) yet so slender that they increased the already noticeable impression of cruelty. Once unbuttoned, his flap fell forward over his parts like a child's bib. His eyes were shining. His face and even his hair were gleaming with hate.

'That's what I said, chum; it's the first time and I meant it. Better not try to warm me up too far.'

This sudden outburst of anger only served as a spur to Norbert. With his wrestler's muscles tensed for action and ready to recoil, he said in the same harsh tone of voice:

'Don't pull any of that stuff with me 'cos it won't work, see! You think I'm easy, but you're wrong. I got your number all right. You tried to bluff me.'

And, with the full force of his massive frame added to the strength engendered by rage at finding himself defied, he came close enough to Querelle to touch him with the whole of his body, from forehead to knee. Querelle did not draw back. In a still deeper voice, Norbert rapped out:

'What's more, it's good enough as it is, don't you worry. It wasn't me who asked you to turn round, so fucking well get ready to take all of it.'

This was a command such as Querelle had never before received. It came from no recognizable authority - like the conventional word of command from without - but issued from some imperative authority deep within himself. It was his very own strength and vitality commanding him to bend over. He felt a strong desire to strike out with his fists. The muscles of his body, arms, thighs, and calves, were braced for action and became tight, taut, flexed to the last pitch. Almost in Norbert's very teeth, his very breath, Querelle said quite simply:

'You're wrong, you know. I wanted your wife.'

'Tell us another.'

In an attempt to make him pivot round, Norbert seized him by the shoulders. Querelle tried to push him away, but his now unbuttoned trousers slipped down a little. To hold them up, he opened his legs a bit wider. The two men looked at each other. The matelot knew himself to be the stronger, even in spite of Norbert's more athletic build. None the less he pulled up his trousers and stepped back a pace. His face muscles contracted. He raised his eyebrows and puckered his forehead, while making a slight movement of resignation with his head.

'Good,' he said.

The two men, as they stood facing one another, suddenly relaxed their muscles and simultaneously put their hands behind their backs. This double gesture, so perfectly synchronized, and so in accord, astonished them both; it had in it an element of fellow feeling. Querelle smiled deliciously.

'You were a matelot.'

Norbert sniffed as he answered good-humouredly enough, but in a voice still reflecting his rage.

'Zephir.'

Querelle's attention was struck by the exceptional quality of the proprietor's voice; it was solid. It was, at one and the same time, a marble column issuing out of his mouth, holding him in position, and against which he could lean. It was, above all, this voice that conquered Querelle.

'What's that?'

'Zephir. The African Battalion, if you prefer.'

Their hands moved to unfasten their belts, and sailors' belts are for practical reasons buckled behind their backs – to avoid, for instance, any roll of the stomach when wearing a tight-fitting rig. Thus it is characteristic of certain bright sparks, for no other motive than that it reminds them of their Navy days or the time when they were completely under the spell of naval uniform, to keep or to have adopted the craze for fastening them in that way. Querelle softened perceptibly. Having established that Norbert was of the same race as himself, of the same family tree with roots stretching far down into the same shadowy and perfumed background of the past, the scene about to be enacted might well have turned out to be as ordinary as any of those goings-on in the miserable hutments of the Bat d'Af, of which no mention is made when the two men concerned meet again in civvy street. Enough had been said. Querelle had to go through with the act of self-execution. He resigned himself.

'Get down on that fucking bed.'

All anger had subsided, like a sudden dropping of a wind at sea. Norbert's voice was flat. Querelle, from the moment he uttered the word 'Good', felt his cock beginning to rise. He had by now unstrapped the fastenings of his leather belt and was holding it in his hand. His trousers had slipped down over his calves, leaving his knees bare, and, on the red carpet, they were like a sort of muddy puddle in which his feet were bogged.

'Get a move on. Turn round. It won't take me long.'

Querelle faced about. He had not been able to catch sight of Norbert's prick. He bent over, supporting himself on his clenched fists – one hand holding the belt – on the edge of the divan. With his flies open, standing facing Querelle's buttocks, Norbert felt himself to be alone. With one finger he lightly, unemotionally, freed his cock from his short pants and held it for a moment, heavy and at full size, in the grip of his hand. He looked at his reflection in the glass opposite, and guessed it must be about the twentieth time in this room that such a performance had taken place. He was strong. He was the master. Total silence reigned in the room. Norbert disengaged his balls, and for a second let go of his cock so that it flipped up against his belly with a smack; then, advancing calmly, he placed his hand over it as if he were hanging on to himself.

Querelle was waiting, his head bowed and the blood mounting to his face. Nono looked at the sailor's arse; the parts were small and hard, round and smooth, covered with almost a fleece of light brown hairs which continued on round to his thighs and – but there more sparsely spread – up to the small of the back, where his striped vest was just peeping out from under his rucked-up jersey. The shading on certain drawings of female backsides is achieved by a few incurving strokes of the pencil after the style of the different coloured circles on old-fashioned stockings, and it is desirable that the reader should thus imagine the bare parts of Querelle's thighs. What gave them a look of indecency was that they could have been reproduced by this process of incurving strokes which lays special emphasis on rounded curves, the very texture of the skin and the rather dirty grey of the hair where it curls. The monstrosity of male love affairs is contained in the discovery of that part of the body, especially when framed by vest and trouser-tops.

Norbert smeared some spittle on his prick with practised speed.

'That's the way I like to have you.'

Querelle gave no answer. The whiffs from the opium packet lying on the bed unnerved him. And already the tip of the prick was getting to work. He recalled to mind the Armenian he had strangled in Beyrouth, his softness, his sleekness, and his reptilian undulations. Querelle wondered whether he should try to entice the executioner with caresses. Having no fear of ridicule, he might as well try out the gentle insinuations of the murdered pederast. 'All the same, can't help thinking that old bugger called me by the fanciest names I ever did hear. One of the softest, he was, too.' But what expression of affection could he give? What sort of caresses? He had no idea which muscles to flex to achieve the required curves.

Norbert took him by storm. Starting gently enough he pushed home his rigid weapon right up to the hilt of his erection until his stomach came slap up against the cheeks of Querelle's arse. He had been drawing him on, and both his hands, so suddenly possessed of terrifying strength, were gripped tightly round the sailor's belly. Querelle's cock, no longer crushed against the velvet cover of the bed, sprang up and beat against the stomach in which it had its roots, and against Norbert's fingers, but he was quite indifferent to the contact. Querelle's erection rivalled that of a man hanged. Gently at first, Norbert went through the appropriate movements. He was surprised at the warmth inside Querelle's fundament. He pushed up further with every precaution, the better to savour his enjoyment and his strength. Querelle was amazed at suffering so little pain. 'He's not hurting at all. I must say he knows how to work his way up.'

What he felt was a new *nature* entering into him and there establishing itself, and he had the exquisite satisfaction of knowing that it was having the effect of subtly traducing him and changing him into a catamite. 'What'll he say to me when it's all over? That's supposing he does want to talk.'

His feet having slipped a little, his stomach was once again being crushed against the edge of the divan-bed. He tried to raise his chin up a little, to lift his face now buried in the black velvet, but he was overcome by the whiffs of opium. In a vague way he was thankful to Norbert for affording him protective covering. He felt some sort of affection for his executioner. He twisted his head round slightly, hoping thereby, despite his anxiety, that Norbert might kiss him on the mouth, but he could not succeed in craning far enough to see the Boss's face, who for his part felt no reciprocal affection, nor would it ever have entered his head that one man should kiss another. Silently, with his mouth half open, Norbert was getting down to it, as if engaged on some grave and important business. He was hugging Querelle with the same apparent passion as a female animal clings to the dead body of her little one – the attitude by which we understand what love is; the knowledge and understanding of separation from one particular being, of what it means to be divided, and knowing that we are able to look at ourselves through our own eyes. The two men heard nothing but the sound of their respective breathing. Querelle felt like weeping over his past self now sloughed off – but where? at the base of the outer wall of Brest? – with eyes that yet remained open and dry in one of the hollow folds of the velvet cover. He gave a further backward thrust with his buttocks. 'This is the moment that I pay off.'

Raising himself a little higher on his wrists, he gave an even more energetic shove with his buttocks – almost to the point of lifting Norbert off his feet – but the latter exerted the full power of his strength to crush him down, and, suddenly pulling the matelot to him after pommelling him on the shoulders, he gave an almighty thrust, then a second, and a third, as many as six at increasingly longer intervals but diminishing in power, till they ended in total prostration. At first Querelle whimpered quietly, then more loudly, till he was unashamedly groaning, for the first had seemed strong enough to kill him. So keen was the expression of his pleasure, that it was proof to Norbert that the matelot was not completely male, in the sense that at the very moment of ecstatic enjoyment he had not known how to restrain himself nor shown the natural male's sexual shame. The murderer felt supremely ill at ease, so much so that he could hardly find words to express his feelings. Was he a proper brown-hatter, he wondered.

Almost at once he felt floored by the full weight of the French Police Force: without always being clearly defined, Mario's features struggled to take the place of those of the man who was crushing him. Querelle ejaculated on to the velvet. A little higher up on the coverlet he softly buried his head with its strangely disordered and untidy, lifeless curls as dead as the grass on an upturned sod. Norbert never moved. He opened his mouth to unclench his teeth from the downy nape of Querelle's neck, which he had bitten at the ultimate spasm. At length the Boss's massive bulk, with infinite delicacy, withdrew from Querelle. He stood up straight.

Querelle had never let go his belt.

The discovery of the murdered sailor provoked no panic and very little stir. Crimes are no more rare at Brest than anywhere else, yet owing in part to fog, rain, and thick low clouds, to the greyness of the granite, the memory of the convict hulks, the presence, not so very far outside the town but beyond the city walls – and for that reason all the more stirring – of Bougen gaol; and, by the same token, owing to the convict-prison, to the invisible but solid thread that binds together old shipmates, admirals, ratings, and fishermen in tropical climes, the atmosphere there is such, heavy and yet radiant, that it seems not merely favourable, but even essential to the flowering of a murder. Flowering is the exact word. It is self-evident that a knife slashing the fog at almost any conceivable spot, or a revolver bullet boring a hole in it, might well strike a goatskin – say at about the height of a man – and spill the claret all down along the runnels and gutters behind the wall of vaporous fog. No matter where the blow fell, the fog would be wounded and spattered with blood.

In whatever direction you stretch out your hand (already so far from your body that it no longer belongs to you) invisible, disowned, and anonymous, the back of your finger-joints and your knuckles will brush against, or maybe your fingers themselves will grab hold of the naked, warm, unwrapped-from-shirt-folds and ready for action, strong and pulsating penis of a stevedore or matelot who, burning hot yet ice-cold, transparently erect, is waiting to spurt a jet of spunk into the blanket of fog. (Oh these overwhelming body-fluids; blood, sperm, and tears!) Your own face is so close to another's that you feel his emotion rising to colour it. All faces are handsome, softened and refined, by being imprecise, velvety with imperceptible dewy droplets sprinkled delicately on downy cheeks and ears; but bodies are thicker and heavier, and become quite extraordinarily hulking. Under their thin and patched blue linen jeans (let it be added, to heighten the excitement, that the men on the waterfront still wear red linen pants similar, as far as the colour goes, to the trousers worn by those condemned to the hulks) the dockers and stevedores usually have on another pair which gives to the outer pair the heavy look of marble folds on statues, and so you will perhaps be even further surprised when you find that the phallus hardening under your hand has managed to penetrate so many layers of material, and surprised that the thick and horny hands have with such care undone this double row of flybuttons to meet your desire, and that this twofold garment has thickened the profile of the man's parts.

The corpse was brought back to the morgue in the naval hospital. Autopsy revealed nothing that was not already known. It was interred two days later. Admiral de D . . . du M . . ., commanding the port, ordered the civil magistrate to hold a secret court of inquiry and received the report of the day-to-day proceedings. He feared that the scandal might besmirch the whole navy. By the light of torches, police inspectors scoured wood and thicket, marshland, and every blade of grass along the fortifications. They searched meticulously, turning over every cow-pat. They passed close to the tree where Querelle had sat in judgement on himself. They discovered precisely nothing, neither knife, footprint, shred of clothing, nor a single strand of fair hair. Absolutely nothing, with the single exception, on the grass close beside the dead body, of the commonplace lighter which Querelle had held out to the young sailor. The police could not determine whether this had belonged to assassin or assassinated. An enquiry as to its ownership on board the *Vengeur* proved fruitless. It so happened that Querelle had picked up this lighter on the eve of the crime, quite automatically, from among the bottles and glasses on the table where Gil Turko was singing. It belonged to Gil. Theo had given it to him.

Since the crime had taken place in the woods around the ramparts, the police had the notion that it might have been committed by a homosexual. When one comes to consider with what horror the public recoils from any idea that remotely approaches the idea of homosexuality, one can only register amazement that the police should so easily have reached this conclusion. In the ordinary course of events, once a crime has been committed, the police immediately put forward the two motives of monetary interest or passionate love drama; but once someone who is or was a sailor is concerned in it, then they simply say to themselves, 'sexual perversion'. They fasten upon this idea with almost pathetic precipitation. To society, the police are what a dream is to the daily round of activity; and what it fights shy of in so far as it can, polite society authorizes the police to bring to light. Possibly this may account for the mixed feelings of disgust and fascination with which they are regarded. Under orders to sift the evidence of dreams, the police retain the dregs of their drag-nets. This may well explain why the police bear such a close resemblance to those they hunt down. It would certainly be a mistake to suppose that it is the better to trick, scent out, and track down their game more effectively, that members of the CID can be so easily confused with their quarry.

If we were to make a careful examination of Mario's personal habits, we should note at the start his frequent visits to the brothel and his friendship with its owner. Doubtless he found in Nono an informer who was in some sort a bond of union between the law-abiding society and the world of suspects, from whom he learnt all the same, if he had not already picked them up with amazing facility, the manners and slang of the underworld – manners and language which he exaggerated when in danger. Finally his natural yearning to indulge in unnatural love with Dédé would be another strong indication; this form of love placed him at a far remove from the police force, where conduct beyond reproach is a prerequisite. (These propositions are apparent contradictions. We shall see how true they are in actual fact.) Up to their necks in work not always strictly official, the police, and above all the secret police, who, under cover and protection of the dark blue uniform worn by the CID, seem to resemble nothing so much as thin-skinned translucent blue lice, small fragile objects easily crushed between finger and thumb-nail, whose very bodies have become blue from feeding off the dark blue of their jerseys. Working under this curse only serves to make them redouble their efforts. No sooner do they get the smell of a possible case of homosexuality than they rush headlong forward, happily without any chance of making either head or tail of its mysteries.

The inspectors had a confused idea that the murder of a sailor in the precincts of the ramparts was something beyond the ordinary run of events. It would have been less exceptional if they had discovered that a 'quean' had been murdered and left there despoiled of money and valuables. Instead, they had found the body of the logical murderer, with money in his pockets. This anomaly doubtless worried a few members of the Force, and upset the natural trend of their thoughts, without, however, causing them too much of a headache. Mario had not been instructed for any special duties at the court of inquiry. He had only taken a small hand in the case to start with and had hardly bothered his head over it, being more concerned with his own danger as a result of Tony's discharge. Why should he interest himself in a crime which, neither more nor less than any other, he would never have thought of attributing to homosexual motives? Indeed, neither Mario nor any of the chief characters in this book (with the exception of Lieutenant Seblon, but then Seblon is not *in* the book) is a real homosexual, and for him such fellows were either those who let themselves be had or those who were ready to pay them, that is to say, queans and others. Suddenly he became engrossed in the case. He wanted to get to the bottom of the plot, which he imagined carefully and subtly organized, and to be directed against himself.

Dédé had come back without bringing any precise information, yet Mario felt certain that he was a marked man; not but what, he went out, courting death, with the crazy idea at the back of his mind that by his strength, agility, and speed he would outwit death, and that even if he were killed, death would simply pass through him. He imagined that, by putting such a bold face on the matter, he would dazzle danger. All the same, secretly, he reserved the right to make a pact with the enemy along the lines that will soon be made apparent. Mario was merely awaiting his opportunity. And, for that very reason, he put on a bold face.

The police officers made enquiries among the known queans. In Brest these don't amount to more than a few. Despite being a big naval base, Brest has remained a small provincial town. The avowed homosexuals, self-avowed that is, have no difficulty in remaining inconspicuous. They are peace-loving citizens of irreproachable outward appearance, even though, the long day through, they may perhaps suffer from a rather timid itch for a bit of cock. No detective in his senses could possibly suppose that the murder discovered in the neighbourhood of the ramparts was the violent and inevitable outcome - judging by the time and place - of a love affair that had developed on board a tough and loyal battleship.

There is little doubt that the police were aware of the world-renowned reputation of La Féria, but as for that of the Boss himself, his was clearly unassailable: they had never heard of any of its clients - dockers or otherwise - who had buggered him or whom he had buggered. Moreover, its reputation was legendary. But Mario did not get on to this till much later, when Nono, as a joke, made a self-confessed admission of his relationship with Querelle.

The day following was the famous occasion when Querelle emerged from the coal-bunkers and came up on deck as black as a sweep. A thick but light coating of dust lay sprinkled over his head, stiffening each hair, turning every curl to stone, and powdering his face and naked torso, his blue linen trousers and his bare feet. He had to cross the deck to reach his quarters aft. 'I mustn't get all hot and bothered,' he was thinking as he walked along, 'there's only one thing to get the shits about and that's the guillotine. Things aren't so terrible. They're not going to kill me every day.' The act he was putting on served him in good stead. Deep down inside, Querelle was already beginning to think about - and for the first time with an eye to getting something out of it - the sorry state of Lieutenant Seblon, who had given himself away by his puckered brows and the sudden severity of his voice. Querelle was deceived by these at first. Since he was just a simple sailor, he understood nothing of the mental processes of his lieutenant who punished him for no valid cause and on the slightest pretext. But one day the officer, who happened to pass too close to the engines, contrived to get his hands covered with grease. He turned to Querelle, who was standing close by. In suddenly humble tones he asked: 'Have you a handful of waste?'

Querelle produced a clean handkerchief, still folded, from his pocket and held it out to him. The Lieutenant wiped his hands with it and kept the handkerchief.

'I'll have it washed for you. You'll have to come and fetch it.'

A few days later, the Lieutenant found an opportunity of approaching Querelle and, he hoped, of wounding him. In a dry voice, he said: 'Don't you know it's forbidden to pull your cap out of shape?' At the same time, he seized hold of it by the pom-pom and snatched it off the sailor's head. The officer came within an ace of giving himself away when he found that he had unwittingly displayed such a wonderful head of hair to the sun's rays. His arm went limp half way through the gesture, and, in a changed tone of voice, he added as he held out the cap to the astonished sailor:

'You enjoy looking like a ruffian, don't you? You deserve . . . (He hesitated, hardly knowing whether he should say 'every knee should bow down before you, that you should be fanned by wings of all seraphim, perfumed by all the lilies in the world . . .') You deserve to be put on a charge.'

Querelle looked him in the eye. In a calm voice that was cruel, he said simply: 'Have you finished with my handkerchief, sir?'

'Ah! I'd forgotten, it's true. Come and fetch it.'

Querelle followed the officer to his cabin. The latter made a pretence of looking for it, but did not find it. Querelle stood strictly at attention and waited motionless. Then Lieutenant Seblon took one of his own clean handkerchiefs, of embroidered cambric, and offered it to the rating.

'I'm sorry, but I can't lay my hands on yours. Will you please accept this one?'

Querelle made a non-committal gesture with his head.

'I'm certain to come across yours. I've had it washed. I feel pretty sure you never would have known how to do it yourself. You haven't got the head for such things.'

Querelle was struck dumb by the officer's harsh look as he pronounced this phrase in an aggressive and almost accusing tone. All the same, he smiled.

'You're wrong, sir. I know how to do everything.'

'I'm amazed to hear it. Surely you take your clothes to a little sixteen-year-old Syrian girl so that she can bring them back smoothed . . . (here the Lieutenant's voice quavered a little. He guessed he had better not pronounce the words that he knew perfectly well he would pronounce, for after three seconds of silence he added) . . . smoothed and ironed out by hand.'

'No such luck. I never found any girls in Beirut. And as for my smalls, I do 'em myself.'

Without understanding what it implied, Querelle noticed a palpable weakening in the officer's rigid bearing. Spontaneously, with the astonishing sense that young men, to whom deliberate airs and graces are unknown, have of surreptitiously exploiting their attractions, he had given his voice a slightly caddish inflexion and, by relaxing the rigidity of his body from neck to calves – due to the almost imperceptible change in stance of one foot put in front of the other – he induced a series of short-lived sinuous ripples that were extremely graceful and made Querelle fully conscious of his thighs and shoulders. He was suddenly delineated by moving broken lines, and, to the officer, delineated by the hand of a master.

'Oh?'

The lieutenant looked at him. Querelle stood perfectly still, yet still maintained his grace of movement. He was smiling. His eyes were shining.

'Well, in that case . . . (The lieutenant casually drawled his words) . . . W-e-l-l . . . (and by an intake of breath he finally succeeded in continuing without betraying too much of his uneasiness) . . . if you really work as well as that, I should like you to act as my steward for a while.'

'Suits me very well, Lieutenant, only if I left the stoke-hole, it would mean I'd no longer be paid my "hard-lying" money.'

Querelle said this quite simply, just as he had quite simply accepted the idea of becoming a steward. Totally unaware that it was love that inspired them, simultaneously and at a single stroke, he was conscious only of witnessing the transformation of all tentative, and all effective, punishments meted out by the Lieutenant. These would tend to lose their primary meaning and take on that of 'relations', which, he now saw, had for some time past been leading to a union, a proper understanding between the two men, and was already halfway to fulfilment. They had each their memories. As from this very day, their pact of agreement could be said to have begun.

'Why should it? I shall arrange to have it made up to you. Don't worry, you won't lose a day's special pay.'

The Lieutenant fondly believed that he had never revealed his love, while hoping at the same time that he had made it abundantly clear. The true situation became perfectly understandable to Querelle the following day when he came across – in a place where, logically, it ought never to have been, namely in an old crocodile-skin wallet – his own grease-stained handkerchief, far stiffer, it seemed to him, than grease alone could have made it. Querelle derived a certain amusement from these little games of hide-and-seek and saw through them perfectly well. On the day in question, he was sure that his suddenly blackened face would not only stand out more provocatively under its light coating of coal-dust, but at the same time be enhanced with such astonishing beauty that the officer would be bound to lose all self-control. Would he, perhaps, 'declare himself'?

'I'll jolly well soon find out. P'raps he never caught on!'

Within this astonishing body, uneasiness was giving rise to the most exquisite emotions. Querelle appealed to his star, which was his smile. The star appeared. Querelle moved forward, putting his broad feet flat on the ground. He gave a slight swing to his hips, narrow as they were, and this sent a gentle ripple along the tops of his trousers where they were overlapped by his white underpants, both being held up by a wide belt of plaited leather buckled at the back. He had, of course, with his usual cunning, not failed to notice that the Lieutenant's gaze often enough wandered down to this part of his body, just as he knew instinctively the most effectual seductive points about himself. He was gravely conscious of these; sometimes they would bring a smile to his face, his typical, hauntingly sad smile. He also gave a slight shrug of the shoulders, but this movement, like that of his hips and his arms, was more discreetly under control than usual, closer to himself, more within him, one might say. He moved as compactly as possible; in a phrase, 'Querelle was playing a neat game.'

As he approached the cabin, he hoped that the Lieutenant would have noticed the abortive theft of his watch. He longed to be taken up on that. 'I'll explain it away, but I fucking well deserve to stop a packet over this.' But, in the act of putting his hand up to knock on the door, he longed for the watch, that he himself, when he had come on board, had replaced in its secret hiding-place in the Lieutenant's drawer, to have stopped of its own accord – either by going wrong or because the spring had run down, or again, he dared to think, by a special dispensation of destiny and even by a particular kindness on the part of the watch that had already fallen under his spell. 'And what about afterwards. If he says a word on the subject, I'll fuck him good and proper, give him the whole works.'

The Lieutenant was waiting for him. From the very first glance, from the kind of lingering caress of the brief survey of his face and body, Querelle was confirmed in the certainty of his power; his body was emitting the penetrating rays that entered through the eyes but ran down to the officer's stomach. This handsome, blond creature, secretly adored, would very soon appear, naked perhaps, yet clothed in majesty and splendour. The coal dust was not so thick that it hid the brightness of the hair, the eyebrows and the skin, nor the rosy pinkness of his lips and ears. It was merely that they were momentarily veiled. And this veil Querelle occasionally removed playfully, by blowing on his arms or ruffling a curl of his hair.

'You do your work well, Querelle. You do certain duties without warning me. Who told you to coal?'

The Lieutenant spoke in dry enough tones. He was fighting against his emotions. His eyes were making pitiful and useless efforts not to rest too obviously upon Querelle's flap and thighs. One day when he had offered him a glass of port, Querelle had said that he couldn't touch alcohol on account of having a dose of clap. (Querelle had lied. On the spur of the moment and further to whet the lieutenant's desires, he had pretended to be suffering from a disease of males, of 'out-and-out womanizers'.) Seblon, ignorant of the whole truth, had a vivid vision under the blue linen of an ulcerated penis, running like a guttering Easter candle to which five grains of incense had become encrusted. He was already incensed himself at being unable to take his eyes off those muscled and powdered arms, whereon particles of coal dust remained clinging to hairs that were still curly and golden. He thought, 'Can it really be Querelle who murdered Vic? But that's impossible. Querelle is by nature already too beautiful to add the further beauty of a crime. What use can he make of this new adornment? Vic and he were not buddies. Therefore all manner of things must be invented about them, such as a secret relationship, secret meetings, embraces and clandestine kisses.'

Querelle gave him the same answer as he had to the Captain at Arms: 'But . . .'

Querelle caught the surreptitious look, rapid as it was. His smile became still broader and, by shifting the position of his foot, he sent a flashing ripple down his thigh.

'You don't care for your work here, then?'

The fact that he had not been able to prevent himself giving such a humble, routine explanation put the officer in a happier frame of mind, and he blushed to observe Querelle's black nostrils quiver tremulously, and the lovely dimpled little hollow between his nasal membrane and his upper lip crinkle with quicker and more subtle twitchings, which were all too clearly the delicious outward signs of a considerable effort to restrain a smile.

'But I do. Suits me. I was only doing someone a sub. Colas, in fact.'

'He could easily have found another substitute. You're in a fine pickle. Are you really so keen on this job, that you must breathe in all that coal dust?'

'Of course not, but then, you see, being me . . .'

'What's that? What d'you mean?'

Querelle gave way to his fullest smile.

'Nothing.'

The officer was properly caught. It only needed a word, a simple word, to send Querelle to the showers. They remained for a few moments very ill at ease, both of them in a state of suspense. It was Querelle who brought matters to a close.

'Is that all you had to say to me, sir?'

'Yes, why?'

'Oh, no reason.'

The officer thought he detected a hint of impertinence in the rating's question as well as in his answer, though both had equally been made in the sunshine of his blinding smile. His personal dignity bade him dismiss Querelle on the spot, but he could not pluck up courage to do so. Supposing Querelle were prompted by some unlucky chance to go down to the bunkers, his lover would have followed him there. The presence in his cabin of this half-naked sailor was driving him frantic. Already he was sinking down to hell, slowly descending black marble steps almost to the bottom of the well in which the news of Vic's death had precipitated him. He wanted to take Querelle with him on this ceremonial adventure. He required him to play his part in it. What secret thought, what dazzling confession, what exciting new light lay concealed beneath this pair of trousers, blacker than trousers had ever been before? What shadowy phallus hung enshrouded there, its sooty stem pendulous among withered moss? And what strange matter encased the whole? No doubt it would prove to be nothing else but a little coal dust – stuff one knows all about and of what it is composed – and yet this simple ordinary stuff, so liable to dirty hands and face, enhanced this fair young sailor with all the potent mystery of a faun, of an idol, of a volcano, of a Melanesian archipelago!

He was himself, yet he was so no longer. The Lieutenant, standing there in front of Querelle, whom he desired, but did not dare approach, made an almost imperceptible gesture with his hand, quickly and nervously withdrawn. Querelle noted all the waves of uneasiness passing across the eyes fixed firmly on his, without letting one of them escape him; and then, as if some great weight had, by crushing Querelle, caused his smile to broaden more and more, he kept on smiling under the gaze and impending weight of the Lieutenant to the point of growing stiff in his efforts to support it. He understood, none the less, the gravity of his gaze and that the whole despair of the man was at this moment concentrated in his eyes. But, at the same time as making a sweeping unintentional movement of the shoulders, he thought: 'He's a queer.'

He despised the officer, yet he kept on smiling, allowing himself to be lulled by the vague and half-formed idea revolving in the back of his mind round the word 'queer'. 'Queer! What exactly does it mean? He's a queer! Well, suppose he is?' And gently, while his mouth was gradually closing, the corners of his lips began to curl up in disdain. The phrase in the back of his mind was beginning to induce a vague feeling of torpor: 'I've been buggered myself, if it comes to that!' Again, a thought he found great difficulty in formulating, one which did not revolt him. Yet he realized how saddening it was when he found that he was compressing his buttocks so tight – or so it seemed to him – that they were no longer touching the seat of his trousers. This passing yet disconsolate thought let loose up his spine an immediate and rapid flood of waves which quickly spread out over the whole surface of his soot-blackened shoulders and covered them with a shimmering shawl of shivers. Querelle raised his arm to smooth back with the flat of his hand the lock of hair that had fallen over and behind his ear. His gesture was so beautiful, disclosing as it did an armpit as pale and dappled as the belly of a trout, that the officer could not help his eyes betraying the fact that he could scarcely hold out any longer. His eyes begged for mercy. The look in them displayed greater humility than if he had gone down on his knees. Querelle was conscious of the full force of his powers. If he despised the Lieutenant, he felt no impulse, as on other days, to laugh at him. It seemed to him futile to exert his charms to the full, so strong was this belief that he belonged to an entirely different species. It had raised him from the depths of hell, yet from nether regions where bodies and faces are beautiful. Querelle derived the same pleasurable feelings from the coal dust on his limbs as does a female when conscious of the feel on her arms and hips of the folds of a material that makes her look like a queen. Such a make-up, by leaving his nakedness virtually unsullied, turned him into a god. He took pleasure in exaggerating his smile. He was now quite sure the Lieutenant would never speak to him about the watch.

'What are you going to do now?'

'I don't know. I'm waiting for your orders. Only, my mates are all alone below.'

The officer made a quick calculation. To send Querelle to the showers would be to destroy the most beautiful object his eyes had ever been given the opportunity of feasting on. Since the sailor would be here again the next day, close beside him, it was better to leave him covered with that precious stuff. Perhaps he might find, in the course of his daily routine, the opportunity of going below to the bunkers and there taking by surprise, in the full flush of uncontrolled physical desire, this giant emblem of the nether regions.

'All right then. You'd better be off.'

'Very good, Lieutenant. I'll be there again tomorrow. So long.'

Querelle saluted and turned on his heel. With the anguish of a shipwrecked mariner watching island shores recede, and in wild surmise at the ambiguous and allusive tone of Querelle's parting words – endearing as the first use of a Christian name – the officer followed with a lingering glance the spruce and dazzling buttocks, the splendid figure, shoulders and neck as they vanished from sight irrevocably, and long enough for him to call up the vision of innumerable and invisible outstretched hands enfolding the treasures committed to their protection with infinitely tender solicitude.

Querelle went back to the bunkers, as had become his habit ever since he had committed the murder. If on the first occasion he had had the idea that he would thus escape detection by possible witnesses, on subsequent occasions he was sufficiently reminded of his own astonishing powers to search out any such intruders, blissfully aware of the protection it afforded him to be powdered in black from head to foot. His strength lay in his extremely handsome appearance and in his daring to add still further to that beauty the cruel disguise of a mask; his strength lay – and how calm and invisible it was, crouching in the shadow of his innate power, in the remotest corner of his personality! – in his being powerful enough to cause fear and yet to know himself to be gentle; his strength lay in his being a Negro savage, the member of a tribe in which murder ennobled a man.

'And so what! Bugger it all, I have my jewels!'

Querelle knew that the possession of money, and above all gold, gave one the right to kill. To kill, thereafter, became a 'State affair'. He was a

Negro among white men, and more mysterious by far, monstrous, outside the laws of this world, since he owed his peculiarity to a make-up that could hardly be said to have been applied at all and was so commonplace, simply coal-dust. Querelle was therefore the proof that coal-dust was something out of the ordinary, since it had the power to transform the soul of a man by no other means than by being sprinkled over his skin. His strength lay in his being a pillar of light to himself, an apparition of darkness to others; his strength lay in his being at work in the lowest hold of the ship. Lastly, he was finding out how pleasant objects and things funereal could be, and how light their weight. He had come in the end to veiling his face, and, after his fashion, wearing the mourning appropriate to his victims. However much he might have dared on former occasions, today he was unable to recount the details of his murder. He must be on his guard against one particular sailor on coaling duty, whose good looks, and as cruelly painted as his own, might well extract a sigh of confession from him. On his way back to the bunkers, he said to himself, 'He never mentioned the watch.'

Had the lieutenant not been doing his level best to embroil Querelle in everything connected with Vic's murder, while he was working out the story in his imagination, perhaps he would have been more than stupefied at the exceptional fact that his steward chose to endure of his own free will, at the end of this day, the self-imposed task of coaling. But he was too stunned by the last scene to put the proper interpretation on the double mystery. And when the two police officers in charge of the inquiry on board came to interrogate him about the men, he did not advance his theory that Querelle could be guilty. But the interview gave rise to the following: if the suddenly caressing inflexions of the Lieutenant's voice and his preciosity of language and gesture passed for signs of distinction in the eyes of his fellow-officers – accustomed as they were to the unctuous and flexible tones of their blessed families – the police officers were not to be taken in by these traits, and at once recognized him as a homosexual. For there was no doubt, whatever illusion he might still hold as to the opinion of his ratings, whether they criticized him for the metallic harshness of his voice, or for exaggerating the crispness of his orders – which he sometimes reduced to telegraphese – no doubt at all that the police had thrown him off his balance. Face to face with them, with their authority, he felt guilty and gave himself away by indulging in the gestures of a mad girl, and by other self-evident confessions of guilt.

Mario took it upon himself to put the first question:

'Excuse me if I am disturbing you, Lieutenant . . .'

'That's a very sound idea.'

But this reflexion, apparently spoken at random, or, at any rate, due to being caught off his guard, made him appear cynical and detached. The police officer thought that he was trying to be witty and this annoyed him. While the Lieutenant's embarrassment tended to increase, Mario, likewise affected, interrogated him more brutally. To the perfectly harmless, 'I suppose you have never noticed anything queer between Vic and any particular one of his shipmates?' Seblon made the reply, which was hyphenated by a half-swallow not unnoticed by the interrogators:

'And how do you expect me to recognize a queer?'

This – in every sense – slip of the tongue, made him blush and further embarrassed him. Evidently the strangeness of the officer's answers was all too apparent to Mario. Since his own strength lay in his words – his weakness too for that matter – Seblon still wished to impress by his verbal power, which was being subtly undermined.

'What should I find to interest me in the extraneous relations of these lads? Supposing the rating Vic were murdered in the course of some doubtful imbroglio, I could hardly be supposed to know the ins and outs of it.'

'Of course not, Lieutenant, but sometimes one hears something.'

'You're joking. I don't spy on my men. And, above all, make quite certain of this, that if any of these young fellows do have dealings with the odious individuals you speak of, they do not boast about them. I believe the greatest secrecy is maintained about such meetings . . .'

He noticed that he was well on the way to extolling homosexual affairs. He would have liked to keep his mouth shut; but, realizing that his sudden silence would seem strange to the inspector, he added in negligent tones, 'These disgusting characters enjoy a marvellous organ-i-za-tion . . .'

That was really overdoing it. He himself noticed the ambivalence of this opening sentence and especially of the word 'organization': he had laid such stress on the first two syllables, closely followed by 'I say', seeming almost to strike a note of delirious defiance. This was sufficient for the police officers. Without exactly being able to lay their finger on what it was that betrayed him, they were perfectly aware that by his choice of language he condoned certain practices that were forbidden by law. Their thoughts might be expressed in such ordinary phrases as: 'He refers to them sympathetically,' 'He doesn't rate them as beneath contempt.' In short, he was suspect in their eyes. Fortunately for him, he had an alibi, for he had been on board the night of the crime.

When the interview was terminated, but before the two police officers had left his cabin, the Lieutenant had the idea of putting his blue cloth cape close over his shoulders, but he introduced such airs and graces into the gesture, which he at once and clumsily attempted to correct – that 'fitting it closely on his back' would be too strong an expression perhaps – and he himself found the word 'enveloping' sprang spontaneously to his lips. It was torture for him to think of, and he made up his mind once more never to touch the thing again in public.

Querelle gave ten francs towards buying a wreath for Vic.

FURTHER EXTRACTS from the PRIVATE DIARY.

This Journal can be nothing but a Book of Prayer.

God grant that I may envelop myself in my chilly gestures as in a shawl, like a dog-tired Englishman in his travelling-rug, like an eccentric old lady in her wraps. That I may confront mankind, you have given me a sword of gold, gold braid, medals, and the right to command: these accessories are my salvation. They allow me to weave about my person invisible lace of purposely primitive design. The vulgarity of it exhausts me even if it comforts me. When I am grown like an old woman, I shall take refuge in the last resort behind the ridiculous fads of rimless steel pince-nez, celluloid collars, lisping, and starched cuffs.

Querelle tells his comrades that he is victim of posters! I am the victim of posters, and the victim of the victim of posters.

My officer's cap casts a shadow over my face. Hiding my forehead, it gives an added importance to my mouth and the two long lines framing it, which are severe, almost old-maidish. But my most feminine feature is my forehead; I remove my cap and, straight away, these wrinkled lines appear flabby and soft; pendulous.

Once again I have dragged the door-curtains in with me quite unwittingly. I felt that they *wanted* to envelop me in their folds and I could not resist making a grand sweeping gesture to free myself of them. The gesture of a swimmer sweeping aside the waves.

I come in. I think again of the life of that cigarette held between the fingers of the sailor. A compact cigarette. It was being smoked, it underwent various little movements between Querelle's almost motionless fingers, and he had no conception of the strange life he was giving to this dog-end. I was no more able to take my eyes off his fingers than off the object to which they lent the grace of motion. And by what a graceful life they were animated, by what elegant movements, so neat and nimble! Querelle was listening to one of his mates talking of the girls in the brothel.

'I have never been able to see myself.' Have I charms another could fall for? Who other than myself is subject to the charms of Querelle? How would it be possible for me to turn into him? Shall I be able to graft on to myself his most lovely features: his hair, his testicles? His hands even?

In order that they may not hamper me in masturbating, I turn back the cuffs of my pyjamas. This simple manipulation makes a wrestler of me, a stalwart. In this guise I confront the image of Querelle, in front of whom (or which) I appear as an animal-trainer. But it all ends tamely with a paltry flick of a towel on the stomach.

(The purpose of this book is not to pick out two or several characters – or heroes since they arise from a fabulous realm, that is to say they have their origin in the fable, fable or limbo – all of them systematically odious. And that the reader may regard it rather as a series of adventures unfolding in the deepest, most asocial recesses of his soul, the creator of this story has breathed life into his creatures, and by voluntarily assuming the burden of the sins of the world devised by him, he saves and delivers it and at one stroke places himself above and beyond sin. Whether or not the reader is to escape sin will depend upon how he reacts to the words of the text and upon the extent to which he discovers these heroes already lurking in himself.

Querelle! All Querelles of the Fighting Navy! All handsome matelots, you have the delicious flavour of wild oats.)

A reception on board. The ship's decks are decorated with green plants and red carpets. Ratings in white come and go. Querelle pays little attention to what is going on. I look at him without his seeing me: he stands there, hands in pockets, the jut of his bum arched and the thrust of his neck like a bull's (or a lion's, or a tiger's) on an Assyrian bas-relief. The entertainment means nothing to him. He smiles and whistles.

Querelle making fast a heavy launch to the quayside; four ratings are pulling on the rope, extending their chests with the effort, the rope passed under and round their left shoulders; but Querelle faces the opposite way. He pulls while walking backwards: no doubt, so as not to give the impression of a pack animal. He noticed that I was looking at him. It was I who had to take my eyes off his.

The beauty of Querelle's feet; his feet when they are bare. He plants them firmly on the deck. He walks with even-spaced long strides. Despite his smile, his face is sad. His sadness reminds me of the look on the face of a good-looking lad, very strong and very much the man, who has been apprehended; like a kid on a grave charge and utterly crushed in the witness-box by the severity of his sentence. In spite of his smile, his beauty, his insolence, the radiant vigour of his body, his boldness, Querelle seems to carry the indescribable signs of a profound humiliation. This morning he was downcast. He had a tired look.

Querelle was asleep on deck in the sun. I stood and looked down at him. My eyes remained riveted on him and I drew back almost immediately for fear that he should see me. To moments of quiet, assured, and lengthy leisure, when perhaps we might be able to sleep in each other's arms, I prefer moments of discomfort, passing moments all too quickly ended by having to shift a leg that can no longer support one in a reclining position or because one is lying on an arm, or because of a badly closed door, or a twitching eyelid. I make the most of those instants, and Querelle ignores them.

Admiral A gave a reception on board; a tall, thin, old man with very white hair. He rarely smiles, but I know that behind his severe and rather haughty exterior he hides a gentle nature and a heart of gold. He made his appearance up the gangway closely followed by a marine, a huge strapping fellow dressed in full fighting equipment – gaiters, belt, chin-strap, and all. He was acting orderly. This apparition caused me the most profound and astonishing emotion, and I enjoy wallowing in the recollection of it. The delicate, fragile outline of the old man with his neat gestures, supported by the magnificent carriage of his orderly! In days to come I shall be an elderly officer, bedecked and bedizened with gold braid, delicate, framed by the superbly solid muscular dimensions of a young soldier of twenty.

We are at sea. A tempest hits us. If we are shipwrecked, what would Querelle do? Would he try to save me? He does not know that I adore him. I would attempt to save him, but I would far rather try to make him save me. When shipwrecked, each man seizes upon what is most precious to him: a violin, a manuscript, photos . . . Querelle would seize upon me. I know that, first and foremost, he *would save* his beauty, and then I could die happy!

He was watching a sailor scrubbing the decks. Lacking anything else on which to lean, Querelle leant upon his two hands, one over the other as they were, tucked into his belt above his flap. The whole of the top part of his body was bending forward on them, and, under this weight, his belt, together with the top of his trousers, was flexed like a taut rope.

I could cry at having no prick to hold in my hand. I howl in my frustration to the sea, the night and the stars. I know that in the quarters aft there are some magnificent specimens which I shall never be allowed to touch.

The admiral gives an order perhaps, and docilely the stalwart who accompanies him everywhere enters his cabin, unfastens his flap and presents to the expectant lips a penis correctly enlarged to regulation size and proportions. I can imagine no more elegant a couple, nor one more perfectly complementary, than that of the admiral and his blond beast. They are beautiful.

Querelle has left his jersey behind in my cabin. Here it lies on the floor as he left it. I do not dare so much as to touch it. This striped naval jersey has all the strong and powerful appeal of a leopard skin. And more besides. It is the very animal lurking there, entirely wrapped up in itself and showing only its outward form. 'Of course, he had to throw it exactly there!' But I have only to stretch out my hand to touch it and it will immediately swell up and fill out with the strength of Querelle's muscles.

Querelle is sewing on his buttons. I watch him brace his arm the better to thread the needle. This gesture is in no sense ridiculous in one who was yesterday evening cuddling a girl, pushing her up against a tree with a conquering smile on his lips. When he drinks a cup of coffee, Querelle will often swill the cup to dissolve the sugar to the last granule with the same rotary motion of his right hand, from right to left (that is, anti-clockwise), as most women, and five minutes later he will reverse the motion and rotate it as men do. Thus, even the least significant of Querelle's acts is filled to overflowing with the humanity, the gravity of the nobler act preceding it.

Looking up the word 'pederast' in the dictionary, I came across this extract: 'Sometimes will be found in their rooms a large number of artificial flowers, crowns and garlands, intended, without any doubt, to be used as ornaments and personal adornment in orgiastic revels.'

Gil was asleep, lying on his stomach. As on every Sunday morning, he woke late. Even though the workmen were in the habit of indulging in a long lie-in on this day of the week, some of them were already up. The sun was already high in the sky and piercing the fog. At the same time as feeling a strong urge to piss, Gil was undergoing the agonizing thought of having to face the coming day and its atmosphere thick with his shame, and, in order to swallow it at the earliest possible moment, he opened his mouth very wide. He delayed the moment of getting out of bed. Above all he must take the greatest care to remain unnoticed, since he would have to invent a whole new code of behaviour to enable him to start on a life which would henceforward be lived under the shadow of contempt. Consequently, as from this morning, he would have to start on new and different terms with his mates in the shipyard. Stretched out under the sheets, he remained motionless; not with the intention of going to sleep again, but in order to think more clearly of what lay in store for him, to 'accustom himself' to the new situation, to give it careful thought before taking part in it physically. Gently, with his eyes shut as though still asleep, in the hopes of putting anyone off the scent if all eyes happened to be watching to see when he woke up, he turned round in his bed. A ray of sunlight from the window shone straight on to the coverlet on which some buzzing flies had settled. Without having seen in any detail exactly what it was that attracted them, Gil knew that it had to do with the exposure of some secret. With as little commotion as possible, he pulled his slip down under the sheets to find that it was slightly stained with shit and blood at the back, and it was this, with the help of the sunlight, that had been attracting the flies. They buzzed off with such an infernally droning hum that the room was filled with the sound of it, drawing the attention of all and sundry to Gil's infamy and proclaiming it with the majestic splendour of an organ voluntary. Gil was pretty sure that Theo was all out for his revenge. He must have ferreted out this disgusting slip tucked well away in Gil's haversack, and left it lying there while the young mason was asleep. His mates would have watched these preparations with grave and silent approval, knowing Theo to be a violent character, the better to appreciate what game was afoot. It wouldn't be such a bad thing if a young 'un against whom they had so little should be pushed around in the shit. And there was no doubt that sun and flies, on whose support Theo had certainly never counted, were for their part at concert pitch.

Without raising his head from the pillow, Gil moved it over to the left: he felt something hard under his cheek. Proceeding with the utmost caution, he slowly guided his hand up towards the object and pulled down under the sheets against his chest an enormous aubergine. He held in his hands something strangely beautiful, terrifyingly large and round, violet in colour. All Gil's compressed venom - visible in the taut muscles beneath his smooth white skin, in the vacant stare of his green eyes, in his alert intelligence, in his uncomfortably smiling mouth and his unfinished smile that, in its refusal to disclose any other teeth but his incisors, was as tight-stretched as a cruel length of elastic that must inevitably flip back mercilessly when released; in his crisp hair, sparse and pale; in his uncommunicativeness; in the icy, purely glacial ring of his voice; in fact, in every single one of the outward manifestations which led people to refer to his 'uncontrollable rages' - all Gil's smouldering rancour was wounded to the quick, bruised like a sleepy pear, and to such an extent that it all but brought tears to the poor lad's eyes. To the extent, that is, that he felt they had their knife into him, so he was feeling pitiably weak and woebegone, and ready to die. From his little toes to the corners of his dry eyes, Gil's body was shaken by profound sobs, which completely broke down all the elements of cruelty in it. His need to piss became more and more intense and concentrated all his attention on his bladder. But, in order to reach the latrines, he would have to get out of bed and cross the room under an incessant hail of mockery. He remained lying there at full length, thinking only of his violent physical necessity. Finally he decided to live down his shame.

There was no adequate gesture for throwing back the sheets. His fists clutched at the folds without his hands obtaining any firm grasp – the proper grip of his wrists was denied him – like a humble-browed Christian, a miserable sinner showing only his ashen-grey neck, unworthy of any applause. Humbly he raised his head without daring to use his eyes and almost on all fours he collected his socks and put them on without showing his legs. The door was suddenly opened immediately in front of him. Gil did not lift his eyes.

'Isn't it warmed up yet, boys?'

It was the voice of Theo who had just come in. He went over to the stove where a can of water was heating.

'Is this mess going to be made into soup? There's not much in it!'

'That's not for soup, I'm going to shave with it,' someone called out in answer.

'Oh! I'm sorry. I was only thinking . . .'

And, with a faint note of resentment in his voice, he went on:

'It's true, of course, that you can go a bit too far and spoil soup with what you put into it. We must draw in our belts, I'm thinking. Don't know how it's to be done, seeing as how there's no vegetables knocking around.'

Gil blushed as there came to his ears the sound of five or six sniggers. One of the very youngest masons took up the answer:

'That's because you don't use your eyes.'

'Is that so?' said Theo. 'You ought to be able to get hold of some without much trouble all the same. Aren't you the guy who stuffs them now and then?'

This was greeted by a general shout of laughter. The same mason replied with a smile:

'You're making a big mistake there, Theo. I don't go much on that.'

This ghastly game of repartee might go on for ever. Gil had got his socks on by this time. He raised his head and waited a moment without moving, hunched up in the bed, his eyes fixed straight ahead of him. He saw that life would be unbearable, but it was by now too late to fight Theo, for now he would have to take on the whole mob; they were all in league against him. All of them were thoroughly worked up over a swarm of flies now dispersed and executing a lively sun-dance. His pent-up wrath must find an outlet; all the masons must be made to feel the sting of it. Gil thought of setting fire to their quarters, but the idea soon evaporated. His rancour, his rage, must be vented on them at once. It simply had to take the form of some desperate deed, even if this should turn out to react on his own guts and cause a haemorrhage. Theo went on again:

'Well, you can never tell. There's some chaps as likes it. They don't mind *pumping up* that hole.'

(This is a joke against Gil and his bike tyres.)

His urge to piss was stronger than ever; it was as violent as the pent-up power behind a steam-engine. Gil would have to be pretty quick about it. He had an obscene feeling that all his courage and audacity somehow depended on his being quick, so tense had his pressing need made him. He was sitting on his bed with his feet on the floor and the look in his eye grew less wild as he slowly let his gaze come to rest on Theo.

'So you've made up your mind, eh, Theo?'

He drew his lips tightly together as he pronounced this last word, and gave his head a slight toss:

'Have you made up your mind? You've been trying to take the piss out of me too long.'

'You're wrong there, young fellow-me-lad. I'd rather stop you shitting.'

When the rather shifty laughter this answer had caused among the none too concerned onlookers had died away he went on:

''Cos there's times enough, it seems, when you don't mind taking it, and for my part, I'm not saying I wouldn't mind giving it you.'

Gil stood up. He was in his shirt. In his stockinged feet he went across to Theo and then, turning to face him squarely, he said, pale, icily self-possessed, terrible:

'You want to fuck me, do you? Very well, get on with it, don't let it go to waste.'

And with a single movement he swivelled round, pulled up his shirt tails, bent down and proffered his backside. The masons were watching closely. Only yesterday Gilbert had been a workman like the rest of them, neither more nor less than any of the others. They had no cause to bear him malice on any account, the reverse rather. They could not see the desperation in the lad's face. They laughed. Gil stood upright again, let his glance run over them, and said:

'You get a kick out of this. You made up your minds to take the piss out of me. Isn't there any of you wants to have a go?'

The words were spoken in ringing tones, scathingly. They made the whole scene into a fantastic ceremony and the lad into a magical character about to perform a rite as thrilling as a sorcerer's, in which obscenity has to enter in if a cure is to be effective. Gil went through the same performance again in front of the masons, still further adding to his enticements by parting the cheeks of his arse with his hands and at the same time calling out to the floorboards in a lugubrious voice like reeking fumes:

'Come on then, why don't you? I'd have you know I've got piles, so get on with it. Bang into it! Wallow in the shit!'

He straightened up again, he was red in the face. A husky lout came up to him.

'Come off it! If you and Theo there have been mucking about, it's nothing to us.'

Theo sneered. Gil gave him a look, and said in the coldest tones:

'You've never been able to get my ring and it's that that's ribbing you.'

He turned on his heels. Clad in his shirt and socks, he went back to his bed and there dressed in silence. He then left the room. Close to their quarters there was a small wooden shed where the masons kept their bicycles. Gil went straight there and up to his bike. It had a yellow frame and the nickel plating shone brightly. Gil loved its lissomness, the low, wide curve of the racing handle-bars which obliged him to bend right over the top of them. He loved the inner tubes; the shining rims; the mud-guards. Every Sunday, and sometimes during the week in the evening after the day's work, he polished it. With his hair falling over his eyes and his mouth always half-open, he unscrewed the bolts, took off the chain and the pedals and stripped down his bike as it rested upturned on saddle and handle-bars. This occupation brought out the best in Gil. Each operation was carried through with scrupulously neat perfection, whether with a greasy duster or a monkey-wrench. Every action was good to watch. Squatting on his heels or bending over the free-wheel to set it spinning, Gil was transfigured. He radiated joy by the very perfection and delicacy of every movement he made.

And so he went straight up to his bicycle. But no sooner did he put his hand on the saddle than he felt ashamed. Today it was quite out of the question for him to get busy on it. He was unworthy of becoming the character his bike turned him into. He leant it up against the wall and went out to the shit-house. When he had wiped his arse, Gil put his hand between its cheeks to feel the knobbly little excruscence of his piles and felt happy to have them under his hand, the outward and tangible sign of his recent outburst of anger and violence. Once more he let the tip of his forefinger touch them. He was proud and happy in the knowledge that here lay a source of self-protection. It was a treasure to be revered piously, since it had given him the opportunity of being himself. Until further orders, his piles were himself.

Once the sun had disappeared that evening, the town was buried in fog. Gil was fairly certain of running into Roger on the esplanade. He wandered up and down there for a few minutes. At four o'clock in the afternoon the shop fronts became illuminated. The Rue de Siam glimmered feebly. Gil walked for a while across the almost deserted Dujot Square. He had not yet decided upon a plan. He had no very precise idea of what would be happening in an hour's time, yet his vision of the world was clouded by heavy anxiety. He was walking in a world where each form was immature and larval, and it would need a prick from a stiletto before he could re-enter the bright world where one dared to think. This in parenthesis, for if murder requires a pointed instrument with a keen edge, or simply of a certain weight, to assuage the murderer as he slashes through some kind of other-worldly texture that seems to be holding him captive, poison, it seems, cannot bring a similar relief. Gil was suffocating. It's true that the fog, in conferring invisibility on him, did afford him a certain comfort; but he was incapable of dissociating this from the day before and certainly the day to come. With a little imagination Gil would have been able to put paid to the past, but as his resentment was dry and arid, he was bereft of imagination. The next day, and during the days following, he would have to continue living in shame.

'Why the hell didn't I bust his face in right away?'

In his raging fury, he repeated this empty phrase over and over again, putting every possible accent of interrogation on its syllables. He saw again Theo's wickedly mocking face. At once his fists became automatically clenched in his pockets and his nails bit into the palms of his hands. If he was quite unable to put the proper questions to himself, let alone answer them, he could at least pursue a desultory line of thought, so that when he reached the balustrade in the emptiest corner of the square, his spirits had reached their lowest and most humiliating ebb. There he turned his head in the direction of the sea, and, in a loud voice, which not but what was half-swallowed back into his throat so that only a squawk emerged, he shouted:

'Oh!'

This brought him a few moments' comfort, but his black mood was on him again in a trice.

'Why didn't I smash that shit's face in then and there? I don't care a fuck for his friends. They can think what they like, fuck him. Only, as for him, I ought to have . . .'

When Gil had first gone to work in the shipyards, Theo had shown a paternal interest in him. Little by little, by coming to accept a drink now and then, the lad gradually accepted the mason's authority over him. Not that there was anything deliberate in it: it was due rather to a sort of weak submission to the fact that Theo gained in strength by paying for the rounds. Querelle could show the most brazen cheek as far as the officer was concerned, since he did not speak the same language. No doubt he joked about it, but with a restraint that gave rise to the fear or the disdain behind which Querelle guessed at the existence of a violent unconfessed desire. To Querelle there were no half measures between weakness and audacity. Even if the officer had not shown any timidity, the rating would have openly despised him. In the first place because he felt the officer's love placed him at his mercy, and in the second because the officer wished his love to remain hidden. Cynicism was possible in Querelle's case. Gil was defenceless when faced with the cynicism of Theo, who spoke the masons' language, full of lewd jests, who had no compunction in airing his habits nor feared being given the sack at the yards because of them. As Theo had taken upon himself to pay for a drink now and then, Gil sensed very clearly that he would never have paid him a sou for love. Finally, what had placed him still further under the mason's power was the friendship - however slight it might be - which had united them over the past month. The greater his realization that their friendship was leading nowhere and would never attain to the goal he desired, the more venomous Theo became. He refused to believe that he had been wasting his time and trouble, and consoled himself in attempting to believe that he had started out on this friendship with the express purpose of leading it to the tortures to which Gil was now submitting. He now hated Gil, and all the more because he could see no other valid reason for hating him, except for the motive of making him suffer. Gil hated Theo for having dominated him to such an extent. There was an occasion one evening when, on coming out of a bistro, Theo had off-handedly pinched his bottom and Gil had not dared to land him one. 'After all, he's just paid for a snifter', he thought to himself. So he simply relied on pushing away his hand and nothing more, smiling to himself as if he were enjoying the fun of it. Over the next few days, almost unconsciously, because he sensed the strong desires of the mason enveloping him, he indulged in rather skittish behaviour. He exaggerated the most provocative poses. He strolled about the yards bared to the waist, he extended his chest, he pushed his cap a bit further back on his head to let more of his hair show beneath it, and, when he made sure that Theo had caught on to his tricks, he would smile. When Theo returned to the assault another day, without any sign of annoyance, Gil made it obvious that he did not care for such things.

'I'd like us to be pals, see; but for the other line, there's nothing doing, mate.'

Theo flew off the handle. So did Gil, but he dared not show fight because of the drink he'd just had at the mason's expense. From that time on in the yards, both while at work and during the knock-off periods, in the quarry, at table and even sometimes when he was in bed, Theo would crack terrible jokes at the expense of Gil, who could find no appropriate answer. Thus little by little the gang, from laughing to start with at Theo's cracks, ended by laughing at Gil. He did his best to rid himself of his provocative gestures once he recognized that every one of Theo's sallies bore a pointed reference to them, but he could in no sense destroy his intrinsic beauty. The too sprightly, vivacious shoots, burgeoning within him and scenting his young manhood, did not wilt and die, since they were permeated with and drew their nourishment from the sap of youth. Without their taking any proper account of it, the rest of the gang let the lad sink in their estimation. Step by step, Gil began to lose their esteem and word by word his standing, till he had become little more than a laughing-stock. He no longer possessed, owing to the constant affirmation from without, any certainty of being what his own inner feelings told him he was. Now this certainty was sustained only in his heart of hearts by the presence of shame there and by the fact that its livid flames were rising fast, as if fanned by the wings of revolt. He allowed himself to fall victim to it.

Roger never showed up. What could he have been going to say to him? That Paulette was not going out with him any more? That he would not be able to see her again? She was no longer the barmaid at that little bistro and it was difficult to find her now. And if she were to turn up by a stroke of bad luck, an even more scorching shame would have set Gil sizzling. He trusted that she would not put in an appearance.

'And all this because I never bust that mug of his.'

He was being crushed by a more oppressive feeling of uneasiness. Had he been better adapted – and also less virile – he would have understood that, far from cissyfying him, a flood of tears would have delivered him from this feeling. So deep sunk in despair was he that he was far from knowing of any other method than that of parading the pallid features of all young men who refuse to take on their opponent, the crucified countenance of nations who prefer not to join in the struggle. He closed his jaws firmly, clenching his teeth.

'Why the hell didn't I smash that cunt's jaw for him?'

But never for an instant did he think of doing so. The time for that was past. His words lulled him. He heard himself going over them very calmly. His rage had now turned into a great sorrow, heavy and burdensome, issuing from his breast and infusing his body and spirit with the infinite sadness that would never again be lifted from him. He walked on a few paces in the mist, his hands in his pockets, always certain of the elegance of his step, and happy even to have this to comfort his loneliness. Gil thought of Roger. He could see his face lighting up with the smile that always appeared so joyously when he listened to a song. It was not exactly Paulette's face. Her smile was never so brilliant, but was clouded by the femininity, which destroyed its natural affinity with the smiles of Gil and Roger.

'Between the legs, good God! Yet think what Paulette must have between her legs!'

He thought, all but murmuring loud: 'Her pussy! Her little pussy! Her gash!' And, as he thought of it, he put an almost insane tenderness into the words, which turned them into a desperate imploration. 'Her little dribbling crimson slit! Her little tits! Her hips!' He expanded his thoughts – 'I mustn't call them her little hips, for Paulette has very beautiful hips. She has great big lovely legs, and there between them her little quim tucked away in its fur.' And he found that he had an erection. In the midst of his sadness – or shame – and obliterating it, he was convinced of the existence of a fresh certainty, one that he had already experienced. He was *refinding* himself. His whole essence was flowing into his cock and making it erect. It was not greater than he, but it possessed a terrible vigour, a providential power capable of nullifying his shame. It worked as an antidote, in effect, by drawing off the shame which was oozing from his body, instead of replenishing the spongy tissues, and seeped into the base of his cock. Gil could now feel it growing harder, stronger, and more arrogant. There could be no doubt it was the moment to call to his aid all the fluids which bathed his organs. The hand in his pocket held his prick close pressed against the fleshy part of his thigh. Instinctively he went in search of the darkest and most out-of-the-way spot on the esplanade. In his mind's eye, Paulette's smile was vying with that of her brother. Animated by a rushing, galloping madness, Gil let his greedy glance slip down as far as her legs and tweak up her skirts: there were her garters. Under these – now his thoughts were more hesitant – the skin was white, till it was suddenly darkened by the presence of a fleece of hair. He became desperate at not being able to keep his imagination fixed upon it under the blazing sun of his desires. By a stretch of the imagination, after running up under Paulette's dress and undies, his cock came out again at just about the level of her breasts: he would be able to see better with the tip of his prick.

Turning towards the sea, Gil leaned up against the balustrade. Out in the road the lights of *Dunkerque* glimmered feebly. Gil let his thoughts rise higher, from the breasts to the pink and whiteness of the neck, the chin, to the smile (Roger's smile and then Paulette's). He dimly realized that the femininity which shrouded the kid's smile had something to do with what lay between the thighs. This smile belonged to the same natural cause as – he couldn't find the right word: yet it was, though so remote, the subtlest and most powerful, and, since it came from such a distance, the most disturbing of the waves that emanated from the deep and cunning apparatus between the thighs. With the speed of lightning, his thoughts flew back to the little tart: 'Oh! the little bitch with her pretty little cunt, that's where I'm going to dip my wopping great wick.' His attention was fluctuating between Paulette's mouth and her cunt. He imagined that he was pressing up close against her, hugging and kissing her. In a flash, the image of Theo came between them for long enough to interrupt Gil's reverie, already well on the way to achievement, and fill him with hatred of the mason. This short break was enough to unnerve his erection. He badly wanted to dismiss all ideas of Theo, whom he felt to be quite close behind him, rubbing up against his bum with an enormous prick, twice the size of his own. Such a fury took possession of him, and so completely, that it used up all his fluid, transferring its potency from his pintle to his eyes. To get a hard on again, he tried his best to recapture his more tender feelings. At the same time, to frustrate the atrocious idea of Theo getting up him, he underwent, through the medium of his cock, a momentary spasm of defiance.

'I'm a man, I am,' he shouted into the fog. 'Why, I shove it up men. I'll slip you a length!'

In vain he tried to envisage the scene where he was buggering Theo. In his imagination he got as far but no further than the mason's dusty and unbuttoned clothes, with his slacks down and his shirt tucked up. That his joy might be fulfilled, his pleasure made certain, he must continue to visualize every detail – and derive enjoyment from that detail – of Theo's face and bum, but, finding it impossible to imagine that anything but – as indeed they were in reality – covered with hair, he substituted the vision of another male face and downy back – Roger's. When he realized the change-over through the stiffness of his prick, Gil knew that he would enjoy an excess of pleasure. He held fast to the image of the boy, which had blotted out the mason's. In an outburst of violence, thinking he would like to be addressing Theo in such terms, and no doubt desperately enraged at the same time at finding that he was inevitably to have the young 'un, he let fly: 'Come on, then, show us your bum, for I'm going to stick it right up you, little bitch that you are! Now, at this very moment, and no mistake about it!' He was holding him from behind. Gil heard the words of his song come floating across the jumble of glasses and broken bottles:

'He was a gay and laughing sod,
'Afraid of neither man nor God . . .'

And then he smiled. He arched his back and his legs. He was aware of his full masculinity when facing Roger. His hand let go its hold. He did not discharge. The overwhelming sadness born of shame once more took possession of him; but Roger's smile was there in response to his own to keep him company.

'Why, oh why, didn't I break his jaw?'

For a moment Gil imagined, because his feelings were so concentrated against the mason, that they must be adversely affecting him and harrying him so as to allow him no rest.

Roger would not be coming along now. It was too late. Even if he were to come along, Gil would never see him through the thick fog. Not daring to think that the lad might be fond of him, he was yet incapable of understanding that he had had to call up Roger's words and gestures to justify his own love for the lad by the lad's love for him. Much as he wanted to think of Roger, the memory of Theo persisted in cutting across these thoughts.

Almost without thinking what he was doing, he went into a bistro and ordered a *fine*. The sight of the array of bottles gave him something different to think about. He started to read their labels.

'Another *fine*, please.'

Since he drank only red or white wine as a rule, he was not accustomed to spirits.

'Another, please.'

He put down six in all. A self-assertive, strengthening clarity of vision began to dispel little by little his muddle-headed confusion and his sadness, to clear the heavy air in which his brain was functioning, and, generally speaking, to bring clarity to his thoughts. He went out. Already he was able to think undistractedly of his desire for Roger. At moments he would call to mind the pale, colourless features and thighs of Paulette, but these quickly gave place to Roger's smile. All the same, he was still in the shadow of Theo's dominance, whose haunting figure became all the more aggravating, in that it refused to be obliterated despite the fact that its power was on the wane. 'The shit!'

He thought of the young lad as he went down towards Recouvrance.

'It's just as easy as that,' he thought to himself, assuming in a vague way that Theo was no longer so much in the forefront of his mind. 'I can make him disappear when I wish.'

Tears were running down his cheeks. He saw quite clearly that the mason was spoiling his love for Roger; and again, that his love rid him of Theo, but not completely. For the mason was still lurking in a corner, microscopical. By compressing his love like a gas, he hoped to crush, to asphyxiate what remained of Theo's ghost, of the idea of him; and the idea became confounded with the physical Theo, so that he tended to grow smaller and smaller in relation to Gill.

Had he not run into the lad coming through the fog, Gil would probably have sobered up by climbing the steps up from the Rue Casse. Then, once back among the masons again, he might well have resumed his life of mourning. As it was, he uttered a howl of joy, at the same time quickly wiping away his tears with the back of his hand.

'Roger, my boy, we're going to have a drink together!'

He grasped the lad round the neck. Roger smiled. He gazed at the cold wet face separated from his own by only the thinnest wisp of fog dispersed by their breaths.

'How goes it, Gil?'

'Well enough, pal. Don't be mad with me. The old 'un's no longer in the show. It's easy enough to get rid of him. Don't get me wrong, I'm no copper. He's not a man, he's a shit, a lousy shitbag. D'you hear, Roger, a dirty shitbag. A tapette, if you prefer. And we're two pals, two brothers. We're going to do just what we like. We've a right to, seeing we're brothers-in-law. We're all in the same family, we are. And he's a dirty shitbag!'

He spoke very fast so as not to falter, and walked very fast so as not to stumble.

'Tell me, Gil, haven't you had a few too many?'

'Don't you worry, kid. I paid for it myself. As for his dough, shit it. I said we're going to have a drink together, on me. Come along there.'

Roger was smiling, he was happy. His neck was proud under the rough but gentle hand of Gil.

'There's no room for him. He's a mosquito. I tell you he's a stinging mosquito. And I'm going to swipe him.'

'Who are you talking about?'

'About a dirty shit, if you must know. Don't you worry. You'll see for yourself. Then you can make up your mind. And he'll not trouble us much longer, I can tell you.'

They went down the Rue du Sac and turned off at the Rue B . . . Gil went straight to the bistro where he knew Theo would be. They went in together. Those sitting inside, eating or drinking, looked up on hearing the glass door open. As in a cloud and very far away from him, Gil saw the mason sitting alone, with a glass and bottle in front of him, at the table nearest the door. He dug his hands deep down in his pockets and said to Roger:

'D'you see him, that fellow there?' and then to Theo: '*Salut*, lad,' as he went up to him.

Theo was smiling.

'Won't you offer us a drink, Theo? I'm with a pal.'

At the same time he seized the bottle by the neck and, with a gesture as swift as forked lightning, broke it against the table. With the jagged shard, twisting it like a gimlet, he struck the mason right through the throat, shouting:

'I tell you, there's no longer any room for you!'

By the time the *patronne* and the other drinkers, stupefied and stupid, thought to intervene, Gil was outside. He was soon lost in the fog.

Towards ten in the evening the police went to look for Roger at his mother's. They let him go again the following morning.

The twin escutcheons of France and Brittany, interlinked, form the principal ornament of the majestic front elevation of the convict-prison of Brest, the other architectural features all derive in origin from the days when the Navy was comprised of sailing ships. Bracketed together, these two shields of oval stone are not flat but convex, protuberant. They have the importance of a sphere which the sculptor did not bother to carve into shape, and the sum total so dominates its individual parts that it composes an absolute whole. They are the two halves of a fabulous egg, laid perchance by Leda after she had lain with the swan, and contain the germ of a power and an opulence both natural and at the same time supernatural. This is no casual masterpiece, no clumsy execution contributes the slightest suspicion of puerile decoration; it is, on the other hand, strikingly puissant and worldly, based on moral and armed force, despite the ermine and the fleurs-de-lis. Had they been flat, they could never have possessed this fecund authority. In the morning, from a very early hour, they are gilded by the sun, which later in the day slowly glides over the full façade. When those destined for the galleys clanked out in their heavy chains from the prison doors, they stayed for a while in this paved courtyard, which stretches as far as the Arsenal buildings, where they overlook the Penfeld quayside. Symbolically perhaps, and to render the captivity of the inmates more evident and mayhap lighten it, here stood a row of stone posts connected together by chains, of which the links were heavier than those of an anchor-chain and so weighty that they gave the appearance of being much lighter than they really were.

In this place, to the hiss of a cat-o'-nine-tails, the gangs of rowers were selected and detailed off to the accompaniment of strangely formulated shouts. Slowly the sun crept up over and down the harmoniously proportioned granite face of the front wall, glowing like a noble Venetian palazzo, to spread out over the surface of the cobblestones in the courtyard, over the crushed and encrusted toe-nails and the bruised ankles of the convicts.

Facing this, Penfeld would still be slumbering in a golden and sonorous mist behind which Recouvrance and the poorer houses could be guessed; and quite close behind that again le Goulet, the Brest Roads, already alive with barques and larger ships of the line. From early dawn the sea would present its shifting pattern of hulks, masts and rigging to the still sleep-blurred eyes of the men chained together in pairs. The rowers shivered in dirty grey linen clothes (the faggot). A weak and tepid soup was distributed among the men from a wooden bucket. They rubbed their eyes a little to unstick the lashes sealed by the secretions of sleep. Their hands were red and calloused.

They could see the sea. That is to say, that in the depths of the fog they could hear the cries of the captains and the sailors who were free, the creak of the oars and the oaths rolling across the water, and could distinguish after a time the swirl of the sails swelling out with all the importance – the valiant and vain importance of the double escutcheon.

Cocks were crowing. Every morning day dawned over the Roads with a more poignant beauty. With bare feet on the wet round cobblestones, the rowers waited for a further short time in silence or murmuring among themselves. In a few moments they would be going aboard the galley – to row. A silk-stockinged captain, with lace cuffs and cravat, passed through their ranks. The surrounding atmosphere grew brighter. Carried thither in a sedan-chair, which suddenly emerged from the vaporous fog, he might have been taken for its tutelary god; indeed, he appeared as its incarnation since the mist was dissipated as soon as he approached. It was as if he must have been there all through the night, so inseparably was he part of it, himself becoming as it were the encircling gloom (yet lacking something – a certain particle of radium which, eight or ten hours late, would galvanize around him the most attenuated elements of the fog and transform him into that hard, violent, veneered, sculpted man, like the carved figurehead of a frigate).

The rowers are dead, of despair perhaps. They have not been replaced. At Penfeld today, specialist workmen are employed on ships of steel. Another kind of rigidity – even more formidable – has replaced the hard hearts and features that always made this locality so pathetic. There can still be seen the fugitive's fleeting beauty, revealed by fear and illuminated by a delicious flash from his inmost being, as well as the beauty of the victor, whose serenity is accomplished, whose life has achieved fulfilment, and who has earned the right to remain immobile. Both on the water and in the midst of the fog, the presence of metal is cruel. The façade and frontal elevation still stand intact, but within the prison itself are coils of five-stranded cables and tarred rope – and rats.

When the sun comes up, revealing the *Jeanne d'Arc* lying under the cliffs of Recouvrance, the younger generation are being drilled. These clumsy children are the monstrous progeny of the chained and coupled convicts, but are themselves feeble and delicate. Behind the training ship, up on the cliff, can be seen the unserried ranks of the School of Aspirants. And all around us, to left and right, are the Arsenal construction yards, where the *Richelieu* is on the stocks. The sound of voices and hammering can be heard. You can guess the whereabouts in the Roads of those monsters of steel, hard and rigid, yet somewhat softened by the nocturnal humidity, and now by the first timid caress of the sun.

The Admiral is no longer, as was once, in days gone by, the Prince de Rosen, a Lord High Admiral of France; today he is simply a Port-Admiral. The convexity of the double escutcheon no longer carries any significance. No longer does it bear any relation to the swelling of the sails, to the curve of the hull, to the proud bosom of the figurehead on the prow, to the sighs of rowers in the galleys, to the magnificence of naval combats. The interior of the prison-house, that immense granite edifice, divided into cells open on one side where the convicts lay on straw and stone, is now nothing more than a store-house for rope. Each room of rough-hewn granite still contains its two iron rings, but houses only huge heaps of tarred rope, left there by the Admiralty and seldom visited, since it is well known that, preserved by the tar, they can remain there for centuries. Nor are the windows, in which almost all the glass is out, ever opened.

The main gate, the one already mentioned that opens on to the sloping courtyard, is fastened by several locks, and the enormous key of forged iron hangs from a nail in the office of the Second-in-Command assigned to the Arsenal, who never looks at it. Another door there is, ill-fitting, to which nobody ever gives a thought, so obvious is it that not a soul would steal the hanks of rope piled up behind it. This is equally massive and armed with an enormous lock, and is to be found at the northern extremity of the building, opening direct on to a little street, narrow and seldom used, which separates the prison from the Naval Hospital. This lane threads its way between the various hospital buildings and finally loses itself, choked up by weeds, somewhere amongs the ramparts.

Gil knew all about these dispositions. Still dazzled by the sight of blood, he ran very fast for a few minutes, only stopping to regain his breath, and, once sobering up, found himself overwhelmed by the enormity of his crime, knocked out, so that his first idea was to search out and take the darkest and most deserted streets to make his escape through some door and find himself somewhere outside the wall of the town. He did not dare to return to the shipyards. Then he remembered the old, forsaken convict-prison and its easy-to-open door. He hid himself for the night in one of those rooms of stone. Behind the coils of rope, he cowered in a corner. Fear laid hold upon him: he seized upon fear. He lived his despair.

Worldly-wise and of a certain dignity, Madame Lysiane, when seated at the receipt of custom, was capable of maintaining a charming smile, while her eyes were busily employed in checking the number of passes or in making sure, without so much as uttering a word to the more nervous of her girls, that their dresses of pink silk or tulle did not catch against a table-leg or on the heel of their shoe. When she dropped her smile, it was to pass her tongue more comfortably over her gums behind closed lips. This simple mannerism was a sure sign of her independence, of her rightful sovereignty. On occasion she would raise a head bedecked with curls and artificial wisps. She felt herself to be an integral part of the luxuriously illuminated rooms, dazzling lights and strains of dance music, and at the same time to be evolving her very sumptuosity at every outlet of her breath, the warm breath emanating from the depths of the breast of a remarkably opulent woman.

There exists a state of male passivity (at the point when virility could well be characterized by lack of response or indifference to the attention lavished upon it, caused by the body's detached period of waiting, no matter whether pleasure is being offered to it or obtained from it) which makes the person allowing himself to be sucked less active than the person sucking, just as later the latter becomes passive when being poked. The real passive quality already met with in Querelle was to be found in Robert, who allowed Madame Lysiane to make love to him. He permitted the maternal instincts of this woman, who was both strong and tender, to take control over him. He floated and swam in the element in which he had at times sought oblivion. As for the Madam, she had at length found the opportunity of revolving round an axis or completely enveloping it, of bringing about 'the proper marriage of sail and mast'.

When they were in bed together, she dragged her too heavy breasts and her face over the indifferent altar of her lover's outstretched body. As Robert's desires were slow in awakening, Madame Lysiane, in the opening stages of the game of love, alone played the active role, and thereby was the only one to be fully satisfied; after pecking at the base of her lover's doodle, she would suddenly pop the entire organ greedily into her mouth. Incapable of fighting against the tickling sensation, Robert invariably ended up by ejaculating and, whisking his weapon from this warm, wet mouth, he plunged it, moistened with saliva, right up to the hilt.

As soon as she caught sight of the face of Querelle coming through the door into the salon, she experienced the same disturbing feeling that had so worried her when she first noticed that the two brothers' features were both united, as it seemed in one face, so exactly alike was the cast of each. Often since that day, a sharp anguish had cut across the regular and gently-flowing stream of her peaceful conscience and, because of this, Madame Lysiane came to be aware of the cause of the overwhelming effect that the surface ripples exerted upon her. So powerful was the resemblance between Querelle and her lover that she even went so far as to suppose, without really believing it, that Robert must have disguised himself as a sailor. Querelle's features, as he smilingly advanced towards her, upset her considerably, yet she was totally unable to take her eyes off his face. 'What's the answer? They're two brothers, aren't they, so it's only natural', she kept on saying over and over again to calm herself. But the monstrosity of his so perfect resemblance took possession of her thoughts.

'I am a repulsive object. I have loved him too deeply, and too great a love sickens one.

Too strong a love moves the bowels of compassion and disturbs the organs to their depths – what bubbles up to the surface gives one a feeling of nausea.

The two halves of your face are the discs of cymbals, which are never clapped together, but glide in silence one over the surface of the other.'

Querelle's crimes had multiplied the facets of his personality, each in turn contributing a fresh facet that did not obliterate the previous ones. The latest 'killer', born of the last assassination, shared the company of his noblest friends, of those who had preceded him and whom he, in turn, surpassed. He therefore bid them welcome to the ceremony, which was given the name of 'a blood-marriage' by old-time cut-throats: the accomplices all planted their knives in the same victim, a ceremony similar in its essential points to one that comes to mind:

'Rosa said to Mucor:

"This is a trustworthy man. You may remove your socks and serve the kirsch.'

Mucor carried out his orders. He placed two socks upon the table and poured into one of them a little sugar handed him by Rosa; then after pouring some kirsch into the bottom of a vase, he picked up the two socks and, holding them over the vase, let them down into it with the utmost precaution so as not to let the kirsch moisten any part but the tips of the toes, after which he handed them to Dirbel, saying:

'Take your choice and suck either the one with the sugar or the one without. Don't be put off by them. This is the test for entering into the fraternity; to eat and drink from the same bowl. There must be honour among thieves".'

This latest manifestation of Querelle – born fully-fledged at the age of twenty-five, arising defenceless from some murky region in ourselves, strong and solidly built – was inclined at the same time, with a joyous shake of the shoulders, to return once again to the smiling, happy and younger generation of the elect. Each of the older Querelles regarded him with sympathy. In his moments of sadness he was aware of their presence all around him. And, since the fact that they were creatures of memory partially veiled them, this veil endowed them with a special grace, with an almost feminine gentleness as they bent in his direction. Had he actually possessed the requisite courage of his imagination, he would have called them his 'daughters', as Beethoven termed his symphonies. By 'moments of sadness' we refer to those instants when the elder Querelles pressed around this latest athlete, when their veils were made of crepe rather than of white tulle, and when he himself already felt upon his body the light touch of the folds of oblivion.

'There's no telling who can possibly have struck the fatal blow.'

'Did you know the victim?'

'Certainly. We all knew him, but he was no pal of ours.'

Nono said:

'This mason must have been like t'other one. Might well have been the same kind of bugger.'

'What mason?' (Querelle pronounced the syllables slowly, laying special emphasis on the 'a' in 'mason'.) He said:

'What mason?'

'Haven't you heard?'

Querelle and his brother were now talking among themselves, the boss leaning forward with his elbows on the counter. He was looking at the pair of them, and especially at Querelle, to whom Robert was explaining Gil's onslaught. A very considerable feeling of hope, the spring of hope eternal, was gradually mounting in Querelle's breast. An exquisite feeling of freshness was spreading all through him. More and more he felt himself to be an exceptional creature, endorsed with grace. His limbs and his movements were invested with a great strength and with a neater elegance. He felt himself becoming full of grace and he recorded the fact with gravity, all the while preserving the habitual smile upon his lips.

The two brothers had been fighting for a good five minutes. Not knowing where to obtain a grip, since one would always forestall the movements of the other by anticipating his hold, they had started with a series of feints that resembled ridiculous hesitations. Rather than wanting to fight, they had seemed to be backing away from each other and to be avoiding each other with the greatest success. The sparring ceased. Querelle slipped clumsily and was able to clutch hold of Robert's leg. From this moment on the battle became fast and furious.

Dédé had stood to one side to prove to the man who was longing to develop deep down within him, where he was slumbering and germinating, that there is nothing to be gained from interfering in a settlement of accounts between man and man. The street became a passage from the Bible in which two brothers, under the direction of two fingers of one and the same God, hurled insults at each other and fought to the bitter end for two reasons which were in reality but one.

For Dédé, the street was cut off from the rest of Brest. He was waiting for the moment when a soul would fly up heavenwards from it. The two brothers fought in silence, with an increasing fury as they became exacerbated by the silence that allowed them to hear nothing but the formidable sound of their ferocious attacks and counter-attacks and the snuffling of their quick intakes of breath: increasing, too, as their strength began to fail and their lassitude increased, with the threat that they would both go down fighting, that they would both resort to giving in the end one last final, dirty blow, and this perhaps with such tenderness that it would cause the victor to die of exhaustion. Three dockers were looking on, cigarette in mouth. Secretly, in their heart of hearts, they were ready to bet first on one and then on the other. Any prognostication as to the outcome was difficult to maintain, so equally matched in strength were the combatants; an equality considerably helped by their close resemblance to each other, equating their chances and harmonizing their movements as might a dance. Dédé, too, was an onlooker. If he knew every inch of his pal's rippling muscles in repose, he was unaware of their power in a rough and tumble – above all when matched against Querelle whom he had never seen fight before. Querelle suddenly bent himself double and, head down, charged straight at Robert's stomach, knocking him flat on his back.

While making up his mind to strike his brother Robert had savoured a moment of pure freedom, an instant of the briefest duration in which he had to decide whether to fight or to refuse. The sailor's cap had fallen to one side of the scrapping pair, Robert's to the other. With a view to maintaining his rightful superiority and so justifying his part in the fight, Robert took it into his head to proclaim out loud, in the heat of the battle, his scorn for his brother. The first words which sprang to his lips were:

'You dirty bugger!'

But this only sounded like a death-rattle. There followed a whole string of confused expressions blurted out between intakes of breath, which acted as a stimulus to his spirits.

'Fancy being fucked by the boss of the brothel! Filthy little cunt! That stamps you, all right. That gives a pretty good picture of what you're really like . . . that puts you among the pigeons . . . talk of the Bey of Algiers! . . . A nice reputation I'll get, having a brother who takes pricks up his bum . . .'

For the first time, he dared to think in words far obscener than he had ever been in the habit of uttering, or even hearing.

'A nice reputation, you cunt . . . was my face red! . . . When I think of Nono's phiz grinning there . . . the shit . . . while he told me the tale.'

The three dockers shifted their ground. Dédé saw Robert's head being squeezed between Querelle's strong thighs, and being pummelled with both fists. Suddenly, one of Robert's felt-slippered feet pushed Querelle's face back so that he had to open his legs and let go his hold. Dédé hesitated for a moment before bending down to pick up the sailor's cap. He held it in his hand for a second and then deposited it on the top of a stone post. If Robert was going to be defeated, he must certainly not be given the further disappointment of seeing his disconsolate little pal decorate his own head with his blatant beret, which would make him shine like a powerful projectile; no more than must he be allowed to catch sight of him favouring the victor and making as if to crown him with an equally significant laurel wreath. His indecision did not last long, although for Dédé it had seemed fraught with a deep deliberation which astonished him. It astonished him, and his choice brought with it a feeling at once as painful as a sharp cut and almost as voluptuous. He was utterly stupefied to find – having a moment beforehand made up his mind that the incident was in no way any concern of his – that it had become a matter of importance for him. The importance lay in the fact that it had revealed to the kid's inner conscience that he was free to choose. That set him thinking. The previous evening he had, while kissing Mario, cut across the gentle, even flow of some movement started long ago, and this act of audacity had for the first time given him a foretaste of freedom of action, made him a little tipsy and given him sufficient strength to make a second attempt. But this attempt to test his freedom – successful though it turned out to be – caused the withdrawal of the man inside him, whose presence we have already remarked, and who bore some resemblance both to Mario and, in a greater degree, to Robert.

Dédé had known Robert, in fact, since the days when the latter had been working in the docks. Together they had committed several petty thefts in the warehouses and, when from being a docker Robert had become a ponce, Dédé had carefully concealed from him his relationship with the police agent. All the same, because of their old friendship, and out of respect for the success it had brought them, Dédé never so much as thought of acting the spy with Robert, but had arranged for him to meet Mario.

The street was illuminated by the rippling reflections of the brothers' sinuous movements, where before it had been obscured by the strength of their hate, by the dark depths of their invisible eyes and by their breath. Querelle had drawn himself up and now stood erect. Dédé had watched his buttocks contract like a taut bow. A mocking but appreciative voice had shouted:

'What a piece of cake! Anyone want to try his hand?'

Under the blue cloth of Querelle's trousers, Dédé could imagine the expansion and contraction of muscles from his intimate knowledge of Robert's legs. He knew all the interplay and various reactions of buttocks, thighs and calves. He was almost able to see through the stuff of his jersey and appraise the backbone bosses, the true shape of shoulders and arms. Querelle appeared to be fighting against himself. Two women had come up to see what was going on. At first they spoke no word. They kept their shopping baskets, filled with provisions and long, thin loaves of bread, pressed close to their bodies. Then at length they asked why the two men were fighting:

'What's it all about? Don't any of you know?'

But none of them did know. Nobody knew anything. It was a fight for some family reason, it seemed. They did not dare continue on their way for the street was blocked by the fight, and their eyes became fascinated by this human knot of rumpled, dishevelled, tousled, sweating manhood.

Closer and closer grew the resemblance between the two brothers. The look on their faces had lost all its cruelty. There was no outward sign of the transition brought about by fatigue or the desire - not to win, but simple desire - a sort of innermost desperate longing not to finish the fight, which was in a sense a means of uniting the two of them. Dédé remained perfectly calm. It was a matter of indifference to him which was the victor since, whatever the outcome, it would be the same face and the same body which would pick itself up, shake out torn and dusty garments, use a hand for a comb - and that with the most negligent abandon - before placing one or other of the caps on a still tousled head. These two faces so exactly alike had just finished taking part in a titanic but idyllic struggle - of which this combat was merely the vulgar projection visible to men's eyes - a struggle to remain single individuals. Rather than attempting to destroy one another, they appeared to want to become united, to melt into a unity which would create, from the two characters in question, a very rare animal indeed. They were jousting rather in the lists of love, where not a soul would dare to intervene. One felt that the two antagonists would at once unite in league against any would-be mediator who might - in reality - simply be inspired to intervene in order to take a hand on the party. Somehow Dédé was dimly aware of this. He was equally jealous for both the brothers. Each was putting up a terrific resistance. They tore at each other, pulled each other to pieces, and chewed each other up in order to achieve their mutual embodiment; their double put up a stiff resistance to every new move. Querelle was the stronger. When he had made absolutely certain of his victory, he hissed into his brother's ear:

'Say that again! Go on, say it!'

Robert was struggling under the determined pressure, struggling in the toils of the impossible-to-loosen muscles of Querelle. He looked down at the ground. He bit the dust. His assailant, flames, smoke and lightning issuing from his nostrils, mouth and eyes, murmured into the nape of his neck:

'Repeat what you said!'

'No, I won't!'

Querelle felt a sense of shame. And now whenever he stepped back to lunge out at the legs or the body of his brother, he delivered a blow all the harder because of the shame he felt at having struck him at all. Not satisfied with beating his opponent and humiliating him, he hurled himself upon the whole thing which, crouched in the dust or upright, detested him. Traitorously, Robert had managed to get his knife out. A woman gave a piercing shriek which brought the whole street to the windows. Out popped heads of women with their hair down, in petticoats, all but showing their breasts, leaning out, hanging right out over the spot where they usually leaned their elbows on the balustrade of their balconies. They did not possess the strength of mind to tear themselves away from the spectacle and go to fetch a pail of water from the tap to throw over these two males as they might over a pair of panting, lubricious dogs, clamped together in the heat of their fury. Dédé himself was now afraid. So much so that he basely told the dockers that they had better put a stop to the fight.

'Leave them alone, why can't you! They're grown men, aren't they? What's more, they're brothers; they know their own business.'

Querelle broke his hold. He was in mortal danger. For the first time in his life, the murderer himself was threatened with death, and deep within him he felt the early stages of a cramping numbness which he did his best to overcome. In his turn, he whipped out his knife, and, retreating till his back was against the wall, he was ready to leap upon his rival.

'It seems they're brothers! Stop them going on!'

But the people of the street, watching from their balconies, were unable to catch a far more moving exchange of words between the pair. (Translator's Note: The following dialogue is barely articulated, being more the ebb and flow of mental reaction than the actual words ejaculated between sobs for breath.)

'I'm going to wade a foaming stream. Give us a hand – I must get to your side . . .'

'Not much, brother mine, you're too tough a proposition.'

'Speak up, can hardly hear what you say.'

'Jump on my smile. Take a chance; don't funk it! Jump now!'

'Don't lose heart. Try.'

The trumpets blare.

'They want to kill each other! You men there, separate them!'

The women whimpered. The two brothers watched each other closely, eyes skinned, fingering their knives, their bodies very stiff, magnificently calm, as if they were going to march one against the other ceremoniously to exchange, with raised arm, the Florentine oath which is never sworn without a poniard in the hand. Perhaps they were about to prick each other's skin as a symbol of grafting or sewing together one body on to the other.

A police patrol put in appearance at the end of the street.

'Break it up quick. Beat it!'

Shouting these words gruffly and rapidly, Mario hurled himself at Querelle, who did his best to hold him off; but Robert, after taking one look in the direction of the patrol, shut up his knife again. He was trembling all over. Uneasily and in a breathless voice, he turned to Dédé – for the intervention of a mediator was still indispensable – and said:

'Tell him to get out of this.'

Meanwhile, to save time and that he might at a quick stroke free himself from all the magic formality imposed by the theatricality of the scene (the implications of which are profound), just as an Emperor, discarding the panoply and etiquette of war as well as the interventions of his generals and ministers, might hurl invective in the teeth of his enemy, he addressed himself directly to his brother. With a curtness and an authority which only Querelle was capable of understanding, the secret familiarity between them excluding the comments of the street and the bystanders, he said:

'Pipe down. I'll catch up with you. We'll settle this another time.'

Thereupon they parted in silence, without even looking at each other, on either side of the street on opposite pavements. Dédé followed Robert without uttering a word. He threw a glance or two in the direction of Querelle, whose right hand was blood-stained.

* * *

Face to face with Robert, Nono resumed his true virility which had not been at full potency when he was with Querelle. Not that he took on the character and gestures of a homo, but in the presence of Querelle he ceased to think of him as a womanizer and permitted himself to bathe in the special atmosphere that always is excitingly induced by a man who likes his own sex. With such men, and for them alone, a whole world comes into being – with its own set of laws and its own secret, invisible relationships, and it had affected the boss in particular. Tenderness is not quite the right word to express that strange mixture of intimate feeling with regard to all the parts of the body from which a man derives his several pleasures, but it does embrace the various after-effects of those pleasures – the all-enveloping sense of dissolving sweetness as the pleasure gently ebbs, the physical lassitude, even the sense of disgust which drowns yet assuages, submerges yet keeps afloat the man who has taken his pleasure; and finally the infinite sadness – and thus this gleam of tenderness – subject, as it were, to intermittent dull and feeble flashes, does continue to play its part in even the most simple relationships between men. Not that these can ever be said to approach anything like genuine love between man and woman or between two beings, one of whom is feminine; but the very absence of women in the world does oblige the two men to discover whatever feminine streak there may be in their make-up, to invent the woman in them. It is not necessarily the weaker or the younger, or the more gentle of the two, who succeeds the better; but the more experienced, who may often be the stronger or the older man. They are united by a mutual complex; but, since it arises from the absence of a woman it has the power to evoke and sustain the idea of a woman who, by the very fact of her not being there, acts as a link uniting them. Thus there need be no misgiving, no false modesty, no dissimulation on this aspect of their relationship, no need for them to be anything but what they really are: two male specimens, glorying in their virility, who perhaps feel a touch of jealousy for each other, even a genuine hate, but never love.

Almost without giving thought to the matter, Nono had blurted out the story to Robert. From the apparent comfort he derived from so doing, from the fact that he no longer felt any inward rage when he recalled the brief passage of words between the two brothers: 'I'd like to be in your job' – 'It's not so bad', it is evidence that his confession was to rid himself of the shame that had obsessed him ever since the famous evening. Never had Nono attempted to catch out Robert. Never had Robert, perfectly versed in the rules of the game, so much as hinted that he was going with his wife. Besides, when he first came to the brothel as a client, he had paid no attention to Madame Lysiane until she picked him out herself. Once Nono had confirmed Robert's complete indifference to the fact that his brother had slept with him, he was overjoyed. In some roundabout way, he encouraged him to hope that it might bring Robert closer to him, and even to recognize him as his brother-in-law.

Two days later he made a full confession, feeling his way to start with:

'I think I'm quids in. Everything's hunky-dory with your brother.'

'Come off it!'

'Honest to God. But not a word of it yet – not even to him.'

'Couldn't care less. But you'll never make me believe you slipped him a length.'

Nono smirked, po-faced, but triumphant.

'You got there? On the level? You surprise me, I must say.'

Madame Lysiane was good and gentle. To the pleasing softness of her skin was added the ineffable feminine quality of which the essential function consisted in watching over the vicious, and treating them as if they had been charming invalids. Her advice to her 'girls' was to be a ministering angel to these gentlemen; for the official from Police Headquarters in love with Carmen, to be deprived of his jam; to the old Admiral, who strutted about naked gobbling like a turkey-cock, a feather stuck out of his behind and pursued round the room by Elyane dressed up as a farmer's wife; an angel to Mr Clerk who liked to be rocked to sleep; an angel to the man who was chained to the foot of the bed where he would bark like a dog; an angel to the strange, secretive fellows who were stripped bare to their very soul by the gentle warmth of the brothel and Madame Lysiane's ministrations. All this only goes to prove that she exuded a sort of lullaby of lushness and the beauty of the Mediterranean countryside.

'It is most fortunate that the vicious do exist, girls, for otherwise the poor devils who've been unfortunate in love might never come to enjoy its delights.'

In fact, she was a good woman.

Robert broke into a smile still incredulous.

'Supposing I were to say I believed you. But aren't you piling it on?'

'It's as I'm telling you.'

The deeper the boss entered into the story, recounting every detail, including the fraudulent trick over the dice, the more indifferent became the expression on Robert's face. He began to rage with fury inwardly. Shame made him clench his teeth and suck in his cheeks, while throughout the telling he became more wretched in front of Nono, as if he had had the guts knocked out of him.

Except for the limitations of the sea and Penfeld, Brest is surrounded by thick, solid ramparts. They are composed of a deep ditch with a steep embankment. This embankment – both on the inner side and the outer – is planted with acacias. All about the inland extremity of the town winds the lane where Vic was murdered and left abandoned that night by Querelle. The ditch here is impenetrably overgrown with brushwood, brambles, and here and there rushes where the marshland has encroached. Here they tip cartloads of manure. From summer to autumn, all sailors ashore for the evening, if they have missed the last liberty boat – it goes at 22 hours – go to get a bit of kip there while waiting for the six o'clock in the morning boat. They lie down on the bare ground among the brambles. Ditch and banks are then littered with sailors sleeping on the leaves and moss. They are to be seen in the strangest positions, for the most part cramped for adequate space for their limbs by roots, trees, bushes, and by the indispensable protection of their clean uniforms. Before stretching themselves out or curling up in a heap, they have squatted on their haunches or spewed. Out to the wide, they doss down close beside the spot they have befouled. The ditch is spotted with turds. In the midst of these, the sober prepare some sort of summary lair for themselves and bed down. The branches resound with their snores and deep breathing. The freshness of dawn awakens them. In certain places along the ditch there are often gypsy encampments, caravans, and a few fires, cries of verminous children, and quarrels. Gypsies abound in the country thereabouts, since the Bretons are simple creatures and the girls coquettish and brash enough to be dazzled by baskets full of odds and ends of pieces of machine-made lace to which they readily fall victim.

The masonry of the ramparts is solid. The wall supporting the slope on the town side is wide and nowhere breached, intact save for a few stones that have been loosened by a tree seeded and growing between the interstices.

It was on the sloping bank thick with trees, not far from the Hospital or the convict-prison, that the buglers of the 28th Regiment of Colonial Infantry held their practice on every week day. On the day following the murder, Querelle before going to La Féria, took a turn along the ancient fortifications, being careful never to approach too close to the scene of his crime, for fear the police might have posted guards all around it. He was looking for a spot where he could bury his jewels. The wide world over he had had these secret hiding-places, carefully noted down on scraps of paper which he kept in his ditty-box: places in China, Syria, Morocco, and Belgium. The notebook containing these maps and plans was something very much like the 'Register of Crimes' kept by the police.

SHANGHAI: Maison de la France. Garden. Behind the grill of the bath-house.

BEIRUT, DAMASCUS: Female pianist. Wall to the left.

CASA: Alphand Bank.

ANTWERP: Cathedral. Bell tower.

Querelle had a very clear memory of all the details connected with these treasure store-houses, even those of the general surroundings had been observed with scrupulous precision, aided by that of the attendant circumstances that had led up to the discovery and choice of the exact spot for depositing his swag. He could remember every crack in the stone, each root, the insects, the smell, the weather, the triangles of shadow or sunlight; and every time that he evoked these insignificant scenes, they appeared in precise and astonishing detail in the light of an exact memory, all of a piece and illuminated, as if they had been a fairground – dazzlingly huge and precious. These photographic details of any one of his hiding-places would leap to mind in a flash and simultaneously. They appeared in relief, clear-cut as if picked out by a bright sun which lent them the precision of a mathematical solution. Querelle revelled in the memory of his little treasure-stores, but tried his hardest to forget the contents of each, so as to savour the joys of surprise to the full when he came to make the World Tour expressly to collect them. His imprecise knowledge of the entombed riches was like a sort of radiant nimbus that shone above each chosen hiding-place, above each malevolent fissure stuffed full of gold, and these clouds little by little floated away from the source of their burning intensity to bathe the world in a deliciously soft, golden light in which his soul could take its ease and experience the ineffable joys of freedom.

Querelle derived great strength from the feeling that he was rich. At Shanghai, behind the grill of the bath-house, he had concealed the booty resulting from no less than five robberies and the murder, in Indo-China, of a Russian dancer; at Damascus, in the ruins of what he had come to call the Lady at the Piano, he had buried the profits of a murder committed in Beirut. Attached to this crime was the memory of the twenty years hard labour awarded to his accomplice. At Casablanca, Querelle had hidden a fortune stolen from the French Consul in Cairo. To the memory of this was added the horrid knowledge of the death of an English sailor, again his accomplice in crime. At Antwerp, he had managed to discover a place in the bell-tower of the cathedral where he had hidden a small fortune, the residue of several successful thefts in Spain, and linked with the death of a German stevedore, his victim as well as his partner in the crime.

Querelle was wandering about amongst the brambles. He could hear the delicate sound of the wind whistling through the tips of the grasses, that he had heard so clearly the previous evening after the crime. He felt no fear, no traces of remorse, and this will come less as a surprise if it is admitted that Querelle had already come to believe that he carried the crime in him, not that he had taken part in the crime. This calls for a short explanation. Suppose Querelle had suddenly found himself, still possessed of his habitual everyday modes and gestures, in a world transformed, he would have felt a certain sense of loneliness and fear: the sense of his strangeness. But the idea of murder was more than familiar to him, and by his acceptance of it it became his body's exhalation and the world he knew was bathed in it. His movements were not without an echo. Thus Querelle felt a quite different sense of loneliness; that of his creativeness, which singled him out from the rest. All the same, let it be remembered that we shall discover that our hero was capable of turning this quite unscrupulously to his own account.

Every crack in every stone of the ditch wall was subjected to careful scrutiny by Querelle. At one spot the brambles grew thicker and closer to the wall. They were caught by the foot in the masonry, as it were. This spot he examined more thoroughly. It appealed to him. Nobody had followed him there. Nobody was behind him, nor was there anyone on top of the slope supported by the wall. He was all alone in the ditch that formed part of the fortifications. With his hands stuck deep in his pockets to protect them from being scratched, he began deliberately to force his way into the undergrowth. For a moment he stood stock-still under the wall: he made a survey of the masonry. He could see the stone which would have to be removed before he could begin to hollow out a little of the wall behind it: the small sail-cloth bag which held gold, rings, broken bracelets, earrings, and a few Italian gold coins did not call for much space. For a long time he stood staring. He became hypnotized. Soon he had induced a form of sleep, of self-obliteration, which allowed him to become part of his surroundings. Finding that he could now enter into the wall, every detail of which was burningly impressed upon his mind, in imagination his body was not long in following his sight. There were eyes in the tips of his ten fingers. Even his muscles seemed endowed with them. Very soon he became the wall and for a moment he remained the wall, feeling every detail of its stones alive in him, their sharp edges causing wounds and invisible streams of blood to flow from them mingled with the silent cries and anguish of his soul. He could feel a spider tickling the tiny cavern where two of his fingers joined, and a leaf sticking delicately to one of his moist stones. At last, realizing that he was pressed so close against the wall that the damp, rough contours indented his hands, he forced himself to break away from it, to remove himself out of it. He came out of it, bruised for ever, indelibly scarred by the particular spot he had picked out along the ramparts, and these stigmata would remain in his bodily memory. Now he would be certain to find the place again five or six years later.

As he turned homeward, his thoughts reverted to another crime which had been perpetrated in Brest, but he attached little importance to it. He had seen a photograph of Gil in the morning papers and recognized the smiling face of the young mason with the voice.

Aboard *Le Vengeur*, Querelle lost nothing of his sulky arrogance or irritability. Despite his duties as steward, he preserved a redoubtable elegance. Without appearing to put too much into his work, he paid the greatest attention to all the Lieutenant's affairs. Seblon no longer dared to look Querelle in the face, after his unequivocally ironical answer given with the perfect assurance of his power over one who was in love with him. Querelle dominated his shipmates by his strength and harshness and by a mounting prestige, which increased when they found out that he went every evening to La Féria. This did not go much further than the fact that some of the matelots had seen him shaking hands with the owner and with Madame Lysiane.

The reputation of the owner of La Féria had spanned the seven seas. Sailors spoke of him among themselves, as we have said, as they do of ducks in China, as they do of Crillolla, Bousbir and Bidonville. They were impatient to get acquainted with the whorehouse, but when first they clapped eyes on the dark, dank street with its small ramshackle house, filthily squalid, its shutters permanently closed, they were both astonished and a little uneasy. Not many dared to enter its studded door. That he had become a regular visitor added considerably to Querelle's stature. Nobody went as far as to presume that he had diced with the boss. Querelle was powerful enough in his own right for his reputation to remain unsullied, and even for it to be further enhanced by the frequent visits he was known to pay. That he was never to be seen about with a tart was only further proof that he didn't go there as a client, but as a friend or pimp. To have a woman of his own inside made a man of him, and no longer a matelot. He had as much authority as if he had a stripe up. Querelle felt that he was surrounded by immense respect, and bathing in this reflected glory sometimes made him forget himself. He became more arrogant with the Lieutenant, whose express desires he well knew.

Querelle maliciously tried to exacerbate him. He had an astonishing natural gift for finding the most provocative poses. Either he would lean up against the door with one arm raised, giving a full view of his armpit; or sit on the table, taking great care to keep his thighs pressed tight against it, while he pulled up a trouser-leg to show off the smooth muscles of his calf; or else he would throw out his chest, or again, when replying to the officer, assume a pose far more outrageous and suggestive, answering his call by coming forward with his hands thrust down in his pockets and pulling so hard on the flap of his trousers from the inside that it was drawn tight over his cock and balls and showed off his stomach in all its insolence.

This drove the Lieutenant almost insane: he did not dare to complain or reprimand him, or even to exclaim in adoration. The most upsetting memory of all – and the one he most frequently called to mind – took place at Alexandria one afternoon when he caught sight of the rating coming up the gangway. Querelle was so obviously laughing, showing all his teeth, yet making no sound. At that time his face was bronzed, or rather bright gold in colour, the true golden tint that goes best with fair hair. He had just returned from the garden of some Arab where he had broken off five or six sprays covered with tangerines. Not to encumber his hands, which he liked to be free while walking the better to swing his arms from the shoulder, he had put these inside his white shirt. They were bubbling out behind his shiny black silk and almost rubbing against his chin. For the officer, this vision was the sudden revelation of all that was most secret about Querelle. The foliage that seemed to be growing quite naturally out of the neck of his shirt was doubtless what the sailor grew on his broad chest in the place of hair, and haply attached to each one of these precious and personal branches would be tantalizing testicles, both hard and at the same time yielding to the touch. Hesitant for a split second as he stood at the top of the gangway before putting his foot on the scorching metal deck, Querelle came forward towards his mates. Almost the whole ship's company was on shore leave. Those who were left on board, overcome by the heat of the sun, were lying stretched out under the awning. One lad shouted to him:

'What a cow! Talk of being in pod! You've not got the guts to carry them!'

'You bet I wouldn't! Everyone'd think I was on the way to my wedding.'

Querelle had the greatest difficulty in disentangling the branches, which kept catching in his striped jersey and in his silk. He never stopped smiling.

'Where did you get them?'

'From a garden. I broke in.'

Even if Querelle's murders had grown up, as it were, into a charmed hedge around him, this did not prevent him from feeling sometimes that they had so diminished in size as to be not much higher than insignificant iron spikes. This feeling was terrible. Bereft of his loftiest protection – though he could never be too sure of their reality, since they were outside his mental control and occasionally capable of being reduced to his insignificance of metallic form – he suddenly felt poor and naked among his fellow men.

With an effort, he collected his wandering thoughts. As he took the first step on the scorching deck of *Le Vengeur*, he was already climbing back up to those regions of the Elysian Fields where he would find, grouped about him and in their proper form, the victims of his past savagery. Despair at finding himself despised and rejected had caused him previously to multiply cruelties where he intended caresses. This had gained him the reputation among the ship's company of having a wicked temper. Since he possessed the facility neither for friendship nor companionship, he had come to regard himself disparagingly. He would suddenly wish to win over his mates with a joke, but only succeeded in hurting their feelings. Wounded, they were quick to take offence. Querelle would stand his ground, dig in his heels still deeper, and fly into an almighty temper. But there is nothing like hate and cruelty for engendering the real seeds of a genuinely sympathetic relationship. There was no doubt that Querelle was hated, for all the admiration his effrontery might win him, and, what is more, this concentrated hate began to eat its way into the marble of his features and to mould the beauty of his form.

He noticed that the Lieutenant's eye was on him, and, smiling, he made his way towards him. The remoteness of the Motherland, the comparative freedom accorded to the lower deck on his 'off' day, the blistering heat, the general air of festivity aboard the ship at anchor in the Roads, all contributed to the relative relaxation of discipline between officers and men.

'Would you care for a tangerine, Lieutenant?'

The officer went forward with a smile. The next moment witnessed a synchronized double gesture: for as Querelle raised his right hand to break off one of the tangerines, the Lieutenant took his from his pocket and slowly held it out to the rating, who placed his gift in it with a vivid smile. The harmony of these two simultaneous actions greatly affected the officer.

'Thanks, matelot.'

'Don't mention it, Lieutenant.'

Querelle turned round again to his mates, pulling off and chucking them a few tangerines as he went. The Lieutenant moved away slowly, negligently, almost affectedly, peeling the skin off the fruit as he went and telling himself with resurgent joy that his affection for Querelle was perfectly pure. The first foretaste of their union had just taken place, following the laws of so concerted a harmony, that there could be no doubt it was ordained expressly by their twin souls or, better still, by a unique entity – Pure Love – a single altar lit by twin rays. He glanced warily to left and right and then, finally turning his back on the knot of sailors after making sure that he could be seen by none of them, he stuffed the tangerine into his mouth whole and kept it for a moment in the hollow of his cheek, thinking, 'It might well be the balls of any handsome young "skin" who deserves to be gobbled by old sea-dogs like me!'

He turned round surreptitiously. Querelle was standing with his back to him, in front of all the sailors who were lying stretched at ease, merged into one large lump of virility. The Lieutenant was just in time to see him flexing his powerful legs in their white ducks, hands on buttocks, in the act of straining every muscle in the effort (he could imagine the high colour of the matelot's face and the anticipatory smile as he waited for the Great Relief, his eyes bright and a set smile on his lips) the culminating effort that would unloose down wind a series of loud farts, short, sharp, and dry, as though the famous white ducks (Querelle called them his farting-gales) had been rent from top to bottom; a performance to be greeted by a thousand cheers and streamers waving, and a burst of laughter from his mates. Shocked to shyness, the Lieutenant quickly averted his head and turned tail.

Querelle performed the most dangerous of his crimes without wittingly or wilfully committing an error, but, no sooner had he committed a theft, a murder even, than he perceived the nature of his error – sometimes of his errors – which had slipped in unawares. Often enough it was next to nothing. A slight flaw in the perfect crime, an unsure hand, a cigarette-lighter left behind in the dead man's fingers, a shadow cast by his own profile on some clear surface that he imagined might prove to be indelible, insignificant things, in all conscience, though sometimes he was seized with anguish lest his eyes, which themselves had witnessed the scene, might not so reflect the image of his victim as to make it visible to others. After each one of his crimes, he passed in review, detail by detail, the course of the event in its entirety. In this way, he hit upon the error. His quite amazing retrospective clarity of vision enabled him to spot the smallest mistake. There was, in every case, at least one. And so, in order not to be completely swallowed up by his despair, Querelle, with a smile, was in the habit of offering up this error to his protecting star, while repeating some such phrase as, 'We shall see, all in good time. For, to be sure, I did it on purpose. On purpose. And that makes it far worse.'

But instead of being stunned by fear, he became uplifted by it, inspired by a profound, violent, and to all intents and purposes, organic belief in his lucky star. It was to win its favour that he was always smiling. He felt convinced that the divinity protecting a murderer was a joyful one. So the sadness, which others as well as he himself found in his smile, flowered only at moments when he was aware of the absolute loneliness which a destiny as particular as his imposed upon him.

'What should I do if I hadn't got my star?', this was as much as to say, 'What should I be if I hadn't got it?' 'You cannot be *only a sailor*, for that – that function – is what you believe it to be; but it must be what you cannot see, if you really want to amount to someone.' The smile intended for his star had repercussions over the whole of his body and enveloped his personality in the light and tenuous gossamer of a spider's web, so that it flowered into a galaxy of twinkling stars. Gilbert Turko thought of his piles in very much the same way.

When Querelle left the garden in Alexandria, it was too late to throw the broken-off branches over into the road as he waited behind one of the supports, keyed up in nervous tension for a favourable moment to leap over the wall. For where would they land? Perhaps there would be a beggar huddled in the dust on the other side of the wall, or else some Arab urchin might catch a glimpse of a French sailor discharging his cargo of tangerine-covered branches. The best plan seemed to conceal them on his person. Querelle wanted to avoid taking any exceptional step that might call attention to himself; and so it came about that in the end he determined upon an uninterrupted progress from garden to ship, humouring himself by slipping some branches into the opening of his shirt, but allowing the leaves and one or two of the tangerines to remain sticking out so as to make, in his star's honour, a delicate, temporary altar of his manly chest. But once aboard, he was aware of the risks he was still running and would continue to run until he no longer felt the efficacy of the rapture that always came to him after committing a crime. Thus it was that, with one foot poised on the companionway and the other still poised in mid air, he smiled a mystic smile at his night-enfathomed star.

In his trouser pocket were the necklace of gold coins and the two bangles he had stolen from the villa where he had picked the tangerines. The gold gave him weight and security on earth. When it came to distributing the fruit and branches among the sailors lying stretched out and bored in the intense heat, he had felt purified and so transparent that he had to keep careful watch over himself on the way back to his quarters not to take out the stolen jewels in full view of the ship's company. Much the same feeling of lightheartedness, though he was torn between complete faith in his guiding star and the certainty of being lost to all perdition, had sustained and lightened his steps as he made his way along the rampart ditch, until, in a sudden blinding flash, he was struck by the inspired revelation, based on the news that the police had found a lighter beside the murdered sailor, and that this lighter, according to the papers, belonged to Gil Turko. The discovery of such a dangerous clue made him so cock-a-hoop that it might have been the touchstone to the wide world. It was the point of contact that enabled him to perform his act all over again, only backwards, in reverse order; to take it to bits as it were, but, as the result of this piece of evidence, he was able to divide up the pieces into separate and distinct parts, all of which went to prove that the whole disentangled skein had been referred to God, or some other judge and jury. Querelle realized that the act was indeed a terrible mortal sin. He discerned the presence of Hell in his act, yet almost at once, to combat this thought, saw that it pointed towards a dawn as pure as that corner of Heaven adorned by a blue-robed and innocent Virgin, who made her appearance through a rent in the fog in the side-aisle of the church in La Rochelle where are to be found the votive ships. Querelle then knew that he would be saved. Slowly, very slowly, he recovered himself. He had gone very far towards losing himself deep in those realms where in secret he was at one with his brother.

Clearly there is no reason to speak of the tenderness of brotherly love in this case, but rather of what is currently known as sentiment, or presentiment (the usual sense of the prefix). Querelle had a presentiment of his brother. Despite the fact that he had only shortly beforehand fought with him in a fight that might have proved fatal to one or the other, the hate engendered by the heat of the fight never for a moment prevented him from rediscovering the presence of Robert in the deepest recesses of his own inmost being. What Madame Lysiane had suspected turned out to be true: their good-looking faces growled and showed bared teeth, hate twisted their features, and their bodies were entangled in mortal combat – yet the mistress of neither of them would have stood a chance of coming out alive had she intervened. Already in their youth, when they fought together, one couldn't help believing that behind their agonized faces lay a region far removed where their astonishing resemblances were united as in wedlock.

It was in the shelter of these outward appearances that Querelle was always able to rediscover his brother Robert.

When they reached the end of the street, Robert had turned to the left spontaneously, in the direction of the brothel, Querelle to the right. He gritted his teeth. His brother, drunk with fury, had said to him almost under his breath, and in front of Dédé: 'Bastard, you let Nono fuck you up the arse. Why did your bloody ship have to bring you here? You shit!'

Querelle had blanched and looked Robert straight in the eyes.

'I've done worse things and I'll do as I please. And get out of my sight or I'll show you who's the shit.'

The kid had never moved. He had expected that Robert would defend his reputation as a male with the last drop of his blood. The two men lived to fight again.

Nonetheless, in turning to the right, Querelle was already searching for a motive that would allow him to hurl back his scorn in his brother's pallid face, and now that they were quits as far as their apparent – and indeed real – hate was concerned, this would enable him to become one with his brother again in his innermost being. With head erect and looking straight in front of him with unwavering eyes, lips a mere line, elbows tight pressed into his sides, in other words with an altogether shorter and neater step than was his wont, he perforce followed the dictates of his mood in the direction of the ramparts, or more precisely to the very spot along the walls where he had hidden his jewels. The nearer he got to their whereabouts, the quicker his bitterness began to melt away. No exact memory of the acts of daring that had gained him the possession of them came to his mind, but the jewels themselves – their very proximity was sufficient for that – were an effective proof of his courage and of his existence. On arrival at the slope facing the consecrated wall now invisible in the fog, Querelle stood stock-still, legs apart and hands deep in the pockets of his oilskin coat: he was but a short distance from one of the many altars he had erected in various parts of the globe and within the orbit of their special radiance. Since his treasures were a refuge where he could glory in his power, Querelle was already making them over to his hated brother in a theoretical will. He was feeling a little downcast and gloomy that Dédé had been a witness of the brawl. Not that he had felt a sense of shame in the youngster's presence, but he had a vague fear that he was not to be trusted; Querelle realized that he was by this time a celebrity in Brest.

Lucubrations of Lieutenant Seblon.

Night – looking out to sea. Neither the sea nor the night bring me peace. The very reverse. A sailor has only to throw a shadow as he passes . . . for him to be good-looking. In this semi-darkness, thanks to it, he cannot but be good-looking.

Within its flank the ship holds many a delicious brute, clothed in blue and white. Every shadow is for me desirable. How can I single out any one male among so many, each one more beautiful than the other. Scarcely shall I have let go one before wanting another. I derive what peace I can from the sole thought that there is but one sailor; *the sailor*. And each individual one I see is but the momentary representation, fragmentary at that, a pale shadow of THE SAILOR. Each type has something of him in embryo, be it his strength, endurance, beauty, cruelty, a hundred other qualities, all save the one authentic personality. Every sailor who passes by serves as a touchstone for THE SAILOR. Were all the sailors to appear live and present before my eyes at the same time; yes, all: yet not one of them separately would be the sailor created by their sum total, who can but exist in my imagination and who can exist only in me and through me.

I am comforted by this idea, for I alone possess THE SAILOR of my imagination.

Querelle's anger led to his being insolent to the Quartermaster, in the following manner:

'I'll take you on the quarter-deck.'

'And I'll piss up your arse and wash your brains out!'

I took pleasure in signing Querelle's charge-sheet. All the same, he shall not go before a Court-martial this time. I wish him to remain in my debt and to be aware that he is in my debt. He gave me a smile. All of a sudden, I was struck by the full force of the expression, 'He's still alive', with reference to a wounded man - perhaps mortally wounded - who is transfixed by a sudden spasm.

Querelle, to his mates: 'It's blowing,' or 'It's blowing a gale.' He then advances, swaggering, as sure in his progress as a ship under full sail.

A master hand has moulded each curl, triumphantly sculpted and chiselled each muscle, eye and ear.

The least line or wrinkle, the faintest shadow on his body, holds an exciting message for me: the bending of a finger-joint, the intersection of the lines of his arms, his neck, each severally is capable of inducing an emotional state during which I come off as I dive down deeper to the delights of his belly, as soft and smooth as a woodland bank strewn with pine-needles. Does he know the full beauty of his form? Has he any conception of its power?

Throughout the length and breadth of the docks and arsenals he peddles by day his load of darkness, his shadowy cargo on which a thousand eyes delight to feast, refreshed and comforted; by night his shoulders bear a hod of light, his conquering thighs drive back the breakers of his natal seas, the very ocean rolls back to rest at his feet, his chest is perfume-laden with scented waves.

On board this ship, his presence is just as astonishing – and as efficacious and normal – as would be a carter's whip, a squirrel, or a clod of turf. I cannot say whether he saw me this morning as he passed by, but he pushed his cap back on his head with the two fingers that held a lighted cigarette and spoke aloud in the bright sunlight for the benefit of the Lord knows whom:

'That's the ticket when you're chokker.'

His whole forehead was aglow with his love-locks, fair and brown, mingled in a perfect uprush of ordered beauty. I looked at him disdainfully. At this very moment, no doubt, he was parading bunches of sunlit or moon-ripened grapes stolen from the harvest of the sea already garnered by laughing maidens after they had first prinked and preened in the glassy mirror of each gloriously gleaming grape.

I love him. The officers bore me. If only I were a rating! I remain in the wind. My forehead aches with cold and migraine, crowned with a metal tiara. I grow bigger and bigger and finally founder.

THE SAILOR is my one and only love.

I saw the most lovely poster of a white-uniformed Marine. Leather bandolier and belt; gaiters; bayonet against his thigh. A palm tree. A flag. His features were hard and scornful. He scorned death . . . and at eighteen! 'Quietly to give the order to these proud and stalwart lads to go to meet their death! Slowly the disabled ship begins to founder, and I alone standing up in the prow – perhaps upheld by this Marine who will perish only with me – shall witness the drowning of these lovely lads?'

One speaks of a ship *sinking to the depths*.

Do my fellow-officers, I wonder, spot my troubled state of mind?

I'm afraid some inkling of it must have seeped through in my relations with them during the course of my service. Throughout the morning, my thoughts were really haunted by *ideas concerning young men*: thieves, bloodthirsty warriors, pimps, bloodstained but smiling scrappers, etc . . . Their presence is not so much visual as conjectured in my mind's eye. Of a sudden, they form a picture, only to fade away again almost as quickly as they came. They were simply *ideas concerning young men*, as I have just put it, that embalmed my thoughts for a moment or two.

O that he would so position his thighs that I might sit down and rest my hands upon them as on the arms of a chair!

Naval officer. Barely out of my 'teens, a mere Sub-Lieutenant, never did I give a thought, when I chose the life of a sailor, to the perfect alibi that career would provide. In it the bachelor is self-justified. Women do not ask you why you are not married. They like to tell you with a sigh that you can know nothing of true love since perforce all you have experienced are passing fancies. Sea and solitude. 'A wife in every port.' There is nobody to feel concerned as to whether I am engaged or not; neither my shipmates nor my mother. We chart our own course through life.

Since I have come to love Querelle, I tend to take my duties more lightly. Love makes me flinch. The more I love Querelle, the more clearly defined become my feminine traits and the more tender I become and the sadder that my love is unfulfilled. No matter how strange may be the various turns and twists of my relationship with Querelle, they only add so many more mental upheavals to my sum total of unhappiness, that I am forced to cry out, 'What's the use?'

Another glimpse of Admiral A, a widower now for twenty years or more. He has become his own gently smiling widow. The stalwart who accompanies him everywhere (chauffeur, not orderly) is the living reincarnation, gloriously endowed, of his own flesh and blood.

I am recently returned from six days at sea. My first meeting with Querelle has the effect on me – and on all around me in the sunny air – of a slight shock, a faintly tragic clash. The whole day has floated along in a sort of bright steamy atmosphere caused by the heaviness of this *re-turn*. Return for good and all. Querelle knows that I'm in love with him. He knows from my never taking my eyes off him, and I know that he knows from his wickedly provocative and sometimes insolent smile. But everything about him goes to prove that my attachment to him is taken for granted, and everything he does seems to show all too clearly that he would like this attachment to be strengthened. And all the awkwardnesses that exist between us give us a still clearer insight into the exceptional merits and virtues of this particular day's events. Supposing he had wanted it, it would have been beyond my power to make love to Querelle tonight, and certainly to anyone else. The whole reservoir of my collective affections flows out in the pleasure of return and swamps my happiness.

I have just had the most terrifying dream. I can thus far describe it. WE were in some sort of stables (with a dozen or so unknown accomplices). Which of us (I have no idea which) would have to kill HIM. One of the young men took on the job. The victim in no way deserved death. We watched the carrying out of the murder. The self-chosen murderer time and time again dug deep into the greenish back of the wretched man with a pitchfork. Suddenly a looking-glass made its appearance immediately above the victim, for the express purpose of allowing us to see our faces blanch. The more blood we saw on the back of the murdered man, the paler we became. The executioner struck and struck again in desperation. (I am certain that I am transcribing this dream faithfully, though its details may have escaped my memory, for as I write, I live through it once more.) The victim - and be it remembered that he was innocent - however atrociously he might be suffering, always helped the murderer. He contrived to show him where to strike the next blow. He took an active part in the drama, despite the reproachful look of agonized misery in his eyes. I can still see the beauty of the murderer, the whole full horror of the curse under which he was labouring. My whole day has been splotched with blood as a result of this dream. Yes, quite literally, this day has been for me an open wound.

Robert had come to rely on Madame Lysiane, and, to his shame, he found himself more and more under her sway. The Madam was now sure of her power over him. One evening, as she was almost swamping him under the sumptuous curves of her body, he gave a sudden shake of irritation to rid himself of her hair which was tickling him. In wheedling and furtive tones, she murmured:

'You don't love me.'

'What d'you mean, I don't love you?'

This sulky, heavily reproachful cry of Robert's ended by his seizing his mistress' head in both hands and plunging his knob deep into her mouth and there working it to and fro. When he withdrew it, they both burst out laughing, so overcome were they by this precipitate and perfect proof of their mutual love. One must recollect, all the same, that Robert detested this little piece of fun so dear to the heart of Madame Lysiane. Moreover, it was he himself who, on the spur of the moment, had chosen this way to protest against the accusation of his mistress, and by so doing he revealed the childish side of his affection for her, as well as his surrender - all the more heroic in that it had been provoked - to the motherly love of La Féria.

Querelle's hand was thick and strong, and Mario, without having really thought much about it, had imagined when he came to hold out his own in response that he was about to shake an effeminate and therefore crushable hand. His muscles were in no way prepared for the handshake he received. He took a closer look at Querelle. This good-looking chap, despite a day's growth of beard which in no sense detracted from his perfect features, had the very looks and athletic build as Robert; his general appearance was manly, with a touch of devil-may-care brutality about it. (The strength and brutality were still further emphasized by a sparing use of gesture.)

'Is Nono about anywhere?'

'No, he's gone out.'

'Are you in charge of the joint, then?'

'There's the Madam. Don't you know each other?'

As he put this question, Mario looked Querelle straight in the eye and a sneer came over his face, and though his mouth might have an ironic twist, his look was hard and pitiless. But Querelle suspected nothing.

'Yes . . .'

He spoke this 'yes' with prolonged emphasis, giving the word such an unquestionably circumstantial tone that it seemed the most natural thing in the world for them to be acquainted. At the same time, he put one leg in front of the other and took out a cigarette. Everything about his person seemed bent on proving to the world in general that the importance of this particular moment lay not in his affirmative response, but in the most insignificant and futile gesture.

'Care for a fag?'

'Don't mind if I do.'

They lit their cigarettes and each inhaled a first puff; Querelle exhaling his with a touch of pride, mostly through the nose, thus suiting his action to the word by celebrating in his magnificent smoke-ejecting nostrils his own victory over himself, till now unexpressed, that had given him the courage to speak familiarly to a 'tec who, to all intents and purposes, was an officer of the law.

It had not taken the police long to make up their minds that both murders were the work of Gil. They became convinced of it when the masons were shown, and identified as his, the lighter which had been picked up in the long grass near the murdered sailor. At first the police considered the crime to be one of vengeance, then to be a love-drama, and finally they settled for the idea of sexual perversion.

From every room in the Brest Headquarters a curious feeling of desperation emanated: yet, more often than not, this proved to be a consolation to them, though it can hardly be said the police officers grew accustomed to this all pervasive atmosphere. On the walls were pinned up a number of photographs from the Criminal Anthropometry Department and a few notices giving descriptive details of wanted criminals who were suspected of having reached a port. The tables were littered with dossiers containing past records, or further more precise and important details.

As soon as Gil enters this room at Headquarters, he will be submerged by a sea, a very ocean of desperate and overwhelming sense of heaviness. He had become fully aware of this sense of heaviness from the moment of his arrest by Mario: when the officer had laid hold of him by the sleeve, Gil had wrenched himself free, but Mario, as though he had foreseen this, and almost without allowing it to interrupt him in the course of his action, began all over again - or, to be more exact, continued more forcefully by grabbing his forearm in such a grip of authority that the young mason was forced to give up struggling. It is in such fleeting moments of liberty as exist between two arrests of this nature - the first a failure and the second successful - that is contained the full measure of the power behind the game, of the chase, of the irony, and its cruel methods and final justice, everything that goes to make up the astonishing weight of the Police. In this particular case, the Power behind the police officer caused Gil's complete eclipse. He stiffened, to prevent himself from succumbing altogether, and, because he noticed the expression of flushed anger and pleasure at his capture on the face of the young inspector accompanying Mario, Gil said, 'What d'you want with me . . . ?', and added falteringly, 'Sir?' The young inspector was quick to answer: 'We'll soon show you what we want with you!'

From the arrogance of it, Gill realized with stupefaction that the young officer derived some comfort from Mario's summary action in fastening a pair of handcuffs round the wrists of a murderer. He could now approach and safely insult or strike the ravening beast, proud while free, but now rendered harmless. Gil turned towards Mario. All the child-like trust in his soul, that had flashed to the surface a moment since, now deserted him. After calling upon a host of a thousand angels to fly to his aid, he might be relying on the accomplishment of God's will. Yielding to the impulse to utter just one resounding phrase before he died – at such moments even silence can count as a beautiful final phrase – one which might achieve the continuance of his life, or bring it to a noble conclusion, or express the fulfilment of his personality, Gil simply said, 'That's life!'

On entering the Police Headquarters, he was immediately overcome by the heat of the room, and little by little he grew feeble enough to imagine that he would die from exhaustion, powerless to make any effort to escape the clutches of the radiator; it was already beginning to hiss in trembling preparation of uncoiling itself like a boa-constrictor to envelop and crush him in its folds, and finally suffocate him. He endured agonies of both shame and fear. He heaped reproaches on himself for not putting up a better show. He began to imagine that the surrounding walls possessed enigmatic secrets bloodier by far and ten times more terrible than his own.

When the Superintendent looked up at him, he was amazed. He had never conceived of a murderer looking like that. While impressing upon Mario the need for prompter action, he had been unable to prevent himself from investing the cut-and-dried criminal of his imagination with all the worst possible attributes. In any case, men in his profession never learned anything from experience. Seated at his desk, fiddling with a ruler, he had tried to evoke the living embodiment of his conception of a criminal sodomite. Mario had given little credence to his words.

'There are precedents for a case like this. There's Vacher, for instance. Such men are characters whose vices lead them in the end to commit some folly. They are known as sadists. And these two murders are the work of a sadist.'

It was in just such superficial terms of deference that the Superintendent had conferred with the Superintendent of Marine Police. Each vied with the other in trying to formulate their ideas about sexual perverts – that is, their physical attributes – and then fit them to the actions of murderers. They invented monsters. The Superintendent had a second search made in the vicinity of the corpse for some unusual clue, something corresponding to the celebrated flask of oil used by a notorious criminal to ease the sodding of his victims, or for traces of fresh excrement near the scene of the crime. Ignorant of the fact that the two crimes were the work of two different people, he tried to connect them, to juxtapose the motives for each. How was he to know that each murder was motivated and carried into execution by its own particular set of laws, and that these amounted to murder as a fine art! To the loneliness of Querelle and Gil as moral outcasts was added their artistic loneliness, which rests on no firm foundations and can only be called to question by a fellow-artist. (It follows from this that Querelle was more than ever his own soul-mate.)

The masons told the tale that Gill was a pederast. For the benefit of the police, they were ready to recount a hundred details to prove that the murderer was a nancy boy - and no mistaking the fact. They did not realize that this was to describe him not as he really was, that is to say a youth persecuted by a man obsessed, but exactly as Theo had wanted them to see the lad, and in the light of his machinations. They were nervous when faced by the police inspectors, and embarked upon descriptions that were crazily at variance - crazy by reason of the halting hesitancy of their evidence - which became more and more exaggerated in the telling. No doubt it dawned on them all that their accusations were without any real foundation, and were nothing so much as a flourish of the imagination that allowed them to speak at length and in good earnest of matters which they had joked about when they put all they knew into swearing extravagantly - or when they sang their songs - yet at the same time the golden opportunity of letting their tongues loose went to their heads like wine. They sensed that the picture that they had portrayed was as swollen as the corpse of a drowned man.

Here are some of the peculiarities that were cited as proofs of Gil's morals by the masons: the almost girlish prettiness of his face; the way he had of singing and trying to give his voice a velvety quality; the gaily provocative clothes he wore; his casual, almost idle, behaviour at work; the way he knuckled under to Theo; the pink and whiteness of his fresh skin; and so on - details that appeared to them altogether revealing from what they had picked up of Theo's and other mates' ribald comments on nancy boys.

'He's more girl than boy . . . he's got a funny little tart's face . . . he's about as fond of work as a kept woman; his best work's done on a bed. Oh! he purrs like a pussy . . . and when he trips along, it's like a pro swinging the bag on the beat in Marseilles . . .'

All these traits, hopelessly garbled as they were, added up to a description of a nance such as no mason had ever set eyes on. They knew about 'queans' and 'queers' from what Theo had told them and from the things they said among themselves when skylarking, and bandying such phrases as:

'He's one of them – a regular brown-hatter! . . . You can have them any way you like, front, back, or sideways . . . Go and stuff it up your own arse for a change . . . You'd best trip along to "your aunt" and get your greens that way!'

But these expressions, straight off the cuff, gave them no precise picture. No amount of such back-chat would ever have been able to teach them anything of lasting importance, so little did the subject interest them. But the fact was that they had become absorbed by it. Their utter ignorance of the real state of affairs may justly be said to have left them in a slightly uneasy state – indestructible by reason of its very imprecision and fluidity, unknown indeed because no name could be attached to it, but partially revealed to them by a thousand reflections, since they could never see it in its proper light. They were all able to guess at the existence of a world at once abominable and miraculous, on the brink of which any one of them might be hovering; in fact, it was fated to remain just around the corner of their minds, in much the same way as an elusive word hovers on the edge of your memory, only to disappear a moment later when you say, 'I had it on the tip of my tongue.'

When it came to the turn of any one of them to have to tell what they knew of Gil, that man would give a touch of caricature to each of his mannerisms which recalled, or might superficially recall to them, what they thought they knew about queers, and do it in such a way as to conjure up the exact portrait of a joy-boy which had a horrible ring of truth about it. Speaking of the relations between Gil and Theo, they said:

'They were always to be seen about together, but sooner or later there was bound to be a flare-up between them. Perhaps it was all because that fellow Gil had been bumming his load with another bloke . . .'

In the opening stages, they never thought of bringing up Roger's name. It was only after one of the inspectors had said:

'And what about that lad who was with Gil on the day of the murder?'

That they recalled to mind Roger's occasional appearances in the masons' yard. They were quick to exploit this new thread of evidence. To the masons, 'them like that' signified an indistinct group, with no specific traits; therefore it was naturally to be expected that a lad of eighteen, fresh from the embraces of a mason of forty, should go on to have an affair with a kid of fifteen.

'None of you ever seen him with a sailor?'

They could not say for sure, but what if they had? In the fog it's none too easy to see clearly. There were far too many sailors in Brest for Gil not to have known some of them, if not several. In any case, he usually wore matelot's trousers.

'You're certain of that?'

'Now that you've mentioned it, there's no doubt. Proper sailors' bags. Flap and all.'

'If you don't take our word for it, we might as well save our breath.'

Being able at long last to give veritable proof of a definite fact, they lost no time in forgetting their fearful and humiliating inferiority when confronted by the police. They began to put on airs. They went all out to furnish proofs of every word they had spoken. To be able to supply the police with an ascertainable piece of evidence, hitherto unsuspected by them, must inevitably make them one up with the Force. The police had mercilessly grilled Roger the whole of one night. All they had found on him was his clumsily-repaired clasp-knife.

'What are you doing with that?'

Roger blushed, but the police officer merely considered this momentary shame-facedness to be due to being found in possession of such a twopenny-ha'penny little knife. He did not press the matter further. He never guessed that the weapon was false and practically useless, and by becoming a symbol, was all the more dangerous. In the sharpness of a real weapon, in its ultimate purpose and its perfect manipulation, there already exists the germ of the idea of the act of killing, sufficiently formed to scare off the child who is afraid (the child who invents symbols is afraid of what is clumsily termed reality) whereas the symbolic knife can scarcely present a practical source of danger, but, since it comes in handy in a thousand imaginary adventures, it becomes a sign of acquiescence in crime. The police failed to see that this knife was the sign of condoning Gil's murder even before he had committed it.

'Where did you go with him?'

The kid denied ever having slept with the murderer, no less than with Theo whom he had only seen for the first time on the day of his death. Only for a moment did Roger hesitate. Then he confessed that one evening he had gone to meet his sister when she left the pub where she worked. Gil had been standing at the bar, joking with her. She had finished at midnight and Gil had walked back home with the brother and sister. The following day he was there again. Five days running Roger had found him there. And from time to time when he ran into him by chance, Gil had offered him a drink.

'He never tried to sleep with you?'

Roger's large eyes opened in utter astonishment and child-like innocence at what could lie behind such a remark on the part of the police.

'With me? Whatever for?'

'He never did anything with you?'

'What do you mean – did anything! Certainly not.'

He let his untroubled eyes rest calmly on the police in their confusion.

'You're sure he never, at any time, tampered with your flies or tried to mess you about?'

'Never.'

They could get nothing out of the kid who, furthermore, adored Gil. He had a childish love for him, in the first place; a child whose imagination is quick and high-flying. Crime had forced him to penetrate into a world where feelings are violent, and a natural love of the dramatic made his attachment to Gil all the stronger, for, without him, there would never have been this drama. Now it was all the more necessary to be linked to the criminal by the strongest and closest of ties, those of love. The bonds of love were only intensified by the effort Roger was making to baffle the police. He had need of this love to arm himself with sufficient strength, and if at first he misled them from the simple need of protecting himself and his dream-life, he very soon came to see that by ranging himself against the police he was inescapably driven to take Gil's side. Deliberately, and in order to get back as close as possible to Gil – who at that moment had attained the height of his glory (on account of his murders and his appearance) – Roger concentrated all his powers of dissemblance. All that remained to him was the shadow of Gil crouching at his feet like a dog. Roger wanted to put his foot on it to keep it there. Secretly, he implored it not to run away, but to stay there beside him as a manifestation and witness of hidden supernatural powers; if only the shadow could be prevailed upon to hover there unseen and detached, to lie down again, stretched out, connecting him with Gil. He was quick to pick up many of love's artful dodges, but in making such skilful use of them he was in constant danger of being hoist on his own petard. The more straightforward he might appear, the more underhand he became, and the purer – that is to say his love and his were pure.

The police let him go as dawn was breaking. They had reached the conclusion that Gil was a sadistic madman and dangerous. They instituted enquiries throughout the length and breadth of France.

Gil had found refuge in the solitude of the ancient maritime convict-prison. He had longed to be alone when in the crowded thoroughfares, where, on the run and regarded almost as a monster, he had felt swollen and puffed out, so that every feature and every gesture he made must inevitably be revealing. So long as he never ventured outside its walls, the certainty of not being discovered inside the prison-house began to act as a solace to his agonized nerves. He felt able to endure a life of misery when he considered all that it was depriving him of, but he could never have put up with a life that was false. Given a little sustenance, he would be able to bear it. He was beginning to feel hungry. His crime had increased his fears during the three days he had been in hiding. His periods of sleep and his sudden awakenings were hideous. He was afraid of rats, but he seriously considered trapping one and eating it raw. He had quickly sobered up and almost at once the futility of the murder he had committed became apparent to him. He even felt rather soppy about Theo. He remembered how matey he had been at the start and all the half-pints they had put down between them. He begged his forgiveness. He was threatened with remorse, which added to his hunger. Finally he gave a thought to the old folk at home. They must almost certainly have learnt about it from the papers and the police. How had his mother taken it? and his father? They were workers too. His old man had been a mason. What were *his* thoughts about his son killing another mason in a crisis of sexual hate? And what were those of his school-mates?

Gil slept on the bare stone floor. Not bothering to fold up his clothes – shirt, vest, and trousers seemed to slip off almost automatically – he was inclined to remain there on his haunches, stripped to the buff, while mechanically and lovingly – but deriving therefrom a sensual pleasure which had nothing to do with erotic excitement – be began to run a light, almost caressing finger over the protruding sensitive veins, supposedly very pale pink in colour, which had once given him the proper knowledge of his masculinity at the time when they were instrumental in preventing Theo from attempting to sully him. There they were, his piles, a faithful and permanent record to remind him of that scene, and their presence gave him the fortitude to be consciously faithful to himself.

'They must have buried Theo by this time. The boys won't care overmuch, they'll all have chipped in for a wreath.'

A wreath for Gil, for it was Gil who was being buried. He crumpled up, but remained in the corner, pressing his knees together between his arms. Sometimes he would walk up and down but always quietly, fearfully, mysteriously hugging the wall, like Baron Franck, as though attached to it by a complicated network of chains running from his neck to his wrists, to his waist, to his ankles, and to the stones of the wall. He took the greatest care in dragging along this heavy and invisible load of metal and was surprised to find out how easily his clothes had dropped off him: his trousers, which ought to have been clinging to his flanks, and his vest, to the full extent of his arms. And he walked quietly for a further reason, from fear of the spectral bird of ill-omen he would have raised from the dust had he walked with a quicker step; it would have spread out to its fullest extent like a billowing sail filled by a breeze, with the lightest puff that blew from nowhere at all. This spectre lay somewhere under his feet: he must do his utmost to stamp it out, to crush it by treading heavily. It was in his arms and in his legs: he must smother it by moving very slowly. Too rapid a twist or turn would have allowed it to escape from him, to unfold a white or a black wing above his head, whence most certainly it would lower an invisible, shapeless head and into his ear – into the very drum of Gil's ear – murmur the most terrifying threats like the grumble of thunder. This special bird was within him and Gil must on no account do anything to let it loose.

Theo's death had in no sense advantaged him. A man murdered is more alive than the living; more dangerous than he was when alive. Gil gave not one moment's thought to Roger, who thought continually of him. All the circumstantial details of the scene of the drama ebbed obstinately from his mind. He knew that he had killed – and killed Theo – but was it really Theo he had killed? Was he really dead? Gil ought to have asked him right away. 'Just tell me you're all right, at least, Theo!' Had he replied that he was, then Gil would have derived incalculable comfort; yet, let us reflect, he would have been no less uncertain. For the dying man was quite capable of replying with direct malice, the more implicitly to commit Gil to a purposeless crime. Theo was more than likely a bloke who wished to implicate him right up to the hilt, a bloke who harboured an unwarrantable hatred towards him. At times Gil got over his apprehensions by recalling that he had noticed the thousand and one little wrinkles and the delicate lines at the corners of his victim's mouth. At other times, he would quake with fear. He had committed a crime which had merely brought him a load of trouble – it hadn't brought him a penny piece. It had been a big mistake, as empty as a bottomless pail.

Gil brooded over the best way of retrieving the position. To start with, huddled up in the corner, crouching there with damp stones all round him, his head sunk on his chest, he tried to nullify his act by breaking it down into a series of actions, each one perfectly harmless in itself. 'What if I did open a door? One has a perfect right to open a door; what if I took hold of a bottle? – one has every right to take hold of a bottle; if I broke a bottle? nobody has a right to stop that; if I put the ragged edges against the skin of the neck? there's nothing so very terrible in that, one has the right to do it. To exert a little pressure and then to press them home a little further? – that's not so terrible, either. If I let a little blood flow? One can do it, one has the right to do it. To let a little more blood, and then a little more still?'

Thus it was possible for the crime to be reduced to next to nothing, to be reduced to such an infinitely small scale of measurement that it was impossible to determine the point of balance at which what is lawful merges – and once it has touched this point of what is lawfully permitted there is no getting away from it – into what is illegal and results in actual crime. Gil did his utmost to reduce his crime to this level, to scale it down to vanishing point. But he could not resolve the question as to why he had killed Theo. This murder remained senseless; it remained a blunder, and one cannot retrieve a blunder.

Whether he should abandon his first scale of measurements for reducing the crime to nothing was what still occupied Gil's thoughts. With the utmost speed, after several false starts and hesitations in reviewing the past events of his life, his mind seized on the following idea: to retrieve this senseless crime it was necessary to commit another (of a similar kind) which did serve some purpose. A crime that would gain him a fortune of some sort and render the precedent effective (like a definitive act) by having instigated the second. On whom could he now lay his hands to kill? The long and short of it was that he didn't know any swells; so then he must get out and about, take a train, get to Rennes, to Paris, where possibly he would find wealthy people walking about in the streets waiting impatiently or impassively for a thief to fall upon them. That the purse-proud would accept and willingly be waiting for such a fate became Gil's obsession. It seemed quite obvious to him that in the big cities the gilded rich were only living in the hopes that some criminal would kill and rob them of their riches. But here, in this dungeon, in this cell, he was anchored by the very encumbrance and uselessness of his first murder.

Several times he thought of giving himself up, self-confessed, to the police. But ever since his childhood he had retained his fear of the police and their sinister uniforms. He was frightened that they would lose no time in sending him to the guillotine. He became maudlin at the thought of his mother. He begged her forgiveness. He cast his thoughts back over his childhood; the time when he was apprenticed to his father; and then his first job in the masons' yard of the south. Each detail of his life seemed to him pregnant with omens and to point, from the outset, to the fact that he was marked down for tragedy. He soon convinced himself that he had only become a mason to fulfil his destiny as a murderer. The fear of the consequences of his act – an act so anti-social – forced him to think things over most carefully and threw him back on the resources of his own mind: in short, made him use his brains. Despair caused him to look into himself, to take stock of his own character. His thought ran along the following lines to start with; looking at the sea through the prison windows, he *lived and breathed* an existence so estranged from the world that he might suddenly have been transplanted to Greece, atop some cliff face, crouched in thought, gazing out over the Aegean. Since his utter misery obliged him to turn his thoughts to the world outside, he began by establishing a relationship between himself and external objects, though these might threaten danger. He concentrated. He looked at himself and began to see himself life-size, twice life-size, since he was in opposition to the whole world.

But now let us return to Mario, whose long night vigils were assuming the wide sweep and amplification of some musical Meditation upon the beginning and end of Time. The impossibility of arresting and charging Gil Turko - of discovering his hideout and linking up all the clues between the two crimes - was giving the police officer a headache, which, in some unaccountably mystic way, he once again attributed to the background threat of Tony. When Dédé came back without having discovered any very exact information, Mario had given way to a similar fit of despair as had caused him, when he left the lad's room, to hesitate before going down the stairs. Dédé noticed this slight hesitation and said to him:

'You've no reason to fear anything. He's not got the guts.'

Mario checked an oath. Supposing he were to go out on his own and not in the company of his usual companion (the young police officer who had made Dédé cry out in astonishment: 'The two of you together make a swell pair,' thereby promoting them to a powerful sexual symbol in the lad's eyes) it would be to blot out the shame of his first fearful reaction, and with the hope thus to provide against any lurking danger by an outward show of bravery.

So Mario chose to go out at night, in the fog, when a crime is quickest committed. He would walk at such time with a sure step, hands in the pockets of his overcoat, or else meticulously adjusting each finger of his brown leather gloves. This simple gesture linked him once more to the invincible might of the Police Force. On the first outing, he did not take his revolver, hoping by so extreme an act of candour - of purity - to disarm the dockers who were out for his blood; but the following day he took his gun as an additional aid to what he now termed his valour, which was nothing else but his belief, firm and unshakable, in the Law and Order of which his revolver was the symbol. To arrange a meeting-place with Dédé, he traced a street name in the mud under the windows of the Police Station, which the young urchin scraped through as he went by, for the lad still persisted in his determination to discover the headquarters of any gang of hooligans pledged to pass judgement on the police officer.

As for Gil, having done the deed, he wished to justify it by proving it to have been inevitable, and to this end he *stepped back again* into his past life. He went about it in the following way: 'Supposing I'd never met Roger . . . Supposing I'd never come to Brest . . . Supposing . . . etc; etc.', until he reached the conclusion that supposing the crime had been running in the blood of his body and down the veins of his arms, then its source must be somewhere outside him.

This method of getting to grips with his crime plunged Gil into a fatalistic frame of mind, and it remained an obstacle to his longing to surmount the crime by *willing* it deliberately. In the end, he left the convict-prison one night and succeeded in reaching Roger's home. Brest was asleep, totally obscured by fog and sea mist. After many a circuitous detour and by keeping his eyes skinned, Gil arrived at Recouvrance without having run into anyone. Once outside the house, he wondered anxiously how best to let Roger know of his presence there. Then suddenly, on tenterhooks to see whether his ruse would be successful, for the first time in three days he smiled wanly and began to whistle:

'He was a carefree, laughing sod,
Afraid of neither man nor God,
The lilt of his singing down in the glen
Melted the hearts of the sternest policemen.'

A window on the first floor opened cautiously, and Roger's voice whispered: 'Gil!'

Gil came forward on tip-toe. When close up against the wall of the house, he raised his head and once more whistled the same tune, only more softly. The fog was too thick for him to see Roger clearly.

'Gil, is that you? . . . Roger here.'

'Come down, I want a word with you.'

Roger closed the window again with infinite precaution. A few moments later, he opened the door into the street. He was in his shirt and barefooted. Gil went in without making a sound.

'Speak as low as you can because sometimes the old woman doesn't sleep any too well. Nor does Paulette for that matter.'

'Got any grub?'

They were in the main room where the mother slept, and they could hear the sound of her breathing. In the dark, Roger took hold of Gil's hand and whispered:

'Don't budge an inch, I'll go and look.'

He eased off the lid of the bread-bin, making as little noise as possible and came back with a crust which he gropingly put into the hands of Gil who was still standing motionless in the middle of the room.

'Look, Roger, you'll come along and see me tomorrow, won't you?'

'Where?'

Question and answer were little more than a breath passed from mouth to mouth.

'In the old disused convict-prison . . . I'm lying doggo . . . The way you come is along through the Arsenal gates. I'll be on the look-out for you towards dusk. But don't let yourself be spotted.'

'You can count on me, Gil.'

'Nothing's popped yet? The cops haven't questioned you?'

'They did, but I didn't squeal.'

Roger went closer, and taking Gil by both arms he murmured:

'I swear to you, I'll come along.'

The little mason pressed the lad close to him, and the touch of his breath on his eyes worried him as much as if he had kissed him on the cheek or mouth. He said:

'Till tomorrow, then.'

Roger opened the door again with even greater precaution. Gil went out into the street. On the doorstep he held Roger back for a moment and asked, after a slight hesitation:

'Did they grill you?'

'I'll tell you all about it tomorrow.'

They let go each other's hand, and Gil went back to the convict-prison almost on tip-toe, devouring the crust of bread as he went.

After that, Roger went to see him every evening – when the fog was at its thickest. Surreptitiously, he pilfered a little food from his home: later on he went so far as to steal a few pennies from his mother to buy bread. He would hide a loaf under his shirt and pick his way along fortifications to the cell in the disused convict-prison. Gil was on the look-out any time after six. Roger gave him all the news. The papers had already dropped the story of the double murder and the killer was supposed to have fled Brest.

Gil alone would eat and then have a smoke.

'What news of Paulette? What's become of her?'

'Nothing much. She's in and out of a job mostly. She's at home with us.'

'D'you ever talk to her about me?'

'But I can't. You don't know the half of it. There are times when they ask me where you are, and sometimes they shadow me.'

He was only too pleased to find an excuse for keeping his sister out of this fabulous friendship that was at present bringing him into closer and closer relationship with Gil. Beside him, in the narrow confines of the granite cell, he felt astonishingly calm – the reek of tar all round them. He would crouch by his side on a cotton dust-sheet filched from the lumber room and feast his eyes on his hero while he smoked. He would look long at the smooth planes that built up the face on which the beard was already strong. He was full of admiration for him. In the early stages of these prison rendezvous, Gil had seldom drawn breath, pouring out a flood of words; and to anyone other than this hero-worshipping lad, such a continuous spate would have been a sure sign of the bluest of blue funks. Roger recognized it solely as the sublime outpouring of an inner tempest. This was exactly how his hero should carry on – as a creature of crisis, crime, and stress. Gil's advantage of three years over Roger made a full-grown man of him. His pallid features had hardened at all points where the muscles showed through (muscles the very sight of which floored Roger as speedily as those inherent in a boxer's mitt) and made Roger conscious of the muscles and sinews of his own body – solid and sufficiently developed to do a man's job in the yards.

Roger himself was still wearing shorts, and, though his thighs were strong, they had not the developed firmness of Gil's. Lying as close as he could possible contrive and supporting himself with one elbow on the ground, he would gaze at the face grown pale and drawn by the hateful conditions imposed upon it. Roger leaned his head against Gil's legs.

'Must wait a bit longer, don't you think? Best to hold on a while before I get out?'

'Says you! The cops are still on your tracks. They've had your photo published.'

'And what about you – they've said no more to you?'

'Not to me, no. Nor to anyone at home. Only I mustn't stay here too long.'

And all of a sudden, Gil let himself go in a sigh that ended in a hoarse moan:

'That sister of yours! It's at times like these that I want her so bad. She's pretty, you know, so pretty.'

'We're very much alike.'

Gil knew it. But, not wanting to let Roger see that he appreciated the fact, and also to give the lad an inkling that he didn't think too much of him either, he said:

'Only she's ten times prettier. You're quite like her, only ten times uglier.'

Roger felt that he was blushing, even in the gloom. However he looked up at Gil with a wistful smile.

'I don't mean to say you're ugly, far from it. What's more you have the same little mug.'

He leaned over towards the lad and took his face between his hands.

'Oh! if only I could be holding her as I'm holding you. Give me skates, and I'll be off to her in a twinkling.'

Of its own accord, as it was being squeezed between the vice-like grip of Gil's cupped hands, the lad's face rose closer and closer to his hero's. To start with, uttering a slight groan, Gil brushed his lips against Roger's forehead. Then the two noses touched and for a few moments rubbed against each other playfully. Because in the sudden discovery of the striking resemblance between brother and sister he was overwhelmed by a violent wave of emotion, Gil could hide his feelings no longer. Pressing his mouth to Roger's, he whispered all in one breath:

'It's a shame you're not your sister.'

Roger smiled:

'D'you really mean that?'

Roger's voice was clear, limpid, unruffled. For a long time now he had loved Gil; he had longed for this moment and was ready for it, yet he did not wish to appear to be moved by any other emotion than friendship. The self-same wariness that had made it possible for him to fool the police with his bland, innocent expression now compelled him to answer Gil in an unemotional voice. Since Gil had been the first to give way to his emotional strain, it made things easier for the lad proudly to display his own self-control. However, he did not yet know enough to recognize the tell-tale signs of uncontrollable desire and that this can be gauged to some extent by the sensual rumblings in the throat.

'Honest – you've every bit as juicy as a jane.'

Gil again pressed his mouth against the lad's, but he drew back with a smile.

'Are you scared?'

'Oh, no!'

'Well then – what d'you suppose I wanted to do?'

Gil was embarrassed that his kiss had miscarried. There was a sneer in his next words:

'Perhaps you're none too happy to be with a bloke like me?'

'Why? Of course I'm happy, otherwise I wouldn't have come here.'

'You wouldn't think so.'

Then, in severer tones, as though the fresh idea which had just occurred to him was one of such importance that it must needs o'erleap the one preceding it, he said:

'Look here then, you've got to go and see Robert. I've been thinking things over. Only he and his pals can get me out of this place.'

Gil was simple enough to believe that the corner boys would welcome him with open arms and let him join their gang. He was certain there existed a dangerous gang, a secret society out to fight society itself.

That evening it was a very downcast Roger that left the prison. He was happy that Gil (albeit by confusing him with Paulette) had for a moment desired him physically, and he cursed himself for having drawn back from his embrace; he was proud in the knowledge that his friend's magnificence was about to be recognized and that it was he – Roger – who had been specifically chosen to beard the Powers-that-be.

Now it so happened that whenever a chance offered, Querelle would go, about dusk, for a discreet stroll in the neighbourhood of his buried treasure. A sadness clouded his expression. He felt that his limbs were already garbed in convict uniform and that, dragging the cannon-ball chained to his foot, he was walking slowly and painfully in a landscape of monstrous palm-trees – a landscape of dreams or of death – from which neither a wakening nor mortal acquittal would have the power to release him. Convinced that he was living in a world which was the silent counterpart of that world where to all intents and purposes he moved and had his being, Querelle became possessed of a sort of disinterestedness which gave him the power to have immediate and complete knowledge of the essence of things. Being by habit totally indifferent to plants and objects – but was it not he himself who was responsible for their proximity? – he now had a complete understanding of them. Every essence or taste can be isolated and determined by a unique trait which the eye first distinguishes and then passes on to the palate. Thus, hay is hay (that is, it can be characterized by its 'hayishness') primarily by virtue of its characteristic grey-gold powder which the sensory organs sample before approving. The same is true of every species of the vegetable kingdom; the mental processes challenge, and the palate approves. What deceives the eye, the mouth detects. And Querelle was now slowly entering a highly-seasoned realm, advancing from clue to clue, sampling, testing, approving. Then, one evening, he came across Roger. It did not take the sailor long to discover who the lad was and to succeed in worming his way into Gil's hide-out.

With one ear applied to the vibrant lid of his jewel box, Querelle was listening to the Offices for the Dead, performed in all its pomp and importance for him alone. He had prudently cut himself off from the outside world the better to receive the Recording Angel's verdict. He was crouching amidst the black velvet grasses, arums, and bracken, surrounded by the palpitating darkness of his own particular Isles of the Blest. He kept his eyes wide open. The Spirit that incites to murder had gently passed a cloying tongue over the delicate, open countenance which Querelle was so intimately offering, without even causing him a tremor. His bright gold hair alone was touched with emotion. Sometimes his Watch-dog of Desire, that kept guard between his legs, reared up on its hind legs and pressed close against its master's body, becoming part of the muscles in his shoulders where it lay hidden, ever on the watch and growling. Querelle knew that he went in danger of his life; he further knew that he was protected by this beast. Said he to himself: 'With a snap of the jaw, I'd sever his jugular,' without knowing precisely whether he was referring to the Watchdog's or the white neck of a child who happened to be pissing close by.

As he made his way into the depths of the convict-prison, Querelle felt assuaged by fear and by the weight of responsibility he was taking on his shoulders. While walking beside Roger without a word passing between them as they went along, he was aware of all the portents of a violent adventure welling up within him till they blossomed into full flower and scented every part of his body. He was ripe once more for a life of danger. He was assuaged by the perils ahead and by fear. What would he find in the depths of this disused prison-house? He held fast to his own freedom. The very least surrender to ill-temper would have made him afraid of this naval dungeon, for he felt - by a tightening of his lungs - that its massive walls were ready to crush him and against them he therefore pitted all his strength, buttressing himself to fend them off as he fended off his rage, by exerting a similar effort and almost a similar muscular movement as would a sergeant of the guard in the act of barricading, with both hands and the full weight of his body, the gigantic gates of a citadel. He was groping his way towards a defunct but happy former existence. Not that he thought seriously that he had once been a convict, nor did his imagination become involved in such kinds of fantasy, yet he felt a delicious sense of well-being, a presentiment of rest and quiet at the idea of entering as a free man - as a conquering hero - the gloomy precincts and thick-set walls. They had contained for years on end such a wealth of suffering in chains, so much physical and moral agony, so many bodies twisted by torture, wasted by disease, tasting no joy in life except the memory of wonderful past crimes whenever a bright beam transfigured this vale of shadows, or a shaft of sunlight illuminated through some hole in the walls the dark place where they had been committed. What exhalations of these past murders could remain clinging to the stones, lurking in the corner, or hanging in the damp air? Even supposing these thoughts were not clear in Querelle's head, at least all that brought them to life so vividly under our pen would have caused him heavy and disturbing thoughts and confused and troubled his brain unmercifully.

At least Querelle was going to meet, and for the first time, another, a brother criminal. Up till then he had dreamed vaguely of finding himself face to face with a murderer about his own size, shape, and weight – his own brother, he sometimes hoped for a second or two; but his brother was too close a reflection of himself – one who had quite a different crime sheet to his credit than his own, but just as beautiful, just as grim and reprehensible. He could not exactly say by what he would have recognized him had he come across him in the street, by what signs; and at times his loneliness was so great that he thought – but only in a passing flash – that he would get himself arrested, that he might meet in prison some kindred criminal or other who had been mentioned in the papers. He very quickly dropped his idea, for the mere fact that such men had no longer anything to hide made them at once uninteresting. His resemblance to his brother was capable of affording him a twinge of regret for this would-be friend. When he was beside him, he sometimes wondered whether Robert really was a criminal. He both hoped and feared that he might be. Hoped, because it would be so wonderful if such a miracle could take place and exist in the world; feared, because it meant he would lose his sense of superiority in respect to Robert.

So very strange was this brotherly affection! There was no clear reason for supposing that two young men – brothers in the strongest sense possible – might love each other, united by murder, united not only by the blood which flowed in their veins, but by that which had flowed over them. For Querelle the question did not arise in this form: 'love' meant something different to him. For him there could be no question of love between man and man. There were women for that kind of thing. For better or worse.

But the question of friendship did arise: friendship for him being what completes a man, who without it is split in two from top to bottom. Certain that he could never derive any requisitely sumptuous benefit from sharing a secret with his brother – 'He's too much of a cunt for that' – Querelle had shut himself up instead within the confines of his own loneliness: and this he had built up into the strangest of ivory towers, all the more beautiful because of this inner derangement, this disharmony caused by the absence of a real comrade-in-crime. Now, at last, in the disused convict-prison, he was going to find a lad who was a killer. The very thought touched his heart. This murderer was a clumsy clot, a killer without motive for his crime. A bloody fool. But, with Querelle's aid, he would become endowed with a real murder, and things could be made to look as if the sailor had been deprived of his share of the swag.

Querelle assumed an almost paternal feeling towards Gil before he went to see him there. He had already lent him one of his murders by making a full confession of it. All the same, Gil might turn out to be nothing but a pal who could never become for him the promised comrade-in-crime. These thoughts, (not in the final state in which we report them, but in their original shapelessness) rapid and shifting, jumping over one another, mutually destructive yet recreated continuously, broke over him like a wave, over every limb and sinew of Querelle's body, rather than issuing from his brain.

He strode along the high road in better spirits, yet swayed by this storm of shapeless thoughts, never the same for two minutes running, but leaving behind them an uncomfortable feeling of discomfort, insecurity, and fear. Querelle never lost his smile, as he stared at the ground in front of him. Thanks to this smile, he was free to dream and idle away his time without any danger befalling his body. Querelle did not know how to dream. His lack of imagination made him fix his attention on what had actually occurred and kept it there.

Roger turned round.

'Wait here, I'll be back soon.'

The boy was really going on an ambassadorial journey into the presence of his Lord and Master the Emperor, and he wanted to make certain that all was properly prepared for this meeting of two monarchs. New thoughts were stirring in Querelle's mind. He had not expected all these precautions. He could see no entrance into the cavernous regions. The road simply took a turning and disappeared behind a slight mound. The trees were not thickly planted nor was their foliage denser than elsewhere. However, once Roger had disappeared, Querelle felt himself to be in some 'mysterious region', some place more precious than any he had ever visited. It was the boy's absence that made this astonishing difference, and that made him so suddenly important. Querelle smiled, but he could not prevent himself from worrying over the fact that this boy was the active go-between of these two murderers, and that his work was performed so rapidly and effectively. He passed through this mansion of which he was the congenial spirit, able to prolong or shorten the journey at will. Roger was going along at a smarter pace. Once away from Querelle he walked with more certain step because he knew that he was carrying to Gil the essential Querelle, that is to say, he vaguely understood the natural desire of Querelle to come into close contact with Gil. He recognized that he himself, a lad not yet used to long trousers and with legs not yet fully developed, was conducting the ceremonial rites usually performed by accredited ambassadors – and one could understand why such delegates are more finely apparelled than their Lords and Masters by taking one look at the innate gravity of this boy's bearing. Upon his delicate person, loaded with a thousand insignia of authority, Gil's almost haggard eyes feasted as he sat crouching in his cavern, while Querelle's remained fixed in astonishment, as though he were standing at the Gates of Hell.

Querelle lighted a cigarette and then put both his hands back in the pockets of his oilskin coat. He made no further surmise. His imagination boggled. His thoughts were in a state of suspense, fluid, waiting to assume some definite shape, but a little troubled by the sudden importance of the lad who had left him standing there.

'It's me – Roger.'

Quite close to him, Gil whispered:

'He's here?'

'Yes, I told him to hang on. D'you want me to go and fetch him?'

His nerves on edge, Gil answered:

'All right. Fetch him along – make haste.'

When Querelle had advanced till he stood immediately in front of the hole which led to Gil's hiding place, Roger firmly and loudly proclaimed:

'All's well, here he is. Gil, here we are.'

The lad had the miserable feeling that the world was coming to an end for him as he spoke these words. He felt himself to be shrinking, to be losing his identity. All the treasures, rich and rare, which for the past few minutes he had carried so proudly, were now evaporating, and all too quickly. He was aware of the vanity of man, and how, of a sudden, it melteth away like wax. Piously he had set himself the task of bringing these two together, only to find himself annihilated at the climax. His whole life had culminated in this gigantic achievement – all over in less than ten minutes – and now the glory was departing and would soon disappear, taking with it the joyful pride which had served to *puff him up*. As far as Gil was concerned, this lad had merely enabled him to get in touch with Querelle whose story he had told and whose words he had repeated: while for Querelle, he was merely the tool by which to get into contact with Gil.

'Here you are, I've brought you some smokes.'

These were Querelle's opening words. In the semi-darkness, he held out a packet of cigarettes which Gil took hold of with groping fingers. Their handshake closed over the packet of fags.

'Thanks, fellow, that's real decent of you, I shan't forget it.'

''Nuff said. It's the least I could do.'

'All I've got to offer you is some meat and a bit of pie.'

'Put them on the packing-case here.'

From another packet, Querelle pulled out a cigarette and lighted it. He wanted to have a look at Gil's face. He was astonished to find it thin and hollow-cheeked, dirty, and covered with a thin growth of fair beard. Gil's eyes were sparkling; his hair unkempt. The light of the match added a pathetic appeal to his face. Querelle beheld a murderer. He held the match so that he could see all round him.

'Do you have to take your daily shit in here?'

'I'll say – it's not too funny. But what else is there to do? Where else can I go?'

Querelle stuck his hands in his trousers pockets and all three remained silent for a moment.

'Aren't you going to have a snack, Gil?'

Gil was hungry, but he dared not make this obvious to Querelle.

'Light the candle – everything's hunky-dory.'

Gil sat down on a corner of the packing-case. He started to eat in a casual way. The kid squatted at his feet, while Querelle remained standing, his legs apart, smoking without taking his cigarette from his mouth, surveying the scene.

'I'm in the hell of a mess, eh?'

Querelle answered with something like a sneer:

'Can't say things look any too good, but it won't last long. You've nothing to fear while you're in here, surely?'

'No. So long as I'm not shopped, nobody'll ever find their way in here.'

'If that's meant for me, you've got me wrong. The narks and I don't run in harness. Still, I don't know how you're going to rig things. You've got to get out some time. How, I haven't a clue.'

Querelle knew that he wore an expression of cruelty, the very marks and lines that stamped his features the days when the ship's company bore arms and he stood on guard with the triangular steel bayonet fixed to the rifle planted firmly in front of him. At such times his face could be termed steely. As he stood at attention behind it, himself its steely counterpart, his bayonet became the soul of a flesh and blood Querelle. To the officer inspecting his men on deck, this bayonet was exactly in line with Querelle's left eyebrow and eye, which seemed to shine with the sinister glow of an arms-factory.

'If I'd a little cash, I might get myself over into Spain. I know a bloke not far from Perpignan. I done labouring in those parts.'

Gil went on eating. For the time being, he and Querelle could think of nothing further to say, but Roger knew instinctively that they had established an understanding between themselves in which he had no share. They were now two grown men who talked, and talked seriously, of things that any lad of his age only vaguely touches upon when on the borderline of sleep.

'So you're Robert's brother – do you go to Nono's place?'

'Yes, I'm pals with Nono too!'

Never for an instant did the nature of his relations with Nono cross Querelle's mind. There was not a trace of irony when he had said he knew him well.

'No kidding! Is he one of your pals?'

'What if I said "Yes"? Why d'you ask?'

'D'you think that he . . .' Gil was tempted to say 'that he'd be willing to help me?' . . . but it would have been too unnerving, he realized, if the answer turned out to be in the negative. So he hesitated before adding, '. . . that he couldn't perhaps help me?'

In placing him outside the law, the murder had, of course, encouraged Gil to look for a helping hand among prostitutes and ponces, among people – so he believed – who live just, but only just, within the law.

A worker of considerable repute had been wiped off the slate by this murder. Such a deed, on the other hand, would harden Gil's character and illuminate him from within; it conferred on him a prestige which he could not otherwise have attained, one which, did he not possess it, might have caused him extra suffering. This prestige was doubtless set off by the momentary recoil of Gil's thoughts as he sought by means of the chain of cause and effect to unburden himself of his crimes. Having come full circle in this recoil only to find that the burden of the crime was still upon him and that remorse was still gnawing at his soul, weakening him and making him tremble and bow his head in shame, it became all the more necessary for him to obtain – and not merely as a justification – a full understanding of the truth of this murder by approaching it from some different angle. There would then be granted him, by an inverse movement to that of self-justification, the fullest explanation possible: a movement towards the future, starting out from the point of accepting the fact that he had committed murder of his own free will. Gil was a young mason, but he had never had the time to be so much in love with his job as to identify himself with it. He still indulged in vague dreams, which were quite suddenly turning out to be true. ('Dreams' are isolated indications of what is 'marvellous', expressed in one particular action such as the rolling of hips or shoulders; calling attention to oneself by cracking fingerjoints; blowing out cigarette-smoke from the corner of the mouth; lifting the trouser-belt on the hip with the flat of the hand, etcetera, and such details as a special choice of words; the preference for slang, the jaunty way of wearing certain articles of clothing – a plaited belt, thin-soled shoes, pockets known as 'bellyachers' – the whole giving sure proof that the adolescent in question is thoroughly conversant with these more or less precise traits of human vanity, which are the proud attributes of the criminal world.)

Yet, when he came to realize the full splendour of this significance, the lad could not help being mortally afraid. He would have found it easier to accept, had he become, the following day, the actual thief or accomplice which every street-urchin aspires to become. To be a murderer was making too great a demand upon the soul and body of a lad of eighteen. At any rate he could derive some benefit from the prestige attaching to it. In his simplicity, he believed that lads of the underworld were happier when imbued with such prestige. Querelle, on the other hand, felt certain that the very opposite was the case. For him, the act which finally moulds the murderer was something so strange and peculiar that the man who commits a murder assumes the rôle of a sort of hero. He must remain unscathed by the mud-slinging mob. Since street-urchins are activated by baser motives, real murderers are seldom found among their ranks.

'I'll go and see. I'll have a natter with Nono. Then we can decide what must be done.'

'But what's your idea? I've proved my worth.'

'I'm not saying you haven't. Come what may, you can count on me. I'll give you all the news.'

'What about Robert? I could work in with Robert.'

'You know his half-section?'

'Dédé, I know. We used to be pals. I know they're pretty thick. Mario doesn't go much on that all the same. But he says nothing. If you're seeing Robert, see whether I can't fix it to work with them. But don't tell them where I am.'

These words were music to Querelle's ears, not because he was exploring the cavernous realms of evil, but because he was now in possession of a secret far more profound than the one Gil had just revealed to him.

There exists, somewhere deep within us, a secret room with an armour-plated door. It contains, along with several poor caged dogs, other monsters of which the most alarming is the one that is to be found in the very middle of the room. This is the living reproach at the centre of our innermost being. Enclosed within a huge glass case, corresponding almost exactly to the shape of its body, this creature is mauve in colour and soft, almost gelatinous in substance. It would resemble a great fish, were it not for the very human sadness of its head. The keeper who watches over these monsters harbours the greatest contempt for this one, which, we know well, would find a degree of peace and comfort in the embrace of another of its own kind. But it has no like. The other monsters differ from it in a few minor details. It is lonely, unique, and yet it loves us. In hopeless, doggy devotion, it waits for a friendly look from us, one we shall never accord it. Querelle lived his whole life in the company of this disconsolate creature.

In the most casual, off-hand manner, Querelle said,

'But how come you killed the matelot? I can't seem to get the hang of it.'

So heavy was the hypocritical and insinuating 'But' at the opening of this matter-of-fact phrase, that, accustomed to sarcastic innuendo as he was, it immediately put him in mind of Lieutenant Seblon's sardonic manners and his laboured form of approach. Gil felt himself grow pale. His very life – his inner essence – flowed into his eyes and dried their tears, fled from them in a look of desperation, finally to be absorbed into the shadowy gloom of the cell. He paused before anwering, not from the sort of hesitation during which, with supreme self-possession, pros and cons are weighed in the balance, but from a kind of indolence as if punch-drunk, and aggravated still more by a feeling that it would be useless to deny the charge. He found it prevented him from opening his mouth. So grave was this accusation that he sought by what means it could possibly be made to apply to him; he held his peace, he did his utmost to put the whole of himself into the glance of his eyes, and to such effect that he felt the muscles moving furtively in his eyeballs and their lids. He stared fixedly at nothing. He drew his lips tighter and tighter together.

'Yes, that matelot is what I said. Whatever came over you?'

'He never did him.'

As though through the semi-consciousness of a waking dream, Gil listened to Querelle's question and heard Roger's answer and was not in the least disturbed by the sound of their voices. He remained staring straight ahead, intent only on the fixity of his look and absorbed by that alone.

'Then who done it, if it wasn't him?'

Gil let his fixed stare swivel round till it rested on Querelle's face.

'I give you my word it wasn't me. I can't tell you who it was, for I don't know sweet FA about it. But I swear, sw'elp me God, it wasn't me.'

'The papers make it pretty clear they plump for you having done it. For my part, I believe you, but you'll always be able to explain things to the cops. They found your lighter beside the corpse. No matter what it costs, I'd say you'll have to stay doggo.'

In the end, Gil became resigned to this other crime. The monstrosity of his act blurred his vision, and to begin with he seriously thought of going to the police. He believed that once they had recognized his innocence in the case of the second crime, they would release him, provided he kept quiet about the first. The police, he believed, would respect the rules of the game. The lunacy of such thoughts was very soon apparent. What's more, little by little Gil began to feel the weight of the sailor's murder on his own shoulders. He began to rack his brains for the proper answer. He began to wonder now and again who the real murderer could be. He searched in vain for the reason why and how it had come about that he had dropped his lighter close to the scene of the crime.

'Who can have done that? I hadn't even noticed that I'd no longer got my lighter.'

'I'm telling you that you must keep well under cover. We'll see what can be done about you when I've had a talk with the lads. I'll come along and see you just as often as I can. I may even get hold of some cash to give this young pal of yours so as he can bring you some good kip and smokes.'

'You're a good pal, I'll say!'

But, the moment before, in the effort of losing himself, of concentrating the whole of himself in his glance and letting it trickle out into the gloom, Gil had used up too much of his strength, and now he was quite unable to collect a sufficiency to invest his gratitude with the full warmth of his being. He was tired. His face was veiled and the corners of his lips were drawn down by a terrible sadness - the lips that Querelle had noticed were moist and gaily smiling. His body, slumped on the edge of the packing-case, was sunk in an attitude which all too clearly gave expression to, 'What the fucking hell am I to do with myself now?' He was on the verge, not of despair, but of grief, comparable to that of a child left for an instant on the threshold of night. He was fast losing strength, his true essence was ebbing. He was no murderer. He was afraid.

'D'you think I'm for the high jump if they get me?'

'There's no telling. It's a toss-up. But don't go getting ideas into your head, they'll only get you down.'

'You're my pal, you know. What do they call you?'

'Jo.'

'You're my pal, Jo. I'll never forget you.'

At long last his whole soul went out to meet Querelle, who soon would be on his way out back into the world again, to resume a normal life, and who was strong, even with the strength of a hundred million men.

Behind his dungeon walls, the early morning or twilight scenes of the outside world penetrated to Gil's ears only through the filter of the blocks of stone, and the shouts and din of the naval dockyard would then revive many a happy memory. Shut off from the world by ashlar, murder and adolescence, suffocated by the agonizing smell of tar, his imagination developed with amazing vigour, and struggled impetuously against the encircling obstacles, determined to battle with them to the bitter end. Gil could pick out, from the noisy confusion of sounds, the high-pitched grinding squeal particular to the cranes and pulley blocks. His gang had been working at Brest quite long enough for the noise and bustle of the naval yards to have become impressed indelibly on his memory. Strong were the evocations of certain clear ringing tones, corresponding to vivid sunlight striking on the brass ramps of companion ladders or on a splinter of glass; on a dressed launch as it flashed rapidly past with its array of gilded officers; on a white sail out in the Roads; on the slow manoeuvring of a cruiser; on the peripatetic play of candescent spume atop the waves. His incarceration enhanced a thousandfold each one of these noises and invested them with far more stirring qualities than ever they had possessed in real life.

If the sea is the natural symbol of liberty, then every image that evokes it is charged with symbolic power: indeed, is peculiarly charged with the whole symbolic power of the sea; and the more commonplace the image evoked in the mind of a prisoner, the more disturbing the open wound it causes. It would be perfectly natural for a spontaneous glimpse of a steamer in mid-ocean to cause the inner consciousness of a child the deepest sense of despair; but in this case the images of steamer and sea were far less evocative: for Gil, by far the most portentous was the characteristic sound of a chain. (Can it be that the grinding of a chain does release all the attributes of despair, a simple chain with rusted links?) Gil was undergoing – without being in the least aware of it – a painful initiation into the mysteries of poetry. The image of a chain would cut right across a fibre and this incision widen sufficiently to admit the passage of a ship, to let in the sea, the world, till finally it would destroy Gil by taking him out of himself, he who had no other possible existence but in the world which had just administered his death-wound by cutting him off in his prime and obliterating him utterly.

Squatting for most of the day behind the self-same coil of rope, he developed a strong attachment to this coil, a sort of friendship for it. He had made it his own. He grew to love it. It was precisely this coil, and it alone, which he had chosen especially. Whenever he left it to go over for a minute or two to the paneless window, or with panes rendered opaque from filth, he never altogether detached himself from it. Crushed, and squatting in its shadow, he would listen to the golden song of the port. To this he gave his own interpretation. The sea lay beyond these walls, calm and familiar, harsh yet gentle to lads in his position, to those who have 'taken a hard knock'. Motionless for minutes on end, Gil would stare at the strand of rope his fingers were fiddling with. He would concentrate his gaze on its end. He became attached to a particular tar-coated tress. A disconsolate spectacle, though one which deprived Theo's murder of all its magnificence, for this it was that had led its author to so wretched a ploy, to the lamentable vision of the black, frayed, sticky end of a coil of rope being rolled between his dirty fingers. This was, however, preceded by periods of morose morbidity. Gil's exacting and microscopic vision forced him to pass through the horrors of despair to win through to serenity. While seeking to penetrate the simple mystery of his tarry rope, his gaze would sometimes become confused – on account of the utter desolation of the scene – and he would conjure up some happy memory again. Then it was that Gil would return to the coil of rope – his consuming interest in it no longer followed the dictates of reason – and start to interrogate it in silence. This habit amounted to a routine. Alas! it had the effect of inducing the unfortunate ability of apprehending violently and at once the essence of things, and led him slowly, stage by stage – it wasn't long before he became capable of grasping the essence of granite, of a piece of material, the tang peculiar to a metal plate with rough edges that cut the lips – towards living a scorched existence, scorching the very marrow of his bones. On occasion, tears welled up in his eyes. He would think of his relations. Were the cops still interrogating them? During the course of the day he would listen to the drum-and-fife band of the cadets of the military school playing, and hear the double time ring out and the marching songs. To Gil, for ever enclosed in darkness, these performances became a monstrous cockcrow announcing a whole long day on which the dazzling sun would never rise. He was thrown into despair by these cries which had no power to tear asunder his everlasting night. Any cry heralding a dawn was a false cry.

Suddenly Gil got to his feet for no special reason. For a time he walked to and fro, avoiding every patch of light on the floor. He waited for nightfall, food, and Roger's kisses. 'Poor kid – so long as he doesn't let me down. So long as he isn't got down himself! What would become of me then?'

Gil did his best to carve his initials on the granite with the knife Roger had left him. He often slept. As soon as he was awake, he knew at once where he was – fleeing and hiding from every police force in the world on account of a murder, or two. In this way did the full horror of his situation come upon him: no sooner had he accepted the fact of his total solitude, than he put it into the following words: 'Gil, Gil Turko, that's me, and I'm all alone. To be the real Gil Turko, I've got to be utterly on my own, and to be all alone I have to be on my own. That's to say, left out in the cold . . . O shit! The old folk give me the shits! What do the old folk mean to me, for fuck's sake? They're real bastards! All that really happened was that my old man shot it off into my mum's great cunt and nine months later out I came. What'd that to do with me, for fuck's sake! A come-by-chance. A stray gob of spunk made me. Fuck my parents, they're shit-bags!'

For as long as possible, he kept himself keyed up to this pitch of sacrilegious aggression which provided him with the armourplate of pride and revolt and made him hold his body upright and his head high. Gil longed for this to be his habitual state of mind: to hate and despise his parents in order that he might no longer be crushed by the sorrow they caused him. In the early stages of this experiment, he would always allow himself a minute's day-dreaming or so, during which, huddled up on himself, head pressed to his chest and enclosed in his arms, he became once again the submissive child adored by his parents. He undid the evil of his act, elaborating a life which would run on gently, simply, his crime expunged. Then he would come back once more to his work of destruction. 'I coshed Theo and I was right to do it. If I had my life to live again, I should do the same as I did before.'

Gil became desperate, and killed – or attempted to kill – every ounce of pity there might be left in him.

'Poor chap – he's bully enough, tip-top in fact, but just what does he know about a hard knock? Nix. What a north-and-south! No, to hell with it all!' so his thoughts ran on Querelle. He did not mince his words, but a deep if hardly formulated feeling, in which he could wallow, made him lean restfully on this tough guy whose calm, age, position in the world, and certain security in society, were for Gil a raft to cling to for support in the sea of his despair. Querelle, as early as his second visit, had shown a certain joviality. He had joked about death, till Gil was left with the impression, that, for the matelot, the death of a man was of small importance.

'So you think pretty bad of me for fixing that bloke?' (In Roger's absence, he could let himself go a bit. He no longer had to play the man.)

'What, me? It takes more than that to worry me, chum. You don't look at it the right way. To start off with, he made you chokker. He was out after your ring. No proper bloke can stand for that. You'd the right to do him.'

'That's what I said to myself. Only the judges won't see it that way.'

'There's not much hope of them understanding. They're all fatheads, specially in these parts. That's why you've got to lie doggo. And why your pals must help you. If you want to be a real tough guy.'

In the gleam of the candle, Gil thought he saw the suspicion of a smile on Querelle's face, as though seeing him through tissue-paper. It gave him confidence. With all the strength at his command he wanted to be a tough guy. (With all the strength at his command is to say that Querelle's smile provoked in him a wave of enthusiasm and exhilaration that made him forget even his own body.) Querelle's presence thus afforded him a friendly and efficacious comfort, as exciting as the advice one sportsman gives another – sometimes even his rival – in the heat of a race: 'Take deeper breaths.' 'Keep your lips closed.' 'Flex your calf muscles,' in which can be seen the whole wealth of secret solicitude for the beauty of action.

'What have I got to lose now? Nothing no more. The old folk are gone. Nothing's left me no more. I've got to start a new life for myself!' And he said to Querelle:

'I've got nothing left to lose. I can do as I please. I'm free.'

Querelle hesitated. All of a sudden, he was faced with the concrete image of what he had been five years ago or more. He had killed a bloke in Shanghai accidentally. Sailor's pride plus national pride had urged him on. Thus the crime was quickly committed. A young Russian had insulted him. Querelle struck out and with one stroke of his knife he had whipped out his eye. Sickened at the sight and to rid himself of the horror of it, he had cut the lad's throat. This drama had taken place at night, in a lighted back street, and he had dragged the corpse into the shadow and so arranged it that it stayed in a crouching position, propped up against a wall. In the end, spontaneously and in a sense to flout the dead man who could so dangerously haunt him, he took a brier pipe from his trousers pocket and stuck it in his victim's mouth.

* * *

Madame Lysiane forbade her 'young ladies' the right to wear black lace undies. She tolerated salmon-pink, green, and pale yellow, but, knowing how well she herself looked in these dark point-lace drawers, she could never bring herself to allow her girls to adorn themselves with black cami-knickers. It was not so much because they set off to advantage the soft, milky whiteness of her skin that she preferred black, as because black gave an altogether frivolous note to her undies – at the same time conferring a certain note of gravity – and Madame Lysiane had need of this super-frivolity for the following reason. In her bedroom, she took her time over taking off her attire. As if nailed to the floor by her high heels, she stood planted in front of the looking-glass over the chimney-piece, and would begin by unhooking her dress with her right hand. It fastened down the left side, along an opening that started on a curve behind the shoulder and ran down from the neck line to the waist. In so doing, she made full use of quick little rounded movements that drew particular attention to her ample curves and to the nimbleness of her fingers as she lingered lovingly on all the most alluring, sugary, and comfortable parts of her body. It was the prelude to a Cambodian ritual dance. Madame Lysiane adored the sinuosity of her arm movements, the acute angle of her elbow, and she was certain that it was just such points that distinguished her from the general run of tarts.

'My God, how vulgar they are! So contemptibly commonplace! To think that Régine considers it no longer fashionable *to wear a fringe*! Would you believe it! All of them – no matter what they're worth – imagine that clients prefer their girl to look like a strumpet, and that couldn't be more wrong, for the very opposite is the case.'

She looked at herself in the glass as she spoke, a wild look in her eye. From time to time, she let her glance wander to Robert as he undressed.

'Are you listening to what I'm saying, ducky?'

'Can't you see I'm listening?'

He really was listening to her. He did admire her elegance, and the fact that she showed herself to be a cut above her girls and their sluttish appearance, but he was not looking at her. Madame Lysiane let her sheath-like dress slip down to her feet. She peeled it off her body. Her shoulders were the first to emerge, white, marked or rather cut across by the line of velvet or black satin shoulder-straps that held up her slip; then her breasts under the black lace and pink brassière; finally, she stepped out of the folds around her feet: she was then ready for action. In her Louis XV shoes – even higher-heeled than those of the period by reason of their narrow, thin lines which gave them a sharper look – she went towards the bed into which Robert had slipped the moment before.

Running her eyes over him without thinking, she suddenly turned round again, saying, 'Ah!', and went straight back to the mahogany dressing-table. There, after snatching the four rings off her fingers, she began to let down her hair with ever ampler and more gracefully sinuous arm movements. As, at the sudden trembling of every sinew in a lion's body when it appears on the edge of the desert, the whole expanse of forest vibrates, so the whole room vibrated, from the threadbare pile of the carpet to the least fold of the window curtains when Madame Lysiane shook her head, her angry mane, her alabaster shoulders. Every evening she set out to reconquer the already subjugated male. She returned to the brink of the stream, under the palm fronds, where Robert puffed away at his cigarette, seeing nothing but the ceiling above his head.

'Can't you even let me see it?'

Casually he threw back a corner of the sheets so that his mistress might slip into the bed. Madame Lysiane was hurt by his lack of gallantry; and on each occasion this hurt was a balm to her, for it was proof that she must bring some fresh ruse to rouse him during the ensuing struggle. She was a woman full of courage, but enslaved. The ostentatious display of her physical charms, the overflowing wealth of her breasts and hair, the full opulence of her body, even by the very reason of this opulence – for all opulence offered is virginal – were already offered and of easy access. No mention need be made of her beauty. Beauty can be a more terrible defensive weapon than barbed wire; it presents lurking perils front and back; it can send forth its squalls; it can kill at a distance.

Madame Lysiane's opulence of flesh was the visible form of her generosity. Her skin was soft and white. No sooner was she stretched out, (Madame Lysiane had a horror of the expression 'in bed' and, out of respect for her delicacy, no mention will be made of it when speaking of her, but we shall touch on her 'delicacies' and other forbidden words), no sooner was she lying down than she looked all round the room. Slowly she let her eyes pass from object to object as they wandered over her rich possessions, lingering on each one in turn: the chest-of-drawers, the glass-fronted hanging cupboard, the dressing-table, the two armchairs, the gilt-framed oval pictures, the glass vases, the chandelier. The room was her oyster and she its royal pearl, surrounded by the soft, nacreous opalescence of the blue satin, the bevelled-edge mirrors, the curtains, the wall-paper, the varying lights and shades. The pearl of her bosom (while thinking of it with delight, but, to evoke its appeal, one must imagine her assuming a mischievous air, a cupidinous smile on her lips and her little finger uplifted to them), and, let it be said, the twin pearls of her crupper. She was by nature happy and perfectly worthy of the heritage of those who have gone by the names of fallen women, kneelers, sluts, prostitutes, strumpets, punks, misses, demireps, jades, skits, mopsies, drabs, rigs, frails, or loose women.

Every evening, in order to abandon herself completely to love and the sun, almost going as far as self-immolation, Madame Lysiane had recourse to checking over her terrestrial riches. This gave her the assurance that on waking up she would find herself among the marvels of a cave of harmony worthy of her bodily endowments, of the good fortune that would permit her the next day to find love again disseminated among the warmest folds of the room.

Slowly, almost negligently, as if they were a liquid wave, she insinuated one of her legs between Robert's hairy legs. At the bottom of the bed, three feet – striving almost in desperation to be for an instant the sensible extention of a corporate body whose each foot was the expression of a differing and inimical sex – three feet came together and became entangled with as much dexterity as their wretched joints permitted.

Robert stubbed out his cigarette on the marble top of the night table, turned to Madame Lysiane and kissed her; but no sooner had she been kissed than she put her two hands flat over his ears, pushed back his head and looked at him.

'You're handsome, you know.'

He smiled. Having nothing to say in answer, he tried another kiss. He did not know how to look at her except with lovelight in his eyes and the awkwardness of his expression gave his features a thoroughly virile severity. At the same time, his mistress's almost trembling precipitation and the fact that he broke her adoring glances as he received the impact of them on his face, left him extremely happy.

'Perhaps he'll allow himself!' She was thinking to herself.

She meant to say, 'Perhaps he'll allow himself to remain passive, though he's violent enough.' He did remain so. The wild light already shining in her eyes was beginning to play upon and caress the beetling rocks of his impassivity. (Madame Lysiane had lovely eyes.)

'My beauty.'

She threw herself upon a new embrace. Robert was beginning to show signs of excitement. Slowly – and bringing him peace together with the certainty that all the wealth of the room was still his – warmth entered into his prick. It began to show signs of rising. From now on – till the moment of his fullest pleasure – nothing would remind him that he was once a docker, sadly going about his work, spare and lazy, or that he might again go back to being one. From now on he was a king, an emperor, well-nourished, clothed in coronation robes, in robes of peaceful and pregnant power that were in direct contrast to the conqueror's breeches. His erection increased. It was stiff. At its hard and vibrant contact, Lysiane gave her pink and white flesh the order to quiver.

'You're so handsome.'

Then she waited for all the preliminaries of the real work ahead, for the moment when Robert would go down under the sheets, his mouth agape like a pig's snout routing in the dark earth, black and truffle-scented, and, after parting the hairs round her cunt, insert his tongue to titillate it. She looked forward to this moment without letting her thoughts get the better of her. For she wanted to remain pure, in order to feel superior to the girls under her command. Were she to encourage such perversions among the others, then she would be half-way towards admitting her own addiction to them. It was essential for her to remain normal. Her fully-rounded and heavy buttocks were the seat of her foundation. She loathed the instability induced by immorality and licentiousness. She felt herself in a strong position, owing to the beauty of her thighs and crupper. They were her security. The appropriate word, her 'arse', would have shocked her no more, had it sprung to her mind, than if a docker had loosened up her slit. Madame Lysiane's sense of responsibility, her self-confidence, resided in her arse.

She clung all the closer to Robert as he edged his body nearer to hers and gently, quite simply, without using his hand, inserted his prick between her thighs. She sighed. She smiled, as an offering to the star-spangled velvety night that was titillating her body all over, right up to her mouth, in the same way that she offered her pearly white skin shot through with blue veins. As a rule, she abandoned herself at once, but for several days now, and most of all this very evening, she had felt beset by anguish caused by the strong resemblance between the two brothers. Her anxiety prevented her being a happy mistress: all the same, she stretched out her arm most gracefully to turn out the light.

'At night, you are both alone in the world, in the solitude of an immense esplanade. Your twin statue is reflected, each half in the other. You are both utterly alone and exist in your twin solitude alone.'

She could stand it no longer. She sat up and turned on the light. Robert looked at her in astonishment.

'You've only to say what you want, pal . . . (Robert's ineptitude, his indifference to women, gave him no taste for words appropriate to the sex, though he was at least polite. To speak to a female tenderly, even to address her as a woman, would have been to make himself ridiculous in his own eyes) . . . pal, but you're far from easy . . .' (again he hesitated for an adjective, aware that he was searching for something more feminine in his words of reference) . . . 'you're not easy at all. Jo and me are like that, 'cos we are, see. Ever since I can remember . . .'

'That's what worries me so much. I can see no reason for keeping it to myself.'

She was acting the Madam. For too long this resemblance had been murdering her, persecuting her so lovely flesh. She was in charge here. The House was worth a great deal to her. If Robert was a handsome fellow – 'and one who'd allow himself' – then she was a strong woman, strong by virtue of her money, of her authority over her girls, of the solidity of her arse.

'It's draining me, draining me, draining me, this likeness between the two of you.'

She was aware that her cries were as shrill and feeble as those of an easily moulded woman.

'You're surely not going on moaning, are you? There's nothing I can do about it, as I've told you before.'

Robert was abrupt. At the beginning of the scene, not being conversant with her mood, he had thought that his mistress was making allusion to the very delicate emotions that a woman as 'posh' as she alone could feel and then, as the scene dragged on, he had got fed up. Incapable of gauging what all the fuss was about, he had relapsed into his habitual coldness.

'I can do nothing about it. When we were tiddlers, there was no telling one from t'other.'

Madame Lysiane drew a deep breath for a sigh that might prove to be her last. Immediately before and while in the act of making this remark, Robert realized confusedly that he would cause her terrible pain; but, without exactly desiring it, yet maliciously conscious of being both clear and muddled, he added still further details to bring suffering to his mistress, more to strengthen his position and at the same time cut himself off from the world in the company of Querelle, whom, for the second time, he had found to be so profoundly wrapped up in his own inmost being. Madame Lysiane scouted yet provoked these further details. She waited for them. She secretly hoped for the most monstrous revelations. As they lay together, and without very well comprehending it, the two lovers had a presentiment that the cure would eventually come, when, like juice, the malady had been totally squeezed out of their bodies. The pus must come out. Robert's presiding genius forced from him a terrible phrase, which contained the idea of one *single* being.

'. . . when we were still nippers, *folk couldn't tell us apart.* We wore the same togs, the same shorts, the same shirts. We had the same little phiz. We could never be parted from each other.'

He detested his brother – or thought he did – but he plunged with his full weight deep down into his relationship with him, a relationship that seemed, so far away in the distant past was it, to be like a pool of treacle in which their two bodies were tied and bound to each other. At the same time, the fear of Madame Lysiane discovering what he considered to be his brother's vice made Robert exaggerate this relationship and do his level best, thanks to his ever more naïve look, to endow them with a demoniacal quality.

'I'm sick of the whole thing, Robert. I'm sick of you and your filthy ways!'

'What filthy ways? There was no dirt between us. We're brothers.'

Madame Lysiane was stupefied at having let slip the word 'filthy'. It was obvious that there was nothing wrong (as one says 'that's wrong' meaning 'that's not clean') in the fact that the two brothers resembled each other. The wrong lay in the invisible operation that took place before her very eyes, which made but one of two persons – an operation which is known as love when the two persons do not resemble one another – or which made two persons out of a single being by the magic of an undivided love: that's to say, her own love – and she hesitated to pronounce the word 'for' even to herself – her love for Robert or Querelle? For a moment she remained nonplussed.

'Yes, your filthy ways. Exactly what I meant when I chose those words. D'you think I was born yesterday? Even then, I've been long enough in charge of a House to know all that goes on in it; and make no mistake, I'm sick of it.'

She addressed this reproach to God, and beyond, higher than that, to life itself that was tearing at her hot white flesh and her milk-nourished soul. She was certain now, so much was she in love with them, that they must have felt the need for a third person who would make each let go his hold on the other and cause a diversion. She was so ashamed to realize that this person was none other than herself. Self-accusing, and in a plaintive voice, she offered up a prayer.

'You only think of things as concerning yourself. I no longer exist. I no longer exist in any way. What am I? How am I going to be able to get in between the two of you? Tell me that, tell me!'

She was shouting. It hurt her to shout so loud, and yet not so loud as all that. Her voice became louder and louder, shrill yet muffled. Robert looked at her with a smile.

'Does it make you smile? You, Sir, live in your brother's eyes – in your precious Jo's eyes. Oh yes, he goes by the name of Jo, doesn't he? And you, Sir, live in your brother.'

'Don't come it so strong, Lysiane. That's not the sort of thing to shout about.'

She threw back the sheets and got out of bed. The whole room stood out clear to Robert's vision, soft and menacing. All its sumptuosity had come rushing to her assistance, yet almost at once each individual piece of rich furniture began to fade and disappear, carried away on a wave of distress. Madame Lysiane was standing white and upright in the midst of her retreating furniture. A sudden access of hate brought Robert a glimmering of understanding. He sought and found the cause; his mistress was hateful and ridiculous.

'Are you through with your moaning?'

'In your brother. You live in each other's body.'

The harsh tone of Robert's voice and the suddenly inhuman glint in his eyes began to hurt her more cruelly than ever before. She hoped he would really go as far in his liberating anger as to throw up on the sheets all his love for his brother and his affiliation with him.

'And, of course, there's no place for me. For me to come in between the two of you would be to make myself a sight too small. You'll throw me over. I'm too fat. Oh yes, that's what it is, I'm too fat!'

Standing there on the carpet, her bare feet flat on the floor, her figure no longer had the impressive extra height afforded her by her high-heeled shoes. The plump curves of her thighs had no meaning now that they no longer were swathed in and swayed beneath the heavy folds of a silky dress. Her bosom was less provocative. All of this she felt instinctively, and also that anger could be expressed in the real tragic manner only when properly supported on the theatrical buskin, and could increase only with the body tightly swathed, allowing no pendulous part of it to appear. Madame Lysiane regretted the time when women were set on a pedestal. She regretted the days of buss-bodices, stays, whale-bones that stiffened the body and gave it authority enough to rule over conduct, and sufficient ferocity. She would have liked to be able to squeeze together the edges of a stiff and flexible pair of pink stays, at the bottom of which would be dangling four suspenders, flapping against her legs. But she was stark naked, her feet planted firmly on the floor. Something just as monstrous in its inconsistency as this inner monologue began to undermine and upset her poise. 'Shall I be shamed into thinking myself a clumping Big Bertha in carpet slippers? But I am . . .' Thereupon her spirit failed her and she was overcome with terrible confusion as the vision of two febrile muscular bodies came forcibly yet inescapably before her eyes, and, facing them, the softly crumbling mass of her own too fat body. She stepped into her shoes and regained something of her former stature.

'Robert, Robert, do look at me, Robert! I'm your mistress! I love you. You don't seem to know how I feel.'

'What d'you want then? I can't open my mouth without you flying into a tantrum.'

'You see, my love, I only want you to be absolutely your own self. If I'm unhappy, it's because I see you as two. I'm frightened for you. I'm frightened that you're not free to be yourself. Can't you see that?'

She stood naked under the lighted chandelier. At the corners of Robert's mouth were two faint lines, the vestiges of his all but vanished smile. Already his eyes were taking on a fixed expression as they stared at Lysiane's knees, through them, and on to a far distant horizon.

'Why did you have to speak of my filthy ways? Just now you said, "I'm sick of you and your filthy ways!"'

Robert's voice was as distant as his stare, but it was unruffled. Lysiane, watching her lover's reactions, felt there to be an underlying desire for some geometrical explanation: hidden at the back of his voice was an instrument - an organ rather - whose function was to see. His voice possessed an eye determined to pierce through the dark. She did not answer him.

'Eh! Didn't you say "I'm sick of your filthy ways!" Why filthy?'

His voice was still unruffled. But in the depths of his being a strange emotion welled up as he forced himself to get out the word 'filthy'. At first this was obscure enough. The conception of his brother obviously was absent from his thoughts; the idea of 'filthy' alone prevailed. Robert was not thinking of anything. He was staring too rigidly in front of him and holding his body too stiffly to be able to think intelligently. He did not know how to think. But the slow way he had spoken, his outward calm, palpitating though it was with hidden emotion, and the fact that he repeated the word 'filthy', only increased the obscurity within him and had the hoodoo effect of a lament of misery whose refrain hauntingly harks back to the desolation in the most secret purlieus of unhappiness. He was worried by the idea of filthiness which smirched his ideas of family life. Sadly he thought to himself, 'The family flue-pipe!' He felt himself guilty in some vague way, rather deeply involved, in fact. Lysiane had said nothing. She had suddenly taken on a crazy, disabled look. With uncomprehending eyes, she had looked at her lover speaking from beyond the grave. She was afraid of losing him.

Whenever he was alone with himself, and above all when he was taking one of his twilight strolls, circling round his treasure, Querelle felt himself conditioned by the docker's remark . . . 'What a piece of cake! Anyone want to try his hand?' . . . If he was walking on grass, under the trees, in the mist, with sure foot and set expression, his thoughts all the while wandered round this phrase, as if working over some obscure problem. He had been raped. Little Red Riding Hood all on his own, some wolf stronger than himself had popped his hand into his provision-basket, into his small little basket; like a charming flower seller, when an urchin snatches some of her carnations after rummaging his hands about among her wares, with a smile on his face as he seeks to deprive her of her treasure, so Querelle felt uneasy as he approached his hidden treasure. Anguish gripped his stomach. So, too, Madame Lysiane had watched Roger piteously trying to digest his expression, as though it was some sort of pill he was dissolving. She trembled lest he melt away to nothing before her eyes.

'Because, after all, you did say filthy habits.'

'I said all that the way I did because I was so unhappy, you know. Forget it, my love.'

He stared at her. She had dropped all the female authority of the Madam; her claws were sheathed, her face composed. It was now simply that of a mature woman, with no make-up and no beauty, but it overflowed with loving-kindness, full of deep reserves of tenderness it could scarcely contain. These were trembling on the brink and ready to flow over into the room at the slightest provocation, first over the spell-bound Robert's feet, in warm rolling waves where sported subtle and quizzical small fish.

Lysiane was shivering with cold.

'Get down under the sheets again.'

The scene was played out. Robert snuggled up against his mistress. For an instant, he did not know whether he was her son or her lover. He kept his lips close-pressed to her still powdered cheek down which tears were flowing.

'How much I love you, darling. You're my man.'

'Put out the light,' he whispered.

Their feet were frozen. At the extremity of their single body, they were the one snag that prevented the lovers from sinking down into the wild intoxication whence there is no emerging. He pressed her very close to him. Madame Lysiane was burning with desire and he was soon hard.

'I'm all yours, you know, my ducky.'

She had made up her mind and, that this decision should not be vain or useless, she had made her voice sound as inviting as she possibly could. One veil that had never before yielded was this evening being torn asunder. She would be losing a real virginity by sacrificing, at the age of forty-five, her modesty and, like other virgins, she dared at this moment to commit obscenities almost unheard of in their audacity.

'Do whatever you would like best, ducky.'

She made an imperceptible movement of the body to go down under the bedclothes. A quite astonishing feeling of emotion it was, soft and reprehensibly tragic. To mingle her life with that of the ridiculously confused brothers that she might later put her own choice into action, and to test the living and pure elements of that life, her love had instructed her to descend to the furthest cavernous periods, in order to return to that indecisive, protoplasmic, foetal state, the better to flow in between the other two and thus mingle with them like the white of one egg with the white of others. Her love might well consume her utterly, reduce her to nothing, to zero, thus destroying her moral armament that made her all she was and conferred what authority she possessed. At the same time a feeling of shame floated away from her (more exactly reducing her to a state where she felt no shame), and thus, aspiring to retain the figure of a man less monstrous, keep only this single half of a double statue, one which further would have the inestimable advantage of knowing how to manage money affairs and have no other occupation than of relieving her of her everyday practical affairs, and this evoked in her a momentary nostalgia for Nono. To be lorded over and compelled to occupy herself with the basest chores was one thing, but to be relieved of these would give her back a truer, more certain and more essential life.

Already the hope of mixing freely in the life of the two brothers was waning; she would in future slip down only for her pleasure. With her mouth glued to the neck muscles of her lover, she whispered:

'My love, my great big lover, I'll do whatever you wish.'

Robert squeezed her very tight, and then released the tension to enable his mistress to continue her downward glissade under the sheets. She slipped a little way further, inch by inch. Robert braced his body slightly as he pulled himself up in the opposite direction. Lysiane went down still further. Robert came up a little more. Then she moved again, having decided that the moment had come for Robert, imperious and radiant, to push her down firmly by the shoulders. With fumbling clumsiness, she applied her lips to her lover. She swallowed the spunk. Robert restrained himself from uttering any moan: he was a male and refused to 'let himself go'. By the time she brought her head out from under the sheets, daylight was filtering through the ill-fitting curtains. She looked at Robert; he was calm and indifferent. Through the dishevelled hair falling over her forehead, she smiled at him so sadly that he kissed her out of compassion, and this she understood and resented.

Then he got out of bed. It struck her forcibly that everything was changed. For this was the first time in her life after making love – giving a man his pleasure – she did not wash herself, did not want to leave the bed at the same time as her lover to go to the bidet. The uniqueness of such an event troubled her as she waited: lying alone on the edge of the bed – having it all to herself – while Robert went to wash himself. What part of her would she have washed? To have rinsed out her mouth or gargled would have been laughable after she had swallowed the spunk. She had the feeling of being unclean. She watched Robert washing his cock, soaping it and covering it with suds where the base disappeared into his body, soaking it and drying it carefully. A crazy thought entered her head and by no means cheered her. 'He's afraid my mouth's poisoned him. The poison oozes from him, yet it's I who infect him.'

She felt the burden of loneliness and old age. Robert was washing himself in the white china basin. She could see the movement of his muscles as they rippled over his shoulders, arms, and calves. It was growing more and more light. Madame Lysiane let her thoughts dwell on what Querelle's body must be like, for she had only seen him dressed as a sailor. 'It's the same! surely not – surely there must be some spot somewhere – perhaps he's got a different prick' (we shall see where these thought were to lead her). She felt tired and utterly alone. Robert turned, calm and solid, in the middle of his brother, in the middle of himself. She said 'Light the curtains' intending to add 'my darling', had not some sort of humiliation, arising from the idea of her uncleanliness, forbade her to soil this man already so brightly shining; this man so tender after his revelations during the night and so soft after taking his pleasure, or wound him by a too insulting intimacy. Without noticing her lapsus linguae, Robert drew the curtains. The pale light of day 'undid' the room, as one says that a woman undoes her hair, or that a face is undone, a sure sign of great misfortune or nausea. Then it was that Lysiane craved death. She felt it imperative to die, that is to say, her left arm became a giant shark's fin and she longed to enwrap herself in it. In much the same way, Lieutenant Seblon wished to wear a great black flag as a cape so that he might furl himself in it and then be able to masturbate within its folds. This garb would cut him off from the outside world and confer a mysterious hierarchic attitude upon him. He would no longer require arms. We read in his personal diary:

'To wear a tippet, a cape. To have no arms and so little leg. To become an embryo again, a swaddled babe, and still secretly keep all one's members. By virtue of this garment, I should imagine that I was being rolled in a wave, borne along in it, buckled into its crest. The world and its happenings would stop at my door.'

Querelle's murders and his belief in his own personal safety in the midst of them, his calmness while performing them, his lack of fear among the shadows, all combined to make him a solemn character. Deep down within him, his thoughts evolved with methodic solemnity. He felt sure that he had experienced the limits of danger, so much so that he had nothing to fear from any revelations concerning his habits. Nothing could prevail against him. Nobody would be able to discover his errors, to decipher, for example, the signs carved on certain trees along the ramparts. Sometimes he cut deep into the wet bark of an acacia with his knife, carving a highly stylized design of his initials. Thus all round the secret resting-place where his treasure slept – like a sleeping dragon – were woven strands of lace corresponding in their guardianship to the special virtue prevalent at the moment of their manufacture. Querelle kept a double watch on himself. He re-endowed tokens long in disuse with a new meaning. The oriflamme or embroidered church linen were to him a token at every moment of his prowls. The number of points, each strand of the network, corresponded to a thought offered to the Holy Virgin. Around his own altar, Querelle wove a protective veil on which was embroidered, as the gold-thread 'M' on blue altar-cloths, his own monogram.

When Madame Lysiane found herself facing him, her eyes could not help wandering downwards to his parts. She knew very well that they could never hope to pierce the dark blue material, but it became imperative that they should be reassured on that impossible point. Perhaps this evening the coarse serge would be less opaque, less stiff, and would outline his private parts more boldly, allowing her to verify a profound difference between the two brothers. She hoped that the sailor's prick would turn out to be a little smaller than Robert's. Sometimes she found herself imagining the reverse and dared to hope that it prove true.

'But then, what difference would that make? If Robert's turned out to be smaller, it doesn't mean . . .'

She was unable to finish the sentence, for she was overcome by a maternal concern for a Robert less well endowed than his brother.

'Then I'd twit him with the fact, just for the fun of hearing him create. Only if it made him look sad and he answered me in gentle, trusting tones, 'That's not my fault'; if he said that, then it wouldn't help matters at all. It would mean that he recognized his infirmity and came for comfort under my wing as his own was broken. Then what should I do? If I kissed him at once, smiling at him as he had smiled at me, as he had kissed me when I poked my dishevelled head out from under the sheets, then he would realize how cruel can be the pity of somebody one loves. Does he love me? I should myself go on loving him more tenderly, but less magnificently.'

Madame Lysiane felt that her desire to love more tenderly (in short, her desire to love) would be incomparably less intoxicating than the irresistible force that must inevitably precipitate her into the arms of the more virile of the two young men, above all when the latter had the same body, the same features and the same voice as her wounded lover.

Querelle chucked away his lighted cigarette. It fell at some distance from him, but close enough, this smoking weapon, white and delicate, the fatal sign indicating that war was declared, that it no longer depended on him if, by burning a little further down the butt, it should blow the world to smithereens. He kept his eyes off it, but he was well aware of what he had just thrown aside. The solemnity of his gesture was impressed on his conscience and bade him – irresistibly, for the fire was not far from the powder – not to stop there. He stuck his hands deep into the two pockets tailored at a provocative angle across his stomach, 'stomach-ache pockets', and stared at Mario fixedly, rather wickedly, scowling, his words forced out between clenched lips.

'What's that you're trying to say? Yes, you! What are you trying to say to me? What do you mean, could you take Nono's place?'

Mario felt afraid in face of the sailor's calm. If he were to go to the full lengths of the plan he had initiated, he would forfeit all prestige as a copper. Querelle would simply regard him as a copper who wanted to keep a closer eye on him. With an unconscious and hardly preconceived slickness of thought, concerning suspicions of contraband and theft even – the only suspicions that could account for a copper hanging about La Féria, and no doubt due to something said by one of the girls – Querelle made up his mind to pile it on thick. He would do his best to work on the one simple fact in order to dissemble that of murder, about which a copper, just because he was a copper, must always be concerned, sometimes in the most cunning manner. That was why it was all the more necessary to lead on this 'tec in the first place, before extricating himself to his full advantage. So, to start with, he must implicate himself. He must force Mario's attention from the beginning by a thousand dazzling effects: effects to be achieved by a crisp tone of voice, clenched teeth, harsh looks, and a wrinkled brow.

'Come on now . . . spit it out!'

With a single sentence, such as 'I wanted to find out if you had any snow on you,' Mario could have restored calm, but the forcefulness he felt in Querelle communicated itself to him, not by strengthening his own physical vigour, but rather his audacity, his firmness of purpose. Querelle's attitude, frightening by reason of his unexpected, icy resolve, communicated to Mario a fervently acceptable strength of mind which bolstered him up, since it prevented him fading out in a single ringing word to mark his retreat, and backing out of the whole affair. *Querelle confirmed the copper's own convictions.* Eye to eye with Querelle, the sharp overtones of his voice splintering on Querelle's still visible over-emphasis, Mario answered:

'I said what I said.'

Querelle did not answer or shift his ground at once. Keeping his mouth tight shut, he drew in so deep a breath through his nose that his nostrils quivered. Mario felt a desperate desire to bugger the tiger in its fury. Querelle allowed himself a few seconds to scrutinize Mario more carefully; to hate him into the bargain, and at the same time to put himself in a more advantageous physical and moral position the better to fight it out. It would be necessary for him to concentrate, therefore, the full force of his passion upon this one incident, born of the suspicions held by Mario concerning his thefts or contraband, and let any idea of the crime expire of its own accord through lack of any intuitional support, which would be used up already by these soothing suspicions. He half-opened his mouth like a fish, and at once it was filled with the inrush of wind, the exact cylindrical size and shape of a well-developed penis.

'Ah!' he exclaimed.

'What is it?'

Querelle transfixed Mario with a look that had the pointed rigidity of an umbrella spoke.

'If it doesn't put you out too much, you'll come along with me now. I've got something to say to you outside.'

'Right you are.'

Mario racked his brains for words and expressions that went down well with the corner boys, with whom he often liked to associate himself. They went out without a word. Beside him, a little behind, Mario kept his hands in his pockets – the left already squeezed round the ball of his handkerchief.

'Will you be going far?'

Querelle stopped and looked at him.

'What do you want with me?'

'Why, haven't you guessed?'

'What proof have you?'

'Nono's told me about it, and that's good enough for me. And if you let yourself be pounced by Nono, there's no reason why I shouldn't join in the hook-up.'

Querelle felt his whole bloodstream flowing back into his heart from the very tips of his fingers. He grew so pale as to be almost transparent in the semi-obscurity: this copper was no proper copper. Querelle was neither a killer nor a thief: he could live his life without fear of danger. He opened his mouth to burst out laughing; but he did not laugh. He was engulfed by an enormous sigh fetched from his guts up to his gullet, where it remained blocking his mouth like a great wad of cotton-waste. He wanted to kiss Mario, to give himself to him, to shout aloud and sing: all this was but the work of a second and took place within him.

'Oh, yeah!'

His voice was hoarse: it sounded husky to Querelle. He turned away from Mario and took a few steps. He couldn't be bothered to clear his throat. When he came face to face with him, the copper's fury ought to be strong enough to serve some purpose, to provoke, perhaps the unrolling of another drama just as necessary – if not more so – than the one which had never taken place. It would then be essential that the threatened storm be accompanied by solemn music. Since Mario seemed to be so determined, so conclusively set on his purpose, and further, since he was clearly thinking of something very different from what Querelle had at first supposed, then whatever it was still necessitated an equally tense determination.

'No need to go as far as the North Pole! If there are some little games you don't go much on, you've only to tell me.'

'Yes, I've . . .'

Querelle's fist struck home on Mario's chin. Happy to be scrapping – for he was fighting bare-fisted – he was convinced that he was matched against nothing that could not be defeated by hands and feet. Mario parried the second blow and replied with a straight left to the jaw. Querelle stepped back. For an instant he hesitated then sprang forward. For a while the two men fought in silence. Unclinching, they were able to break apart to just outside close range, never more than two yards separating them, and there they stood, looking each other over before suddenly leaping forward for another set-to. Querelle was happy to be fighting a copper, and it was not long before he was well aware that this combat in which he was shaping so finely – his youth and suppleness standing him in good stead – was comparable to one where the flirtatious advances of a girl are provoking proof that she intends to give way while resisting to the bitter end. He perpetrated the most daring, the most punishing, the most virile assaults, with never a thought of putting Mario off or an idea of letting him think that he had made a big mistake, but with the intention of bringing home to him all in good time that he had been up against a man of mettle and defeated him fair and square, whittling down his resources, and slowly, delicately, *despoiling* him, one by one, of his male qualifications.

They fought on. The noble attitudes struck by Querelle in the end inspired Mario to rival nobility. At the outset, finding that he was playing second fiddle to the sailor, both as regards good looks and peace of mind, the policeman had cursed the beauty and noble bearing of his opponent in order not to feel compelled to despise himself for not possessing similar grace and elegance. He wished to prove to himself that it was *precisely* against this very thing that he was battling, the better to possess it; and he opposed it with his own weight and vulgarity, while rejoicing in them. It was then that he took on a new beauty of his own.

On they fought. Querelle was the more agile and ever the stronger. Mario half thought of drawing his revolver and polishing off Querelle, all in the course of his duties; he would have liked to arrest the sailor, for he had threatened him. And besides, a wonderful, heaven-scented flower round which a golden swarm of bees hovered, was blossoming within him, cockled up as he was, shrivelled and sad, his mouth set firm, his chest heaving, short of breath, his arms heavy and awkward; he whipped out his knife. Querelle guessed this rather than saw it with his eyes. Mario's whole bearing had changed: his movements were quite different, more calculating, concealed, his behaviour more catlike, more classically tragic, and Querelle could discern in everything about him an irrevocable and dearly-gained decision, a will to murder, at the moment unaccountable in its determination – in its gravity even. This increased proportionately as his opponent, armed with a lethal weapon, since a copper, of course, carried a 6.35, became more ferocious and human (an infernal ferocity, totally outside the lust of battle, far beyond the idea of vengeance and insult that they had hurled at each other), so much so that Querelle quaked in his shoes. It was at this very moment that he guessed, from Mario's palpitating and flurried appearance, the presence of a knife in his hand, the lethal, sharp, metallic blade. This alone, though invisible, could furnish the closed hand and twisted wrist with a suppleness, a look so alarming and self-assured, and the body with the appearance of being heaped up on itself – like an accordion deflated without visible motion, and not being inflated again, to sustain the required long note – and, in the eyes, a look of a desperado's irrevocable calm.

Querelle could not see the knife, yet he had eyes for nothing else, for it became, by its very invisibility and its paramount importance to the issue of the fight, (it could easily mean two corpses) of vast proportion. Its blade was white, milky, and of almost a fluid substance. The fact that it was sharp did not make the knife dangerous: it was the fact that it became the symbol of death in the night. Being this symbol, death-dealing simply because it was what it was, it terrified Querelle. It was the idea behind the knife that struck terror into him. He opened his mouth and had the marvellous, life-saving shame of hearing himself stammer:

'You're surely not out for my blood?'

Mario did not budge. Nor did Querelle. Because of the idea of blood involved, because he allowed himself to entertain hopes, the imploring tone in his own voice made his own blood circulate more freely, yet he hesitated to break his rigid immobility. He was afraid, so strongly did he feel attached to him by a multiplicity of threads, that a single one of them – and the very slightest might well release some fatal mechanism, so evident is it that fatality hangs by the most tenuous of threads – that a single one of his movements would inevitably call forth a corresponding action from Mario. They were in the centre of a patch of fog in which the knife nestled, unseen but inevitable. Querelle had no weapon on him. In deep and ringing tones, by their suddenness profoundly moving, he addressed the Prince of the Night and the encircling Trees.

'See here, Mario, I'm alone before you. I've no defence whatever.'

He had spoken the 'Mario' in a loud voice and already felt himself to be bound to him by the gentlest of bonds, by a feeling comparable to what we feel at night-fall while waiting beside a window in a hotel bedroom and hear a boy's nervous voice shouting, 'Get out, you filthy brute, I'm only seventeen!' He centred all his hopes on Mario. The sentence started as a timid note, hardly infringing the silence and the mist (it was rather the delicious vibration of both) and little by little it grew stronger without losing anything of the simple and precise tone of a commonplace announcement, yet one devised by a barker of miraculous powers, attempting to bewitch death and riffling the depths of his memory for a word that escapes him, read perhaps in some newspaper taken from an officer while he was speaking to another officer. Querelle repeated,

'I'm defenceless; I've nothing in my hand.'

One. Two. Three. Four. In the silence, four seconds sped by.

'You can do what you please, for I've no blade. If you draw blood, I'm as good as done for. I've got no defence.'

Mario stood his ground. He felt himself the master of terror, and of life, which it was in his power to cut short or allow to continue. He rose above his policeman's calling. He took no great pleasure in his powers, for he never paid much attention to his inner calling and was little given to extolling it. He made no movement, being at a loss to know how first to move, but chiefly because he was fascinated by his moment of victory, which inevitably would be destroyed by and for one possibly less intense, one less happy, he couldn't tell, but one that would certainly be irremediable. Having achieved what he wanted, it was no longer a question of choice. Yet Mario was aware that a choice was hanging in the balance. He was at the ultimate centre of freedom of choice. He was ready to . . . except that he couldn't remain in this position for long. To lie down on his side, to stretch this or that muscle, would already be to make a choice; that is to say, to limit himself. He must therefore keep up this state of suspense if only his muscles did not tire too quickly.

'I should have asked you what you were after, but I never felt like it.'

The voice was beautiful, a gentle sing-song. Querelle was also at the centre of the same freedom of choice and he realized the danger that lay behind Mario's instability. It communicated itself to him above everything else, putting him in a state of funk that endowed him with a marvellous zest for the game, a tight-rope walker's fragility and hesitant step, above all invincible strength. Thus funk could well make him hurl himself from the flying trapeze, to which he was clinging with glass claws, and hurtle down among the caged panthers. Death lay there, watching out for him, just as he had so often been the lurking death for his prey. He could see himself in Mario's face and attitude, both so new to him. What uncanny power – in the guise of a police officer standing with legs apart, the upper half of his body stiffly braced inside a light blue sports shirt – had fled from his own body and was now confronting him? Without danger to himself, so long as it was inside him, Querelle had harboured this poison now projected on the wall of fog in front of him. Tonight he was being threatened by his own poison. He was mortally afraid, and his fear was pale as the death whose efficiency he well knew, and he was doubly afraid of being suddenly abandoned by it.

Mario shut the hasp of his knife. Querelle sighed, knowing himself defeated. The weapon born of man's intelligence had soon cheapened the effect of the body's nobility, of the warrior's heroism. Mario drew himself up to his full height and put his hands in his pockets. Facing him, but with a shiftiness due to his recent humiliation, Querelle did the same. They came a little closer to each other and exchanged troubled glances.

'I never meant to harm you. You chose to settle matters according to your own rules. I don't care a fuck if you go with Nono. Why should I fucking well care? You can do what you like with your own arse, but there's no need to go at it head down.'

'Listen, Mario. What if I do go with Nono? That's my business and mine only, and there's no need for you to take the piss out of me in front of the whole brothel.'

'I've never taken the piss out of you. I simply asked you if I couldn't take his place, joking like. I'd have you know there was nothing at the back of that. And, what's more, there were no witnesses to hear what I said.'

'Right you are then, nobody heard, but get a load of this. I don't care to listen to jokes of that sort. You're right, I can bloody well please myself what I do. That's my concern and I can do as I please. For get this straight, Mario, you only won because you had the whip-hand just now, or believe me you'd never have got me down.'

They disappeared into the fog, walking side by side like brothers, feeling themselves isolated by the swirling mist, their low voices almost confidential in tone. They turned to the left in the direction of the ramparts. Not only did Querelle no longer feel afraid, but little by little the emanation of death, having so mysteriously escaped from his body, found its way back into it and thereby armed him once more with an impenetrably flexible armour-plating.

'Come now, say you see I wasn't trying to get at you. I didn't mean the half of what I said. There was no offence meant. I whipped out my knife, but I could have shot you down with my 6.35. I had every right. I could have invented anything I liked and told the tale, had I wanted. Only I didn't want.'

Once again Querelle was aware that a policeman was walking at his side. He was lost in silence.

'You may be wondering how well I know Nono! You can ask him. I go to La Féria as his pal, not as a copper. And make no mistake about it, I'm on the level. There's not one of the chaps who won't tell you the same, believe me. Come to that, I've never picked up one of the lads, never, d'you hear! That won't mean much to you, I dare say. You're in the navy, my lad, and I've known lots of your chaps who like a bit of navy cake, I can tell you! That doesn't stop 'em playing the man, take it from me.'

'True enough, but don't you go thinking that because a chap's been with Nono he's one of those.'

Mario gave a clear, ringing, youthful laugh. He brought out a packet of cigarettes from his pocket and silently held it out to Querelle.

'Come, come, no need to keep your end up with me.'

Querelle laughed in his turn and through his laughter came out with: 'Honest, I'm not trying to kid you.'

'I've told you, you can do what you please. I know life, don't fool yourself with these here – what do they call them? – "special morals". Your brother now, he's different, he plays safe by going with the girls. He doesn't hold with specialized habits – you see what I know. Best not mention it to him.'

They had climbed almost as high as the fortification without having met a soul. Querelle stopped. He touched the policeman's shoulder with the hand holding his fag.

'Mario!' and, staring straight into his eyes, he added in severe tones, 'I've been with Nono, I won't deny the fact. Only don't get me wrong. I'm not like that, I'd have you know. I like going with girls. You believe that, don't you?'

'I'm not saying that I don't. Only, according to what Nono himself has to say, he's slipped you a length all right. That you can't deny. You certainly didn't snatch his ring.'

'Agreed, he did it to me, only . . .'

'Then why the heck keep belly-aching about it? As I've said before, I can draw my own conclusions. There's no need for you to keep telling me you're a real he-man. I can see that for myself. If you were a nance of any sort, you would soon have changed your tune. But you're not one to try that game.'

He put his hand on Querelle's shoulder, forcing him to walk on. He smiled, and so did Querelle.

'Listen. Here we are, two men together. We can talk as we like. You cased up with Nono, that's no crime. The main point is that he fucked you and you stood for it. Isn't that so? Don't go telling me you didn't lap it up!'

Querelle still wanted to put up some defence, but his smile defeated him.

'I'm not saying I didn't. Doesn't matter what sort of chap you are, you could get a stalk on.'

'There you are then. As long as you get some sport out of it, there's no harm done. And Nono must have enjoyed it too, because he's hot enough and you've a decent phiz.'

'No more than any of the others.'

'Come off it now. I should have said you and your brother. Sorry, mate. I can just see Nono – he must have been as randy as a rutting stag. Tell us, is he a good hand at the job?'

'Nark it, Mario, can't you?'

But he was smiling as he said this. All the while the copper had kept a hand on his shoulder as if to guide him gently but surely to the gallows.

'Why do you ask? Does it make you randy? Do you want to have a go yourself?'

'Why not? If it's really so good, give us a wrinkle. How does he go to work?'

'He's pretty keen on it. Satisfied? Look here, Mario, you're not trying to make me shit myself all this time, by any chance?'

'We're enjoying a chat. There's nobody to hear us. Between pals, did you really get the horn? Did it make you feel pretty good?'

'You've only to try it.'

They laughed together. Mario took care to lean more heavily on Querelle's shoulder.

'And why not? Only you haven't come clean yet. How did you find it?'

'Not so bad. You don't giggle as it goes up; after that, it's all right.'

'Honest? it's a bit of all right?'

'My life! It's the first time it had happened to me. I never thought it'd be like it was.'

He laughed rather awkwardly. By this time, he was getting a bit worried, and all the more at the policeman's heavy hand on his shoulder. Querelle did not yet know whether Mario was really out to feel his collar or his arse. He was put off by the volley of questions as precise as at an interrogation, by the tone of urgency, by the insinuating voice and its multiple insistence on some sort of confession, no matter what it was. He was exercised by the strangeness of his immediate surroundings, by the thickening mist and darkness which further united the straying policeman and his victim, by enclosing them in solitary companionship and thus having the effect of adding to their complicity.

'He's got a big prick, surely. The fellow's well-loaded. How did you like his cock?'

'You're barmy. It meant nothing to me. I'm not as far gone as all that. Come off it now, talk of something else.'

'Why? Does it shake you a bit? If you're browned off, I'll say no more about it.'

'No, I'm not chokker. I was only joking.'

'Just to talk of it gives me a hard. Cross my heart.'

'Nark it, you're kidding!'

Querelle intended to convey by this exclamation – as by his previous remark, 'I'm not chokker' – a series of light taps, as it were, constituting a game and a come-hither approach, which must inevitably end in the action he feared and that meant the end of freedom for him. He was not ashamed of having accepted to go along this narrow path; but, at the same time, he was amazed at his own craftiness in rolling up like a prickly hedgehog and so reaching the peak of his secret desire. At least he felt a slight sense of shame at performing face to face with a he-man, unaided by the pretext of superior strength, an act which he might have dared to try out with or on a queer without letting himself down, or with an ordinary man, but only under the compunction of an irresistible pretext.

'So you don't want to believe it?'

'Don't flannel me! You've never got a hard on from what we've just been saying! Tell that to the Marines!'

'It's the truth, I give you my word.'

'Come again! I don't believe you – it's too bloody cold. There can't be much there!'

'See if it isn't so! Feel for yourself!'

'Not bloody likely, not me! There's nothing of it there. It's more likely frozen stiff.'

They had come to a standstill. They grinned as they looked at each other, each mistrusting the other's smile. Mario arched his eyebrows to their highest extremity and wrinkled his forehead, wishing to give full expression to the fact that he was flabbergasted at the idea that a chap like him should have an erection at such an hour, in such a place and for such poor reasons.

'You'll soon see if you feel it.'

Querelle made no movement. His smile was more winning, subtler, even more mocking as it slowly faded out, making his lips tremble as it left his face.

'No, I tell you. You're having me on.'

'What I say is, see for yourself. It's queer, it's as stiff as my baton.'

Without taking his eyes off Mario's, a smile hovering on his trembling lips, Querelle did little more than let the tip of two fingers rub against the cop's flies, but against the material only. Then he explored further, but only the merest fraction, till he touched the stiff, burning prick. Almost falteringly, and lowering his voice against his will, he said,

'There's nothing to write home about that I can feel. Is that what you call a hard?'

'You've not felt it properly. Grab hold of it. It's not a bad piece of meat at all.'

'Only when it's got your shirt wrapped round it. That puts a bit on, I dare say: it's all that clobber round it.'

'Put your hand inside and you'll soon see.'

Querelle stretched out his hand and drew his fingers back hesitatingly just as they came in contact with the bulging material. This hesitation of his troubled each of them deliciously.

'Undo them. Then you'll see that I'm not shagged out as you seem to think.'

They kept up a pretence of innocence – one as much as the other – though both were well aware of the game they were playing. They were afraid of dashing forward too precipitously to meet the truth and take their pleasure in the unveiled symbol of their mutually accepted excitement. Slowly, with a smile always playing about his lips, so that Mario might suppose it a matter of supreme indifference to him, proper poppycock, yet certain that he would not for a moment be taken in by such flimsy pretences, and keeping his eyes fixed on Mario's, Querelle undid one, two and then the third of the buttons. He slipped in his hand, taking a tentative hold of the penis in the first instance; keeping it between thumb and forefinger, before grasping it firmly in his whole hand as if to appraise its proper size. In a voice he wanted to sound clear, but which still kept traces of his frayed emotions, he said:

'You're right, it's not bad.'

'D'you like it?'

Querelle withdrew his hand, but he never stopped smiling.

'I've told you, it doesn't interest me, no matter what size it is.'

With the free hand thrust deep in his trousers pocket – the other never for an instant letting go of the sailor's shoulder – the copper flipped out his prick from between his open flies. He stood thus, firmly planted on both feet, set wide apart, face to face with a matelot who was looking at him and smiling.

'Come on, give us a rub!'

'Not here. Can't we find some other place?'

From all points of the compass, that night, intimations of crime were being wafted down exposed paths on dusty feet. Querelle was aware of this creeping approach. His ear was trained to catch every whispered adulation. Orion's Belt was above him. He bent down: there in the dark shone the opalescent tip of Mario's formidable erection. Close to his ear, Querelle could hear the faint suck of the saliva in the policeman's mouth. His moistened lips were smacked apart in preparation for a kiss, perhaps: his tongue was ready to flicker into an ear and there let itself go in impetuous excavations. The whistle of a locomotive pierced the night. Querelle listened to the train's approach, almost heard it snort. The two men had reached the cutting that overlooked the railway. The policeman's face must have been very close, for Querelle could still hear the same sharp sound, now more like the sizzling of saliva against his lips. This seemed to him to be the mysterious preparation for an amorous orgy such as he had never dreamed of. He was not a little worried at distinguishing so personal a characteristic of Mario's, at seeing so clearly into his secret habits. Although he had opened his lips and moved his tongue inside his mouth in the most natural way, the policeman had seemed to be anticipating the pleasures to come with prurient delight. The hiss of the saliva alone was sufficient - so close was it to his ear - to isolate Querelle in a world of silence which remained unpierced by the passing train. With a terrifying roar, the express rushed past them. Querelle was in the clutches of so powerful a feeling of abandon that he allowed Mario to do what he liked. The train sped on into the night with unmitigated desperation. It was speeding towards the serene, peaceful, and terrestrial unknown, to something so long denied to the matelot. The sleeping travellers alone would be witnesses of his affair with a policeman, leaving the pair of them behind on the brink, as if they had been outcasts or lepers.

'Come on, here goes.'

Mario did not manage it. In a flash Querelle turned round and squatted down. At the very moment that the train plunged into the tunnel before entering the station, the policeman's prick, as if fated, plunged deep into his mouth.

For the first time in his life, Querelle was kissing a man on the mouth. It seemed to him that he was pressing his face against a mirror that gave back his own image and that his tongue was excavating the inside of a statue's granite head. Yet, this being an act of love, of culpable love, he knew that he was committing evil. His erection hardened. They kept their two mouths soldered together with tongues either crushed or the tips of them in sharp contact, neither daring to place them on the rough cheeks where a kiss would have been a sign of tenderness. Each pair of eyes looked into the other with ironic surprise. The policeman's tongue was very hard.

The fact that he was a steward neither humiliated Querelle nor lowered his prestige in his mates' eyes. He performed all the duties demanded of his job with a simplicity that is the hall-mark of nobility and he would be seen on deck every morning, squatting on his haunches, polishing the lieutenant's shoes, his head bent over his task and his hair falling over his eyes. Occasionally he would raise his head and smile, a brush in one hand, a shoe on the other. Then he would jump lightly to his feet - presto, like a conjurer - collect all the utensils together into their box and go below. He walked with fast, well-balanced steps, his body radiating happiness.

'Here you are, Sir.'

'Good. Don't forget to fold up my clothes.'

The officer did not dare to smile. In front of such strength and happiness, he never dared to show his own unhappiness, so certain was he that if he let down his hair for a moment in Querelle's presence, it would be to deliver himself body and soul to that wild animal. He was fearful of him. No matter how severe he was, he had never succeeded in casting a blight over Querelle's smile or his body. However, he knew his own strength. He was taller than the rating, but he was aware of a certain feebleness deep down inside. It was something almost concrete that sent out waves of fear along his muscles and swelled his body.

'Did you go ashore yesterday?'

'Yes, Sir. It was starboard watch ashore.'

'You could have reminded me. I wanted you. Next time let me know before you go.'

'Certainly, Sir.'

The Lieutenant watched him dusting the desk and folding away his clothes. He looked for a pretext for addressing him in icy tones, in such a way that familiarity was fore-doomed. The previous night he had gone aft to the sleeping quarters as though he wanted him for something. He had hoped to see him coming in or going out in his blues and jumper. The five men who were there got up when he put in an appearance.

'Is my steward not there?'

'No, sir. He's ashore.'

'Where does he sleep?'

Automatically he walked towards the hammock indicated, as if to leave a letter or a note upon it, and automatically patted the pillow, as though wishing to give special care to the sleeping-place in the absence of the beloved owner. With this gesture, lighter and gentler than a wisp of hay, his tenderness evaporated. He went out more disillusioned than before. It was there that slept someone beside whom he would never sleep. He reached the upper deck and leaned over the rails. In the midst of the fog, looking out towards the town, he was alone, happy in imagining Querelle on the spree, drunk and grinning, singing with the girls, with other lads – colonial troops or dockers with whom he was pally before half an hour had gone by. From time to time perhaps, he had left the smoke-filled café for the slopes of the fortifications. That was where he stained the bottom part of his trousers. The Lieutenant followed Querelle's movements both inside his own mind and by projecting his thoughts out to where those stains were picked up.

One day, while passing a group of sailors, one of whom had referred to the stains on Querelle's trousers, the Lieutenant had overheard him answer rakishly, 'Oh, them's my decorations!' His 'decorations!' More likely his 'spew'.

Querelle's face and body began to fade away. He made off with long strides, proud of the frayed bottoms of his trousers and the stains all round the back of his calves which he wore with the most glorious shamelessness. He would probably be going back to the café, where he would drink red wine, sing, shout, and go outside again to lend his prick to whoever might so desire it. Many a time, at this and other ports of call, the Lieutenant had gone ashore to cruise about the districts frequented by sailors in the hopes of taking part in the mysteries attended by the lower deck, and with luck catch sight of Querelle's flushed face in the smoke-ridden, noisy crowd. But he owed it to his braid to pass quickly by, hardly sparing time for more than a cursory glance. He virtually saw nothing; the clouded windows were too opaque with the smoky atmosphere, but what he guessed to be going on behind them was far more exciting than reality.

To give a proper edge to an insult, we must have self-confidence in our mother wit, in our command over language. Since Lieutenant Seblon's cowardice was due to little else than physical recoil when faced with a strong man, and still further to the certainty of his own defeat, he had to seek compensation in an insolent attitude. On the occasion of his decisive meeting with Gil at Police Headquarters, (which, by prevailing force of logic, has to be placed at the end of this book) his conduct was haughty, and finally insulting to the officers of the law. It was all too evident that he had already recognized Gil as his aggressor. That he determined to deny the fact was out of fidelity to the 'unscrupulous' thought process to which he had been subject ever since his first contact with Querelle. This had been some little time in coming to light, but later it had begun to grow at a fearful, devastating, break-neck speed. The Lieutenant proved more unscrupulous than all the Querelles of the Fleet put together: there was not a man among them to touch him. His controlled harshness was possible so long as his mind and not his body was called into play. No sooner did he set eyes on Gil, sitting on a bench with his back against the radiator, than he recognized at once that what was expected of him was to heap contumely upon the lad. But deep within him a very light wind began to blow, at ground level: ('a slight breeze, hardly more than a zephyr', he wrote in his private journal) and this gradually began to inflate him, to puff him up, till it escaped in generous gusts through his vibrant mouth – in other words, his voice – in a torrent of words.

'Now then, do you recognize him?'

'No, Sir.'

'Excuse me, Lieutenant, I can well understand the feelings which cause you to act in this manner, but it is a question of Justice. It goes without saying that I shall overlook it in my report.'

The detective's prompt recognition of his generosity only spurred the officer to further sacrifice. He felt elated.

'I do not understand what you are driving at. You may rest assured that my deposition will equally be dicated by my sense of Justice. And I cannot accuse an innocent man!'

Standing beside the desk, Gil was hardly able to hear, body and soul were dissolving into a greyish vapour, which was exactly what he felt himself turning into.

'Do you really think I should not have recognized him? The mist was not so very thick, and his face was so close to mine . . .'

No more needed to be said. A metaphorical bodkin passed through the brain of each of the three men and at once they were connected by the thick white thread of sudden comprehension. Gil turned his head. The recollection of his face against that of the officer cast light upon his memory. As for the superintendent, intuition convinced him of the truth as soon as he heard the voice alter its tone on the words 'his face'. For a few seconds, perhaps less, the three of them were united in intricate connivance.

The police officer, however – and this will seem strange only to readers who have never experienced such momentary revelations – dismissed this insight from his mind as though it might have been of danger to himself. He suppressed it, he buried it beneath thick layers of other thoughts.

The Lieutenant went on acting his part in his own private monologue. He all but overplayed it. He now felt certain of success. He linked himself in an increasingly mystic way with the young mason; the more he narrowed the distance between them the further he seemed to be moving away from him, not merely by denying his aggression, but, in self-defence, by defending the lad by his emphatic generosity. By denying his generosity, he destroyed it at its source, leaving in its place a feeling of indulgence towards the criminal, and, further still, a sense of moral participation in the crime. This sense of culpability could only lead to his downfall. Lieutenant Seblon insulted the officer of the law. He dared to strike him. He himself felt that reprehensible acts of insubordination are the fiercely beautiful beginnings of a work of art. He caught up with Gil and outstripped him. The same thought-process that now permitted him to deny Gil's aggression had formerly made him base and cowardly with regard to Querelle.

'Clear out of it, Jack! Cough it up or I'll strangle you! The pitch has been queered. Five against one!'

He was fond of this last expression, and it fitted exactly his present attitude. He was *proud* of fearing nothing and nobody, of being safe from any reprisal in his gold-braided uniform. In this cowardice lay his strength. Besides, it only required a slight twist for this cowardice to confront another enemy (to be precise, its opposite), for it to confront itself. From the way he vexed Querelle or punished him for no good reason, his cowardice could be inferred. Yet in the middle of his act, he was aware of a force or will – his strength: it was this strength that allowed him – when he discovered and cultivated it at the centre of his cowardice – to insult the inspector. In the last resort, carried away by his 'gentle zephyr', supported by the illuminating presence of the real guilty party, he accused himself of the theft of the money. When he heard the inspector give the order to arrest him, Seblon made secret appeal to his prestige as a naval officer, but when he found himself handcuffed in one of the cells, certain that the scandal would create an uproar on board, he felt happy.

Nono's face was composed of commas: the curve of his eyebrows; the shadow cast by the curves of his nostrils; his lips; and the two ends of his moustache. The supreme formula of the structure of his head had its essence in the comma. To bugger those who went with his wife sufficed to give him peace of mind. 'She only goes to bed with the buggered. Those buggered by *me*, by the boss. And don't you forget it.'

Mario was gracious enough to be indulgent. The physical bulk of the brothel-keeper was crushing and almost enough to knock the breath out of him. As for Nono, he was riveted by the severity of the copper, by his ferocious quality, like that of cold steel as he stood before him, needle-sharp, as rigidly severe and polished as the triangular blade of a bayonet.

When he had buggered the lad who was after his wife, his spent passion diminished at the same speed as his erection. With his dropped trousers clinging round the calves of his legs, he lifted the front tail of his white shirt with one finger so as not to dirty it, and paraded the flabby, shit-spotted knob of his penis.

'Look, that's what you've done – you've given me a shitty prick. Get moving – pull up your slacks again and piss off to the Madam. If I've helped to give you a bit of a hard, you can finish it off with her.'

At the time of the murder of the Armenian, Querelle had relieved the dead man of all valuables. Only in rare cases does the idea of robbery become divorced from the idea and the act of murder; perhaps only in cases where the motive is less debauched. It is rare for a tough, after striking the queer who has accosted him, not to take his wallet. He does not strike him in order to steal his wallet, but he takes it *because he has struck him.*

'You're a cunt not to have taken that stone-mason's dough. It'd come in handy for you now.'

Querelle waited. He was still hesitant. He had pronounced these last words on a slightly timid note, noticeable only to himself.

'But I couldn't. There was a crowd in the boozer. I never even gave it a thought.'

'Fair enough. But with t'other one, with that matelot. You'd time enough that time.'

'Jo, I swear I never done it. I swear.'

'See here, Gil, don't throw me that line. I've not come along here to preach to you. You may have your reasons for keeping it to yourself. It only goes to show you're growing up. If you say so, it's good enough for me. Only it's not worth doing a bloke if you don't get nothing out of it. You want to become tough - I'm telling you, lad.'

'So you don't think I could be a real tough guy, eh?'

'We'll see.'

Querelle was still afraid. He did not dare to say what he meant. We must look upon Gil as a young Hindu whose beauty prevents his attaining celestial bliss at such an early stage. His fetching smile and his lascivious look provoked the randiest thoughts in himself as well as in others. Like Querelle, Gil had committed murder by chance - by mischance - and it would have delighted the matelot to mould the lad in his own image. 'It would be grand if a poor little bugger of a Querelle was knocking about in the fog in the streets of Brest.' There remained the question of getting Gil to confess to one murder which he had not wished to commit, and to another in which he had no hand. In such fertile ground, Querelle was about to plant a Querelle seed which would grow and prosper. The matelot already felt *his power* in Gil. He felt himself to be as procreative as an egg. Gil must be forced to accept the act of murder. He must take it as a matter of course. What was aggravating was the need to keep under cover. Querelle got up.

'Don't take on, young 'un. Nothing's gone wrong yet. For a beginner you've not done so bad. You must go on as you've begun. It's up to me to put you right. I'll have a natter with Nono.'

'You've not said anything to him yet?'

'Don't you worry. He can't take you in La Féria, mind you. Some of the girls rabbit too much; doors aren't too thick there, anyway. And too many cops get around the place. But we'll look after you. No matter what happens, don't put yourself on the spot. It's not because of your crime that the boys'll make you welcome. You'll have to show 'em you can get away with a good few hold-ups. 'Cos your racket's a classy one. Don't let that worry you, that's my business. So long for now, young 'un.'

They shook hands and, just as he was going Querelle turned round, saying,

'What about the kiddo of yours, has he been along lately?'

'He'll be here any time now, you bet.'

Querelle grinned.

'You're not telling me there's no funny business between you and that bambino?'

Gil blushed. He thought the sailor was ribbing him, remembering the real story behind the murder of Theo. He was in the grip of an agonizing constraint. He answered tonelessly,

'You must be crackers. It's because I'd had a rub at his kid sister, that's why. You're crazy, Jo. Don't take all you hear as gospel. I'm all for the girls myself.'

'That's fine with me, even if the kid is your winger. I'm a matelot, don't forget. I know a thing or two. I'm not greedy any more. Well, so long, Gil. Keep smiling.'

As soon as he got back home, Roger looked at his sister with feelings of mixed irony and respect. Knowing that she would want to find in him something of Gil, he did his best to simulate him, to use his little tricks with a girl; in all innocence and at the same time rather wickedly he tried running his hand through her hair and tweaking up her skirt a bit over her hips. There was a touch of irony when he studied her reactions, for he was happy to think his body was receiving and intercepting her devotion for Gil, and a touch of respect, too, because she was the repository of Gil's most heart-felt emotions and the altar of the temple of which he was the High Priest. In the eyes of his mother, Roger had attained a singular maturity from the fact of being mixed up in a crime – so closely and so simply – which sprang from certain *habits*. She dared not make further enquiry for fear of hearing pour from his lips some wonderful tale in which he figured as the hero in a love drama. She could not be sure whether, at the age of fifteen, her son was already acquainted with the mysteries of love, not to mention those of forbidden love, of which she herself was ignorant.

Madame Lysiane was far too opulent a character for Querelle to regard her as a sister-in-law. His imagination boggled at the idea of his brother having sexual relations with so sumptuous a female. In his eyes, Robert was still a pimp who had set his mind on being kept and protected. This was not at all surprising to Querelle. For her part, Madame Lysiane did her best to be perfectly simple with him. She spoke to him as kindly as she could. She knew of his relations with Nono. Caught up in the enchantment of her strange jealousy, she paid little heed to her increasingly insistent preoccupation with the essential difference between him and Robert.

One evening, however, she was deeply moved by a sudden burst of laughter from Querelle – so fresh, so boyish, that it could never have come from Robert. Her eyes remained riveted on the corner of his wide-open mouth, which showed his brilliant teeth, and later on the play of the contracting lines round it as he closed it. It was clear to her that this young fellow was enjoying himself. It gave her an almost imperceptible shock, causing a slight crack through which her mixed feelings began to trickle. Unknown to her girls, who were used to seeing her eyes bright and her features composed and to being under the spell of the melancholy and majestic carriage of her body on its heavy haunches (spreading, and, in the best sense of the word, hospitable, destined in reality for motherhood) there floated continuously within her, whose flanks were outwardly dignified and calm, long, wide, black veils of soft yet curiously thick material, like mourning handkerchiefs with shadowy folds, ever twining and untwining according to some mysterious emotional cause. There was nothing within her except the sometimes agitated, sometimes slow rippling movements of these tenuous, black, floating pennons. It was equally impossible for her to extract these through her mouth and air them in the sun, as it was to evacuate them through the ordinary channel, as one does a solitary worm.

'All the same, things have come to a pretty pass! And a woman of my age can't afford to fool herself. I'm certainly not the kind to be fooled, in any case. Nobody's going to fool Josephine. All the same, I shall be fifty in five years' time. Above all, I mustn't let myself go just because of an idea I may have. And I have an idea. When I say *they* resemble each other and there is only one of them, in reality "they" are two. There is Robert on one side, and Jo on the other.' She found these day-dreams soothing during leisure moments and when not preoccupied with her duties in the salon, but they were incessantly interrupted by questions that arose in her daily routine. Slowly Madame Lysiane had come to regard life with its thousand and one little inconveniences as something altogether insignificant, without anything like the importance she attached to this all-absorbing phenomenon, of which she was the witness as well as the moving spirit. 'Two soiled pillow-slips? What have two soiled pillow-slips got to do with me? They've only got to be washed. What do they suppose I've to do with them?' And she speedily abandoned this degrading idea to occupy her thoughts with the fascinating interplay of her mourning weeds.

'Two brothers who love each other to the extent of being indistinguishable – that's one piece. I can feel it. It's moving. It's waving ever so gently, unfurled by two naked arms with closed fists, tight-clenched within me. It's rippling. Now another, also black, but of a different texture, is obstructing the first. The new piece of stuff seems to be saying "Two brothers who resemble each other so closely, to the extent of being in love with each other." This piece is also eddying about in the vat and covers over the first. No, it's the same piece back to front! Another piece, of a different black. It seems to be saying, "I love one of the brothers, only one . . ." Then another saying, "If I love one of the brothers, then I love the other . . ." I must put my finger on the truth and make an end of it all. But one really cannot conceive and give birth to a piece of stuff. Do I really love Robert? Surely I do, for we've now been lovers for six months. That means nothing, it would seem. I love Robert, I don't love Jo. How come? Perhaps I do love him. They both love each other. I can do nothing about that. They adore each other. Do they make love together, then? where? where? They're never together. So they must do it in secret, and make love somewhere else. Where, though? Where in the world? They have a go-between . . . That little nipper is their go-between . . . I may be crazy, but even though a dress does count for very little beside my pieces of stuff, I simply must give that Germaine a bit of my tongue for sweeping the floor with her dress. My principles demand it. If only she could walk properly. Why is it that a woman like me can never take things calmly?'

For many a year, Madame Lysiane had waited for the dawning of love. Men had never made any great appeal to her. Not until she was forty did she feel any fancy for a fellow with hardened muscles. But at the very moment when happiness was within her grasp, she was seized with a deep-rooted jealousy which she could not impart to anybody. Nobody would have understood it. She loved Robert. She became randy at the thought of him. Thinking of his hair, the nape of his neck, his loins, her breasts hardened; stood out at the thought of coming into contact with the image she evoked, and all through the day, in feverishly happy anticipation of desires that were never out of her thoughts, Madame Lysiane prepared herself for her nights of love. Her man! Robert! He was her man. Her one and only true love. If these two brothers were in love with each other, did they really make love? Like queers, then. Queers were despicable. To make mention of their name in her brothel would be comparable to calling out that of Satan in the choir of a cathedral. She despised them. None of them ever came to her place. It was certainly true that she did admit clients with peculiar tastes; even though they might smack of homosexuality, tastes that demanded certain practices of her girls which they were not ordinarily accustomed to perform. Since they went upstairs with the girls, then they must like them. They could do as they pleased. But queers, never!

'What am I trying to discover in all this? Robert's not a nance.' The face of her lover, hard and relentless, reflected his mood: a face whose peculiarities became confused with those of the sailor, and quickly enough to make her giddy so that, as the mood changed, Querelle's face became Robert's, and Robert became Querelle, Querelle, Robert: the expression of the face itself never changed; the cold look; the severe mouth; the firm chin; and, on top of all that, an air of complete ignorance of the confusion it never ceased to create.

Querelle did not dare mention Mario's name. He wondered sometimes whether anyone suspected their goings-on. But why should he speak of it? Madame Lysiane didn't seem to know anything about it. After the first time he clapped eyes on her, Querelle never bothered to look at her again. But she, little by little, in her usual possessive way, focused her thoughts on him and cherished him in her innermost heart, emphasizing his every contour, his every movement, and enhancing their fullness and beauty. Rising from the finely-balanced mass of his virility swirled a vaporous mist which enveloped Querelle without his being aware that he was under her spell. He gave a casual glance at the golden locket chain hanging down over her bosom, at the bracelets on her wrists, and, even vaguely, felt that he was basking in opulence. Sometimes he thought, when he saw her in the distance, that the Boss was lucky to have such a fine-looking wife and his brother such a fine-looking mistress: but, as soon as she came close to him, Madame Lysiane became little else than an astonishingly warm and richly productive fountain-head, almost unreal by reason of the magnetic charm she radiated.

'You wouldn't have a light, by any chance, Madame Lysiane?'

'Yes, ducky, I can give you one.'

With a smile, she refused the cigarette offered her by the sailor.

'Why don't you? One never sees you smoke. It's a Craven A.'

'I never smoke down here. I allow my girls to do so because it doesn't do to appear too rigid, but for me – never! Just imagine what would happen if the Madam took to smoking.'

She did not appear shocked. She answered him quite simply, as if expressing an irrefutable fact, which brooked no further discussion. As she brought the match flame closer to his face, she saw that his eyes were fixed on her face. She was a little put out by his look, and without thinking of what she was saying, she came out with the phrase her tongue had tripped over a few moments beforehand, and which had remained stuck to the top of her palate.

'There you are, ducky.'

'Thanks, Madame Lysiane.'

Neither Robert nor Querelle was sufficiently interested in copulation to seek out new ways of performing the act. They simply regarded it as a satisfactory hygienic outlet. Nono regarded his antics with Querelle as the violent, almost swaggering expression of lechery in which he recognized a reflection of his own nature. This matelot, crushed under his weight upon the coverlet, presented a tight-drawn and shaggy arse from the midst of quilted mushrooms of velveteen, on which he performed with him an act akin to convent orgies where, it is said, the nuns are poked by a goat.

It was a huge joke, but one which enabled him to square his shoulders. Nono would remain on his feet facing the dark anus, bushy with hair, freely offered to him on long and heavy brownish thighs rising out of the folds of feet-entangling trousers. He would rip his flies open and, taking out his already erect penis, pull aside his shirt tails to free his testicles so as to appear the complete male. For several seconds he would study himself in this posture, as if he were about to embark upon an adventurous exploit in battle or the hunting field. He knew he was running no risks, for no feelings of sentiment entered into it to spoil the essence of the game. No passion either.

'It smells a bit high,' he would say, or 'it's a nice piece of cake,' or again, 'I must say, it's pretty fetching.'

It was nothing but a game, not to be taken too seriously. Just two stalwart men with a smile on their faces, one of whom – without any fuss or flapdoodle – was offering his bum to the other. 'It's jolly good sport.' And he went on to talk of the fun of hoodwinking girls. 'If they only knew that two pals can get rid of their dirty water together without their help, they'd kick up a hell of a row. No sailor in his senses is likely to let on. He gets too much of a kick from letting me enter the pearly gates. So there's no harm done.'

In the end, Norbert got to the point of having Querelle just for the fun of it. It seemed to him, not so much that the matelot was growing keen on him, as that he really had need of it to go on living. Norbert did not despise him: firstly because he had reason to know that he couldn't carry on his traffic in opium without him, and also on account of his physical strength. He was unable to prevent himself from admiring the youthful, lithe suppleness of the sailor's body, for it had the effect of stiffening his prick. He applied the spittle with his hand before bending over slowly and then, resting his weight on Querelle's back, he inserted his member. Querelle no longer winced from the pain. He simply felt the hard round knob trying to force its way in and then slipping gently right up as far as it would go. Nono kept it there for a few seconds without moving, thereby affording his friend a little respite. Then he began to work it up and down like a piston. It was very restful, very comforting, to feel oneself so deeply possessed and to sense inside one such a sovereign presence. There was little chance of it slipping out. Locked together, they turned over a little on their side and continued. Nono grabbed hold of Querelle under the arms and drew him against his body. The sailor let himself be pulled backwards, pressing heavily against Norbert's chest.

'Not hurting, am I?'

'No, go on as you're going.'

They whispered together - disjointed words, disjointed thoughts, words like nebulous gold-dust breathed out from their half-opened mouths. As Querelle gently agitated his buttocks, so did Norbert more forcefully his loins.

It is an intense sensation to be held fast by a penis, to retain within one's body, and by the penis, a stalwart who cannot free himself except by discharging inside one's fundament. At intervals Querelle was aware of the sudden throb of the solid weapon within him to which his own, tight squeezed in his hand, responded with a similar pulsation. He tossed himself off calmly, in no great haste, determined to relish every thrust and counter-thrust of the huge big-end.

When they had buttoned up their trousers again, they looked at each other with a smile.

'Well, what d'you know! We're a proper couple of cunts, and no mistake!'

'Why cunts? We're doing no harm to nobody.'

'But do you really mean to say you enjoy putting your chopper up my bum?'

'And why the hell not, I'd like to know. It's pretty good. I can't honestly say I go much on you. I'd be a liar if I did. I've never understood one bloke having a crush on another. Mind you, it does happen. I've known cases. Only I'm not much that way.'

'Same here. I let you get up me 'cos I don't care a fuck. It's a bit of a skylark, like. But don't ask me to get sweet on another fellow.'

'Ever tried breaking a bit off with a young 'un?'

'Never. Not my line at all.'

'Not a nice, soft, velvet-arsed boy? Doesn't that say anything to you?'

Querelle, having lowered his head to fasten the buckle of his belt, raised it again and shook it from side to side, pulling a long face.

'So what you like best is to be rooted good and proper.'

'Have it your own way. You were asking what I got out of it, and I'm telling you, it's just a way of having a good skylark.'

Norbert expressed no love for him, yet more and more Querelle felt that something new was coming into his life. Some feeling or other bound him to Nono. Perhaps it had to do with the difference in age between the two. He refused to admit that Nono had the whip-hand because he slipped him a length, though that might account for some part of it perhaps. Besides, nobody can go on playing what he fondly imagines is no more than a sexy game every day of his life and not end up by taking to it.

There was a further contributory factor to this new feeling – or rather this over-all atmosphere of easy connivance – and that lay in the form, gestures, and jewels of Madame Lysiane, in the way she looked at him, and in the very fact that she had addressed him twice on the same night as 'ducky'.

Now it happened that since he had been overwhelmed – in every sense – by the intervention of the police officer, Querelle had ceased to find any enjoyment in his sexual escapades with Norbert. He had submitted on a further occasion purely from habit and almost without thinking, but – and Norbert's now too obvious pleasure had been part cause – he was beginning to detest him. All the same, it seemed impossible to extricate himself entirely from what he had brought upon himself, so he set about wondering how he could secretly slip out of it and, for a start, thought he would get Norbert to pay him. Eventually, owing to the smiles and encouragement of the Madam, he began vaguely to consider another possible justification for it. But he soon dropped the idea: Norbert was not the sort of man to let himself be intimidated. We shall see how Querelle never altogether abandoned this idea, but made use of it rather – indeed it was instrumental – in compassing the downfall of Lieutenant Seblon.

The daily papers still carried the story of Gil – the double murder of Brest – and the police redoubled their search for the murderer whom the press reports built up into a terrifying monster, whose devilish cunning was more than likely to keep the police guessing for some time to come. Gil was beginning to achieve something of the hideous reputation of Gilles de Rais. For the populace of Brest, his elusiveness turned him into the Invisible Man. Could this be entirely due to the fog, or was there some quite other, more supernatural reason?

Querelle never missed a single paper and brought them all along to Gil. The young mason went through strange emotions on seeing his name in the headlines for the first time in his life. It was on the front page. At first sight he thought at one and the same time that the name referred to someone not himself, yet to him alone. He smiled as his face grew red. In his excited state, his smile developed into a long soundless laugh, and this struck him as touching on the macabre. The name printed in bold type was that of a murderer, and the murderer who bore that name was at large in flesh and blood. He was part and parcel of everyday life, side by side with Mussolini and Mr Eden; cheek by jowl with Marlene Dietrich. The papers mentioned a murderer whose name was Gilbert Turko. Gil held the paper at arm's length and turned his eyes away from it that he might relish the image of that name deep down in the recesses of his own conscience. He wanted to become familiar with it, that is to say, to establish as an immediate fact that the name there registered would be read and written for many years to come. To this end, it was necessary to see it again and become letter perfect. Gil made his name – new in the sense that it was now somebody else's name under this novel and irrevocably definitive form – run through the deep night of his memory. He wandered with it into the darkest corners, circuitously winding and unwinding it, turning it this way and that to get the full effect of its myriad scintillations and taking its multi-faceted sparkle into the dim and inmost recesses of his conscience, before setting eyes on the paper once again. Thereupon he experienced a new shock in rediscovering his name so *truly* printed there.

A similar shiver of modest shame gave him goose-flesh, for it seemed to him that he was naked. His name exposed him, exposed him stark naked. It was a fearful glory – and terrible in its shamelessness – to pass through the gates of scorn. Gil had never altogether accustomed himself to his own name. He was not even certain whether it was really a question of one simple murder, or of a double. Gilbert Turko was a character of whom henceforward the papers would always speak. Yet, as each day went by, familiarity began to strip the articles of their magic.

Gil was soon able to read and discuss them dispassionately: they had ceased to be poems.

It became clear that they indicated a danger soon discovered, savoured even, by Gil. Sometimes he enjoyed melting into this danger, thus proving to himself - not only a sharper, almost painful consciousness of being alive, but a sort of forgetfulness, a self-abandon and loss of faith in himself, much as when he used to rub his finger over the indubitably pink flesh of his piles; or again when, squatting as a child by the roadside, he used to trace his name in the dust with his finger and derive a curious delight, no doubt provoked by the soft feel of the dust and by the rounded shape of the letters. There were times when he so far forgot himself as to feel utterly heart-broken, to feel his heart turn over, almost to the extent of wanting to lie down on the top of his name and go to sleep there, despite the passing traffic. Yet all that happened was that he would end by rubbing out the letters and demolish their fragile rampart of dust by gently scattering it with his outspread hands.

'No matter what happens, the beaks will see clearly enough . . .'

'See what? What beaks? This is not the moment to give yourself up! That would be bloody foolish. Firstly, you've already been under cover far too long for them to think you're not guilty. And secondly, you see what the papers say, that one chap you killed was a queer and the other a matelot. There's nothing you can do about that.'

Gil let himself be won over by Querelle's arguments. He was in the mood to be won over. He no longer felt like taking too dangerous a risk, for, after all, he had been saved simply *by staying put*. Some little bit of him was going to remain since his name would remain, being in print, and thus eluding Justice since it was designated by Glory, even though he himself savoured the bitter taste of despair intermixed with that glory. Gil felt that he was lost for ever, since always and everywhere would his name be coupled with the word 'CRIME'.

'I'm going to put you wise and give you the griff. You'll first get hold of some cash and then get yourself over into Spain. Or to America. I'm a matelot, and I'll manage to get you on board a ship. Just you leave that to me.'

Gil was only too happy to entrust himself to Querelle. A sailor by his calling must be well in with all the navies of the world, in closest personal touch with all the secret workings of navigation, indeed with the sea itself. Gil delighted in this idea. He liked to wrap himself up close and warm in anything that brought him consolation, and the more safe he felt inside, the less he wanted to talk about it.

'What have you got to lose? If you steal and get caught on the job, they won't bother to mark it up against you, for what's robbery beside a murder?'

Querelle never brought up the question of the sailor's murder now, so as not to excite Gil's recriminations. This would merely have led to the innate sense of pure justice – common to everyone – rising forcibly to his lips in a torrent of self-justification. Coming to him from the world outside with his mind clear and calm, there was something agonizing in the young mason's attachment. Gil gave himself away by his anxiety, for it betrayed the smallest fluctuation in his character and made him vibrate, in much the same way as does the needle of a gramophone passing over the rough surface of a record and transforming the roughness into waves of musical frequency. Querelle picked up each of these variations and derived pleasure from so doing.

'Supposing I didn't happen to be a matelot . . . but as it is, there's nothing I can do about it. Yes there is though; I'll tell you what . . . I could stop you. But it happens I have complete faith in you.'

Gil listened without saying a word. He was now certain that the sailor would never bring him money, nothing other than a hunk of bread, a tin of sardines, or a packet of fags. He pondered deeply over the idea of the two murders, his head bent, a bitter expression on his lips. Overwhelmed by an immense weight of weariness, he was forced to resign himself to them both and admit both, accepting the fact that from henceforth his life lay along the paths that lead to hell. As far as Querelle was concerned, he felt both furiously angry and at the same time completely confident, and in this strange mixture was involved the fear that Querelle might really shop him.

'As soon as you've got some cash and some decent clobber, you'll be all set up for the journey.'

The adventure appeared very attractive and the murders lent point to it. Thanks to them, Gil would be forced to dress himself smartly, as before he had only done on Sundays. In short, it was going to be Buenos Aires.

'You may be sure I see what you mean. I won't say I wouldn't do a job, bust in somewhere . . . but where . . . have you any idea?'

'At the moment, in Brest, I know of only one dodge and that's a bit of thievery. I know better ways when overseas, but in Brest that's the only line I know about. I'll go take a dicker at the prospects; after, if you like, we might do it together. There's nothing to get worked up about. After all, I'll be with you.'

'Couldn't I do it on my own? Perhaps that would be better.'

'You're in a mess, aren't you? No question of it. I want to string along with you. You don't think I'm going to leave you stuck with the dangerous job all on your own, do you?'

Querelle was in his element after night had fallen. He had learnt to turn to his own account every phase of darkness, to people the shadows with the most dangerous of the monsters dwelling within him. He would then subject them to his will by breathing hard through his nose, so that the darkness was entirely possessed by him, and subject to him. He had got used to living in the repugnant company of his crimes; these he enumerated in a sort of mental register of minute details, a catalogue of massacres, which for his own reference went by the name of 'My bunch of flowers'. This catalogue included a plan of the places where each crime had taken place. These rough sketches were childish, and since Querelle had no idea of how to draw, he used a name instead and sometimes he even mis-spelled the name. He had never been properly taught.

As Gil came out of the prison for the second time (the first time had been for the purpose of going over to Roger's place), he had the impression that the night and the surrounding landscape were posted like sentries at the door and would stretch out a hand to his collar and arrest him. He was frightened. Querelle walked on ahead. They took the lane leading in the direction of the Naval Hospital and so, following the line of the ramparts, they entered the town. Gil dared not admit his funk to Querelle. It was a dark night and that at least was encouraging, because, if the darkness could hide the signs of his fear, it should also be able to dispose of other dangers, such as police interrogation. Querelle felt elated, but was careful to hide his excitement. As usual, he looked straight ahead, his head well protected from the cold by the stiff, turned-up collar of his oilskin coat. They went into the narrow alleyway sandwiched between the prison walls and the esplanade which overlooks Brest, just where the Guépin barracks stand. At the end of the alley lay the town of Brest, and Gil knew it well. A squat house of but a ground floor and one storey was built up against one of the bastions of the old Arsenal, an extension of the prison. A café occupied the ground floor, and the front gave straight on to the alley in which they were. Querelle stopped. He whispered into Gil's ear:

'Here we are. Here's the café. The entrance is right on the street. There's an iron shutter. But you can take up your position on the first floor – I'll explain it all to you – it's not difficult. I'm going in.'

'What about the door?'

'It's not locked, never is. We'll both go into the passage – because there is a passage – then a staircase. You'll go up to the top, but make no noise. I'll go into the ship. If things go wrong – if the boss opens the door at the top of the stairs, down you come, pronto. I'll be making my own getaway at the same time. Make for the hospital. If somebody kicks up a row by the time I'm through, I'll give you the high sign. Got it?'

'You bet!'

Gil had never committed robbery. He was astonished that theft could be at once so difficult and so easy. After a quick look round the street which was filling up with fog, Querelle, without making a sound, opened the door into the passage of the house; Gil followed him. Querelle guided his hand on to the banister. His mouth close to his ear, he whispered, 'Up you go', and, turning aside from the lad, he slipped into the well under the staircase.

When he judged Gil to have reached the top landing, he began to make a series of faint scratching noises to show that he had started operations. Gil listened at the door. In imagination, he heard the jingle of the approaching stagecoach which was to be held up to ransom by a posse of highwaymen, of whom he was one. He heard a pistol shot ring out in the heart of the lonely forest, the creak of a broken axle, imagined young women snatching off their veils, and Marie Taglioni dancing, under the dripping trees, on a carpet spread out for the purpose by the gay desperadoes. Gil cocked his ear. He heard a hissing whistle in the darkness. To him this meant, 'Gil, get out of it!' Slowly he came down, his heart thumping. Querelle quietly shut the door behind them. Safe back in the street they had come along, they made off hastily and in silence. Gil was agog to know the results. At last he whispered:

'All according to plan?'

'Yes, let's get on.'

They retraced their steps through the same patches of mist and fog. As the prison came nearer, so Gil felt a returning sense of security and this helped to calm his desperate anxiety. In their lair inside the prison, by the glimmer of a candle, Querelle pulled out the swag from his pocket. Two thousand, six hundred francs. He gave a half of it to Gil.

'It's nothing to write home about, but mustn't grumble. It's the day's takings.'

'It's not so bad for now. I can get myself quite a way out of the shit with that.'

'You're cock-eyed and no mistake. Where do you think you go to now? You've still to get the proper rig. No, my lad, there's still another job to do.'

'OK, I'm with you. Only this time it's me that's going to do the dirty work. I don't want you getting into trouble on my account.'

'Well, we'll see. Meanwhile, hang on to your boodle.'

The sight of Gil putting the money into his pocket was heart-rending for Querelle. The agony it caused him justified the double-cross he was preparing for Gil. There was little doubt that he would be able to recoup a hundredfold, and in a few days, this little sum, which he had made a pretence of stealing from a house he knew full well to be unoccupied; but all the same, it left a nasty taste in his mouth to see how Gil had swallowed the bait - hook, line, and sinker.

Each day Querelle brought along various articles of clothing. Within three days he had been successful in getting a pair of sailor's trousers, a jumper, oilskins, a singlet, and a navy cap. Roger pressed his nose to each parcel in the approved manner of those looking for suspected opium at the docks. The night came when Querelle sprang the news on Gil.

'It's all fixed. You won't panic, will you? Because if at the last moment you're going to funk it, you must tell me.'

'You can count on me.'

Gil would have to go about Brest in full daylight. The uniform would cloak his personality with invisibility. There was very little chance that the police would guess that the murderer was walking about the town disguised as a sailor.

'You're sure the Lieutenant will be easy game?'

'I tell you, he's a nance. He looks sturdy enough and all that, but if it comes to a show-down, you can count him out.'

Sailor's rig transformed Gil, giving him a strange new personality. He no longer recognized his old self. For his own satisfaction, he dressed himself with great care in the dim light. To make himself 'proper tiddly', he carefully tilted his cap and then pushed it on the back of his head with flirtatious swagger. The beguiling and restless soul of the most elegantly uniformed of the Services entered into him. He became one of the members of the Fighting Navy, whose chief occupation appears to be to decorate rather than to defend the coasts of France. In gay and graceful swags it festoons and ornaments the whole length of coastline from Dunkirk round to Villefranche, caught up here and there into bunches and firmly-gathered knots, which are the naval ports and dockyards. The Navy is a superbly appointed organization, composed of young men who are given a full apprenticeship in the art of how to make themselves attractive. While he was still working in the masons' yard, Gil used to come across sailors in various bars. He brushed against them, never dared to hope that he might become one of their company, but all the while respected them as belonging to such an astonishingly gallant and devil-may-care company. Today, during the hours of darkness, in secret, for himself alone, Gil was one of them.

In the morning, he went out. The fog was lying thick. He set off towards the station. He lowered his head, trying to bury it in the turned-up collar of his oilskin coat. It was highly unlikely that any one of his former workmates would run into him, still less that he would recognize him in his present rig. Shortly before reaching the railway station, he turned down towards the road that led to the Docks. The train was due in at ten minutes past six.

Gil had with him the revolver supplied by Querelle. Should he fire it if the officer called out? He went into a small, single-stall urinal, built into the parapet that overhung the sea. The fog blurred his appearance. If anyone came along, they would see nothing but the back of a sailor in the act of relieving nature. Here he need fear neither gold braid nor patrol. Querelle had planned it perfectly. All that Gil now had to do was to wait for the arrival of the train; the Lieutenant would be sure to pass that way. Would Gil recognize him? In his mind he rehearsed the details of the assault. Suddenly Gil was worried by the thought of whether or no he ought to speak familiarly to the officer. 'Surely I should, to impress him!' But, on the other hand, it might be strange for a rating to speak familiarly with an officer. Gil chose familiarity, but with a slight feeling of regret at not being able, on this the very first morning of putting on uniform and coming out in it, to know all the pleasures and consolations that the habitual wearing of it provides by way of assurance and the resulting abolition of self-consciousness. Gil waited, his hands thrust into the pockets of his oilskins. The fog moistened and froze his face, cramping his wish to be brutal. Querelle must still be asleep in his hammock.

Gil heard the train whistle, clatter over the iron bridge, and stop in the station. A few minutes later, an occasional silhouette of women and children passed in front of him. His heart thumped.

The Lieutenant was coming through the fog, and alone. Gil came out of the urinal, the revolver in his lowered hand. When he drew level, he greeted him with:

'Keep your trap shut. Hand over the portfolio or I fire!'

It suddenly dawned on the Lieutenant that he was being given an opportunity of doing something heroic, but at the same time he realized with regret that there could be no witness of such an act who could tell the story to his crew and above all to Querelle. Then he came to see the futility of such a deed and, further, his own dishonour if he did not bring it off; he also realized from the tone of voice, the expression in the eyes, in all the pale agitated beauty of his aggressor, clutching his revolver, that such recourse was out of the question.

(Whatever happened, the sailor would make off with the money.) He hoped for the intervention of a passer-by, but he did not really believe this possible, and he even feared it. All these thoughts came to him in a single flash. He said,

'Don't shoot!'

Could he overwhelm the sailor with a mass of clever talk, tie him down with arguments and little by little gain his goodwill? He was disturbed by the youth and audacity of this young fellow.

'Don't move. Don't make a sound. Hand over the doings!'

In the midst of his fears, Gil was very calm. Fear had given him the courage to speak sharply, brutally. It had made him quick-witted enough to realize that by using short sentences there was no chance of being tangled up in an argument.

The Lieutenant made no movement.

'The cash, or I'll plug you in the belly!'

'Go ahead, fire.'

Gil fired, hitting him in the shoulder, hoping this would make him uncover and drop the portfolio. The crack of the shot made a fearful reverberation in the little illuminated funk-hole where their figures were all too conspicuous in the surrounding fog. As Gil put out his left hand to grab hold of the leather strap of the portfolio and pull it towards him, he pressed the muzzle of the revolver close against the Lieutenant's eye.

'Let go or I'll blow your brains out!'

The Lieutenant let go of the handle and Gil, recoiling slightly, turned round quickly and made off at full tilt. He disappeared into the fog. A quarter of an hour later he was back in his hide-out. The police never suspected him. They instituted identification parades among the naval crews without discovering a clue.

Not for a single moment had Querelle suffered a qualm of anxiety.

As Querelle became a figure of ever greater importance, with sadness in his heart Roger watched Gil drifting away from him. No longer on his arrival did Gil put his arms round his shoulders. He simply shook his hand. Roger felt that everything was taking place on a level above and beyond his age. Without actually hating him, he was jealous of Querelle. He was glad to have enjoyed his own small importance in such a serious adventure. At last, of his own accord, he detached himself from Gil on account of his increasing infatuation with the double beauty of the two brothers. He was trapped in a sort of complicated network of emotion, where the sight of the faces of both Querelle and Robert became necessary to fill his cup to the brim. He lived in the fervent hope of a fresh miracle which would put him in instant touch with the young men, and cause them severally and together to return the love and devotion he bore them.

Every evening he went miles out of his way for the express purpose of passing by 'La Féria', which had assumed for him, to all intents and purposes, the semblance of a shrine ever since the day when he went to see Gil at work and heard one of the masons say, 'I'm off to Mass in the BAG Street Chapel.'

Roger recalled the mason's gusty guffaw, as with huge whitened hand and sharp regular movements he plunged his trowel into a hod filled with mortar and stirred it. He had never bothered his head about the nature of the cult that could make a buck-navvy look so impious and uncouth. Roger knew something of the reputation and the appearance of the brothel, but today 'La Féria' excited him because it was the holy resting-place of his twin divinity (this two-headed monster that caused him such misgivings without his being able to give it a proper name), the inaccessible object that smothered his small soul with devastating charms, to which no doubt the masons went to pay their homage, not with flowers in their hands, but filled with fear and hope. Roger further remembered how at this sally (he did not guess the implication which lay far behind the simple joke) one of the masons had shrugged his shoulders. At first Roger had been astonished that a joke about brothels had made a laughing-stock of a workman standing with his shirt open right down to his belt over a large hairy chest, the hairs on his head stiff and covered with chalk and dust, his arms hard, chalk-powdered, sunburnt; a workman in fact who was definitely a he-man. Today the shrug of the shoulders that greeted both the wisecrack and the accompanying laughter was a sure if disturbing confirmation that a secret cult did indeed exist. It introduced the element of doubt and incredulity, which always accompanies religious beliefs in the heart of a would-be votary.

Roger came to visit Gil every day. He brought him bread, butter, and cheese, which he had bought far away in a dairy in the St Martin area where he was not known. Daily Gil became more demanding. Tasting the power of money, he became a bully. The fortune which he kept hidden close at hand gave him authority enough to tyrannize Roger. In the end, he had accustomed himself to the life of a recluse, had settled down into it, and little by little found that he could move about there with assurance. The day after his assault on the Lieutenant, he tried to find out from Roger what the papers were saying. Not being able to confess to his part in it, or in turn extract anything from him, put Gil into a rage with Roger. Then he began to feel that the lad was drifting further and further away from him.

'I've got to be going.'

'Bit of a hurry, aren't you? Looks like you're going to leave me to get on with it!'

'*Me* leave you in the lurch, Gil! I come here every day. Only my old lady puts up a moan when I come in late. It wouldn't help us much if she stopped me going out of the house.'

'That's a lot of bunk. Can't you get what I'm driving at? Tomorrow make sure you bring me a litre of red wine. Understand?'

'Yes, I'll try to.'

'I didn't say "try". I said bring me a litre of red wine.'

Roger did not take it to heart too much when he was spoken to so harshly. Like the fetid atmosphere of the hide-out, Gil's bad temper increased day by day, but Roger barely noticed the gradual worsening of either. Had he still been under his spell, no doubt he would have been sensitive enough to notice the change in Gil's voice and inflexions, but he came along every evening regularly, as though in obedience to a sort of ritual, while forgetful of its deeply emotional and compelling appeal. In trying to free himself from the burden of his forced term of labour, he centred his thoughts on the double image of Robert and Querelle. He lived in the hope of meeting both the brothers together.

'I've seen Jo. He said not to worry. He said everything's going along all right. He'll be coming to see you in a day or so.'

'Where did you see him?'

'He was coming out of La Féria.'

'What the hell were you doing fucking about in La Féria?'

'I wasn't inside, I was just passing.'

'You certainly were not just passing! It's not on your way home. You weren't trying to get off with one of "the boys" by any chance? La Féria's not for little shrimps like you.'

'I tell you, Gil, I was only passing.'

'Tell us another!'

It dawned on Gil that he was no longer the be-all and end-all for the kid who, once outside the prison orbit, led a life in which he himself had no part. He was in constant fear that this life might prove of greater fascination than his own. In any case, being no longer preoccupied with Gil, Roger could move about in safety and take part in carousals from which he felt himself to be excluded in the heart of the brothel, where the two brothers came and went from one room to another, looking for each other: rooms that he imagined were poorly furnished and of a size far different from what they were in reality, an opinion based solely on the dilapidated exterior. There they would go looking for each other, suddenly find each other (and their meeting would give rise to a command), only to separate again and lose one another, and then again start hunting for each other among the goings and comings of girls dressed in veils and lace.

He dared to imagine the two brothers smiling at him and holding him by the hands. They had exactly the same sort of smile. They would each take him by his arm and spare him a few moments of their time. At home, Roger could not discuss the two brothers, he could not mention thieves and pimps. If he so much as said a word to his sister, she would have repeated it to his mother. His anxious infatuation, however, had such a hold on him that at every turn he risked giving himself away. Besides, he talked about them with an innocent guilelessness. One day he happened to invoke them out loud, 'The Gallant Pair of Chevaliers!'

He could not imagine himself even in his dreams participating in their many adventures. He conjured up a picture of himself offering them both he did not quite know what, but certainly the most precious thing he had to offer. He even had the fanciful idea of sloughing off from his body an exact replica of himself and sending it as a sort of delegate to Jo and Robert, to find out whether they would accept the friendship offered them by his real and essential self, who had remained outside the room in which they were.

Querelle came back one evening when he supposed Roger would not be about.

'Now the time's come. All's set. I've got you a ticket to Bordeaux. The only thing is you'll have to get on the train at Quimper.'

'But the togs? I'll still need some kit!'

'You'll certainly find some in Quimper. You won't be able to buy anything here. You've got your loot and with that you can get yourself out of the shit. That hold-up brought you five thousand francs. That's surely enough to be going on with.'

'I've been more than lucky to have you helping me, you know, Jo!'

'No doubt about it. But now you'll have to keep your eyes wide open not to be picked up. And, what's more, I reckon I can count on you not to spill the beans about me if you get caught.'

'No need to worry on that score, Jo. I can look after myself and the cops won't ever hear a word about you, rest assured on that. Why, I don't even know you. So I'm to get going tonight, is that it?'

'Yes, you must be on your way. It gripes me a lot to see you clear off like this. I don't mind saying, young Gil-me-lad, I've taken a great fancy to you.'

'Same here, I've taken to you too. But we'll see each other again, I'll not forget you.'

'You say that, but it won't be long before you chuck me overboard, I bet.'

'No, pal. Don't say that. That's not my way of thinking at all.'

'D'you mean it? You won't forget me?'

While he was saying this, he put his hand on Gil's shoulder. Gil looked into his eyes before replying,

'Not on your life, I won't.'

Querelle smiled and lovingly put his arm round Gil's neck.

'It's funny the way we've become pals, isn't it?'

'We were pals from the start.'

They stood face to face, looking straight into each other's eyes.

'Here's hoping nothing goes wrong for you.'

Querelle pulled Gil close against his shoulder, without meeting any resistance.

'Good luck to you, whatever happens, you bloody little waster!'

He kissed him, and Gil returned the kiss, but Querelle did not relax his firm embrace. Holding him tight, he whispered,

'It's a shame.'

In a corresponding whisper, Gil said,

'What's a shame?'

'What? Oh, I don't know. I said "It's a shame", but I don't know why I said it. It's a shame I have to lose you.'

'But you're not losing me, you know. We'll soon be seeing each other again. I'll send you word of what happens - you can join me when you've finished your time in the Navy.'

'Will you really remember me?'

'I give you my word, Jo. You're my pal for life!'

These confidences were whispered, and in syllables ever more and more indistinct. Querelle felt that he was entering upon a deep and lasting friendship. He let his whole body sag voluptuously against the unresisting Gil. Again he kissed him and again Gil returned the kiss.

'We're necking like a couple of sweethearts.'

Gil smiled. Querelle continued to kiss him with greater and greater intensity and most cunningly, giving him quick little pecks as he brought his lips ever closer to his ear, which he finally covered with one long kiss. Then he put his cheek against his friend's cheek. Gil hugged him close in his arms.

'Get on with you, you young bastard. I like you a lot, you know.'

Querelle imprisoned Gil's head in his arm and redoubled his caresses. He pressed against him more yearningly than ever, entwining his legs about Gil's.

'We really are pals, aren't we?'

'Yes, Jo. You're my real pal.'

They remained a long time locked together, Querelle stroking Gil's hair and repeatedly giving him passionate kisses.

At last Querelle found himself near to ejaculating. The tenser his excitement, the more he wanted to maintain it and increase his emotion still further. He wanted Gil, he wanted to have him.

'You're a proper winger to me, you know.'

'How d'you mean?'

'You let yourself be gum-sucked like that without squealing or saying a word.'

'Well, what if I do? I've already told you you're my real pal. There's no one to stop us carrying on like this, is there?'

In gratitude, Querelle gave him a sharp and violent kiss on the ear, and then brought his mouth down in line with Gil's. When he reached it, lips pressed against lips, he murmured in one breath: 'You swear you don't mind what I do?'

In a whisper, Gil answered: 'No.'

Their mouths became glued together and their tongues touched.

'Gil!'

'What?'

'You'll have to be my proper mate - for always - got it?'

'Yes.'

'Will you?'

'Yes.'

Querelle knew his friendship for Gil came close to bordering on love. He felt the same kind of feeling of endearment for him as might an elder brother. What is more, like him, Gil had committed murder. It was as if he were a minor Querelle, one who must never be allowed to grow up, to go further, and, looking at him, Querelle experienced a peculiar feeling of respect and curiosity, almost as if he had been brought face to face with an embryo Querelle.

He longed to go to the full length in love-making, for he genuinely believed that his fond feelings would gain strength from it, because it would link him still more closely with Gil and thereby he would be as close as possible to him. But he did not know exactly how to go about it. Having always been made love to, he did not know how to start the ball rolling and bugger the lad. The physical act would have embarrassed him. He thought of asking Gil to guide his penis up his bum. He remembered having had such feelings of endearment for the Armenian pederast; but if, on the spur of the moment, in his ignorance, Querelle had imagined that Joachim had wished to pounce him, today he realized that the queer, both by his tell-tale voice and gestures, had desired fundamentally the opposite. Then again, so far as Nono was concerned, he had never felt any such longing. Nono could go and blow his brains out, he'd be fucked if he cared. Dimly he came to see that love must be a voluntary act. You must want to do it. When you're not properly homosexual, it may give you a certain pleasure to have it done to you, but to do it yourself you must love a man, if only for the actual moment of penetration. In order to love Gil, he would have to get rid of his passiveness. He set to work with a will.

'My little pal . . .'

He let the hand on Gil's shoulder slide down till it reached his quivering buttocks. Querelle squeezed them with his broad and powerful hand. He took possession of them with an immediate and unquestionable authority. Then he slipped his fingers between his trouser-belt and shirt. He loved Gil. He forced himself to love him.

'Isn't it a shame that we can't stop together – just the two of us, all the time?'

'Yes, but we'll see each other again.'

There was a trace of anxiety – even anguish – in Gil's voice.

'I'd like nothing better than to live like this all the time, just the two of us, as we are now . . .'

The vision of utter solitude in which their love could grow increased his affection for Gil to the point where he felt that he could do everything for him, be his only friend, his only relation. He took Gil's arm and forced his hand to touch his penis. Gil stroked it under the trousering and himself unbuttoned the flap. He fondled the stiff penis, so that it became stiffer than before. For the first time in Querelle's life, a man was feeling him. He crushed his mouth against Gil's ear, Gil responded with a similar kiss.

'I've never in my life before loved one of the lads. You're the very first, you know.'

'D'you mean that?'

'Honest!'

Gil squeezed the throbbing penis all the harder till Querelle whispered softly,

'Give us a suck!'

For a moment Gil did not move; then slowly he lowered his mouth. His lips parted and he sucked Querelle while he remained in front of him, four-square on his feet, running his hands through Gil's hair as he bent down in front of him.

'Suck it hard.'

With both hands he pulled Gil's head away from his penis and held it close to his thigh. He would not let himself go to the full length of his pleasure. He pressed his cheek against his friend's head.

'I go the bundle on you – I do love you, you know.'

'Me too.'

When the time came for them to part, Querelle had become honestly and genuinely in love with Gil.

Querelle placed absolute confidence in his guiding star. This star owed its existence to the trust the sailor put in it. It was, if you like, as if his confidence in his absolute trust sent out a beam that swept the skies till it reached to his star. Then for the star to preserve its size and splendour, its full power, Querelle had to preserve his trust in it – that is to say his trust in himself, above all he had to preserve his smile, so that not even the most elusive cloud should slip between him and his star, that its beam should lose nothing of its intensity, that the most shadowy of doubts should not dim its brilliance. He hung suspended from it as he recreated it at every second of his life. In this way it afforded him effective protection. Fear of seeing it snuffed out made his blood run cold. Querelle lived in continual suspense. Since he was for ever concerned with keeping his star alive, he was obliged to execute each action with exquisite precision, which would never have obtained had he led a softer life. For of what use would it have been? For ever on the alert, he was quick to anticipate any difficulty and choose the surest means of avoiding it. It was only when he was exhausted (if he ever were) that he faltered. The certainty that he did indeed possess a star arose from a complex of circumstances (one could refer to it as a stroke of good luck) all the more hazardous for being as multi-faceted as a rose-window of such inspired design that one is tempted to look for a metaphysical explanation.

Long before he joined the Navy, Querelle had heard the ballad called 'Star of Love'.

Every sailor has a star,
That protects him from afar,
While he holds it with his eyes,
No ill-luck can him surprise.

On evenings when the dockers went on the booze, they would pick on one of their number with a good voice to sing for them. The lad would take his time in being persuaded, wait for a drink or two to be poured out for him, and then, rising to his feet in the midst of the crowd of toughs with their elbows on the tables, give voice through irregular teeth to the dreamy sentiments they loved so well.

Nina, of all the stars so bright,
You are the one I choose tonight,
Though all unknown to you to be
My Star to all Eternity.

Thereafter a bloody drama would be unfolded in the encircling gloom, the sad tale of the wreck of a brightly-lighted ship, symbolizing the foundering of love. Dockers, fishermen, and matelots were vociferous in their applause. Standing with one elbow on the bar and his legs crossed, Querelle had no eyes for them. He did not envy them their muscles or their pleasures. He did not even wish to become like them. There is little doubt that he joined up as the result of falling a victim to a poster, but the real cause lay in the sudden revelation of an easy life. 'Join the Navy and see the World'. We shall have more to say later on the subject of posters.

The scene is Beirut. Querelle and another matelot had just emerged from 'The Bugle'. Neither had a sou left in his pocket. They were dressed in the white linen rig that sailors wear in summer – a dress each rating trims to his own satisfaction, knowing exactly which parts of the body to bring into prominence or cover suggestively with some loose floating riband or other. White cap, white shoes.

The evening was unusually mild. The two matelots were walking along in silence and had just reached the brothel when a man of thirty or so crossed their bows. He looked them over closely, paying marked attention to Querelle. Then he went on past them, but at a slower speed.

'What's he want?'

Querelle turned round. His astonishing indifference, his utter lack – not of real warmth, but of sympathetic understanding – were due to his ignorance of what the world calls vice. He really did believe that this man had recognized him, or thought he had.

'Him? He's a queer. There's no mistaking his sort.'

Jonas knew what he was talking about. He was not as handsome as Querelle: a fact that never dawned on the latter, who had no idea of the devastating effect he had on men.

'These customers always have an eye open for a pick-up, far more often than we do, the cunts,' he said, as he slackened his pace.

'Yes, but we're not looking for that. So there you are.'

'Oh, I'm not saying that you have to go along with them; but blokes like him . . . why, they're tarts, not men at all. I'd draw him off one, just for the fun of it.'

Jonas had dropped his voice on this last phrase: for one thing, to achieve a sterner tone (for this would strengthen him in his virility, put paid to the queer, add a bit to his weight, range him alongside Querelle, and save the day for the Navy); and finally, as a precaution, for out of the corner of his eye he had observed the man turn about to retrace his steps towards them. For the next few moments Jonas did not speak. He walked along in the knowledge or belief that 'he was sold', moving with a greater self-assurance and sense of virility (the muscles of his thighs and buttocks stretching his white ducks); but, by working himself up to an artificial indignation, his hackles really did begin to rise, patent throughout his body. It is remarkable how, of all the emotions, anger and fear have the power of visibly affecting every member of the body at one and the same time, so that the lips and calf-muscles are seen to tremble; anger even causes the tips of fingers and toes to tingle with animosity.

He went on to say, with almost a quaver in his voice:

'Chaps like that can go and take a running jump at themselves for all I fucking well care. I'd rather give them a sock on the jaw. What about you?' and he looked at Querelle.

'Me? Same goes for me. I'm with you every time. Too bloody true, I am. But we can't give him a boot up the arse out here. Too many people about.'

Gaining confidence from this, and certain that his pal was with him all the way, Jonas once again lowered his voice.

'Let's make him think we're game.'

He broke off sharp: the stroller was following slowly behind them. Both hands stuck deep in his trouser pockets, Jonas did his utmost to stretch his white ducks tight across his stomach to give emphatic prominence to what, from the little he already knew of the queers' parlance, went by the name of 'a packet' – his private parts. Querelle was smiling. The stroller had turned in passing to give them a very cursory quiz.

'He's swallowed the fly, now we'll have to find out which of us he's after. There'll be nothing doing if we stick together. The best will be for one to stay behind and for the other to follow on after. What d'you think?'

'Yes, I reckon that'll be best. You stay here. All this is a bit new to me. I've never tackled a job like this before.'

'Right you are then. I'm not much of a hand at it myself, mind you, but I'll have a go. I'll try and edge him off towards the waterfront. You tag along without being spotted, got it? Just as we pull alongside him, you make as if you've got to cut along back.'

'Suits me.'

They put on a turn of speed. As they came within earshot of the fellow, each held out a hand, and Querelle said in a ringing voice:

'Till tomorrow then. I'll have to be getting back on board. Think yourself quids in to have all night leave. So long, me old cocky.'

He stepped off the pavement there and then, and with long, swinging strides made off across the street.

Jonas pulled out a cigarette from his pocket while he walked slowly away. Putting heart and soul into the game, he set about making himself 'tiddly', adjusting the drape of his trousers so that the bottoms fell correctly over his white canvas shoes. Querelle's last sentence had allowed him perfect freedom of action and, in a flash, this enhanced his natural ease and grace of movement as he became drawn irresistibly into a sartorial fandango. It was perfectly normal that his unconsciously graceful gestures should be the unpremeditated result of becoming absorbed in this fiesta, and equally normal that this fiesta should have been especially desired by the matelot to give him the opportunity of abandoning himself to such delectable play with the folds of his trousers; of embarking upon this, the most beautiful and evocative of all physical overtures, the boasted pride of the Navy; of entering into the self-communion essential to these personal preparations - the very essence of the sailor - and all the more bewildering when they become subtly involved with the deepening shadows of star-heralded nightfall. He was executing an elaborate *pas seul*. He was dancing before Herod. Behind him he was aware of the gold-dust glances of a tyrant already under his spell and revelling in his miraculously protracted movements, as they became ever more nonchalant, for nonchalance is the pretext for this dance, and its essence.

When the man drew level with him, both simultaneously turned their heads; each had a cigarette out, but whereas Jonas already sported his between his lips, the man kept his modestly in his hand.

'Excuse me . . . Oh, you've not got a . . .'

Jonas smiled.

'No, I haven't a light. Hold on a tick, I may still have a match tucked away somewhere deep down . . .'

He went through all the pretence of delving into the very bottom of his pockets and from one of them he fished out a match. Politely he first held the light to the stroller's cigarette. He saw him to be an essentially delicate fellow with a very white face, made to look longer than it was by two deeply-incised lines on either side of the mouth. He was dressed in a natty fawn suit of tropical silk. As he took the first pull at his cigarette, he never took his eyes off the sailor's bare neck. Jonas was more interested in the weight than the age of the queer.

'Sailors are never caught napping! That's a way we have in the Navy - we always rise to the occasion.'

'Surely it stands to reason that those who sail the seven seas can seldom be caught short - for "caught short" is the right expression, I believe - and it is exactly that which gives them their dazzling charm. You understand, of course, that I dare to say this only about a French sailorman.'

He made a slight inclination of the head in salutation to Jonas. He had spoken in a thin, reedy voice, in trepidation at his presumption in speaking to a sailor so portentously alive - standing in flesh and blood before him - and deigning to lend an ear to all that he was saying.

'Oh, hell! We bods just have to . . . have to find the right answer to everything. There are times when we're at sea for weeks and weeks and never see a soul.'

All of a sudden it dawned on Jonas that he was having to deal with a very prim and proper type, and that he might scare the life out of him by using rough and ready words to express thoughts that were too bawdy. The stranger flapped the gloves he was carrying with a finicky little gesture:

'Weeks on end? By all the powers above! What incomparable nobility, to face the infinite alone! Far from home, far from all affection!'

His voice had become stronger; apart from that, he still kept his dulcet tones to give expression to feeble and artificial little fatuities. It would not have been surprising had this creature turned into a tissue-paper kite with a tail of frilled curling-papers attached to a thread loosely tied round his neck by a hook stuck into his mouth, or had he simply been whisked off up into the air by one of the stars in this myriad-star-twinkling dusk. Without a trace of a smile, he walked along beside Jonas who was still occupied in attending to the folds of his trousers.

'Affection, my foot! That's far too posh!'

'Posh? What do you mean by that? Is it slang?'

'Yes, it's slang - good Parisian slang at that. Why do you ask? Aren't you . . . French?'

'I am Armenian. But I am so thoroughly French at heart. For me, France is Corneille and the divine Verlaine. I was educated at a Marist Mission School. Now I'm in business. I sell soft drinks . . . fizzy lemonade.'

Feeling suddenly freed from oppression, now that the nature of its weight was explained by the fact that he had feared the queer really might have been French, Jonas relaxed. Not that he would have had the slightest scruple if this had really been the case.

The Armenian touched him on the arm, or rather on the stiff linen fold at the bend of his elbow, and even more softly - almost trembling at his own audacity - he said:

'Come along! What are you afraid of? I'm not going to eat you!'

He sniggered, hesitating over the last phrase all of a sudden, and, as he withdrew his benumbed hand, ablaze with glittering sparklers, his whole body shook as if he were shivering with laughter.

Having peered round to see whether Querelle were following, he had seen no one behind them. Since the two matelots had parted from each other in such haste, he had been terrified that they might have concocted some dirty trick against him. Much the same breath of fear, though prompted by a different cause, ran through Jonas as he stood stock still, legs wide apart and hands in pockets, certain that he had adopted the proper attitude.

'Oh, I'm not worried about being adrift, but I can't, that's all. I'm not afraid of the risk. I'm a sailor out on the spree; I mean no harm to anyone. When it takes me to have a bit of fun, I don't have a care in the world. I've an open mind, I have. I'm wise to everything.'

'Oh, how right you are, my dear friend. In this world it's most important to have big ideas. I myself am mercifully free from all preconceived ideas. I adore only beauty.'

'On board I go by the name of "Slaps"; that's to say that I do as I like. Live and let live, that's me! The chief thing is never to tread on other people's corns.'

'I like to hear such sentiments, especially when they are spoken by such a lovely voice as yours.'

He took hold of the sailor's arm and tugged it, exerting every ounce of his feeble nervous energy in the effort, almost to the extent of hurting Jonas.

'You really must come back with me and have a nice liqueur. A French sailorman cannot refuse. Come on, my very dear friend, do come along.'

His features had by this time taken on a far graver expression, and his despairing anguish and longing welled up into his great dark eyes. He persisted still further and added, but in a lower key:

'You're so astonishingly understanding. And then . . .' (his words stuck in his throat and his Adam's apple bobbed up and down as if he were swallowing) '. . . and then you say you don't mind what you do as long as you're happy. I should be so pleased if you would come back to my place for a little while.'

'There's no need to go indoors. We could go for a stroll.'

'But, O my friend, you'll be all on your own at home.'

'We could go down to the waterfront. We could find a spot where there's no one about.'

And off he started on his own for a few steps, after throwing away the stub of his cigarette. The Armenian began to hurry after him.

'My room is so seductive. I should so much like it to harbour a memory of your visit.'

Jonas burst out laughing. He looked at the queer and said in friendly tones:

'You have got it bad, I must say. That's nothing but a declaration of love.'

'Oh, oh! You really . . . oh, goodness, gracious, I do feel embarrassed . . . but don't mind that, don't get upset . . . I've taken a great fancy to you, no doubt . . .'

'All right, all right, I'm not taking it the wrong way. I don't get chokker over a little thing like that . . . why should I? There's no harm in it that I can see. Only I can't, and that's that. There's nothing to be done about it. I can't go back with you, but we could easily go for a stroll. It's a fine evening. We could go down to the beach or to the Public Gardens. We'll be all on our own there and can do what we please.'

'Oh, I couldn't, I couldn't. Someone I know might see me there.'

'And doesn't that go the same for your place, if not more so?'

They were arguing in a vicious circle. The sailor's insistence on going down to the shore greatly worried the Armenian who began to impose his stronger will on Jonas and edged their steps towards the centre of the town. Jonas felt his temper rising. He was fully aware of the almost invincible resistance offered by this little whipper-snapper, who was smouldering with mistrust. He had long known that queers are often prone to defend themselves to the death; and if he went back with this one, he wouldn't trust himself to be responsible for his actions. He thought for a moment. Then he remembered that they often have the nerve to call in the police. He cursed his luck in failing to make the queer go his way, and he feared Querelle's sarcasm. 'He's in two minds about something and must have the jitters.'

It was not possible for Jonas to know that the Armenian had really wanted Querelle and that his regret at seeing him part from his pal had only whetted his desires. He would content himself by going with this other sailor, naturally, but he was in the process of developing a whole mass of minor points of resistance against him that he would never have suspected and which he could not control. Like so many queers, he had a deep-rooted, instinctive fear of being left alone too long with anyone physically stronger than himself. To have gone down to the beach could only have accentuated this weakness still further, for that boisterous element is on the side of the sailor. At home he had had installed an easily-accessible alarm system. And further still, for him there was true poetry to be found in a room decorated with flowers, dark frames encrusted with mother-of-pearl, rugs, ribbons, purple cushions, and shaded lights. He longed to go on his knees in front of this sailor, stripped of all his clothes, and pour forth honied words. These many motives all derived from the one cause of which Jonas was ignorant, that the queer hankered after Querelle and wearily, drearily, hoped that if he let Jonas go, he might somehow find Querelle again. Finally, to all these alarums and excursions one further fear was added; for the stronger his emotional feeling for a lad, the greater his fear of him, and now that he was deeply stirred by Querelle, all the misgivings he might have had on his account were vested in Jonas.

'Well, what's to do?'

'Come back with me.'

'Cut it out, I've had enough. I'm off. So long. We part pals, eh? We'll see each other again, perhaps, one of these days.'

They were standing in a well-lighted and fairly frequented thoroughfare. Jonas seized the hand of the terrified Armenian, grabbed it suddenly - almost brutally - before he made off with a sturdy, rolling gait and a broad expanse of shoulder, to disappear from sight, while the rhythm of his receding steps sounded all the heavier and more ominous the greater the distance he put between himself and the despairing queer, whose heart thumped louder at each diminishing footfall. Jonas did not find his mate again that night. But ten minutes after this scene of farewell, just as the Armenian was turning the corner before reaching his house, he ran slap up against the lofty, striking, white figure of Querelle.

'Oh, my!' he was unable to prevent himself exclaiming. Querelle grinned.

'What's up? Did I put the fear of God into you? I'm not so terrible.'

'Oh, you're so terribly dazzling.'

Querelle broadened his grin. In a flash he felt absolutely convinced that Jonas had got nowhere with this character, without exactly being able to guess what had taken place between them.

'You . . . you shine so bright. For me your face is a beacon of light.'

Grinning ironically, Querelle let out a low whistle, into which he put such natural friendliness and familiarity that the Armenian smiled in his turn. No sooner had he left Jonas than he had got into a regular rage with himself for having allowed a prize so well and truly captured, and so handsome withal, to slip through his fingers. His feelings of rage and despair at having failed to pick up the sailor, whom he had coveted and lost in an evening peopled with silent figures, were now mixed with the breath-taking joy of finding him again, and this induced such a rare paroxysm of audacity that it had the effect of increasing the sailor's grin and polite amusement still further.

'You certainly know how to lay it on thick!'

It did not take the Armenian very long to persuade Querelle to come back home with him. He went through all the mummery he had performed for Jonas' benefit, but he made it shorter, sweeter, and more succinct. He was in the seventh heaven. He threw discretion to the winds, almost to the extent of ridding his thoughts of the persistent and disquieting question as to how this sailor, who had said in his hearing that he was going back on board, had been found again miles from the port.

No sooner was he back in his room than he lighted a joss-stick. Querelle was lost in admiration of this lavishly upholstered, cosily effeminate interior, and thought it sumptuous. He felt lulled by the unaccustomed softness. The cushions were downy, the carpets thick, and the flowers out of this world. The dark wood of the furniture and picture-frames embodied the very essence of repose. He felt crushed under such a superfluity of softness and experienced something of the peace that comes to drowning men. He let his thoughts go wool-gathering.

'You're at home here. You are the lord of all you survey. I am yours to command.'

'Command' Querelle found unsettling, but even this word only added to the general sensation of becoming submerged. Thoughts came to him in disjointed words - for there even seemed to be words floating here and there in a vague, musical background - under the influence of the contorted shapes of the strange exotic flowers, ever suggestively changing and being woven into extenuated garlands or melodies, of which the burden - rising almost to the pitch of anguish at moments of anticipated unease and falling again as any future eventuality became acceptable - was finally resolved into: 'Come what may, I must never let myself go as far as being buggered.' For to Querelle a queer was simply a chap who wants to roger another chap.

Since so much unmitigated hatred - the sort he had witnessed on all sides without having a drop of it in his own veins - was poured on the heads of the fellows whom sailors refer to among themselves as 'brown-hatters', it must be because they wish to treat the sailor they went with as a girl, even though they themselves looked and acted like females. If not - and if the reverse was the case - what reason could there be to hate them so ferociously? Querelle held this candid opinion, which can so easily be mistaken for the purity of innocence. But any anxieties he might have had were short-lived and had little effect beyond making him feel a trifle uneasy. 'We'll soon see,' he thought.

Seated impassively among the pile of cushions, taking long puffs at his cigarette, he watched the Armenian becoming wilder and more abandoned in his actions as the longed-for moment approached. Querelle watched him prink and preen and powder himself, and then, with nervous twitches of his ravishingly small and well-manicured hands, prepare to serve a pink liqueur in the tiniest of coffee cups - such hands as he was later to admire on the Lieutenant of his ship. 'It's a regular skylark. If queers are really like this, I'm quids in.'

'I am called Joachim. And thou, my starry beauty?'

'Me?'

He had been caught napping. All his senses were soothed by that delicious softness that he would one day experience again when, on the naval jetty, Lieutenant Seblon - under the compulsion of the charming weight of his heavy white breasts - was to lean over him thinking: 'My lovely alabaster globes!' These alabaster globes were pendulous and heavy. The officer was certain they were pale, milkyfull moons, pulpy yet firm, and swollen out with the milk he knew beyond doubt would nourish Querelle, who at that moment was beginning to raise his head.

'Yes, thou?'

'My name is Querelle. Matelot . . .'

He went no further, knowing full well that he had blundered. For a second or two he hovered on the brink of an abyss, then took the decisive plunge and said: 'Querelle.'

'Oh, what a beautiful name!'

'Yes, Querelle. Able-Bodied Seaman Georges Querelle.'

The Armenian was on his knees before him among all the cushions. His pale pink kimono, embroidered with gold and silver birds, was unfastened over a perfectly white and smooth body and legs. In his semi-stupor, Querelle saw this strange apparition advancing upon him with all the sudden enormity of things in a dream, and, as it loomed closer, taking on the semblance of a ravening she-wolf, striving to stare so fixedly at her intended prey as to become identified with it. So curious was it that Querelle had to smile. The Armenian's mouth was being raised closer and closer to his own. Querelle bent his head down to meet it half way, having made up his mind to sail straight ahead into the first kiss he had ever had from a man. A momentary giddiness came over him. He was now determined to go to all lengths in this room dedicated to what in reality he was so little alive to, so little awake to. Though smiling, he was deadly serious. The most fitting expression is that he felt as at peace in this room as in his mother's womb. He felt warm.

'Thy smile is as a star.'

Querelle's smile broadened, his white teeth sparkled. Joachim's antics did not worry him in the least, nor did the sight of his white skin – this only happened later on discovering that his skin was powdered and scented all over – but he was shaken by the look of agonized supplication fixed on him from beneath long, curved, fluttering eyelashes.

'Oh! Like stars are thy teeth!'

Joachim let his hand slide as high as the sailor's testicles. He began to stroke them as he murmured,

'These treasures, these jewels . . .'

Fiercely Querelle crushed his lips against the Armenian's mouth. He hugged him very tight in his powerful arms.

'Thou art a star immense and thy light will for ever brighten my life. Thou art a golden star! Protect me for ever . . .'

Querelle strangled him. He smiled grimly as he watched life ebbing under the pressure of his clenched fingers, watched the queer die with mouth agape, tongue lolling, eyes goggling: not a very different picture, he reckoned, from what he must look like at the crisis of his own solitary pleasures. A miraculous wave broke over the silence of his ears. The world was humming. The sea murmuring.

It is the Star of love . . .
. . . every sailor has his star,
That protects him from afar,
While he holds it with his eyes,
No ill-luck can him surprise.

The lights in the Armenian's eyes were suddenly extinguished: they went glassy. At once all singing ceased. Querelle paid strict attention to death and to the significance of sudden change in all things. A little queer was something very soft. It died gently. Nothing got broken in the process.

In order to pay proper respect to the dead by the traditional use of ceremonious ritual, arising in this case from the necessity of disguising the face and nature of the crime – to cover his tracks and falsify the scent, much in the same way as the umbrella that was left open seemingly to protect from the sun's rays the body of the young girl done to death in a hayfield – and the need of putting the finishing false touches to the murdered man with the aid of some object or other, so arranged that it would appear to have held life 'suspended', Querelle, inspired by the ecstatic expression on his victim's face, pushed aside his clothes and placed the lifeless hands in a position suggestive of a self-induced climax. A smile played over his lips. Queers offer a delicate neck to the headsman. One can almost say, as will later be verified, that the victim becomes his own executioner. The eternal chronic anxiety that trembles so querulously in the voice of all queers, even the most arrogant, is in a sense an unconsciously tender appeal to the terrible hands of the assassin. Querelle caught sight of his face in the mirror and it was superbly handsome. He smiled at his reflection, at this double of a murderer dressed in white with a touch of blue, and of black in the silk tied under his collar. He took all the money he could lay hands on and calmly left the room. In the dark shadows of the staircase, he brushed against the figure of a woman.

The following day, the whole ship's company of *Le Vengeur* was paraded on deck. Two young men who had seen Joachim with Jonas the evening before tried to identify the sailor. They picked out Jonas, who for the next six months defended himself in a Court of Inquiry; fought, battled, and struggled violently, despairingly, ruefully to solve the mystery of a black-veiled woman who at first light had passed a French sailor on the stairs of an Armenian gentleman with whom he himself had been seen strolling not so many hours before in the street. And this Armenian had been strangled at the very same time when Jonas was on his way back to the *Vengeur*. Out of deference to a country under French Mandate, and also by reason of the rebellious attitude of the accused, the naval court condemned Jonas to death. He was executed. Querelle's star was in the ascendant.

He left Beirut loaded with spoils. First and foremost was the knowledge of his lucky star and of all the wonderful names the Armenian had bestowed upon him, as well as of the assurance that, hanging between his legs, he possessed a further treasure. The murder had been easy: and inevitable, since Querelle had given his proper name. It was all in the scheme of things that Jonas, one of his best pals, should be put to death. This sacrifice accorded Querelle the absolute right to dispose of, in whatever way he liked and without a twinge of remorse, the whole of the little fortune in Syrian pounds and coin of all realms unearthed from every hole and corner in Joachim's room. It had certainly been acquired at a high premium. And then, as a final contention, if this were a typical queer - a creature so crushable, soft and delicate, a thing so fragile, light and airy, so clear and transparent, a being so melodiously gifted with tender, honey-sweet words - then one was almost justified in killing it since it was made to be killed, in the same way as Venetian glass simply cries out to feel the weight of the fist of a horny-handed warrior who will smash it to smithereens without so much as a scratch being inflicted, unless by some mischance a sharp and glittering splinter insidiously, hypocritically, slits the skin and lodges deep within the flesh. If it was a queer, it was certainly not a man, and nowhere near a man's weight. It was something in the nature of a kitten, a fawn, a goldfinch, a blind-worm, or a dragonfly; something so provocatively and precisely exaggerated in its fragility that it must inevitably invite death. And, what is more, it went by the name of Joachim.

The police seized upon Gil Turko just as he was about to board the Nantes train from the blind side. They had been warned by a ring from a call-box in the station that an individual corresponding - though clearly in disguise - to the description of the murderer of both the sailor and the mason, was attempting to clamber on to the train. It was Dédé who had made the call. The Inspectors found only a few coins on Gil. They took him under escort to the Police Station where they questioned him as to his whereabouts between the date of the second murder and that of his arrest. The young man answered that he had been sleeping here, there, and everywhere, in the docks and out under the ramparts. Querelle suffered pangs of sorrow when he learnt from the papers of Gil's arrest and subsequent transfer to Rennes gaol.

The action of this book must be speeded up. It becomes important to strip the narrative down to the bare bones. Notes and jottings, however, are not sufficient, and for the following reasons. If the reader is 'astounded' - and we use this word rather than 'moved' or 'indignant', since we wish this novel to be demonstratively logical - that Querelle should have suffered a pang of sorrow on reading of the arrest that he had himself provoked on the previous evening, then it stands to reason that he will require more light to be shed on the psychological events that led up to this particular event.

He killed to steal. Once the murder was accomplished, theft became, not justified - one would rather think of hazarding the conjecture that the murder could be said to be justified by the theft - but sanctified. It would appear that it was quite by chance that Querelle came to be aware of some moral strength to be gained from a theft embellished, and absolved, by a crime. If the act of thieving, while temporarily invested with splendour and pulse-quickening, loses a part of its outward significance, sometimes to the extent of being overlaid by the pomp and circumstance of the murder - and, even further, that though not being utterly consumed, it continues to sully the pure act of killing by a noisome breath of corruption - it must of necessity strengthen the willpower of the criminal when the victim is his friend. The dangers he ran - his head at stake - would already have sufficed to give him a sense of self-justification, against which precious few arguments could prevail. But the ties of friendship between him and his victim, who becomes thereby an extension of the murderer's personality, provokes a magical phenomenon best described in the following words:

'I've just run all the risks of an adventure in which one part of myself - that is, my affection for the victim - was called into play. I know how to enter into a pact - non-formulated - with the Devil, to whom I vow, not my soul nor my right arm, but something far more precious, my friend. This friend's death sanctifies my theft. It is not so much a question of any elaborate formality - all the more because in tears, mourning, death, and blood, quite apart from their outward trappings, there exist reasons stronger than those in the penal code – as a question of an act of real magic, by which I become the authentic owner of whatever it is that has been *willingly* exchanged for my friend: willingly because my victim in so far as he is my friend was in some mysterious way – proof positive being the sorrow I feel – flesh of my flesh and blood of my blood; the leaves, as it were, at the extremity of my branches.'

Querelle knew that nobody, unless he committed a sacrilege, which he himself would know how to prevent with the full force of his might, would ever succeed in taking these stolen goods from him, since his accomplice (and friend) whom he had betrayed to the cops to save his own skin, had been condemned to five years' solitary confinement with hard labour. It can hardly be said that Querelle was grieved to find himself the real possessor of the stolen goods; it is fairer to say that he sustained a nobler sentiment – entirely devoid of sentimental affection – a sort of manly devotion to a wounded comrade. Not that our hero conceived of the idea of committing the booty to the charge of his accomplice; it was to preserve him intact from the clutches of man's justice.

On the occasion of each new theft, therefore, Querelle felt compelled to insure himself by establishing a mystical link between himself and the stolen goods. The spoils of battle took on a special significance. Querelle transmogrified his friends into bracelets, necklaces, gold watches, and earrings. If he succeeded in turning a feeling – friendship – into cash, then it was something altogether beyond the judgment of any man alive. The transmutation was his concern and his alone. Whosoever tried to make him 'disgorge' would be held guilty of body-snatching.

We claim the aforesaid thought-processes to be correct in the given circumstances. They are not indeed those of an exceptionally complicated personality, but are universal. With this exception; that Querelle, who further required to make full use of every resource, was forced to draw constantly on the resources of his own contradictions.

When Dédé had recounted the full story of the bust-up between the two brothers, laying special and malicious emphasis on the insults hurled at Querelle by Robert, Mario at once experienced a feeling of immense deliverance, from what, he could not immediately put into words. It developed along the following lines. The vestige of a suspicion drifted into his mind that Querelle must have had a hand in the murder of the matelot Vic: a suspicion, at the time, vague enough to do no more than enlighten the police officer and bring him some comfort. He already had the feeling that in this one single as yet undefined idea lay the hopes of his salvation. Little by little, and as if eschewing all thoughts for his own safety, he pieced together an effective relationship between the murder and what he thought he knew of homosexuals. If it were really true that Nono had put him through it, then Querelle must be 'on the game'. It would therefore be quite in keeping for him to be mixed up in the assassination of the rating. No matter whether Mario's reasonings were false or not, there is relatively little doubt that they enabled him to attain to the truth. Musing upon Querelle and the crime, from the very start he was worried by the idea – accepted as correct at Police Headquarters but impossible for him to refute since he refused to discuss it openly for fear of giving himself away – that Gil was guilty of both murders. From there he quickly launched out into a further daring and precise speculation, as yet no more than guesswork. Finally he applied himself deliberately to the tricky business of hypothetical reasoning.

Mario could easily suppose Querelle gone on Vic, and stabbing him in an access of jealousy: or Vic gone on Querelle, and wanting to kill him. The whole of one day he pondered over these speculations, not one of which could be verified, yet step by step he became convinced of Querelle's guilt. He recalled the pallor of his face despite the sea-tan – so pale and so closely resembling Robert's – a resemblance that provoked a charming confusion, a delicious jumble of thoughts which were very far from being to Querelle's advantage.

It so happened that one evening out on the ramparts Mario had experienced very much the same uneasiness as had Madame Lysiane on seeing the two of them together. He was careful to take stock of and memorize every feature, so that he was able to recompose Robert's face with some ease in his mind's eye. And so absorbed did he become in the process that this face gradually came to take the place of his own. For several minutes he had remained motionless, under cover of the branches and their dark shadows. It was a struggle between the substance before his eyes and the shadow in his mind. He puckered his brows. He wrinkled his forehead. Querelle's face, set and firm before him, confused the image he held of Robert's. The two faces became interchangeable, interrelated, mutually at enmity, and finally identifiable. That evening it was impossible to differentiate between them; not even Querelle's smile, beside which his brother's was a pale reflection, was of any avail. (His smile spread a moving curtain over his whole body, a fine-meshed trembling veil with shadowed folds, and enhanced the freshness of his alert and supple, carefree body, while Robert's melancholy was due to his passionate self-interest, and, instead of casting a shadow over him, it made him glow like a hearth with no direct radiance, but if anything damped down by the fact that his slow-moving and well-controlled body was all but immobile.) The spell suddenly broke. The police officer was left on the horns of a heart-rending dilemma. Which of the two can it be? he thought. But there was little doubt left in his mind that the author of the crime was Querelle. He wondered where his thoughts were leading him.

He refused to let himself be misled by the resemblance between the two brothers that had brought him to such a pretty pass. As far as Querelle was concerned, his rather crafty opinion might have given rise to some such expression as, 'You're trying to reshuffle the cards, my lad, but that won't work with me.' Out of hand he rejected this complicated network that no police cunning could disentangle, a network which after all had not been woven expressly that he, Mario, should become involved in it and attempt to unravel it. In short, it was no concern of his.

All the same, he said to Querelle:

'You're a queer customer.'

'Why do you say that?'

'Oh, no reason - just for something to say.'

If, as we have said, Mario experienced a feeling of deliverance, it was because he had 'seen' all of a sudden the possibility of a reward, supposing the sailor were guilty. Without knowing the reason for it, and therefore unable to put it into words, he saw that he must never breathe a word of his discovery. He swore himself to a secret vow of silence. If he protected the murderer by becoming an accessory after the fact of his own free will, it was possible that this would prove sufficient atonement for his betrayal of Tony. Not that he especially went in mortal dread of vengeance from his old pal and the rest of the dockers of Brest; but rather that he feared the scorn of those around him. If we don't dare to speak of police psychology, we can at least try to show how it is that their 'culture' - the development and use they make of the reactions of the general public - may affect and influence their technique and result in that astonishing creation, 'the cop', the epitome of bluff heartiness.

Among his many characteristic tricks and foibles, Mario had a preference for twisting his heavy gold signet ring round and round on his middle finger. It was set with a large stone with such sharp edges that it slightly bruised the contiguous fingers of his beringed hand. This mannerism was especially noticeable when he sat at his desk and grilled a docker or warehouse pilferer. At Police Headquarters he shared with a colleague, Marcellin Daugas, an office where each had a desk of his own. Mario took great pride in his appearance, and there could be no doubt that his taste was excellent. He liked to look smart and well turned out, laying particular emphasis on the severe cut of his uniform and the natty way in which he wore it. This exactly fitted the stern set of features, which he took pains to cultivate, along with the assured and sparing use of gesture. To be the official occupier of an office gave him an indubitably superior authority in the eyes of the delinquents who came up for interrogation. Sometimes he would leave the room in a state of apparent disorder, just as one has no qualms about quitting something one knows to be perfectly secure. He would get up to go and consult one of the numerous files. This added still further to his importance and authority and was proof that he was in possession of the secrets of thousands of his fellow-beings.

Immediately on leaving the building he would assume a mask; it would never do for people in cafés or elsewhere to suspect that they were hob-nobbing with a police officer. What's more, it was behind this mask, the wearing of which presupposed a face to support it, that Mario recomposed to his own satisfaction his policeman's 'mask'. For hours on end he had to play the part of a man who was to discover all that he can about the little weaknesses of his fellow-men, their inmost secrets, for the slightest indication of these had power to condemn the least suspicious among them to the most fearful punishment. It would be an act of madness were he to descend from such sublime heights to listening behind doors or peeping through keyholes. He never showed a specific curiosity about a man's habits, nor ever went as far as to commit an indiscretion; but once he had detected the slightest suspicion or taint of evil, he had to follow it up, rather like a child with a heap of soap-suds who, with the end of a straw, chooses from among the frothy, evanescent conglomeration one that he can expand into an iridescent bubble. It was at that point that Mario began to feel exquisitely cheerful as he advanced from discovery to discovery, conscious of the crime swelling and swelling almost under the power of his own breath till it broke away from him and floated off by itself up into the air.

No doubt he sometimes told himself that his way of performing his duty was both useful and perfectly moral. For over a year Dédé had been an exponent of the double principle of pilfering and denouncing the pilferers to the police. There was something a little more than strange in this attitude, for in order to encourage the kid's propensities as an informer, Mario had to keep on repeating to him, 'You're very useful, don't you see. You're helping *us* to round up the bad lots.'

The lad never seemed to worry, and this argument touched his pride only by reason of the mention of the word 'us', which gave him to understand that he was participating in an adventure of vast dimensions. It became perfectly natural for him to go thieving with the bad lots and then split on them.

'Does the name Gil Turko say anything to you?'

'Yes. I don't say we were pally, but I knew him.'

'Where's he to be found?'

'Haven't the foggiest.'

'Come off it . . .'

'Honest, Mario. I know nothing of him. I'd say if I did.'

Even before he acted under police orders, the lad had made investigations of his own that had led to nothing. Without exactly putting the proper construction on Gil's amorous passes at Roger, he had at least a pretty shrewd idea of the real meaning behind their smiles and their frequent meetings, though Roger's ingenuous responses lent him a spontaneity usually denied to what is known as a practised aptitude.

'It's up to you to find out where he is.'

It did little to allay Mario's anxiety that he had somehow guessed that the general scorn attaching to his name – he seemed to feel the spray of its first breakers, as we have already observed – might well be increased once he knew the name of the murderer and that his dead body might become the repository of his secret.

'I'll have another try, but I've got the idea he's quit Brest.'

'Nothing's known about that. If he's flitted, he can't have got very far. The police have been warned. What you've got to do is to keep your mince-pies on the simmer and your far and nears open to pick up what you can on the qt.'

Dédé was really shocked to hear these slang expressions and looked hard at the police officer. Mario was blushing furiously. No sooner were the words out of his mouth than he realized that it was unworthy of him to have used terms that might be eminently suitable for the exchange of certain practical ideas, but whose real beauty lay above all in the almost instantaneous transmission from speaker to listener of the otherwise indecisive communications within a close-bound fraternity. They were enigmatic – not in form or content – but by reason of their sheer indecency, their monstrous decency, the contrary essences that constitute the life blood of this language. It was sacrilege for Mario, who was no longer in a state of grace, to have taken upon himself to speak this language, and it gave rise to the scandalous uncertainty that Dédé could now no longer know what he meant when he made use of such ridiculously flowery phrases. For him Mario was no longer simply a member of the police force, but something less than a policeman in that he had no direct contrary, that is to say the direct contrary against which, as a policeman, he was opposed. He could be one only in outward appearance by being opposed to the world he fought against. Inasmuch as he was the policeman, Mario recognized in himself the presence of the delinquent, that is, of the criminal, or at any rate of the corner-boy he might so well have been instead of a policeman; but his betrayal of Tony had cut him off from the criminal world by forbidding him all traffic with it, so that he had to remain in blank ignorance of it as a superficial judge and could no longer circulate among its members or regard them as a sympathetic element capable of being worked upon by him. The love that every artist owes to the material he works in was now denied him by his material. There was nothing for him to do but wait in suspense. At the present time he was apt to connect, in the dawning light of the presentiment of his own salvation, the appeasement of the dockers with the clear proof of Querelle's guilt.

During the day he would joke with his comrades, to whom he never so much as hinted at the dangers that beset him. Almost every evening he would meet Querelle somewhere along the railway embankment above the deep cutting before the track runs into the station. Failing to see that the discovery of the cigarette lighter near Vic's dead body could be explained if Querelle was guilty of the murder and now in league with Gil, Mario never thought to question him on the subject. Querelle passed along this way when returning from the convict-prison. He had had no special liking for the policeman, but habit accustomed him to these meetings, strengthened by the feeling that he held him at his mercy. Above all he regarded himself as protected: he felt the roots growing.

One dark night, he murmured,

'If you caught me red-handed on the job, would you jug me?'

The expression, 'You could have knocked him down with a feather,' if taken literally, can hardly be said to be true, yet the state of fragility to which it reduces the person who provokes its use compels us to use it. 'You could have knocked Mario down with a feather.'

In a devil-may-care spirit, he answered,

'And why not? I should simply be doing my duty.'

'Would it be your duty to put me inside? That's not funny, you know!'

'All right then. And if you murdered someone, it would be the same. I should send you straight to the guillotine.'

'Ah!'

As soon as he was on his feet again, after an intercourse to which neither he nor Mario would have dared to give the name of love, Querelle once more became a man confronting another man. The vestige of a smile played over his lips as he buttoned up his trousers and fastened behind his back the thong he used as a belt; he wanted what he had just been doing to be treated as a joke. Since this scene took place at the time when his affair with the Madam was in its early stages, Querelle was not far from suspecting some form of conspiracy, for he was incapable of disentangling the various intrigues that embroiled him with Nono, Mario, and his brother. He went in mortal terror. The next evening he gave Gil the order to clear out.

As soon as he entered the prison-house, he methodically went through all the motions he had foreseen the night before as indispensable for his future safety and the first was to take his revolver away from Gil.

He set about this in a crafty way, by asking,

'You've still got the gun?'

'Why yes. It's over there, well hidden.'

'Let's have a look at it.'

'Why? What's up?'

Gil did not dare ask whether the hour had come to make use of it, but feared this might be so. Querelle had spoken in such quiet tones. He was having to advance with all possible care for fear of arousing Gil's suspicions. We might almost say that he was playing his part like a great actor. In withholding the real reasons behind his request, yet making it impossible for Gil to refuse, to hesitate even, he had not said, 'Give me the gun', but 'Show it to me! I'll explain . . .' Gil was watching Querelle, gazing at him, both of them carried away by the subdued tones of their voices, tones rendered still softer by the sadness of the surrounding gloom. Their increasingly tender sadness among the shadows plunged them both, naked and scorched, into the same healing waters. Querelle felt real friendship, amounting to love, for Gil; and Gil reciprocated these feelings.

We do not wish to suggest that Gil *already* suspected the nature of the climax towards which Querelle was leading him, the sacrificial and necessary end, our function being to discover what is general in any given phenomenon. To refer to it as a presentiment would be equally misleading. Not because we do not believe in presentiments, but because a study of their origins demands a restriction foreign to a work of art, which has to be free and untrammelled.

There comes to mind an execrable piece of literature written round a picture purporting to represent the Infant Jesus: 'In His eyes and smile can be observed already the despair and agony of the Crucifixion.' All the same, to arrive at the real truth of the relationship between Gil and Querelle, the reader must allow us to make use of the detestable literary commonplace which we so heartily condemn and to say that Gil quite suddenly had a presentiment of Querelle's treachery and of his own immolation. This catchpenny trick not merely enables us to establish more speedily and efficiently the rôles of our two heroes - that of redeemer and redeemed respectively - but it affords us also an opportunity of making further discoveries at the same time as the reader.

Gil made a movement which to some extent freed him from the numbing, cloying tenderness that bound him to his murderer. (This is the place to say that feelings other than hate can, under the eyes of a dismayed and scandalized public, enable a father to address friendly words to his son's murderer and calmly question the man who witnessed the last moments of someone whom he adored.) Gil withdrew into the deeper shadows, and Querelle quite naturally followed him there.

'Have you got it?'

Gil raised his head. He was squatting down, looking for the weapon under a heap of coil rope.

'Eh?'

Then he gave an almost icy laugh.

'I've got it all right,' he added.

'Let's see it!'

Gently Querelle asked for it and gently took hold of it. He believed he was saved. Gil had stood up.

'What are you going to do?'

Querelle hesitated. He turned his back on Gil and went over to the corner where the latter usually took up his position. Finally he said,

'You'll have to quit. Things are getting a bit too hot.'

'No kiddin'?'

Fortunately this participle ending required no glottal stop to emphasize the final guttural, for Gil would not have found it possible to force another consonant from his throat. Terror of the Guillotine, so long repressed, was the cause of this phenomenon, which made every drop of his blood flow back into his heart.

'Too true, they're on your tracks. But don't get the wind up. And what's more, don't run away with the idea that I'll leave you in the lurch.'

Gil strove to understand, vaguely and without determining what ultimate purpose would be served by it, when he noticed that Querelle was putting the revolver away in the pocket of his oilskins. It crossed his mind that treachery of some sort was afoot: at the same time he felt profoundly relieved at being deprived of a weapon that he might so easily be provoked to use, and so be encouraged to further crime. Holding out his hand, he said:

'You're not leaving it with me, then?'

'Now get this straight. I'll explain. Listen. I don't say they'll get you pronto, I'm sure they won't, but you can't be too sure. Far safer to go unarmed.'

Querelle's reasoning was as follows. If Gil fired at the cops, the cops would shoot back. They would either hit him or fluff their shot. If they arrested him, they'd soon find out from the inquest - from Gil himself if he were wounded - that the revolver belonged to Lieutenant Seblon, who must inevitably accuse his steward of its theft. In our desire to give the fullest possible explanation of the psychological ambience of our hero, we cannot help but lay bare our own soul. Please be liberal in your judgment of the attitude we choose to adopt - in view, or rather in *prevision* of any desired end - in that it may lead us to discover the given psychological world which upholds the liberty of choice; but, if it becomes necessary, in the course of deepening the intrigue, for one of our heroes to voice his real opinion, please reflect that we should at once be faced with the dilemma - arbitrary, no doubt - that this character might escape the clutches of his author. He would thereby single himself out. In that case we should have to admit that one component factor would be revealed - after the event - by the author. In Querelle's case, if an explanation is really required, let us hazard one no more detestable or more feasible than any other. It would run as follows. In his almost complete lack of sensibility - conforming to his almost complete lack of imagination - he must inevitably form a bad opinion of the officer who - witness his diary - would far and away have preferred himself to be denounced than to denounce Querelle. According to an entry in Lieutenant Seblon's private notebook, he longed for Querelle to be accused by him of murder, and we shall see the sublime use he made of this consuming desire.

Gil felt that he was going crazy. He could make neither head nor tail of his friend's intentions. He heard himself saying,

'Stark naked, then. I'm to go stark naked!'

Querelle had just laid claim to every stitch of naval apparel lying about. Not one single vestige must remain of anything that might give him away to police.

'You won't go off stark naked, eh! Cut it out!'

Gil was on the point of mutinying, driven to such an extremity by Querelle's quiet and aloof behaviour, and this last particularly wounding expression was almost too much for him to bear. Querelle was admirably aware that, by daring to treat with such scorn the man who could still bring about his downfall, he would prove himself still master of the situation. With consummate skill and cheek, he drove home his advantage, playing a ruthless game by raising the stakes till the most venial mistake would have cost either player his life. Sniffing - the word is apposite - success in this discovery of his, he pushed home his point up to the hilt:

'You're not going to make me shit now, are you, and start to get tough? Your job is to listen to what I'm telling you.'

But by speaking in this way and in this tone of voice, he was courting disaster (a dawning light in Gil's eyes was proof that he had almost reached breaking-point), so he applied himself with greater discernment, with clearer vision and quickened wits, to the thousand and one minor details necessary to ensure his own salvation, by compassing Gil's death and thereby his silence. Alert, quick, already the victor, he tempered his aloofness and scorn, which were capable of cracking - if not upsetting - the balance now weighted in his favour, or at least promising to afford him complete freedom.

(Querelle, let us note, very clearly discerned the mechanism by which he would eventually achieve success, since he was, and knew himself to be, at the very heart of liberty of choice; and therefore he tempered his aloofness and scorn with a touch of good-natured chaff.)

Smiling out of the corner of his mouth, as it were, to make himself believe that in this way he could indicate to Gil the irony, if not the importance, of the whole situation, he said: 'So what, then? A chap like you is never going to give the show away. No kidding, you must listen to me. Get that, eh?'

He put a hand on Gil's shoulder. He was now speaking to him as if he were ill or about to die, and of things that concerned his soul rather than his body.

'You must get into an empty compartment. First hide all your money. Put it under the seat or between the cushions. Don't keep much on you, you understand. Mustn't have too much cash on you.'

'What about my clobber?'

Gil had thought of saying, 'Are you letting me go like this?', but he feared that such a trite remark might only rib Querelle – and this showed that already he felt slightly abashed in the light of their sentimental attachment and the too intimate lengths to which it had gone. He said: 'I must get a change of outfit.'

'No need. Don't give it a thought. The clots have no idea how you're dressed.'

Querelle continued in much the same vein, at once tender and over-riding. Good luck for the future – a sort of affection, in a sense a malady born of high blood-pressure induced by the excitement – still further demanded a more precise turn of events. With his hand on Gil's shoulder, Querelle gave vent to these words, 'Don't lose your head. We'll bring off something else together yet.'

He was referring to their thefts, and Gil understood him in this sense, but the emotions he was going through – let us here put it down to the secret and double meaning imparted by this sort of children's talk, which both gave Gil his instructions and threw his thoughts into a delicious confusion, hovering as he was between being a lover and being an accomplice. For Gil it was the Revelation. We shall call attention to but one error, and it is precisely the one that survivors fall into when they urge courage and hope upon those about to die. Delicately tactful, asking Gil not to betray him if perchance he were caught by the police, Querelle said:

'That won't help you at all, can't you see? Whatever happens, you won't be running any risks.'

From the very bosom of his innocence, Gil asked, 'Why?'

'Why? Because you're already under sentence of death.'

Gil felt his stomach empty, tie itself in knots, fold up, and then be filled again with the whole round ball of the earth. He leaned for support against Querelle, who hugged him tight to his body.

Let us here record that up to the present time Gil had never said a word to the police about Querelle. Before it was decided to send him to Rennes, Mario had contrived to be present at every one of his interrogations. He was more than a little afraid that Gil might mention Querelle's name. If he was certain in his mind that the young mason had committed the one crime, he knew him to be innocent of the other. No sooner was he arrested than he suppressed all memory of Querelle, and, if no thought of him ever entered his head, it was because no one ever suggested Querelle's name to him. Let us not labour the point, the reader will understand readily enough why it was that neither Gil nor the police (other than Mario) could ever perceive the link between the sailor's murder and the more earth-bound existence of a mason's murderer.

Mario's position in this matter becomes stranger and stranger. In order to assign to him his proper, if not definitive significance, we must have recourse to the conventions of the novel. Dédé was – or certainly believed himself to be – in touch with all the little sentimental intrigues and attachments among the youths of Brest. The better to serve – Mario no doubt, and above and beyond him the Police, but above all to *serve* – he became an expert (and this seems to have originated in his physical and moral ability and in his quickness of eye) in speedily summing up the value of his observations. Before he began to feel any qualms of conscience – and of anxiety, let us add – Dédé had become a wonderful machine for registering events. Let us forget for the moment his admiration for Robert. The assignment given him by Mario, that of keeping Querelle under observation, had the profound effect of opening up to him a new, sympathetic relationship between the various corner-boys run in by the police officer and the officer himself. Dédé never plucked up the courage to remind Robert of the pitched battle between the two brothers that he had witnessed. He thought he had found out that Roger was Gil's boy-friend, yet he never thought to

watch his movements or follow him. One day he said to Mario:
'That little Roger was pally with Turko.'
About the same time, Gil said to Querelle, who paid no attention to it, 'I think sometimes, if I was arrested, that perhaps I could get round Mario.'
'Why?'
'What's that? Oh, sometimes . . .'
'Why?'
'You never know, he's a queer. He's pally with Dédé.'

Such a reflection gives rise to a prevalent supposition. No sooner is he arrested than the adolescent thinks to make use of this factor, that is homosexuality. Since we have made mention of the public reaction – something quite outside our own – let us attempt a rapid and controversial explanation. Is the boy ready and willing to give what is most precious to him, or does danger make him yield to his most secret desires? Does he hope to appease fate by this immolation? Is he suddenly aware of some all-powerful fraternity of pederasts and does he put his faith in it? Does he believe in the power of love? We could no doubt learn enough by following Gil's thoughts, but for this we have not the time; nor the inclination. This book has already occupied too many pages and is beginning to become a bore. Let us simply record the young prisoners' profound hope when they learn that their judge is queer.

'Who is this Dédé?'
'Dédé? Oh, you must have seen him often enough with Mario. He's quite a young chap. He's often with him. You never can tell. He's not a nance by any chance, eh?'
'What's he look like?'
Gil described him.
When he met him one evening on the point of leaving Mario, who was on his way to meet him, Querelle felt an old wound re-open. He recognized the lad as the witness of his bust-up with Robert and as his chief rival for Mario's favours. All the same, he held out his hand to him. Querelle thought he saw something rather shifty in his voice, his smile and his general attitude. Soon after the boy had left them, Querelle asked with a smile:
'Who's the kid? Is he your bit?'
With a smile in his voice and almost derisively, Mario answered:
'Why worry your head about that? He's one of them, yes. You're

not jealous by any chance?'

Querelle grinned and had the audacity to say:

'What d'you suppose? Why the hell not?'

'Get on with you.'

In distressed, broken tones, the officer added, 'Give us a gam!' Querelle was seized with such furious passion that he kissed Mario in anger, desperately, full on the mouth. With far rougher fervour than usual – and far greater precision – he insisted upon relishing to the full the deepest possible penetration of the cop's prick to the very back of his throat. Mario was conscious of the despair behind this insistence. To the overall fluctuating terror that the sailor was so beside himself that he might at any moment bite off his penis with one champ of his jaws, the officer further added a continuous flow of erotic ejaculations interspersed with a highly damaging confession, which came out in a series of raucous groans or prayers. Certain that his lover was enjoying being on his knees before an officer of the law, Mario gave vent to his ignominious confidences. With clenched teeth and face reaching out to meet the fog, he hissed:

'Yes, I'm a cop! I'm a shit! I've been with a number of fellows! They're all in the jug now! That's how I like things to be, you know! That's my job . . .'

The deeper his abject wallowing in the mire, the tauter and more hard became his muscles and the more strongly he imposed on Querelle his presence . . . and its imperious, dominating, invincible and beneficial might. When they were once again on their feet, face to face, adjusting their dress, turned back into men, neither dared to make mention of their transports of delirium, but in order to clear the air of the uncertainty that was tending to isolate the pair of them, Querelle grinned and said:

'Come to think of it, you never told me if that lad is your winger.'

'You really want to know what he is?'

Querelle was suddenly frightened. Casually, he said:

'Sure I do.'

'He's my nark.'

'You're kidding!'

Now they could settle down and talk business. Keeping their voices low, but enunciating their words clearly so as not to allow the strange and shameful nature of the conversation to worry them, they reached a point where Querelle declared: 'I can put you on the right road to arrest Turko.'

Mario never batted an eyelid.

'Oh, yes!' he said.

'If you give me your word never to bring my name into it.'

Mario gave his oath. Already he had thrown precaution to the winds and forgotten his mystic reconciliation with the corner-boys: *it was impossible for him not to act as a policeman first and foremost.* He determined not to question Querelle about the sources of his information or their worth. That gave him confidence. Between them they speedily decided on the best plan for keeping Querelle's name out of the whole business.

'You'll have to put your boy wise as to what he's got to do. But he must ask no questions.'

One hour later, Mario instructed Dédé to keep a close watch on all out-going trains and to get in touch with Police Headquarters as soon as he caught sight of Turko. The kid raised no objection. He betrayed Gil. By this action Dédé was put at one remove above his fellows. From that time on, he began to rise in importance, as has already been explained.

On board *Le Vengeur*, Querelle continued to carry out his duties as officer's steward, but his master affected to disdain him, and Querelle suffered in consequence. From having been the pretext of an aggression, the Lieutenant derived sufficient pride to foster the idea of adventure growing within him. From his private diary we cull the following extract:

'*I am in no sense inferior to this marvellous young fellow. I resisted his advances. I offered myself to be killed.*'

In order to recompense Dédé for having been the instrument of Gil's arrest, the Police Commissioner entrusted him with special, almost official, assignments. He was chosen to track down the young fellows, the soldiers and sailors, who stole from the counters of the Monoprix. And so it came about that while going up on the moving staircase, he put on his yellow gloves and felt that he was really 'mounting'. He was now a police agent. Everything carried him away, transported him. He was sure of himself. On reaching the summit of his apotheosis, the room where his career was about to begin, he once more had the feeling of having 'arrived'. He was wearing his gloves; the ground was secure under his feet; Dédé was master of his domain, free to behave as he wished, handsomely or squalidly.

A career in the Army or the Navy offers, to those who are incapable of finding a life of adventure for themselves, a cut-and-dried, fully-developed methodical life, finally endorsed by the thin red ribbon of the Légion d'Honneur. Now, in the very middle of his official adventure, the Lieutenant had just been singled out for another, far graver one. Not that he went so far as to regard himself as a hero! But he experienced the strange feeling of being in direct personal contact with the most despised, the most degrading and the most noble of social activities, that of armed robbery. He had just been found bound and gagged in an out-of-the-way street.

The thief had a charming face. Enchanting as it was to have been the object of the theft, how much more marvellous to have been the thief himself! The Lieutenant made not the slightest effort to suppress any of the mass of fantasies that jostled one another so deliciously among his day-dreams. He felt certain that nothing of this secret history, between himself when face to face with the thief, would come to light. 'Nothing of it can ever transpire', were his actual thoughts. He was secure behind the severity of his outward appearance. 'He ravished me! He is my ravisher! He emerges from the thick mists and kills me. For I defended my wallet with the last drop of my blood.'

For several days he went to the sick-bay for treatment and spent the day writing. With his arm in a sling he ventured out on deck, but for the most part remained stretched out in his cabin.

'Would you care for a cup of tea, Lieutenant?'

'If you like to make it.'

His chief regret was that Querelle had not been his ravisher.

'How thrilled I should have been to struggle with him over my wallet! At last I should have had the chance of showing my mettle. Should I have denounced him? A strange question, one that leads me to ask "which of my many selves?" – always bearing in mind my behaviour during the visit of the police officer. Only by the skin of my teeth did I escape giving Querelle away. I even go so far as to wonder whether I didn't betray him to the officer in my answers and my attitude. I took against that man, and I came very close indeed to giving myself away. He's mad to think it anything but a dream that Querelle killed Vic. Supposing I would like him to be the murderer, it would only bring fresh patterns to my dreams to imagine him mixed up in some love affair. Ought I to offer Querelle my devotion? Pray that he come to confide in me when driven to extremities of remorse by his crime, to extremes of torment, his temples throbbing, and his hair moist with sweat? Ought I to become his confessor and absolve him? Console him in my arms and, finally, follow him to prison? Ought I then to believe in this more implicitly and so denounce him as the murderer in order to offer him at once the benefit of my consolation and to share in his punishment? Without his being in any sense aware of it, Querelle is going to be the greatest danger on board! Little does he know that I was within an ace of betraying him to the police!'

The Lieutenant never imagined that Querelle, cynical though he was – but to whom the expression 'practical joker' did not apply – would extort money. Above all, he never reached the stage of replacing the false sailor's features with those of Querelle, or armed him with a revolver. Had this been so, he would have worshipped him. He would have met with him, joined issue with him in that struggle in the middle of which, while locked in too tight or too loose a hold, they would have learned how best to face up to each other on future occasions. At moments of unbearable loneliness, the Lieutenant indulged in a heroic dialogue, in which he himself would be so subtly transformed that his inmost beauty would be made visible to an astonished Querelle: a short-lived, rather flat dialogue, reduced to essentials. The *sovereign* calm of the Lieutenant's voice would open the proceedings:

'You're crazy, Geo. Put away that revolver. I shan't squeal.'

'Fork out the dough and cut the cackle!'

'No!'

'I'll fire if you resist.'

'Fire.'

For long periods during the night, the Lieutenant paced the deck alone, avoiding his fellow officers, haunted by this dialogue to which he could find no fitting epilogue. 'Won over, he threw down his weapon.' But then my heroism goes for nothing! 'Though won over, he nevertheless fired.' That's to say, out of his esteem for me and to prove he considers himself on the same level. But if he were to kill me, I'd just die stupidly by the roadside. After much deliberation, he decided on the following: 'Querelle fired, but his emotion deflated his aim. He wounded me.' When he came back on board, he would not have given Querelle's proper description (as he had done in Gil's case). Thus he would have been proved stronger than he who should have loved him.

'May I put in a request for forty-eight hours' leave, Sir, please?'

To ask this question, Querelle paused in the act of pouring out tea, raised his head and smiled at the Lieutenant's reflection in the mirror, but the latter precipitately retired within his shell. In curt tones, he said:

'Yes, I'll sign it for you.'

A few days earlier, he had felt a little disturbed. He had wanted to put a few insidious questions to Querelle, to describe ever-narrowing circles round the one essential point till they actually touched upon it here and there, almost revealed it, but never entirely. Querelle was getting on his nerves. His presence in the cabin failed to eradicate the features of the audacious young fellow who had disappeared into the morning mist. 'He was just a young hooligan, yet he had a nerve.' Sometimes he thought rather shamefacedly that even less nerve would have sufficed when making an assault on an aunty like himself. Querelle had had the insolence to say straight out, to the Lieutenant's face, with an exaggeratedly threatening overtone: 'Those lads have a pretty good idea of the type of chap they attack.'

Clearly, the 'ravisher' knew all right of what stuff his victim was made. He had shown no fear. All the same, Querelle felt that the officer was putting a distance between them at the very time that he himself would have allowed himself, slowly it is true and with a thousand reticences, to accept the deep, tender, generous friendship which a homosexual alone can offer. As far as the officer was concerned, this scene gave rise to several reflections, strengthened certain traits, of which some account will be given, and in the end stimulated him to sufficient violence to allow him to conquer Querelle.

'*Loved by Querelle, I shall be loved by the whole French Navy. My lover is compact of all their simple, manly virtues.*'

'The crew of a galley called their Captain "Our Man". One has to remember his soft side as well as his harshness. For I know that he could not help being both cruel and gentle: that is to say, he gave orders for the tortures - not merely with a smile playing on his lips, but also with an inner smile; something corresponding to a soothing potion administered to his secret organs - liver, lungs, stomach and heart. This sedative was noticeable in his voice too, so much so that his orders for torture were given with an overriding gentleness of voice, gesture and look. Doubtless I am constructing an ideally perfect image of the Captain to illustrate my own feelings and desires; one which, all the same, is not simply a figment of my imagination. It corresponds to the conception the galley-slaves must have had of their Captain. This mask of gentleness, no matter on whose atrocious features it was superimposed, was the creation of the eyes - and, to go a step farther, of the hearts of the rowers. By giving his brutal commands, the Captain proved himself cruel. He inflicted deep wounds on their flesh, lacerated their bodies, bashed in their eyes, tore out their nails (he gave orders for these tortures, to be more exact) in order to carry out his instructions, or rather to instil the necessary fear and terror without the existence of which he would not have been the Captain. Now, since he held authority by virtue of his rank - which is also mine! - if he did exact torture, it was with no real hate, (he could not but love his element, thanks to which he existed, and love it by some distortion of love) but, even supposing he did cruelly maltreat the flesh of those delivered to his care by Royal Decree, he maltreated it with a sort of serious enjoyment, with a smile of sadness. I say once again that the galley-slaves looked upon their Captain as having both a soft side and a cruel.'

'"To illustrate my feelings and desires," I wrote just now. If I desire to possess this authority, the admirable outward form possessed by the historic figure of the Captain having the effect of attracting to his person - and with what violence! - the fearful love he aroused in those under his command, then I must arouse such feelings in the hearts of my crew. They must love and fear me. I want to be a father to them and to inflict punishment upon them. I shall leave my mark upon them: they will hate me. I shall remain unmoved in the face of the tortures they endure. I shall not flinch. Gradually I shall be filled with feelings of extreme power. I shall be strong because I have overcome those of pity. I shall be sad, too, because I play such a pitiably comic rôle: that is in view of the sweetness of my voice and of the faint smile as I give my orders.'

'I, too, am a victim of posters. Particularly the one of a Marine, white-gaitered, standing guard over the whole of the French Colonial Empire. His heel is on a compass-card. A red thistle crowns his head.'

'I know that I shall never give up Querelle. My whole life is dedicated to him. Staring at him one day, I said: "You've got a slight cast in one eye." Far from being annoyed or daring to give an impertinent answer, the splendid fellow replied in a voice tinged with sorrow, thus revealing a faint but incurable affliction, "It's not my fault". I realized on the spot that here was an excuse, an outlet for my sympathy. Once the armour of his pride was pierced, Querelle let it be seen that he was not made of marble, but of flesh and blood. In this way, Madame Lysiane showed her goodness of heart and looked after her ailing customers.'

'It is when I am suffering that I cannot believe in God. I am too painfully aware of my impotence to find it in me to offer my complaints to a Being - that is to Him - who is so unattainable. In times of distress, I have recourse only to myself: in those of misfortune I can go to none for comfort.'

'Querelle is so beautiful and to all appearances so pure - yet this appearance is real and sufficient - that I delight in heaping every known crime upon his head. And then, I cannot make up my mind whether I want to sully his name or destroy the evil and render it vain and ineffectual by blending it with the very symbol of purity that lies in his face.'

'The chains of the galley-slaves were called "branches". Think of the clusters dangling from them!'

'What does he find to do with himself when he goes ashore? To what extent do his adventures carry him away? It both delights and worries me to think that he may allow himself to be picked up by any chance admirer, by any stray wanderer, wild-eyed in the fog, who, after some queer precautionary gambit, may offer to walk on a little way with him; Querelle, showing no signs of surprise, smiles and follows on in silence. And then, when they have found a sheltered spot, a convenient angle in the walls somewhere off the beaten track, still smiling and never uttering a word, Querelle undoes his flap. The man goes down on his knees. On rising to his feet again he puts a hundred francs into Querelle's indifferent hand and goes off on his way. Querelle either returns on board or goes off to find the girls.'

'Thinking over what I have just written, this servile function, the use to which this smiling object was put, in no way fits Querelle. He is too strong, and to visualize him thus is only to add to his strength; is to make him into a towering machine capable of pulverizing me without even being aware of my presence.'

'I have said that I could wish that he might turn out to be an impostor; in the solemn and boyish sailor's rig he hides an agile, violent body, and in his body the soul of a cut-throat. That is Querelle, I am certain of it.'

'It was not as a warrior, but rather as some very precious object to be guarded by the soldiery, that I wished to be regarded when I became an officer, and I long to be kept under their surveillance till the time of their death, or even - and in the same manner - to offer my life for theirs.'

'It is thanks to Jesus that we can extol humility, since He made it a hall-mark of divinity. Divinity deep within one - for what reason is there to deny the powers of this world? - opposed to those powers, and strong enough to triumph over them. And humility is born only of humiliation. Otherwise it must be regarded as false vanity.'

This last entry from the private diary corresponds in date to the following incident, which he did not report.

Having rather audaciously felt a young docker, he took him to a thicket below the ramparts, which, as we have already said, were littered with turds. It was the Lieutenant's misfortune that, after dropping his trousers for the sake of convenience, he lay down on the slope of the ditch with his stomach right on the top of a large pat. At once the smell enveloped the two men. The docker fled silently away. The Lieutenant was left alone. With the help of some dry grass happily moistened by the mist, he did his best to clean his jersey. His work began in shame. He found that his beautiful white hands - which became all the more useless as his humiliation increased - were clumsy and unwilling to perform their task. He caught sight of the dark sleeves encircled with gold braid still lying in the mud, which so literally made a bog of the desolate landscape. Since pride can be born only of humiliation, the officer took it very much to heart. He began to take cognizance of his own toughness. When he was once on the road, avoiding all frequented spots like the plague and scouting any place where the wind might carry his smell, he began to realize that the birth in a manger is very significant. (His thoughts of Querelle, being so curiously vague and sullen that they became confused with the smell coming from his belly and made his chore of cleaning so wretched, were now clarified.) In its presence the officer retired within himself after first being overcome with shame, drawn from the farthest bournes and strands of his life into his heart; then, little by little, he dared to think of the sailor in an off-hand way. A little breeze played over him. He thought he could hear a deep voice within him saying, 'I stink, I infest the world!'

From this particular spot of Brest, in the midst of the fog, along the road that runs above the sea and docks, a gust of wind shed upon the world, far sweeter and more fragrant than those rose petals of Saadi, the humility of Lieutenant Seblon.

Querelle at length became Madame Lysiane's lover. All the unease she experienced when thinking of the likeness - for her increasingly perfect - between the two brothers, reached such a high pitch of exasperation that she foundered and sank.

This is what happened. Gil became anxious when Querelle gave up coming to visit him and sent Roger along to find out what the matter was. The kid hesitated for a long time, passed and repassed the spiky door of La Féria, then finally made up his mind and went in. Querelle was in the lounge. Intimidated by the bright lights and the scantily-garbed women, Roger approached him in some trepidation. Still regal in her bearing, though ravaged by her diverted thoughts, Madame Lysiane was present at this meeting. She was unable, therefore, to give her undivided attention or indeed give their proper meaning to Roger's wry smile or Querelle's anxious look of surprise, but she took in their significance. Hardly a minute passed before Robert appeared on the scene and walked across to his brother and the kid, and this gave her an idea that can hardly be termed a thought but can be expressed in the words, 'That's what he is . . . He's their kid!'

Never - not even for that moment - did Madame Lysiane imagine that the brothers could love each other in such a manner that a child could be born to them, yet this physical resemblance, from having put such a difficult obstacle in the way of her love, could itself amount only to love. Besides, this love - she saw but the earthly manifestation of it - had for so long troubled her that the least incident could give it substance. She was not so very far from expecting it to issue from her own body, from her entrails, where it lay enwombed like some irradiating matter. Of a sudden, she saw, two paces from her yet far away, the pair reunited by a young unknown who quite naturally became the personification of this strange fraternal love that was having such an effect upon her and which, in her anguish, she elaborated. When finally she dared to formulate her fantasies, she considered herself ridiculous. She wanted to busy herself over the affairs of her clients and her whores, but she was unable to rid her thoughts of the two brothers on whom she now turned her back. She wasted a little time before deciding, on the pretext of questioning Robert about some wine delivery or other, to take a good look at the kid. He was adorable. He was worthy of the two lovers. She feasted her eyes on him.

'. . . And if the Cinzano turns up, tell the man to wait till he's seen me.'

She made as if to leave the room, but, turning back immediately and pointing to Roger, she beamed, and then smiling even more said:

'I could tell a pretty tale or two on that score. Mind you, this is no joking matter.'

'Who is he?' Robert asked Querelle indifferently.

'The brother of a girl-friend A little girl I've been after in here.'

Not knowing anything about his affairs with men, Robert thought all the same that the little chap must be an affair of his brother's. He didn't dare look at him. Upstairs in the loo, Madame Lysiane worked herself into a frenzy. The resemblance between the pair provoked ripples of anxiety within her. Roger was just as bewildered himself, and when he left La Féria to return to the prison, he was in such a fragile condition - let us make use of an ugly but revealing phrase - that Gil soon 'cracked the pot' for him.

If Querelle, as she told him rather sadly, had failed to get a decent hard-on, at least his prick, about which she had dreamed so often, was not a disappointment to her. It was a thick, heavy, rather massive cock; not the best shape perhaps, but with a good deal of force behind it. At long last some peace was brought to Madame Lysiane's mind, in that it was so dissimilar to Robert's weapon. Now at last she would be able to distinguish them by their pricks.

To start with, Querelle had paid but half-hearted heed to the Madam's advances, yet no sooner did he discover that here was a way of avenging the humiliation caused him by his brother than he hastened the course of his venture. While he was taking off his clothes on the first occasion, his tearing rage, accentuated by the approaching moment of vengeance, gave such an impetus to his haste that Madame Lysiane looked forward with eagerness to the fulfilment of her wildest desires. In point of fact, Querelle entered these lists in defence of his own body. His submission to a real cop in the lists of love had set him free. He felt appeased. If he should chance to come across Nono, now that he no longer wished to seek solace in their secret revels, he would not have been surprised to find him in no hurry to recall the memory of them. Mario, it so happened, had not previously told him that, thanks to him, Nono was informed of all that had taken place. So it was simply a question of Querelle taking his revenge. Madame Lysiane undressed with less haste. The sailor's apparent enthusiasm thrilled her. In her simplicity, she even went so far as to believe that it was solely on her account that he was in such a state of excitement. So long as she was not entirely naked, she hoped that this impatient pricket, already tipped for action, would break through the undergrowth at one bound and leap upon her, bowling her over in a flurry of torn lace.

He lay down close beside her. At length he had the opportunity of affirming his virility and making his brother look ridiculous. Madame Lysiane was only too cruelly, too passionately aware that it was thanks to Querelle that she, like Mario and Norbert, had been taken out of a state of loneliness into which his departure would once more plunge them all. He had sprung into their midst with the sudden surprise and elegance of the joker in a pack. His face might cause confusion, but it added an extra dimension to their lives.

As Querelle was leaving the room, he experienced the strangest of feelings: it hurt him to be leaving her. While he was taking his time over dressing, feeling not a little sad, his eye had lighted on a photograph of the boss pinned up on the wall. One by one the faces of his friends appeared before him – Nono, Robert, Mario, Gil. A sort of melancholy descended on him, an inexpressible fear that without him they would not grow old; and in some vague way, all the while he was being so sickeningly lulled by Madame Lysiane's sighs and by her movements all too clearly visible in the glass of the wardrobe as she was putting on her clothes behind him, he longed to drag them down to the level of his crimes, that they might be fixed there and only be able to love through and because of his presence.

When he went up to her, Madame Lysiane had stopped crying. On her face the stray hairs that had escaped from the clumsily placed pins were plastered down by her tears, and the rouge on her lips had run a little.

Querelle pressed her against his body, rigidly encased once more in his armour-plated blue naval uniform, and kissed her on both cheeks. This throws some light on his subsequent treatment of the Lieutenant, and later of Mario.

Le Vengeur was due to leave Brest. The crew had been informed that the departure would take place within a few days. Querelle received this news with a certain amount of anxiety. Were he to leave the port and the whole network of his dangerous undertakings, he would thereby lose all benefit accruing from them. Every moment that he was unable to get ashore would further accustom him to life on the despatch-boat. He began to be aware of the vast importance of this huge steel object. The fact that preparations might be under way for a cruise to the White Sea, or somewhere even further than the Baltic, made him thoroughly uneasy. Unless he knew for an absolute certainty the exact course, Querelle did not greatly worry his head over any future possibilities.

The incident already recorded in a quotation from the private diary can be dated as the second day of his affair with Madame Lysiane. As he walked through the streets, Querelle played fast and loose with all the girls. He would behave as if he were going to kiss them, and then, if they looked like falling for his charms, he would have no more to do with them. Sometimes he did kiss them, but more often he played them off with a wisecrack or by pulling a face. Above all, his flirtatiousness showed that he wished his proficiency as a seducer not to go unnoticed. He might occasionally stop for a moment with a girl who had been bowled over by his charms, but more often he would continue with his slow, rolling gait. Not so this evening. Happy at having escaped, thanks to Madame Lysiane, from the arid and inhuman practices with Nono, and now with Mario, triumphant and proud of having deceived his brother and slept with a woman, he went whistling on his way down the Rue de Siam. He was in a joyful mood and a little tipsy. Drink had warmed the cockles of his heart and brightened his outlook. He was grinning.

'Hullo there, baby!'

He encircled the girl's shoulders with his arm. She half turned round and let herself be carried away by the bold approach of this great rowdy with his towering body. Querelle did not even wait until they were out of the glare of the streets before he pushed her up against a wall where there was a narrow shaft of shadow between two shops. Excited to such a pitch that she hardly bothered whether or not she could be seen, she flung her arms around his neck and hugged him close to her breast. Querelle blew on her hair and kissed her on the cheeks, whispering indecencies in her ear, making her laugh nervously. He wound his legs about hers and held them fast. At moments he withdrew his face from the girl's to glance rapidly to left and right. It made him prouder to know that he was almost in full view of the street. His triumph was public.

It was then that he saw Lieutenant Seblon coming towards him between two officers from another ship. Never for an instant did he stop smiling at the girl. When the officer reached the line of shadow where the young couple were standing, Querelle hugged her even more tightly and kissed her on the mouth, almost biting her tongue. Then, with the over-riding impulse to continue smiling, he imparted the full significance of the moment to his back, his shoulders, his buttocks; in short, so immersed was he in his will to seduce that all his desires were transferred to that part of his body, which became his real countenance, his matelot's face. He wanted to make it smile and look effectively seductive. Indeed, so strong was this wish that an imperceptible tremor rippled down his spine from nape to rump. This most precious part of himself he dedicated to the officer. He was not quite sure that he had been recognized.

As for the Lieutenant, his first impulse was to go straight up to

Querelle and reprimand him for daring to perform in full view and have him up for indecent behaviour in public. His respect for discipline was in strict accord with his taste for the quarter-deck - and his feelings for wishing to put it into execution, thanks to the force of an order without which his rank and authority would be powerless - but to betray his trust, no matter in how small a way, would be self-destruction. All the same, he remained stock-still. He would not even have attempted it but for the presence of his companions, for, while thoroughly aware of the necessity of respecting this discipline, to infringe it or in any way tolerate its being infringed, gave him the pleasure of freedom of action and of being the accomplice of the defaulter. Finally, he thought it smart and 'excessively tasty' (his own phrase for it) to show a smiling indulgence towards such a ravishing couple of lovers.

Querelle soon left the girl but, not daring to go on down to the port whither the officers were clearly on their way, he went slowly back up the street. He was feeling both happy and discontented. He had not gone so very far when a girl laughingly broke away from a group and ran across the road and had soon caught up with him. She stretched out her hand to touch the sailor's pom-pom for luck and was met with a stinging smack on the nose. Red in the face, as much from shame as pain, the girl remained rooted to the spot while Querelle glared at her in fury. She managed to stammer, 'I never meant no harm!'

Already he was the centre - or, more correctly, the attraction - of a gathering where the lads wouldn't hesitate to smash his face in with their fists. Querelle began to turn his body this way and that without shifting his feet: he was well aware of the mounting danger from the attitude and faces of the young fellows. For an instant he thought of calling all sailors to his assistance, but there was none in sight. Then men began to insult and threaten him. One of them gave him a shove.

'You dirty shit, striking a girl! If you were a man . . .'

'Watch out, you chaps, he's got a knife!'

Querelle looked them over. Drink had dramatized his vision of himself and magnified his danger. Not one of them as yet dared to come forward. There wasn't a woman who didn't yearn for so handsome a brute to be knocked flat by one of the men's fists, torn in pieces, stamped on, that she might be avenged for not being his best girl and under the protection of his strong arm and manly torso, which she was really prepared to believe would prove victorious, thanks to the sole protection of his good looks. Querelle felt that his cheeks were burning. Spittle was already gathering at the corners of his mouth. He was staring at some point beyond the huge transparent face of Lieutenant Seblon who had appeared on the scene after getting rid of his two companions, staring at a dawn rising over some part of the globe, only to spread and link up with other dawns which were rising over each of the spots where he had hidden the result of his thefts or murders, while ever on the watch against any craven and threatening gestures of the crowd.

'Don't make a fool of yourself. Come with me!'

The Lieutenant pushed his way through the crowd and put his hand on Querelle's arm in a gentle, friendly way. Again he had the idea of punishing him for being drunk. Not that he held himself responsible for the proper conduct of the Navy, for in such a case his proper conduct should consist in overlooking rowdyism; but rather because he felt the need for the spiritual power behind his braid to be enforced, mingled with a slight anxiety that some hurt was being done to law and order, and therefore to truth. He saw with absolute certainty that above all things he must not touch the arm holding the knife, and so he put his white hand on the other. This at last gave him the courage to go to almost any lengths. For the first time he was speaking to Querelle in familiar terms, and in the circumstances this seemed to be quite the natural thing to do.

Having written in his private diary that what was of prime importance to him when he became an officer was not so much to be regarded as 'the master', whether feared or not, as a sort of spirit animating these muscular masses, these slabs of raw meat, his anxiety can be the more readily understood. He did not yet know whether this vigorous, all-powerful body, charged and swelling with rage and wickedness, would simply melt away before a single glance from his officer, or, better still, both do this and then permit him to put the rage and wickedness to whatever ends he saw fit . . .

He was already prepared to receive the respect and envy of all the women present, at the moment when he took his departure under their very noses on the arm of this handsomest of brutes, subdued, tamed, and charmed by the sweetness of his voice.

'Go straight back on board! I shouldn't like it if anything were to happen to you. Give me that!'

It was then that he stretched out his hand towards the knife; but Querelle, even if he had submitted to the officer's intervention, was not going to let him confiscate the weapon. He closed the blade by pressing it against his thigh and put the knife back in his pocket. He took a step or two towards the circle, still without a word, and broke his way through. The crowd dispersed, muttering audible curses. When the Lieutenant met him again on the jetty, Querelle was reeling drunk. Mumbling slightly, he came up to the officer and, putting a heavy hand on his shoulder, said to him,

'You're a pal! They're a bunch of cunts. But you . . . you're a real pal.'

Completely overcome by tipsiness, he slumped down on a bollard.

'You can ask what you want of me.'

He swayed backwards and forwards, and to steady him the Lieutenant took hold of his shoulders. Gently he said,

'Keep quiet now. Supposing there's an officer . . .'

'I don't care a fuck. There's only you!'

'Don't shout, I tell you. I don't want you to be put in irons.'

He was pleased at not having succumbed to the desire to punish him. From that moment on he got the better of the martinet side of himself: rid of the disciplinary onus that had weighed so heavily upon him. Then, almost automatically, but exerting the greatest precision, he put his hand up to the sailor's cap and kept it there, lightly at first, before letting it rest more insistently on his hair. Querelle was still swaying and the officer took advantage of this to place his leg under his head so that one cheek was supported on his thigh.

'I should be very sorry to see you taken into custody.'

'D'you mean it? Oh, you just say that! You're an officer and you don't care a fuck!'

It was then that Lieutenant Seblon dared to stroke the other cheek and murmur,

'You know perfectly well that's not true.'

Querelle flung an arm round the Lieutenant, drawing him closer, and, after forcing his head down towards him, implanted a violent kiss on his mouth. With one arm still encircling the officer's neck, he put such a wealth of abandon, such lazy ease, into the motion of rising to meet it that for the first time a flood of femineity, flowing from goodness knows where, transformed this gesture into a perfectly-timed masterpiece of exceptional virile vigour and grace, since the muscled arms – seemingly conscious of forming the handles of a flower basket enclosing a head more attractive than any bouquet – dared to forget their usual function by festooning an object that only enhanced their essential beauty.

Querelle smiled at being so very near the brink of shame from which no escape was now possible, and in which he might well discover lasting peace. He felt so enfeebled, so completely overcome, that the following phrase formed in his mind, born of the desolate autumnal thoughts of all his blemishes, of all his delicate but death-dealing wounds.

'Here's someone who'll follow in my footsteps.'

The next day, as already stated, the police arrested the officer.

'I shall know no peace other than being kissed by him, and in such a way that he shall watch over me, as I lie *struck* down across his knees, as Jesus is watched over in a "Pietà".'

Nono kept up his attitude of placid indifference, while saying to his wife,

'They leapt at each other's throats, they lammed out at each other's jaw. There's no telling what they did.'

'What did they say to each other?'

'You mean to say you don't know? Are you coming over all innocent now? Don't try to make me out a cunt. D'you hear what I say?' And then he added as an afterthought:

'That you go mucking about after two young 'uns don't worry me in the least, all I'm asking you is not to come bringing your troubles to me!'

The boss's voice was severe. He never looked at his wife. He went on putting away the bottles, then added:

'There was no good cause for their scrap and it didn't last long. The blows they struck were scarcely more than scratches. It was more like cats fighting.'

Within her, the drama increased rapidly. Motionless at her cash-desk, facing the empty, brightly-lit room, she was taking a subsidiary part in the unfolding of this drama she most wished to control by making herself familiar with all its most intimate details. At the same time, she never ceased becoming more and more worked up to a pitch of high excitement as her thoughts raced ahead. Totally unable to find any means of justifying her crime in front of the magistrates, she decided to set fire to the brothel. But this fire would have to be explained, and she saw that once she had set the brand to the burning, it could lead only to her own death. In that case, she would strangle herself. She was breathing so heavily that at times her breast, as it grew hard and tight, carried in its expansion her whole being, up and out in a preliminary trial ascent. Dry-eyed behind burning eyelids, she stared at the terrifying emptiness of brightly-lit looking-glasses, while exasperating themes and variations swirled through her brain.

'Even when separated, they will call to each other from the ends of the earth . . .' 'If his brother goes to sea, Robert's face will always be turned to the west. It will be as if I were married to a sunflower . . .' 'Smiles and curses pass from one to the other, uncurl and swirl all round them, become attached to them, and firmly bind them together. No one will ever tell which is the stronger. And that kid of theirs shuttles between them without disturbing any of that . . .'

Madame Lysiane felt that streamers were unwinding from the precious palace of the mother-of-pearl and ivory white flesh of her body, banners of watered silk on which were inscribed in woven embroidery these sumptuous phrases whose inner meaning she deciphered in fear and admiration. She was watching the secret history of lovers whom nothing can separate. Their bouts were riddled with smiles; their games decked with insults. Smiles and insults reversed their meaning. They smiled while cursing each other. And right up to the door of this room, to the very threshold of her own, were they united in their mystic ceremonies. By their expressions, they must be taking part in festive rites. Each minute was a celebration of their wedding-feast.

Back came the idea of arson in more detailed form. To give it better attention, to decide in which spot she would spill the tin of petrol, Madame Lysiane allowed her body to sink back into a kind of forgetfulness; but she pulled herself together as soon as she had made up her mind. She took hold of the ends of her stays by putting both hands under her dress. She drew herself up.

'Above all things, I must hold myself rigidly stiff.'

Scarcely had she conceived this thought than she relapsed into shame. As if crazed, she saw in writing the words she was pronouncing under her breath, but written in her own handwriting. Dreaming of her lovers, this is what she saw: '*They is singing.*'

When face to face with Querelle, Madame Lysiane never again

ever experienced what fencers refer to as 'the sentiment of the point'.

She was alone.